The world c[an't get]
enough of J.[...]

Libraries
ReadLearnConnect

THIS BOOK IS PART OF ISLINGTON READS' BOOKSWAP SCHEME

Please take this book and either bring it back to a Bookswap site or replace with one of your own.

If you enjoy this book, why not join your local Islington Library and borrow more like it for free.

Find out about our FREE e-book, e-audio, newspaper and magazine apps, activities for pre-school children and other services we have to offer at **www.islington.gov.uk/libraries**

'A **fast-paced, superbly crafted story** that is an amazing – and possibly unique – combination of top-notch suspense, detection, and intensely romantic sensuality'
Library Journal

'Robb serves ... **classic whodunit** and noir'
Publishers Weekly

'**Great fun**'
Cosmopolitan

'A **consistently entertaining** writer'
USA Today

'Whether she writes as J.D. Robb or under her own name, I love Nora Roberts. She is a woman who **just doesn't know how to tell a bad story** ... an authentic page turner, with Eve Dallas – tough as nails and still sexy as hell ... If you haven't read Robb, **this is a great place to start**'
Stephen King

Eve Dallas – Personnel File

Name: Eve Dallas

Nationality: American

Rank: Homicide Lieutenant, New York Police and Security Department

Born: 2028

Height: 5 foot 9 inches

Weight: 120 lbs

Eyes: Golden brown

Hair: Light brown

ID number: 5347BQ

Service:
Began police officer training at the Academy in 2046, aged 18.

Family:
Between the ages of eight and ten, Eve lived in a communal home while her parents were searched for. Eve was found with no ID, no memory, and was traumatised having been a victim of sexual assault.

Why Eve is a cop:
'It's what I am. It's not just that someone has to look, even though that's just the way it is. It's that I have to look.'

J.D. ROBB

DELUSION IN DEATH

piatkus

PIATKUS

First published in the United States in 2012 by G.P. Putnam's Sons,
a division of Penguin Group (USA) Inc.
First published in Great Britain in 2012 by Piatkus
This paperback edition published in 2013 by Piatkus

A CIP catalogue record for this book
is available from the British Library.

ISBN 978-0-7499-5517-5

Typeset in Bembo by M Rules
Printed and bound by CPI Group (UK) Ltd, Croydon, CR0 4YY

Papers used by Piatkus are from well-managed forests
and other responsible sources.

MIX
Paper from
responsible sources
FSC® C104740
www.fsc.org

Piatkus Books
An imprint of
Little, Brown Book Group
100 Victoria Embankment
London EC4Y 0DY

An Hachette UK Company
www.hachette.co.uk

www.piatkus.co.uk

Have you read them all?

Go back to the beginning with the first three In Death novels.

For a full list of J.D. Robb titles, turn to the back of this book

Book One
NAKED IN DEATH

Introducing Lieutenant Eve Dallas and billionaire Roarke. When a Senator's granddaughter is found shot to death in her own bed, all the evidence points to Roarke – but Eve senses a set-up.

Book Two
GLORY IN DEATH

High-profile women are being murdered by a knife-wielding attacker. Roarke has a connection to all the victims, but Eve needs his help if she's going to track down the real killer.

Book Three
IMMORTAL IN DEATH

With a new 'immortality' drug about to hit the market, Eve and Roarke must stop a vicious and evil drug dealer and killer – before it's too late.

Head to the end of this book for an exclusive extract from the **NEW J.D. Robb** thriller,

CALCULATED IN DEATH

And I looked, and behold a pale horse:
and his name that sat on him was Death,
And Hell followed with him

THE BIBLE

Cry 'Havoc!' and let slip the dogs of war.

WILLIAM SHAKESPEARE

1

After a killer day at the office, nothing smoothed those raw edges like happy hour. On the Rocks on Manhattan's Lower West Side catered to white-collar working stiffs who wanted half-price drinks and some cheesy rice balls while they bitched about their bosses or hit on a coworker.

Or the execs who wanted a couple of quick belts close to the office before their commute to the 'burbs.

From four-thirty to six, the long bar, the high-tops and low-tops bulged with lower-rung execs, admins, assistants, and secretaries who flooded out of the cubes, pools, and tiny offices. Some washed up like shipwreck survivors. Others waded ashore ready to bask in the buzz. A few wanted nothing more than to huddle alone on their small square of claimed territory and drink the day away.

By five, the bar hummed like a hive while bartenders and waitstaff rushed and scurried to serve those whose workday was behind them. The second of those half-price drinks tended to improve moods so the laughter, amiable chatter, and premating rituals punctuated the hum.

Files, accounts, slights, unanswered messages were forgotten in the warm gold light, the clink of glasses and complimentary beer nuts.

Now and again the door opened to welcome another survivor of New York's vicious business day. Cool fall air whisked in along with a blast of street noise. Then it was warm again, gold again, a humming hive again.

Midway through that happiest of hours (ninety minutes in bar time), some headed back out. Responsibilities, families, a hot date pulled them out the door to subways, airtrams, maxibuses, cabs. Those who remained settled back for one more, a little more time with friends and coworkers, a little more of that warm gold light before the bright or the dark.

Macie Snyder crowded at a plate-sized high-top with her boyfriend of three months and twelve days, Travis, her best work pal, CiCi, and Travis's friend Bren. Macie had wheedled and finagled for weeks to set CiCi up with Bren with the long view to double dates and shared boy talk. They made a happy, chattering group, with Macie perhaps the happiest of all.

CiCi and Bren had definitely *connected* – she could see it in the body language, the eye contact – and since CiCi texted her a couple times under the table, she had it verified.

By the time they ordered the second round, plans began to evolve to extend the evening with dinner.

After a quick signal to CiCi, Macie grabbed her purse. 'We'll be right back.'

She wound her way through tables, muttered when someone at the bar stood up and shoulder bumped her. 'Make a hole,' she called out cheerfully, and took CiCi's hand as they scurried down the narrow steps and queued up for the thankfully short line in the restroom.

'Told ya!'

'I know, I know. You said he was adorable, and you showed me his picture, but he's *so* much cuter in person. And so funny! Blind dates are usually so lame, but this is just mag.'

'Here's what we'll do. We'll talk them into going to Nino's. That way, after dinner, we'll go one way, and you'll have to go the other to get home. It'll give Bren a chance to walk you home and you can ask him up.'

'I don't know.' Always second-guessing with dates – which was why she didn't have a boyfriend of three months and twelve days – CiCi chewed at her bottom lip. 'I don't want to rush it.'

'You don't have to sleep with him.' Macie rolled her round blue eyes. 'Just offer him coffee, or, you know, a nightcap. Maybe fool around a little.'

She dashed into the next open stall. She *really* had to pee. 'Then text me after he leaves and tell me *everything*. Full deets.'

Making a beeline for the adjoining stall, CiCi peed in solidarity. 'Maybe. Let's see how dinner goes. Maybe he won't want to walk me home.'

'He will. He's a total sweetie. I wouldn't hook you up with a jerkhead, CiCi.' She walked to the sink, sniffed at the peachy-scented foam soap, then beamed a grin at her friend when CiCi joined her. 'If it works out, it'll be so much fun. We can double date.'

'I really like him. I get a little nervous when I really like a guy.'

'He really likes you.'

'Are you sure?'

'Abso-poso,' Macie assured her, brushing her short curve of sunny blond hair while CiCi added some shine to her lip dye. Jesus, she thought, suddenly annoyed. Did she have to stroke and soothe all damn night?

'You're pretty and smart and fun.' *I don't hang with jerkheads*, Macie thought. 'Why wouldn't he like you? God, CiCi, loosen up and stop whining. Stop playing the nervous freaking virgin.'

'I'm not—'

'You want to get laid or not?' Macie snapped and had CiCi gaping. 'I went to a lot of trouble to set this up, now you're going to blow it.'

'I just—'

'Shit.' Macie rubbed at her temple. 'Now I'm getting a headache.'

A bad one, CiCi assumed. Macie never said mean things. And, well, maybe she was playing the nervous virgin. A little. 'Bren's got the nicest smile.' CiCi's eyes, a luminous green against her caramel skin, met Macie's in the narrow mirror. 'If he walks me home, I'll ask him up.'

'Now you're talking.'

They walked back. It seemed louder than it had, Macie

4

thought. All the voices, the clattering dishes, the scraping chairs ground against her headache.

She told herself, with some bitterness, to ease off the next drink.

Someone blocked her path, just for a moment, as they passed the bar. Annoyed, she rounded, shoved at him, but he was already murmuring an apology and moving toward the door.

'Asshole,' she muttered, and at least had the chance to snarl as he glanced back, smiled at her before he stepped outside.

'What's wrong?'

'Nothing – just a jerkhead.'

'Are you okay? I probably have a blocker if your head really hurts. I've got a little headache, too.'

'Always about you,' Macie mumbled, then tried to take a calming breath. Good friends, she reminded herself. Good times.

As she sat again, Travis took her hand the way he did, gave her a wink.

'We want to go to Nino's,' she announced.

'We were just talking about going to Tortilla Flats. We'd need a reservation at Nino's,' Travis reminded her.

'We don't want Mexican crap. We want to go somewhere nice. Jesus, we'll split the bill if the tab's a BFD.'

Travis's eyebrows drew together, digging a thin line between them, the way they did when she said something stupid. She *hated* when he did that.

'Nino's is twelve blocks away. The Mexican place is practically around the corner.'

So angry her hands began to shake, she shoved her face toward his. 'Are you in a fucking hurry? Why can't we do something *I* want for a change?'

'We're doing something you wanted right now.'

Their voices rose to shouts, clanging with the sharp voices all around them. As her head began to throb, CiCi glanced toward Bren.

He sat, teeth bared in a snarl, staring into his glass, muttering, muttering.

He wasn't adorable. He was horrible, just like Travis. Ugly, ugly. He only wanted to fuck her. He'd rape her if she said no. He'd beat her, rape her, first chance. Macie knew. She *knew* and she'd laugh about it.

'Screw both of you,' CiCi said under her breath. 'Screw all of you.'

'Stop looking at me like that,' Macie shouted. 'You freak.'

Travis slammed his fist on the table. 'Shut your fucking mouth.'

'I said stop!' Grabbing a fork from the table, Macie peeled off a scream. And stabbed the prongs through Travis's eye.

He howled, the sound tearing through CiCi's brain as he leaped up, fell on her friend.

And the bloodbath began.

Lieutenant Eve Dallas stood in the carnage. Always something new, she thought. Always something just a little more terrible than even a cop could imagine.

Even for a veteran murder cop swimming in the bubbling

6

stew of New York in the last quarter of the year 2060, there was always something worse.

Bodies floated on a sea of blood, booze, and vomit. Some draped like rag dolls over the long bar or curled like grisly cats under broken tables. Jagged hunks of glass littered the floor, sparkled like deadly diamonds on what was left of tables and chairs – or jabbed, thick with gore, out of bodies.

The stench clogged the air and made her think of old photos she'd seen of battlefields where no side could claim clear victory.

Gouged eyes, torn faces, slit throats, heads bashed in so violently she saw pieces of skull and gray matter only added to the impression of war waged and lost. A few victims were naked, or nearly, the exposed flesh painted with blood like ancient warriors.

She stood, waiting for the first wave of shock to pass. She'd forgotten she could be shocked. She turned, tall and lean, brown eyes flat, to the beat cop, and first on scene.

'What do you know?'

She heard him breathing between his teeth, gave him time.

'My partner and I were on our break, in the diner across the street. As I came out, I observed a female, late twenties, backing away from the door of the location. She was screaming. She was still screaming when I reached her.'

'What time was that?'

'We logged out for the break at seventeen-forty-five. I don't think we were in there over five minutes, Lieutenant.'

'Okay. Continue.'

'The female was unable to speak coherently, but she pointed to the door. While my partner attempted to calm the female, I opened the door.'

He paused, cleared his throat. 'I've got twenty-two years in, Lieutenant, and I've never seen anything like this. Bodies, everywhere. Some were still alive. Crawling, crying, moaning. I called it in, called for medicals. There was no way to keep the scene undisturbed, sir. People were dying.'

'Understood.'

'We got eight or ten out – the medicals, Lieutenant. I'm sorry, I'm not clear on the number. They were in pretty bad shape. They worked on some of them here, transported all survivors to the Tribeca Health Center. At that time we secured the scene. The medicals were all over it, Lieutenant. We found more in the bathrooms, back in the kitchen.'

'Were you able to question any of the survivors?'

'We got some names. The ones able to speak all said basically the same thing. People were trying to kill them.'

'What people?'

'Sir? Everybody.'

'Okay. Let's keep everybody out of here for now.' She walked with him to the door.

She spotted her partner. She'd parted ways with Peabody less than an hour before. Eve stayed back at Central to catch up on paperwork. She'd been on her way to the garage, thinking of home when she'd gotten the call.

At least, for once, she remembered to text her husband, letting Roarke know she'd be later than expected.

Again.

She moved forward to block the door and intercept her partner.

She knew Peabody was sturdy, solid – despite the pink cowgirl boots, rainbow-tinted sunshades and short, flippy ponytail. But what was beyond the door had shaken her, and a beat cop with over twenty on his hard, black shoes.

'Almost made it,' Peabody said. 'I'd stopped by the market on the way home. Thought I'd surprise McNab with a home-cooked.' She shook a small market bag. 'Good thing I hadn't started. What did we catch?'

'It's bad.'

Peabody's easy expression slid away, leaving her face cold. 'How bad?'

'Pray to God you never see worse. Multiple bodies. Hacked, sliced, bashed, you name it. Seal up.' Eve tossed her a can of Seal-it from the field kit she carried. 'Put down that bag and grab your guts. If you need to puke, get outside. There's already plenty of puke in there, and I don't want yours mixed in. The crime scene's fucked. No way around it. MTs and the responding officers had to get the survivors, treat some of them right on scene.'

'I'll be okay.'

'Record on.' Eve stepped back inside.

She heard Peabody's strangled gasp, the jagged hitch of her breath. 'Mother of God. Jesus, Jesus.'

'Strap it down, Peabody.'

'What the hell happened here? All these people.'

'That's what we're going to find out. There's a wit of sorts out in the black-and-white. Get her statement.'

'I can handle this, Dallas.'

'You're going to.' She kept her voice as flat as her eyes. 'Get her statement, call in Baxter, Trueheart, Jenkinson, Reineke. We need more hands, more eyes. At a glance, we've got more than eighty bodies, and eight to ten survivors at the hospital. I want Morris on scene,' she added, referring to the chief medical examiner. 'Hold off the sweepers until we deal with the bodies. Find the owner, and any staff not working tonight. Get a canvass started. Then come back in here and help me work the scene.'

'If you talked to the wit I can round up the rest.' Not yet sure she had a solid hold on her guts, Peabody let her gaze skim over the room. 'You can't start on this by yourself.'

'One body at a time. Get started. Move it.'

Alone, Eve stood in the horrible quiet, in the sick air.

She was a tall woman wearing boots that showed some wear and a good leather jacket. Her hair, short, choppy, mirrored the golden brown tone of her eyes. Her long mouth firmed now as she took a moment, just a moment, to block off the trickles of pity and horror that wanted to eke through.

Those she stood over now needed more than her pity and better than her horror.

'Dallas, Lieutenant Eve,' she began. 'Visual estimate of more than eighty victims, multiple and varied injuries. Male and female, multiple races, unknown age span. The scene has been compromised by medical personnel treating and removing survivors. The DBs and survivors were discovered by police at approximately seventeen-fifty. Vic one,' she said and crouched down, opened her kit.

'Male,' she continued, 'severe trauma to the face and head, minor to severe gouges, face, neck, hands, arms, belly.' She pressed his fingers to her pad. 'Vic one is identified as Cattery, Joseph, mixed-race male, age thirty-eight. Married, two offspring, male and female. Brooklyn address. Employed as assistant marketing director, Stevenson and Reede. That's two blocks away. Stop in for a drink, Joe?

'Skin under his nails.' She took a small sample before sealing them. 'He's wearing a gold wedding ring, a gold wrist unit. Carrying an engraved case – credit cards, some cash, ID. Key cards, pocket 'link.'

Bagging the contents, sealing, labeling, working precisely, she focused on Joseph Cattery.

She peeled up his split top lip. 'Teeth are broken. Took a hard one to the face. But it's the head trauma that probably killed him. ME to confirm.' She took out her gauges. 'TOD seventeen-forty-five. That's five before the first on scene.'

Five minutes? she thought. Five minutes before the beat cop opened the door. What were the odds?

She had only to shift to continue. 'Vic two,' she began.

She'd identified and examined five when Peabody stepped back.

'The team's on the way,' Peabody told her, steady now. 'I got the wit's information. According to her statement she was meeting a couple of friends here, and ran late. Got caught at

11

work. She talked to one of them, a Gwen Talbert, at about five-thirty. I confirmed that with the wit's 'link. Everything was fine. She got here about twenty minutes later, and found this. It was done when she opened the door, Dallas. She freaked, stumbled back, screamed, and kept screaming until Officers Franks and Riley got to her.'

'Talbert, Gwenneth, vic three. Broken arm – looks like somebody tromped on it. Slit throat.'

'How could this happen in twenty minutes? Less. How could the entire population of a bar be attacked and slaughtered in under twenty minutes?'

Eve pushed to her feet. 'Look at the scene, Peabody. I've gone over five DBs, and it's my take every one of them was killed with a weapon of opportunity. Broken glass, a bottle of liquor, kitchen knife, bare hands. There's a guy over there with a fork sticking out of his left eye, a woman still clutching the gored, broken table leg it appears she beat the man lying beside her to death with.'

'But—'

Sometimes the simplest explanation, no matter how terrible, was truth.

'There are briefcases, purses, jewelry, money all over the scene. There's good liquor still behind the bar. A gang of chemi-heads gone fucking crazy? They wouldn't be out in twenty, and they'd take valuables to buy more shit. Gang of spree killers looking for major kicks? They'd lock the door and have a party after they'd finished. Added to it, it would take a damn big gang of anything to massacre over eighty, injure about ten more. Nobody gets out, hides, manages to get to their 'link to call for help?'

Eve shook her head. 'And when you do this kind of damage, you're covered with it. Franks had blood on his uniform, his shoes, still had some on his hands and he only assisted the medicals.'

Eve stared into Peabody's stunned eyes. 'These people killed each other, Peabody. They waged war, and they all lost.'

'But . . . how? Why?'

'I don't know.' But she'd damn well find out. 'We need a tox on every vic. What they ingested. I want the sweepers to go over every inch. Something in the food, the drink. Product tampering, maybe. We need to check it out.'

'Everybody wouldn't have been eating or drinking the same thing.'

'Enough of the same, or more than one thing was tampered with. We start with the vics – IDs, COD, TOD, relationships with each other. Where they work, where they live. And the scene, any trace. We get every glass, bottle, dish, the coolers, the AutoChefs, the grill – whatever – to the lab, or we bring the lab to the scene. We check the ventilation, the water, the cleaning supplies.'

'If it's something like that, it could still be in here. You've been in here.'

'Yeah, I thought of that, after the first couple bodies. I tagged the hospital, talked to the medicals who treated the survivors. They're fine. Whatever happened, happened fast. That twenty-minute window. I'm well past that.

'Ingestion's most likely,' she considered. 'Even if only half of them were affected, they could've taken the rest by surprise.' Eve glanced down at her sealed hands, now smeared with cooling blood. 'I don't like it, but it's a theory. Let's work the bodies.'

Even as she spoke, the door opened. She spotted Morris.

As he wore jeans and some sort of silky crewneck shirt the color of ripe plums rather than one of his snazzy suits, she assumed he'd gone off shift. His hair, pulled back into one sleek tail, left his interesting, angular face unframed. She watched his eyes, dark as his hair, scan the room, and for an instant, both the shock and the pity lived in them.

'You've brought me a crowd.'

'Somebody did,' she began. 'I—' She broke off as Roarke came in behind Morris.

He still wore the suit he'd put on that morning in their bedroom: solid, business black, a perfect fit to his long, lean body. The thick, black mane of his hair skimmed above the professional shoulders, slightly mussed, as if the wind had danced through it.

Where Morris's face was interesting, oddly sexy, Roarke's was – Roarke's. Impossibly gorgeous, carved by the strong hand of some clever god and perfected by eyes of bold and brilliant blue.

The two men stood together, and for an instant while it all stood still, she saw that same shock and pity cross Roarke's face, followed by a quick, deadly rage.

Those eyes met hers, and he said, 'Lieutenant.' Even with the rage simmering under the word, the Irish sang through.

She moved to him, not to greet, not to block the view – impossible in any case, and he'd seen more than his share of horror in his life. But she was the officer in charge, and this was no place for civilians or husbands.

'You can't be here.'

'I can,' he corrected. 'It's mine.'

She should've figured it. The man owned most of the world, and half the universe it lived in. Saying nothing, Eve turned a hard stare on Peabody.

'Sorry. I forgot to tell you I hit on Roarke when I scanned for the owner.'

'I'll need to talk to you, but I need Morris first. You can wait outside.'

The rage on his face had gone cold and hard. 'I won't be waiting outside.'

She understood, and wished she didn't. In the two and a half years they'd been together, he'd made her understand more than was always comfortable for a cop. She fought back the urge to touch him – so damned unprofessional – and lowered her voice.

'Listen, this is a fucking mess.'

'I can see that for myself well enough.'

'I need you to stay out of the way.'

'Then I will.' Obviously he didn't see touching as unprofessional as he took her hand a moment, squeezed it despite the blood. 'But I won't wait outside while you wade through this nightmare inside a place I own.'

'Wait.' She turned to Morris. 'I've ... labeled the DBs

15

numerically, the ones we've ID'd and examined. Can you start with One, and I'll be with you in a minute.'

'Of course.'

'I've got more men coming in, any minute now. We'll have more hands and eyes to work the scene and the vics.'

'Then I'll get started.'

'I'm going to turn you over to Peabody,' she said to Roarke. 'You can walk her through security until EDD's on scene.'

'I can tell you there are no cams in here. People stop in for a drink in a place like this, they aren't comfortable with cams.'

No, he thought, they want to relax, perhaps share a private moment with someone. They don't want to be recorded. They don't expect to die a bloody death.

'We have the standard on the entrance,' he continued, 'and standard again for security once the place is closed. But you won't have anything for inside, nothing that would show you what happened here or how.'

Since she hadn't spotted any interior cams, she'd suspected as much, but rubbed her eyes to clear her head again. 'We need a list of employees, and a schedule.'

'I've got it. When I got the tag, I put that together.' He looked around again, trying to understand what couldn't be imagined, to accept what shouldn't be real.

'I've only had the place a few months, but didn't make much in the way of changes. It runs – ran – smooth as far as I know. But I'll know more before it's done.'

'All right. Give what you have to Peabody. I need to work with Morris.'

16

'Eve.' Again, he took her hand, and this time when he looked in her eyes there was more sorrow than rage. 'Give me an assignment, for God's sake. Set me at something to do. I don't know these people any more than you, even those who worked for me, but I have to do something.'

'With Peabody,' she said. 'Start on the vics' 'links. See if any transmissions went out after this started – we've got the time frame. See if there's any video, any audio during the twenty-minute window.'

'Twenty? This happened in twenty bloody minutes?'

'Less than that, that's the outside. Send Peabody back to me once EDD gets here. You can work with them. I've got to get on this.'

Even as she started to Morris, Jenkinson and Reineke stepped in. She swung to them, filled them in, did the same when Baxter and Trueheart arrived.

By the time she got to Morris, he was on the third victim.

'I need to get them in, Dallas. There's defensive wounds, offensive wounds, a variety of both, and of CODs. TODs are, for the first three, within minutes.'

'It all happened fast. In under twenty. One of the vics tagged a friend who was running late, and everything was fine and normal. The friend got here about twenty minutes later, and found this.'

'They did this to each other. From what I can see at this point, they attacked and killed each other.'

'That's my take. Some sort of poison, hallucinogenic, some fucking new rage drug. In the drinks? The bar food? In the ventilation system? There's over eighty dead, Morris, and a handful who survived – so far – in the hospital.'

'They used what was handy – broken glass, forks, knives, furniture, their own hands.'

'There are more downstairs – bathroom area – and back in the kitchen, so it wasn't confined to this space. But I've got nothing to indicate anyone got out, no signs of violence outside.'

'Consider it a blessing. I'll have a team transport bodies as I examine them here, and we'll rush the tox screens.'

'I'll be in when I finish here, after I talk to any survivors.'

'We all have a long night ahead of us.'

'And the media's going to be all over it. I'm going to request a Code Blue, but I don't think a media block's going to stop leaks, not on this. Let's get some answers.'

She pushed to her feet.

Too many people, she thought. Too many dead, and too many cops working in one space. She could trust the team she'd pulled in, but still, so many hands made it too easy for one to make a mistake.

She saw Feeney, EDD captain, former partner, his wiry ginger hair an explosion over his hangdog face, huddled with Roarke. They'd find whatever could be found.

She started down the steps just as McNab – EDD ace and the love of Peabody's life, started up. His bright blue pants, heavy with silver-studded pockets, stood in harsh contrast to the horror. He might've had a half a million shiny rings riding along his ear, but his pretty face was hard, and all cop.

18

'I've got something.' He held out a 'link, held sealed bags of others in his other hand. 'Vic down in the ladies' room, Trueheart did the ID. Wendy McMahon, age twenty-three.'

'She used her 'link.'

'Yeah. At seventeen-thirty-two, she tagged her sister, started off telling her about some guy she met upstairs – Chip – all giddy and happy for the first thirty seconds. Then she says how she's getting a damn headache, and by seventeen-thirty-three, she's bitching at the sister, calling her a whore. The sister cuts her off, but she keeps bitching. It's crazy talk, Dallas, and when another woman comes in screaming, you can hear them going at each other, you can see bits of them fighting when this McMahon drops the 'link. I don't see the second woman down there, so either she killed McMahon and moved on, or got away. The 'link shut off after thirty seconds of no transmission – that's usual.'

Twelve minutes, she thought. Twelve minutes from the first sign of trouble to Vic One's TOD.

'I want that and any others like it back at Central.'

'I've got a couple more. We should be able to put them together for you so you don't have to view them on the individual 'links. It won't take long to do it, and it'll save time. I've got a lot of them to check out first.'

'Keep hunting.'

Eve stepped over the body at the base of the stairs, saw he'd been ID'd and tagged. Trueheart continued to work the area. She imagined Baxter had given him the assignment so the young officer had less misery to pack into his psyche.

Back upstairs, she moved to Roarke. 'Stick with EDD.'

'We're finding some snatches on 'links.'

'McNab reported. I'll be at Central after I talk to survivors. The team can finish here, for now. We're closing you down, Roarke, for the foreseeable.'

'Understood.'

'Peabody,' she called out. 'With me. The rest of you ID and log every body, every 'link, every weapon, any and all of the DBs' personal items. Baxter, see to it I have a list of all vics on my desk asap. We'll be making notifications tonight. I want the security discs from the door. Jenkinson, widen the canvass, four-block perimeter. Morris, have all the vics' clothing sent to the lab and request Harpo on the fibers. All food and drink needs to be transported to the lab, and marked possible biohazard.'

She paused a moment, scanned. Yes, she could trust every one of them. 'Full team briefing at Central.' She checked the time, calculated. 'Twenty-two-thirty. I'm requesting Code Blue, so no chatter. Consider yourselves on this case until I say different.'

She gave Roarke one last glance before she walked out – into cooling air, and the blessed roar of the city.

'The hospital,' she told Peabody. 'Let's see if any of the survivors can talk to us. You drive.'

She slid into the passenger seat, took a breath. Then drew out her communicator and contacted her commander.

2

She hated hospitals, always had. Even knowing the paranoia
stretched back to waking in one in Dallas as a child, beaten,
raped, broken, didn't solve the problem. For her, hospitals,
health centers, clinics, even mobile urgent care outfits all
smelled the same. The smell was pain with underlying fear.

She hated hospitals, always had. Even knowing the paranoia
stretched back to waking in one in Dallas as a child, beaten,
raped, broken, didn't solve the problem. For her, hospitals,
health centers, clinics, even mobile urgent care outfits all
smelled the same. The smell was pain with underlying fear.

Eve lived with the intense dislike, and the fact that her
job so often took her into medical facilities one way or the
other.

She imagined an urban ER never hit the notes of pleasant,
but considered it a sure bet tonight might be a little worse
than usual as the doctors and medicals had been slammed
with ten violently injured people at once.

She moved through the moans and misery, the glazed,
exhausted eyes, the stench of fever sweat and sickness to grab
a nurse. The smiley faces covering the uniform top grinned
in direct opposition to the woman's grim snarl.

'You need to stay in chairs. We'll get to you as soon as we
can.'

Eve held up her badge. Out of the corner of her eye, she
saw a bone-skinny man trembling for a fix slide out of his
chair and jitter his way to the door.

'You had ten injured brought in about ninety minutes ago. I need to see them, talk to them.'

'Wait,' the nurse ordered, and stalked away with her shirt grinning dozens of weirdly perky grins.

Moments later Eve faced a man nearly as skinny as the departed junkie. He wore a lab coat and a look of profound fatigue.

'Doctor Tribido.' His faint musical lilt didn't offset the fatigue.

'Lieutenant Dallas, Detective Peabody. I need to see my vics.'

'Ten came in. One was DOA, two died of their injuries. We got three in surgery now, another in pre-op, and one in a coma.'

'Where are the other two?'

'Holding in Exam Three and Four.'

'I'll start with them.'

'This way. Exam Three's a broken tibia, three broken fingers, a concussion, facial injuries, multiple stab wounds, which the MTs treated on site. Most of the stab wounds were minor, considering. She's one of the lucky ones.'

'Do you have a name?'

'CiCi Way. She's fairly lucid, was able to give us her name, her address, the date, but not how she was injured. We haven't gotten any details on this, Lieutenant. What the hell happened?'

'That's what I'm going to find out.'

She moved through the double swinging doors with him

where a nurse checked one of the IVs plugged into CiCi Way.

The woman on the table kept her eyes closed. Probably couldn't open the left in any case, Eve thought. Not with that vicious swelling. They'd coated her face with gel and patches of Nu Skin so it shone like an oiled mask.

It only made her look more victimized.

Thin casting encased her right arm and hand. Angry scratches and freshly treated wounds showed above her sadly floral hospital gown and along her unbroken arm.

Tribido signaled the nurse as he stepped toward his patient. 'CiCi? It's Dr Tribido. Do you remember me?'

'I . . .' Her right eye slitted open, tracked nervously back and forth under its purpled lid. 'Yes. I think. Hospital? I'm in the hospital.'

'That's right, and you're doing fine.'

'Macie? Is Macie here?'

'I'm going to check on that.' His voice, edged with exhaustion, managed to convey a soft, steady gentleness. 'There's a police officer here to talk to you. Are you okay with that?'

'Police? The police? Because of the accident? The police came, or maybe I dreamed it. The policeman said I was going to be okay.'

'That's right. You're going to be okay. I'll be right outside if you need me.'

'Macie.' Her voice pitched up, sounded strangled. 'Is Macie going to be okay? And, and Travis. And – I can't remember.'

23

'It's all right. You just take it easy.' Tribido turned to Eve, spoke quietly. 'She's asked for Macie every time she's come around. And she's mentioned Travis and sometimes someone called Bren. She came out screaming a couple times. We've got her on a mild sedative for the pain, and to keep her as calm as possible. She's lucid, as I said, but she's spotty on everything that happened after she went in that bar. She'd feel better if we could locate this Macie.'

No, Eve thought, she doubted the woman would feel better knowing Macie Snyder was on her way to the morgue. 'We'll take it easy on her' was all Eve said.

She stepped to one side of the elevated table. 'I'm Lieutenant Dallas, and this is my partner Detective Peabody. What happened to you, CiCi?'

'I got hurt.'

'I know. Who hurt you?'

That single eye began its fearful tracking. 'I don't know. You have to find Macie.'

'She's your friend,' Peabody said in her soothing way.

'Yeah. We work together at Stuben–Barnes. And we hang.'

'You went to On the Rocks with Macie,' Eve asked, 'after work?'

'Um.' Her good eye wheeled again, then focused on Eve. 'Yes. That's right. We work together, and we hang. Me and Macie. She's going out with Travis. They're tight. Macie thinks she might move in with him.'

'So you and Macie went to have a drink after work. Hang.'

'I think so. Yes. Me and Macie, for a drink. It's a nice bar,

24

and they have a mag happy hour. I like the nachos especially. You have to use a fork because they're so . . . '

Her voice shook, and something like terror gleamed in her eye. 'It's close to work. Is Macie okay?'

'It's nice to have a friend to hang with,' Peabody commented.

'She's fun. Macie. Sometimes we go shopping on our day off.'

'But tonight you went for a drink at On the Rocks,' Eve prompted.

'Travis met us there, with his friend. It was kind of a blind date for me.'

'Can you give us Macie's and Travis's last names?'

'Oh. Oh. I didn't think. You need to have their whole names to find them. Macie Snyder and Travis Greenspan. I have pictures on my 'link! I can show you pictures. I don't know where my 'link is.'

'Don't worry about that right now. So the four of you hung for a while, had a couple drinks.'

'A second round. Bren's really cute. Bren!' Her eye widened then closed, and a single thin tear leaked out of the corner. 'I remember now. Brendon Wang. He works with Travis, and Travis and Macie were kind of setting us up. I can't see him very well in my head now.' She gave Eve a weary, pitiful look. 'I'm sorry. My head hurts. I feel sick.' She closed her eye again.

Eve leaned in. 'CiCi, look at me. Look at me now. What are you afraid of?'

'I don't know. I'm hurt.'

'Who hurt you?'

'I don't know! Did we go for dinner?' Her fingers tried to pluck at the sheets, twist them. 'We were going for dinner. Macie wanted Nino's, but . . . Did we go for dinner?'

'No. You were in the bar.'

'I don't want to be in the bar. I want to be home.'

'What happened in the bar?'

'It doesn't make sense.'

'It doesn't have to.' Peabody again, soothing, soothing, even taking CiCi's good hand in hers. 'Tell us what you think happened, and that'll help. We're here to help you.'

'She's a monster. There's blood running out of her eyes, and her teeth are sharp.'

'Who's a monster?'

'It looks like Macie, but she's not a monster. It's all mixed up.'

'What did the monster do?'

'She stabbed Travis in the face. She picked up Macie's fork and stabbed him in the eye – oh God, oh God. And she screamed, and everything was crazy. I had glass in my hand, sharp, sharp, and I stabbed and stabbed, and she screamed and beat at me. It hurts! I have to hurt her, and the other one, all the other ones, but I'm on the floor and my arm! And everyone's screaming and there's blood everywhere. Then I woke up, and somebody was taking me somewhere. Here. An ambulance. I don't know.'

Tears streamed out of her eyes. 'I don't know. I think I

killed somebody, but it doesn't make sense. Please find Macie. She's really smart. She'll know what happened.'

'Let's try this. What were you doing right before you saw the monster?'

'There aren't any monsters, not really. Right?'

Oh, Eve thought, *more than you can count. More than you can name.*

'Don't worry. Just try to remember before. You and Macie and Travis and Bren. You had a table at the bar?'

'A table. Yeah. We got a table. It was close to the bar. I mean the bar in the bar.'

'Okay, that's good. You all had drinks? It's happy hour. What did you order to drink?'

'Ah, I had a house white. It's pretty good. Macie got a Pink Passion. The guys got beers. And we got jumbo nachos to share. But I was afraid to eat them – much – because they're messy. I didn't want to spill because of the blind date.'

'That's good. You were having fun, relaxing after work. You had a drink together. Then what?'

'Um. Oh. Okay. We were talking, and we were going to get another round of drinks. Ah, we – me and Macie, we went to the girls' room. There wasn't a big line, so that was good. And we talked about going for dinner, and how I could ask Bren up to my place if he walked me home.'

The fingers on the sheet moved faster, faster, keeping time with her accelerating breaths. 'I wasn't sure about doing that, but Macie was, and she got, well, a little bit bitchy about it. It's not like her to get bitchy. But she said she was getting a headache. And went back up. Her head must've hurt because she kind of shoved this guy out of her way. I think it was a guy. He'd bumped into her on the way down to the girls' room.'

'The same guy?' Eve prompted.

'I think. I don't know. I got scared when she shoved him, really shoved him. Everything was too loud, too bright, and she was being so mean. And then we sat back down, and I thought I would see if I had a blocker, but she and Travis started yelling at each other. They hardly ever fight, and they never yell, and my head hurt, too. They were yelling, and my head hurt, and Bren looked mad. Mean. I don't know. Then it all went crazy.'

Eve tried a few more questions, walking her back. Had anyone come into or gone out of the bar just before 'the monster'?

But CiCi's memory circled around monsters and blood. They turned her, weeping again, over to the nurse.

The next survivor Eve interviewed stayed calm, almost eerily so. James L. Brewster, an accountant, suffered multiple stab wounds, cracked ribs. A vicious gash ran down the left side of his face from under his eye in a jagged route to his chin, and a violent contusion knotted up in a small volcano on his wide forehead.

He spoke softly, his hands still on either side of his body with the raw, torn knuckles coated with thick gel.

'I go there at least once a week, usually have a client meeting after work. I work at Strongfield and Klein, in the accounting department. It's not officially approved of, but several of us have outside clients. Small accounts. I was meeting a new client. I got there about thirty minutes early, so I could do some work and go over the new client's information. Do you need that?'

'It would be helpful if we had the client's name, the contact information.'

'Of course. MaryEllyn – that's one word, cap E, two Ys. Geraldi. I'm afraid I don't remember her contact information, but it's in my book. I don't know where my book is.'

'That's all right, Mr Brewster,' Peabody assured him.

'I think I got there about half past five, maybe a bit earlier. They know me there, and the waitress – that's Katrina – I don't know her last name – she'd saved me the little two-top over by the wall as I'd called in earlier to let them know I'd be bringing a client in. It's my usual table.'

He closed his eyes – pale, bloodshot blue – a moment. 'Usual. Nothing's usual now. I ordered a soy latte, and started my review. I like to keep as much pertinent information fresh in my head before a meeting. It was crowded. It's not a big place, you understand, but it's friendly and well run. That's why I like to use it, and like the small table by the wall. Katrina brought over my latte, and I was going to ask her for some water as I had a sudden headache and wanted a blocker. Then the bees came.'

'Bees?' Eve repeated.

'Yellow jackets, very large.' His chest rose and fell on a shuddering breath. 'Impossibly large. I was badly stung as a boy, on my grandfather's farm in Pennsylvania. They swarmed me, and I still remember them all over me, stinging, buzzing, and stinging as I ran. I'm deathly afraid of them. That sounds foolish, but—'

'No,' Peabody interrupted. 'It doesn't.'

He gave her a grateful smile, but his chest continued to rise and fall, faster, faster. 'I think I jumped up. I was so startled to see the bees, and I swatted out. They were crawling on Katrina, and I swatted at her to get them off. And then . . . I must have hallucinated. My phobia, I must have hallucinated because Katrina opened her mouth, and bees swarmed out of her. That's crazy. I must've panicked. They swarmed out of her, and her eyes changed, her body. It was – I know this is crazy – it was as if she turned into a huge bee. Like in a horror film. This can't help you.'

'Whatever you remember,' Eve told him, 'however you remember helps.'

'Pretty waitresses don't turn into giant bees. But it seemed real, so terrifyingly real. There was screaming, and buzzing, and everything went mad. I think, I'm not sure, but I think I grabbed my chair and beat at her with it. I've never struck anyone in my life, but I think I struck her with the chair, and tried to run but the bees were stinging me. It felt as if they were stabbing me, and one of them ripped the stinger down my face. I fell. They were all over me, but I must've passed out. When I woke up, there were people lying everywhere, there was blood everywhere. And something – someone – was lying on top of me. I finally pushed him off. He was dead. I could see he was dead. People were dead. Then the police came and found us.

'I don't know what happened to Katrina. She's so young. She wants to be an actress.'

When Eve stepped out of the room she stood a moment weighing options. 'I want you to see if you can talk to any of the other survivors,' she told Peabody. 'If so, I want detailed reports. I want a solid time line. I'm going to the morgue, see what Morris can tell us.'

'I didn't see any bees, giant or otherwise at the crime scene. Or any demons. What would cause people to hallucinate that way, and so intensely for so short a time?'

'We sure as hell better find out. Detailed reports,' she repeated, 'of everything we have so far, everything you get. He hadn't been served yet,' she murmured.

'Who? Brewster?'

'The waitress brought over his latte, he said, and the bees came. So his hallucination came before he'd had anything to drink, anything to eat. It wasn't ingested. I'll hook up with you back at Central.'

She contacted Feeney as she walked out of the hospital. 'Anything?'

'We've got people going in, coming out, normal as you'd expect on the door cam. Female suit, mid-thirties, exits at seventeen-twenty-two. Two women entering ten seconds later. We got a man and a woman – pegged them as mid-late twenties, come out arguing, looks like a hot one. She storms off. He calls after her, starts to go back in the bar. Changes

31

his mind and heads in the same direction she took. That's logged at seventeen-twenty-nine. Seventeen-thirty-two a couple of suits walked out, split off, one north, one south.'

'We'll run face recognition on all of them.'

'We'll do that. On the 'links we're processing, we get a lot of people going off, some starting out easy then screaming or swearing. We've got some audio, and it ain't pretty. It doesn't tell us much.'

'I'm heading to the morgue, maybe Morris has something. Bring everything you find to the briefing. We'll sort through it.'

'It's hit the media, Dallas. Too many people, cops, medicals, bystanders, to keep the lid tight. Nobody has real details. Right now it's coming over as a possible gang hit or bar fight gone seriously south.'

'We stick to "no comment" until we know the direction, and we keep leaks plugged tight in EDD and Homicide.'

'You got that. Your man's got us a list of employees, and who was on. He's working their electronics himself.' Feeney paused, glanced over his shoulder as if checking if any ears were close by. 'Nobody's saying the one thing everybody's thinking.'

Terrorism. She nodded. 'Then let's not say it yet. I'll check back.'

Facts first, she told herself as she drove. Evidence, time lines, names, motives. Just work the case, one step at a time.

CiCi Way and friends, party of four, having cocktails and bar food. Women visit the bathroom, go back. And CiCi's work pal turns into a demon and stabs her boyfriend in the face with a fork.

Brewster, party of one. Comes in, takes his usual table, consumes nothing, and his waitress turns into a giant bee.

An entire bar of office drones and suits turns into a battlefield of makeshift weapons for – given current data – approximately twelve minutes. Result: over eighty dead.

Both survivors interviewed reported a sudden headache, and both came to with blurry memories, but no signs of continued hallucination.

For now, she decided. No telling if whatever had caused it to happen would reoccur.

She walked into the morgue. The long white tunnel, usually quiet, thrummed and echoed with activity. She saw lab coats and protective gear, harried faces, hurrying feet. She could smell the death, still fresh, still bloody as she made her way to Morris's autopsy room.

He had three on tables, and she assumed more stacked somewhere. He wore a clear work cape over his sweater and pants, and had something soft and sorrowful playing on his speakers. Blood coated his sealed hands.

'Busy night,' he commented. 'We love our work, you and I, in our strange and twisted way. But this? This tests resolve, even dedication.'

Delicately, he laid a brain on a scale, programmed for analysis.

'So many dead,' he continued, 'and by whose design? What would cause someone to want so many people, strangers, surely many of them strangers, to slaughter each other?'

'Is that what happened? You can confirm it?'

'Our number two—' He gestured. 'She has flesh under her nails, in her teeth – not her own flesh. Number one, not all the blood on him is his own, and three? He has deep gashes in his palm, his fingers – right hand. Sliced there from a glass shard held this way.'

Morris gripped his hand as if holding a knife. 'His hand's cut to the bone from it. I've people working with other bodies, and reports coming in of the same sort. Offensive and defensive wounds, claw marks, flesh and blood under nails, in teeth, bite marks, some of them savage. We've already found human flesh in some gullets.'

'Jesus Christ.'

'Or whatever deity you might name.' He moved to a sink to rinse blood and God knew what off his sealed hands. 'Your on-scene speculation on COD on these three and the TOD established are accurate. Opinion?'

'Please.'

'Specific COD in these cases won't matter as much as what turned these very likely ordinary people savage. Stabbings, beatings, gashing, chokings, the broken or crushed bones and skulls. It's an ugly variety pack, Dallas.'

'We still need them, every one.'

'Understood.'

Curiously, she lifted the right hand of number three, studied the wide, deep gash. 'A wound like this should've made him scream like a baby, drop the glass.'

'Should have, yes.'

'I need tox reports, as many and as quickly as possible.'

'Also understood. We've been rushing them as we go. The lab's not pleased with us, or you.'

'Fuck Dickhead and the horse he rode in on.'

Morris's lips curved with a combination of amusement and sympathy. 'He's suffering from a broken heart, I'm told.'

'He's suffering from shitheaditis most of the time.'

'Unfortunately true. In any case he and several of his key people have come in to work it, and we have the initial reports on some that expand on what I've been able to process.'

'Down and dirty?' he asked after a pause. 'Or scientific and complex?'

'D&D, for now.'

'Every sample from every victim so far processed shows traces of a complicated cocktail of chemicals – in the nasal passages, on the skin, in the mouth and throat, and in the blood.'

'They breathed it in. It's airborne.'

'They breathed it in,' Morris agreed. 'You have that cocktail – a bastardization of Zeus, LSD in a heightened form, one I've never come across. Add in Rush, pcyote, synthetic adrenaline and testosterone, and an element or two I can't identify, not clearly.'

'That's not a cocktail. It's a freaking stew.'

'Yes, you're right. Stew's more accurate. Measured, mixed, and cooked,' he murmured, 'into a quick-acting virus. In my opinion this strange recipe could cause someone to hallucinate with strong and violent reactions.'

Eve turned to Victim One: Joseph Cattery, she remembered. What was left of him. 'You think?'

He smiled a little. 'The D&D of it? Exposure to such a combination of substances would make a subject bat-shit crazy. I have to assume the elements I've been unable to pin down are responsible, at least partially so, for how quickly it infects.'

'It doesn't last long. The time line's giving it about twelve minutes running time.'

'Time enough. How it was released, how whoever released it escaped the results – if indeed he did – and why the symptoms reversed in a relatively short amount of time? Those are beyond my scope, at least at this point.'

'Released into the air?' Inside, she thought. People in and out, a couple arguing as they left.

Infected?

'No one's reported seeing a cloud of bat-shit crazy descending,' she told him. 'Into the air, carried on it, infecting by inhalation and touch? On two levels, into closed areas like the kitchen, the restrooms. But not outside, as far as we know. Who thinks of this shit?'

'That would be your area, or Mira's. I can tell you these three people were reasonably healthy when they woke up this morning. All three had consumed alcohol and eaten within twenty minutes of death. None shows previous signs of illegals abuse. All have offensive and defensive wounds.'

'What about the brains.' She jutted her chin toward the one still patiently waiting. 'When we dealt with those suicides through mind control, the vics had a kind of burn on the brain.'

'Nothing here.' He moved to the comp, brought up completed analyses. 'Not on these three or any DBs I've gotten reports on. We'll run more tests, but at this point it appears the substance left no permanent damage other than violent death.'

'That's pretty fucking permanent.' She stuck her hands in her pockets, scanned the bodies again. 'I need everything and anything you get as soon as you get it.'

'You think this is the first, but not the last?'

'Unless this was some twisted form of self-termination and whoever did it is on one of your slabs, yeah. It worked so well, why stop now?'

'Then we'll hope he's here. Otherwise, anyone, anywhere, anytime.'

Murder could happen, she thought as she drove to Cop Central, to anyone, anywhere, anytime. She'd seen the worst of what people did to people over love, money, for power, for revenge. Or just because. But mass murder painted a darker canvas, and using victims as weapons made for a particularly twisted mind.

Morris was right. That was Mira's territory, and she needed to bring in the department's top shrink in a hurry. She checked the time, shook her head, and contacted Dr Charlotte Mira at home.

'Eve.' Mira's calm, pretty face filled the screen. 'What can I do for you?'

'There's been an incident,' Eve began.

'We've seen several bulletins. Multiple deaths in a bar downtown.'

'That's the incident. I'm sorry to disturb your evening, but

I need you at Central. There's a briefing scheduled. This is Code Blue. We're not going to be able to hold that very long, but for now. I need you on this, and fast.'

'I'll come right in.'

'Okay.' Eve thought of Dennis Mira, with his mismatched socks and kind, kind eyes. 'Ah, is Mr Mira home?'

'Yes. He's right here.'

'Maybe you could make sure he stays home. Stays in. Just a precaution.'

'Eve, how bad is this?'

'I don't know yet. That's the problem. I'll fill you in at the briefing.'

She clicked off as another thought struck her. Her friend Mavis, Leonardo, the baby. She could contact Mavis, tell her to keep her family home. But for how long?

To soothe herself, she sent a quick text as soon as she'd pulled into her spot at Central's garage.

Can't talk, can't explain. Just stay home until I contact you.

Then she thought of her city, the millions inside it. Going into bars, restaurants, shops, museums, theaters. Using the subways, the buses, the trains.

No way to protect them all, and there never had been. But unless one of the bodies in Morris's house had caused more than eighty deaths, more people would die.

Anywhere. Anytime.

3

She went straight up to her office, ignoring everything else – and did what she rarely did. She shut the door.

Inside the small space with its single skinny window, she dropped down at her desk. And ignored the flashing message light on her desk 'link.

For the next fifteen minutes, if she could manage it, she wanted to concentrate on putting everything she knew, had seen, had confirmed, every detail, every conversation, every speculation into words.

Narrowing her focus, she worked. She backtracked, changed angles, rechecked timing. She scanned a text from Peabody – her partner was on her way.

No time to dump grunt work off, so she printed out stills from her record of the crime scene, of individual victims. She checked her incomings only to add to her list of names: victims and survivors.

Notification of next of kin, she thought briefly, would be a nightmare. One, due to the number, she'd have to share.

She didn't glance up at the knock on the door, but started to snap out when it opened. Swallowed the harsh words as Roarke stepped in.

He looked as tense and pissed off as she felt.

'Word was you were back,' he said briefly. 'I need some bloody coffee, and not that slop they have up in EDD.' He went straight to her AutoChef and programmed two cups as she didn't have one on her desk.

He knew she stocked the blend he supplied her with. And had wooed her with.

'You're busy, I know.' He set her cup down by her computer. 'We all are.'

'We're not going to be able to tell you much more than you already know.' He glanced down at the stills she'd started to organize, sighed once. 'Confirming the time it began, how long it lasted, and the fact all of it was concentrated inside the place. You hear them screaming,' he said quietly. 'You hear a lot of them screaming.'

'I could tell you you don't have to do this, any of this.'

'You could.'

'I won't.'

'It'd be better that way. The fact I own the place is a small part of it. Too small to matter.'

'I don't know that yet. It may be you were the target, some kind of revenge or grievance.'

He passed an absent hand over her hair. 'You don't think that. If it were, why not select a place where I might be? Some restaurant where I'm holding a meeting, or even the lobby area of my headquarters?' He walked to the window, stared out at the busy world of New York. 'It's not me. It's nothing to do with me, really.'

'Odds are slim, but I can't discount it yet. I can't discount any single one of the vics was the reason. Or that none of them were. Not that much time's passed. Someone, or some group, may take credit for it yet. Send us a message, or more likely send one to the media.'

'You hope for that.' He turned back to her. 'Once credit's taken, you'll have a line to tug, a direction.'

'Yeah. Even better will be if we find some screwed-up suicide note on one of the vics, or at their residence, their work.'

He knew her face, her tones, her inflections. 'But you don't think that either.'

'I can't discount it, yet. It would be the best answer.'

'And you and I, cynics as we are, don't believe in answers handed to us on a platter.'

She could say to him what she'd say to few. 'It's not done. I felt it as soon as I understood what happened in that place. Maybe before when I talked to a couple of the survivors. Those who lived through this will carry it with them every day. It's pretty fucking likely each of them killed someone they know, someone they liked. Maybe someone they loved. If and when they fully understand that, how do they cope?'

The cruelty here, she thought, was so bright, so ugly.

'Killing because you have to, to protect a life, to save your own or others? It's hard enough to live with that. We have to start notifications after the briefing. A lot of families will be grieving by morning. So, I think, for whoever's responsible, that's a goddamn blazing success.'

He came back to her because she needed it, whether or not she knew it.

'Did Feeney start facial recognition on the people picked up going out, going in?'

'He'd put someone on that when I left. It shouldn't be difficult to ID the two women going in, their faces are clear. Those going out will take a bit of time, I think, as the camera only caught partials.'

'The women going in didn't come out. They're either dead or in the hospital. So they're not going to be hard to ID.'

He touched her hand, just the lightest of contacts. 'Do you know how it was done?'

'Parts of it. I'll get into it in the briefing.'

'All right.' He moved to her window again, stared out at the air traffic, the buildings, and down to the street. 'When I was a boy in Dublin there were still some pockets of fighting, holdouts from the Urban Wars. Those who were too angry or entrenched to stop. Now and again there'd be a bomb, homemade boomers that were unreliable at best. In a car, a shop, tossed through someone's window. It was a fear you learned to live with so you could go on with your day-to-day.'

He turned back. 'This is more. Bigger place, more people, and a more terrible threat even than a well-placed bomb.'

'We're not calling it terrorism yet.'

A shade or two of the rage she'd seen earlier slid back across his face. 'It's nothing but terrorism. Even if it turns out to be a one-off, it's nothing but. If there's another, or possibly even if not, you're going to have Homeland coming in on you.'

She met his eyes levelly, and thought he had two levels of rage going. 'I'll deal with that when the time comes. They don't worry me.'

He came to her, took her hand. 'Then don't let me worry you either, when it comes to that.'

She thought of what he'd done for her, for only her, by subjugating his need for revenge against those from Homeland. The agents who'd ignored her cries as a young girl in Dallas, her pleas for help as her father had beaten her, raped her. He'd let it go because she'd needed him to.

'I won't. I wasn't.' She gripped his hand tight. 'Don't let me worry you either.'

'You've still hurt places from going back there, from everything that happened only weeks ago. They may not show, darling Eve, but I see them well enough. A bit of worry's my job. Look that up in your famous Marriage Rules.'

'Then we'll deal with that, too. But now I've got to get to the conference room. We've got a hell of a mess on our hands.'

'I'll help you set it up.'

When they got to the conference room, Peabody had already started.

'Your door was closed,' Peabody told her, 'so I got going on this. I've got the time line. And the list of vics. I'll get ID photos and crime scene printed out.'

'Already done.'

'Oh.' For a second, Peabody look mildly put out. 'Okay, I'll match them up. They lost another. One of the ones in surgery didn't make it. One looks good, another's holding, but they don't give her much of a shot. They're working on the one they had in pre-op when you were there. The one in the coma's still out. But I was able to talk to the one guy. Dennis Sherman. He lost an eye. He works at Copley Dynamics. That's the same building, different floor from where CiCi Way works.'

'Small world,' Eve murmured.

'Big city, full of tight districts and neighborhoods. Yeah, small world.'

'I bet he used that bar a lot.'

'You win,' Peabody confirmed. 'It's his regular place. Tonight, he'd come in after work with a couple coworkers. They'd already left, and he was hanging a little longer, talking to the bartender. He's a regular so they know each other, talk sports a lot. And one minute, the best he remembers, they're bullshitting about post-season play, then next, the bartender slams a bottle down, and jabs the shard in Sherman's cheek. He didn't remember a hell of a lot after that, but I got it on record. He talked about the place filling up with water, and sharks everywhere, circling him, drawn to the blood from his face. How he had to beat them off, stab at them.'

'Did you get the names of the coworkers?'

'Yes, sir. I got all I could, but they wouldn't let me talk to him long. The one who didn't make it? The bartender.' She glanced at Roarke. 'Sorry.'

'So am I.'

'Let's get these stills up, and I want to be able to pull any I've printed off the disc and on screen.'

'I'll see to that,' Roarke told her.

'Did you get anything from Morris?' Peabody asked as she and Eve finished with the boards.

'They breathed in a nasty stew of psychotic drugs and illegals.'

Peabody's hands stilled. 'It was in the air?'

'That, and some contact, some trace on the skin. We don't have all the details. The lab's on it. That's the next stop when we're done here.'

It was a long process, pinning the faces to the names, papering the board with scenes of blood and death. She'd nearly finished when the door opened.

And she came to attention for her commander.

'Sir. We're nearly finished setting up.'

'Lieutenant. Your report was brief, but impactful.'

'I wanted to get you as much salient data as quickly as possible. We still have—'

He held up a hand, silenced her, then moved to the boards.

She saw the tension in his stance, a big man with a powerful build. And read the controlled stress on his wide, dark face. Silver threaded though his close-cropped hair. As he scanned the boards, the lines bracketing his mouth seemed to dig deeper.

Every inch of Commander Jack Whitney said command, and every inch carried the weight of it.

'This, all this in under fifteen minutes?'

'Closer to twelve, sir. Yes.'

'Eighty-two confirmed dead.'

'Eighty-three. Another died after surgery, Commander.'

He continued to study the board in silence as Mira came in. Perfectly groomed in a suit of quiet blue, she crossed the room to join Whitney at the board.

'Thank you for coming in, Doctor Mira.'

Mira only shook her head. 'I read your brief, preliminary report.' She shifted her gaze to Eve. 'I appreciate you calling me in.'

They began to filter into the room now: Feeney, McNab, and Detective Callendar from EDD; Trueheart, Baxter, and the rest. Each one scanned the board before taking a seat. For once a room full of cops remained almost silent.

Get it started, she told herself, and walked to the front of the room.

'Shortly after seventeen-thirty this evening eighty-nine people were infected with an airborne substance we must believe was deliberately released inside On the Rocks, a bar on the Lower West Side. Data and witness reports give us a time line for the length of the incident. It lasted from approximately seventeen-thirty-three to approximately seventeen-forty-five – the last TOD, on scene, of any victim so far processed.'

Cops did the math, and there were murmurs as the narrow window of time made its impact.

'As of now we have no confirmation on when the substance was released,' Eve continued. 'We know that this

46

substance caused those eighty-nine people to hallucinate; it drove them to murderously violent behavior. Under its influence these eighty-nine people attacked each other. Eighty-three of those people are dead. Of the six survivors, we have been able to interview three. All their statements bear certain similarities. A sudden headache followed by extreme delusion. Preliminary reports from the medical examiner conclude this substance was most probably inhaled.'

She ran through the mix, using street names, watched the faces of her cops darken.

'Most of you have seen the result of that exposure, on scene. But to keep it in the forefront. Screen One on, display in turn crime scene stills one through eight.'

She waited and she watched as each still flashed on, held, flashed to the next.

'EDD has spliced together some transmissions from pocket 'links recovered on scene. Captain Feeney?'

He puffed out his cheeks, pushed to his feet. 'Some of the vics were on their 'links prior to exposure. We got eleven 'links with some form of transmission, and seven of those continuing transmission during the incident. In all but two of those cases, the other party had already disconnected or the transmission went straight to voice mail. One transmission was made to Freeport, and we've contacted the other party to request a copy of the transmission from their end. As the other party was stoned out of his mind during the transmission and after, we're currently working with the local Freeport PD to obtain. The other was made to an individual in Brooklyn. Detective Callendar was dispatched to speak with the individual, and has just obtained the 'link.'

He glanced at her.

Callendar, in tight red skin-pants and a scooped yellow shirt that showed off her considerable assets, shifted in her seat. 'Schultz, Jacob J., age twenty-four. Single. He was cooperative, and also, if not stoned, considerably under the influence. He believed the transmission, which he replayed for me at his residence, was a practical joke played by his friend. I did not disabuse him of that belief.'

She shifted again so her black hair, done in a mushroom cloud of curls, bounced. 'He was toasted, Lieutenant. You'd have to be seriously toasted to hear and see what's on that 'link and think it was somebody's idea of a big yuck.'

'Can you put it up?'

She nodded at Eve, rose. 'We made a copy. The 'link's sealed and logged.' Moving to the computer, she slid the disc in. 'On screen, Lieutenant?'

'On screen.'

'Vic on screen is Lance Abrams, age twenty-four. Ah, he's number twenty-nine.'

Callendar stepped back as the young, good-looking face came on screen.

'Yo, Jake! 'S on?'

'Decomp time. Might've had a half day, but the fucker was a day and a half. Brew's going down easy.'

'I hear that. Stopped off for a couple, and I got a line on that sweet blonde I told you about.'

'Big Jugs? In your wet dreams, jerkoff.'

'I'm telling you, and she's got a friend. How about it? I said we'd hit a couple of clubs, get some chow. She busted with her boyfriend, man, and she's prime for it.'

There was a long slurping gulp as, Eve assumed, beer went down.

'You want me to come all the way in so you can get laid?'

'She's got a friend.'

'How big are her tits?'

Abrams grimaced, pressed his fingers to his temple. 'Fuck, need a blocker. You want to party or not?'

'I got brew, prime smoke, and I'm tapped till payday. Why don't you bring them here? I'll show you a party.'

'Asshole.' The attractive face became a mask of ugly rage. 'You fucking prick.'

'Got my fucking prick here, too,' Jake said placidly, 'and my good left hand.'

'Fuck up, fuck up, fuck everything up. I'm coming over there and fuck *you* up.'

'Yeah, yeah, you and what ninja army? Take a snap of the friend, yeah? Let me see if I want to get laid. What's with the screaming, man? You at some sex club?'

'They're coming.'

Behind Abrams, blood spattered. Someone ran by, fingers curled like talons, blood running down his face.

'They're coming,' Abrams repeated in a scream, 'for all of us.'

'Who's that? Hey!' There was a moment of concern in

Jake's voice as the screen tilted, as flashes of people – mostly feet now, or those crawling, came in and out of view. 'Hey, man, performance art? Chilly stuff. Where you at, bro, maybe I will come in. Yo, Lance! Nasty!' He laughed as a woman fell into view, clutching at the gash in her throat. Someone tripped over her and was beaten viciously with a broken chair leg.

'Shit man, gotta piss. Get me back.'

Jake clicked off, and the screen went blank.

Feeney cleared his throat. 'We have the same transmission from the vic's 'link, but this gives us the visual. We pieced together some of the others before they were aborted. What we're going to do is dissect the audio, look for any key words, any patterns. But from what we have now, you've just seen the most comprehensive. I can run you the rest if you want it now.'

'It can wait. I want a copy of both. At this point we don't know the method of dispersal, the motive. We don't know if the individual or individuals who released this substance survived, or if survival was their intention.'

'You think this might've been some whacked-up suicide?' Baxter asked.

'Some people don't want to die alone, or easy. But it's low on the list. Think of Schultz's reaction to it. Chilly, he thought. Yeah, he thought it was a show, a joke, but watching people kill each other, it's entertaining. Whoever did this? I think they enjoyed it, enjoyed the punch of causing it. Possibly one or more of the victims was a specific target, but taking out a bar full of people in minutes? Had to be a rush.

Doctor Mira, would you agree with that, or do you have another take?'

'I agree. To kill so many, so quickly, and more to manipulate them, like puppets. Very likely not getting his own hands dirty.'

Her gaze stayed calmly blue as she studied the death posted on the case board. 'Ordinary people,' she added, 'doing a routine, ordinary thing after the workday. It's playing God – a vicious, vengeful God. Intelligent, organized, sociopathic. He, or they, likely have submerged violent tendencies. This was a play. Yes, performance art – the young man wasn't far off. He observes, can't connect. He's unable to connect, except on the surface. He – or possibly she – plans and considers, but enjoys taking risks. He may be envious of the people who come together to enjoy a social hour after the workday. He may, certainly, have a specific target or a particular tie to or grudge against the bar.'

'He would have known the routine, the happy hour business in that location.'

'Yes.' Nodding at Eve, Mira crossed her legs. 'He wouldn't be a stranger there. Unless, and I agree the probability is small, this was an elaborate self-termination, he is also very controlled. He would have walked away. He couldn't stay and watch what he'd created, what he'd caused. What he'd accomplished, and it would be difficult not to see. He'll follow the story religiously in the media. If he can insert himself into it, he will. He'll want that connection – to the power, not to the victims.'

51

'He'll do it again.'

'Yes. And he will likely escalate, try for larger groups. He must have a place, a small lab, where he can create his substance. He must have, or have had, test subjects. Animals, I would think. And if he'd done this before we would have heard of it – I suspect this was his big test. The first on a group of human subjects.'

'It could be political,' Whitney suggested.

'Yes,' Mira agreed. 'The basic profile remains should this be the work of a group or organization. If it is, they will certainly take credit, and quickly. They would crave the attention and the platform for whatever cause they believe in. The fact that it's been several hours now without any group claiming credit lowers that probability in my opinion. The longer without that contact, the higher the probability this is the work of an individual, or a small group with no specific agenda to hype.'

She paused to study the board again. 'He's making a big statement. A public place, a place for society, for gathering. And he kills at a distance. He doesn't need to see, to touch, to feel it.'

'He's better than they are,' Eve suggested. 'Removed.'

'Yes. His targets were primarily white-collar. Executives, those striving to be – admins, assistants. He works with them or for them. He knows them. It's most probable he works or has worked in that area – the area that provides the bar with its after-work clientele, or indeed works or has worked for the bar. He might have been fired, or passed over for promotion.'

'I've checked the firings at the bar,' Roarke put in. 'There's been none since I acquired it. I kept the staff when I bought it. The manager runs it well, and has for two years, which is longer than it's been mine. He wasn't on today. The barman who was among the victims also stood as assistant manager.'

'We'll interview all the bar staff,' Eve said. 'Any who weren't on shift, and especially any who requested off, or don't show up as victims or off schedule. We'll also interview the three people who EDD tagged as exiting the scene shortly before the event, once we've ID'd them. And we'll interview coworkers, family, friends of every vic. It's going to be a long process. I'll assign a group of vics to each of you. You'll work the case individually and as a team. You'll do the notification to next of kin on the vics assigned to you. You'll do the necessary interviews, and work the cases of your vics. Every interview, report, hunch, step, stage, and sneeze is documented and copied to me, the commander, and Doctor Mira. We'll brief eight hundred hours. I'll clear any and all OT.

'Baxter, Trueheart,' she began and handed out specific assignments.

When she'd finished, Whitney rose. 'Lieutenant, if and when you need additional manpower, it will be assigned. While you correctly initiated a Code Blue, it won't hold. There are substantial leaks already – too many people, including civilians, to cover. The department, and the mayor, will issue statements. I'll take point there, at this time.'

'Yes, sir. Considering Doctor Mira's profile, the media attention is what he wants. That may satisfy him, at least long enough for the investigation to earmark a suspect. Or it may charge him up so he does it again — and bigger.'

'I agree.' Mira nodded. 'I'd like to work with you and the media liaison on the statement, Commander. How it's worded, and how it's delivered could buy us time before another attack.'

'We'll get started immediately. Whatever you need,' he told Eve, then turned briefly to the others. 'Good hunting,' he said, and left them.

'Let's get to work. I want all notifications done tonight.' Nobody, she determined, was going to hear they'd lost their spouse, child, father or mother, sister or brother over the damn screen. 'Take a booster if you need it, but I want the interviews started. Be prepared to report, in detail, at eight hundred hours. Dismissed.'

She turned to Peabody. 'This is our briefing room until we close. It's secured when we're not in it. Make that happen. We're going to split the notifications. Take a uniform with you. One you know has his shit together. We've got the top twenty-five in numerical order. You take the last twelve of that. When you're done with that, I want you to go over the reports — crime scene, ME, whatever we get from the lab, anything further from EDD. Write your own report from that, send it to me.'

'Yes, sir.'

'Then get some sleep, and be ready at zero eight hundred.'

'I'll take Uniform Carmichael if he's still around. Otherwise—'

'If you want Carmichael, take him. If he's off shift, tell him he's back on.'

'I'll get him.'

She turned to Feeney as he walked up.

'He got hits on the two women going in the bar.' His gaze tracked to the board, and Eve knew.

'Which are they?'

'Numbers sixty and forty-two. Hilly and Cate Simpson. Sisters. Hilly Simpson lives in Virginia, the other's a buyer for City Girl, some ladies' shop right down from the bar.'

'Sister came in to visit, maybe. They went in for a drink, maybe to meet the New York sister's friends. Jesus Christ.'

'Twenty-three and twenty-six. Age,' Feeney explained, and rubbed at his face. 'Some of them tire you out before you get started.'

'Hit my office for some real coffee.'

'Might just.' He pulled out his communicator when it signaled. 'Here's something. We got another hit. The couple who walked out at seventeen-twenty-nine. Got a hit on her anyway. Shelby Carstein, works at Strongfield and Klein.'

'Same firm as Brewster, one of the survivors.'

'Got an address on her.'

'Send it to me. I want to talk to her.'

'Already sent. Listen, we can't give you much more on the 'links until we have more to work with,' he began. 'You get us the vics' electronics, we'll be all over them. We'll start on their memo books, scan through, see what we can find. But unless one of them was a specific target, or involved, we're shooting in the dark.'

'Understood. I'm going to swing by the lab, see what I can shake loose, then go see Shelby Carstein.'

'If I'm not needed in EDD,' Roarke said, 'I'm with you, Lieutenant.'

'Lieutenant. Sorry.' Trueheart jogged back in. 'We had some people come in. Two of them stated they'd been in the bar, left a coworker there. Another states he's the bar manager.'

'Where are they?'

'The sergeant on the desk put the two in the lounge, the manager in Interview A. He didn't think you'd want them together.'

'He'd be right. I'll take the two, then the one.'

'I'll start on the notifications, Dallas,' Peabody offered. 'From the bottom up. If this takes you longer, I'll keep going until you're loose or they're done.'

'All right.' With her eyes on the board she spoke to Roarke. 'You can come to the lounge, but don't go in with me. Sit nearby. You've got good eyes, good instincts. Get a read on the two I'm going to talk to, then you can do the same from Observation on your manager. How well do you know him?'

'Not well at all, in the big picture,' Roarke admitted. 'I spoke to him extensively during the transition. We did the usual background check, security check, and so on. I also spoke, extensively, with key staff to get a read on him as well as them. He cleared, and very well. Since then I haven't had any personal dealings or contact with him. I haven't needed to. He'd report directly to the coordinator assigned to that property.'

'I might want to talk to the coordinator, depending.'

'I'll arrange it if you need it.'

'Go in first. Get some coffee and—'

'Not in there, I won't.' He managed a ghost of a smile. 'But I know how to cover.'

'Right. I'll be there in a minute.'

She gave Roarke three minutes, then walked to the lounge.

A handful of cops risked the coffee or one of the offerings from Vending. Roarke sat with a cowardly tube of water and his PPC at a table near two civilians.

Both looked tired, fretful. The woman's springy blond hair cascaded down around her shoulders. Her feet snugged into skids to go with the casual pants, the light sweater. The man wore dark pants, a blue shirt, and old boots.

She judged them in their thirties, the man in the early part, the woman headed toward the forty mark.

They weren't wearing suits or carrying briefcases, but Eve made them from the security disc. The visit saved the investigation the trouble of digging for two more IDs.

'I'm Lieutenant Dallas.' She sat down with them, watching them both straighten in the hard plastic chairs.

'Nancy Weaver, and my associate Lewis Callaway. I contacted Lew when I heard the reports on deaths at On the

57

Rocks. We were there, after work. We were right there, with Joe – Joseph Cattery – and Stevenson Vann. I was able to reach Lew and Steve – Steve left before I did. He had to catch a shuttle to Baltimore for an early-morning meeting. But I haven't been able to reach Joe. Lew said Joe was still at the bar when he left.'

Eve let the woman ramble. She did so concisely, like someone used to giving presentations and data, but there were hitches and quavers in her voice.

Deliberately now she shifted her focus to the man. He had a smooth-shaven face and short, straight brown hair. 'You work together.'

'Yes. Marketing and Promotion, Stevenson and Reede. We'd just finished a major campaign. We went in to brainstorm a little on the presentation, and to blow off some steam. Steve couldn't stay long as he was taking point on the meeting in Baltimore.'

'What time did you get there?'

'About quarter to five? I don't know exactly.' He glanced toward Nancy for confirmation.

'We left the office about twenty to five, and it's no more than a five-minute walk. More like three. Steve left after about fifteen minutes. I left around twenty after five, I think. I had an eight o'clock date, and I wanted to get home, change, regroup.'

'Joe and I had one more round,' Callaway added. 'His wife and kids are out of town, so I kept him company for a bit. He talked about going on, grabbing some dinner, but to tell you the truth, I wanted to get home myself.'

He lifted his hands off the table, let them fall again.

'We've been putting a lot of extra hours into this campaign. I was tired. In fact, I was half asleep on the couch when Nance contacted me. I figure Joe probably turned off his 'link, maybe went to a club. You know?'

'Come on, Lew.'

'His wife's away, and you know how tight a rein she keeps on him.' He said it with a hint of a smile, a kind of understood wink. 'He probably just wanted to bust loose a little. But Nance is worried, and by the time she finished, she had me worried.'

'All the reports are so vague, and that makes them more frightening,' Weaver insisted. 'We were there. Right there at the bar. One of the reports said there might be seventy people dead.'

'Take it easy.' Callaway put a hand over hers, briefly. 'You know how the media exaggerates.'

'People are dead.' Her face, soft around the edges, went hard. 'That's no exaggeration. How could that happen? It's a good place. It's not a dive or a joint. Hell, I've taken my mother there. Nobody will tell us anything,' she continued. 'They've all told us we had to wait here, for you. I know who you are. I watch the media reports like a kid eats candy. You're a homicide lieutenant. Were people murdered?'

'I'll tell you what I can. There was an incident at On the Rocks this evening that resulted in multiple deaths.'

'Oh God. Joe?'

'I'm sorry to inform you Joseph Cattery has been identified as one of the victims.'

'Well, Jesus.' Callaway simply stared at her. His eyes, so dark they read black, went blank for a moment. 'Jesus. Jesus God! Joe's dead? He's dead? How? He was just sitting at the bar, having a drink. We were all just having a couple drinks.'

'I'm not able to give you details at this time. Did either of you notice anything out of the ordinary while you were in the bar?'

'Nothing,' Weaver murmured, with tears swimming in her eyes. 'There was nothing. It was happy hour, and most of the tables were full, so we just took the bar. I didn't want anything to eat anyway. We just sat at the bar, talked about the presentation, the campaign. Just shoptalk.'

'Did both of you leave alone?'

'Yes.'

'Yes,' Callaway concurred. 'I actually walked out with somebody else from the company. Not our department. Whistler,' he said to Weaver. 'I didn't know he was in there, and we hit the door pretty much together. Said how's it going, and went our separate ways.'

'How did he die?'

'I'm sorry, Ms Weaver, I can't tell you at this time.'

'But his wife, his kids. He has a boy and a girl.'

'We'll be talking to her. I'm going to ask you not to contact her until tomorrow, until we can make the official notification.'

'There must be something you can tell us,' Callaway

insisted. 'Something we can do. Joe ... we were all there with Joe.'

'I can tell you that we're actively investigating, and we're pursuing any and all leads. We'll be issuing a media release as soon as possible. You can tell me if either of you know of anyone who'd want to harm Mr Cattery.'

'No, absolutely no.' Weaver took a long, steadying breath. 'He's the original Mister Nice Guy. He coaches a soccer team. He's the first one to give you a hand if you need it. He's been married – first and only time – for ... I don't know, twelve years, maybe more. He doesn't forget your birthday.'

'Everybody likes Joe,' Callaway confirmed. 'You have to.'

'How long have you worked with him?'

'I've been with S&R for nine years next January,' Weaver said. 'He came on a few months after me.'

'I've been there almost ten years. We don't always work together,' Callaway qualified. 'We have solo projects, team projects.'

'And Stevenson Vann – related?'

'He's the COO's nephew,' Weaver informed Eve. 'He came on about five years ago. He's good. He's got the knack. He and Joe are pretty friendly, actually. Their boys are about the same age – Steve's divorced, but he gets the kid every other week. They talk kids. They talked kids tonight a little. Oh my God, who's going to tell Steve?'

'I'll do it.' Callaway took a breath. 'I'll tell him.' When Weaver covered Callaway's hands with hers, he patted it. 'I'll get in touch with him tonight.'

'Did you know anyone else in the bar?'

Callaway blinked at her. 'Sorry?'

'You said you walked out with someone you knew. Did you know anyone else in the bar?'

'I . . . I don't know, honestly. I mean to say, you see familiar faces as it's a popular spot for people who work at S&R and in the area.'

'We had our backs to the room most of the time.' Weaver squeezed her eyes shut. 'There could have been other people I knew in there, and I wouldn't have noticed. They might be dead, too.'

After taking their contact information, Eve walked them out. Waited for Roarke.

'Your take?' she asked him.

'The woman's emotional, but knows under most circumstances how to pull it in.'

'Controlled.'

'Yes, and so is he.'

'What's S&R?'

'Cleaning products. Industrial, home, body. They've been around for more than a century. Very solid. And to save you time – Weaver is the VP in charge of Marketing. Vann, Callaway, and your victim work under her. Though Vann heads this current campaign, under her supervision. Callaway and the victim carry the marketing exec title. Weaver's single, with two official cohabs in the past, and Vann's divorced. Callaway's single. And the victim, as you were told, married with family. Vann has a boy, eight – as does the victim, and a girl, five. No children for Weaver or Callaway.'

'You make a good aide.'

'I can get you more, if and when you need it.'

'It's enough for the first picture. Any sense of a thing between Callaway and Weaver?'

'Sexual or romantic? No.'

'I didn't get one either, but he came when she called. Is that an obey the boss thing or a friend thing? We'll see.'

She stopped outside Interview A. 'Tell me about this guy.'

'Devon Lester, forty-three. Second marriage – same sex – no children. He's been in food and beverage for more than twenty years. Worked bars, tables, climbed up the rungs to manager. He's managed the bar for two years. Some minor criminal. Some Zoner busts in his late teens, early twenties. One assault charge, dropped when it was proven he'd attempted to break up a fight rather than start or participate in one. He makes his own brew, and in fact we carry it in the bar.'

'Some knowledge of mixing up a stew – so to speak.'

'You could say.'

'Let's see what *he* has to stay. Observation for you.'

'As you like, Lieutenant.'

4

Devon Lester had what Eve thought of as leprechaun red hair, worn in nappy dreads. It foamed and frizzed around a face the color of bleached burlap, and the face sat round as a beach ball on a neck thick as a tree trunk.

Eyes the color of raisins bulged out of it.

He *rat-ta-tatted* his fingers on the table, kept some quick, inner beat with his feet on the floor. Eve might have assumed he was a junkie jonesing for a fix, but he went still when his gaze latched on hers.

'You're Roarke's cop.'

'I'm NYPSD's cop.'

'I meant, anyway, so anyway, I'm the manager. Roarke tagged me, told me there'd been trouble at the bar. People were dead. I've got a copy of the full crew I gave him.' He pulled it out of his pocket, set it on the table, carefully smoothed it flat. 'Maybe you don't need it since you're his woman.'

'I'm my own woman.'

'I meant – I'm not doing so well.' He rubbed big, wide hands over his beach ball face. 'I can't get my head around it, or my guts. He – Roarke – didn't get real specific. Just the trouble, the dead people, and how I was to send him the names and contacts on all the crew, and who was on tonight, and who wasn't. I figured there'd been a fight or something. We don't usually have much trouble, it's not that kind of place. But that's what I figured until I started hearing the media reports. So I tagged Bidot.'

Eve sat down. 'Who's Bidot?'

'Oh, I figured you'd know all the stuff. The guy who handles the bar business for Roarke.'

'I thought that was you.'

'I'm the manager. He's the one I report to. You don't just tag Roarke every time you need to clear something, you know? A man like him has a lot of balls in the air, right?'

'Sure.'

'You got a pecking order. I report to Bidot, Bidot reports to Roarke if Roarke needs to know. Like that.'

'Okay.'

'Okay.' Devon let out a whistle of breath, as if relieved to have that point cleared up. 'He said, Bidot said, the cops were on it, and it was bad. Really bad. Like maybe—' He paused, swallowed audibly. 'Maybe eighty people, maybe even more. Dead. In my place. My crew. He couldn't tell me about my crew. I came in because I've got to know about my crew. I can't get anybody who was on shift on the 'link. I need to know about my crew, and what – Jesus, lady, what the fuck?'

He was babbling, she thought, but had to give him credit for getting the information out. 'Lieutenant. Lieutenant Dallas. You were off tonight. Is it your usual night off?'

'Yeah. I make the schedule, two weeks running. I like to

be flexible, in case somebody's got something going, wants to change a shift. We run a good, smooth place, and I've got a damn good crew. D.B. was on the stick tonight. He's the assistant manager. I can't get ahold of him. I went by there first, by the bar, but it's sealed up, and there's cops on the door. They wouldn't tell me jack even when I said it was my place. I mean—'

'I get it. There was an incident in On the Rocks this evening that resulted in the deaths of eighty-three people.'

'Mother of God.' The bleached burlap face went lightly, sickly green. 'Mary, Mother of God. Was there a bomb? Or a—'

'We're investigating, Mr Lester.'

'My crew. I got all the names right there. D. B. Graham, on the stick; Evie Hydelburg, that's our cook; Marylee Birkston, head waitress—'

'I have the names. Ms Birkston was in surgery the last I checked. Andrew Johnson – '

'Drew. He goes by Drew. He's a busboy.'

'He's in a coma. They're both at Tribeca Health Center.'

Lester waited a beat, then two. 'The others? What about the rest? I had nine people on that shift.'

'I'm sorry, Mr Lester, those are the only members of your crew who survived.'

'Okay, that's a mistake.' He lifted his fingers, heels of his hands firmly planted on the table as if he needed the anchor. And his voice was all reason. 'That's a mistake. I don't mean to be disrespectful, Ms Roarke, but—'

'Lieutenant Dallas.'

'Whatever.' Suddenly, like a lightning bolt, temper fired his eyes, and behind it crawled fear. 'Seven of my people didn't die. That doesn't happen.'

'I'm sorry for your loss, Mr Lester, and I understand this is hard to accept.'

'Well, I don't accept it.' He surged to his feet. 'Get that? It's not acceptable. I want to speak to your superior.'

Eve rose as well. 'I've just completed a briefing with my commander, and the task force assigned to this investigation. Which I'm heading. I'm telling you seven of your people are dead. Two are in the hospital, and you don't hope any harder than I do that they survive.'

'This is bullshit.'

At the knock on the door, she pulled it open a bare inch. It didn't surprise her to see Roarke.

'I can help here,' he said before she could speak.

She kept her mouth shut, though it took considerable effort, and stepped back. The instant Roarke entered the room, she saw he'd been right.

The heat in Lester's eyes died instantly, and the fear rolled away into grief. 'No. No.'

'Sit down, Devon. Sit down now.'

He obeyed, Eve decided, more because his legs just gave way.

'Just Marylee and Drew? All the others, *all*? They're gone?'

'Yes. I need you to help the lieutenant, Devon. She's going to do her best by them, by all of them. You can help her.'

'D.B. was getting married. He and his woman, they've been together three years, and they're getting married in May. Evie, she just had her first grandkid. Katrina got a callback on an audition. I changed her shift so she'd get off at eight tonight so she could prep for it. She was supposed to go home early tonight.'

Roarke said nothing, just let him talk of each one of the dead, people he couldn't claim to know, but were his as well. His eyes flicked up to Eve's, held a moment – full of sorrow – when she set water in front of Lester.

'What happened to them? Please. God, please. You have to tell me what happened.'

'I'm not able to do that yet.' Eve sat again. 'I need to ask you some questions.'

'All right. All right.'

'You said you had a good crew, but even so, sometimes there's friction or upset. Have you had to discipline anyone? Break up any arguments?'

'Look.' He swiped at his eyes with his forearm, struggled out a couple of steadying breaths. 'Okay, look, there's always drama. Somebody has a fight with the wife, the boyfriend, whatever the hell. Or a customer gets bitchy, right? It's just the way of the business. But my people got along. It's a good place – good pay, good tips. Somebody needs to switch shifts, we switch. Somebody needs a shift covered, somebody covers.'

'You didn't go in at all today?'

'No. Slept in, then me and my guy went to this gallery in

SoHo. He likes the galleries. Had a late lunch, did some shopping.'

'Did anyone from the bar contact you today?'

'No. And that happens, sure, now and again. But not today. First time my 'link rang, it was Roarke. Quirk and I had a quiet day.'

'Have you had any trouble with anyone? You personally, or at the bar?'

'Nothing, really. I mean, our neighbor gave me some grief a couple weeks ago. We had a party and he said we were too loud. He's an asshole. Even his wife can't stand him.'

'What's his name?'

'Oh man, he's just an asshole neighbor.'

'I need to take care of the people who died today, Mr Lester. So I talk to asshole neighbors.'

He gave her the name, the address, then stared down at his hands. 'I'm sorry about before. I didn't give you respect.'

'You lost friends today. Let's both respect them, and that's enough.'

'What should I do?' He looked from Eve to Roarke. 'I have to tell the rest of the crew. Should I go talk to them in person? I don't think this is something I can tell the rest of my people over the 'link. And the families. I've got to tell . . . Jesus, Drew still lives at home with his parents. He's just a kid.'

'We're notifying the families,' Eve told him. 'Leave that to us.'

'You should go home, Devon.' The quiet tone of Roarke's

voice brought Devon's gaze back to him. 'You'll want to talk to the rest of your people tomorrow. Do you want me to arrange for Bidot to go with you?'

'I'll take Quirk. They all know him, and they don't know Bidot so well. If that's okay.'

'Whatever you think best. If you need anything from me,' Roarke told him, 'you can contact me directly. How did you get here?'

'What? Sorry?'

'How did you come to Central?'

'The subway.'

'I'll have a car take you home. You'll have a car,' Roarke insisted before Devon could protest. 'At the main entrance. And you'll have one tomorrow to take you where you and Quirk need to go.'

'Thanks.'

'They were my people, too.'

'Yes, sir. I guess they were.'

Eve let Devon out, said nothing as Roarke made arrangements for transportation. She just sat across from him until he was done.

'I don't have to ask you your take this time,' she said.

'Then I'll ask you yours.'

'You may not like it.'

'It wouldn't be the first time.'

'He knows everyone there. We both know managing people means those people can piss you off – hit buttons, cause frustration.'

'So you solve that by poisoning them all with the goal of mass murder? That's bollocks, Eve.'

'I've done a run on him. He's married to Quirk McBane, an art teacher. Looks clean and tidy.'

'And that's suspect? The clean and tidy among us?'

'He also has a brother. Christopher Lester. The brother's a chemist, with a lot of letters after his name, who heads up a fancy, private lab. The incident happened on his day off. He knows the ins and outs of the place, and could have planted the substance at any time. Maybe it was on some sort of trigger, timer. We don't know yet. Devon's going to personally notify the rest of the staff, and get a lot of attention. He's center there.'

'Christ Jesus.'

'Look, notification sucks. Unless you're telling people when you want the reaction. He spent the day with the art teacher. Nice alibi. I bet we'll be able to confirm with SoHo galleries, with the restaurant where they had lunch. All clean and tidy again.'

'You see him as a potential mass murderer – of people he worked with every day – because his brother's a chemist, and he has an alibi?'

'Did you hear Mira? I agree with her profile. The killer knows that bar, works at it or patronizes it. He'll try to insert himself in the investigation, which Devon Lester just did. His reaction hit all the right notes, sure, and no, it didn't seem faked. But whoever did this would have intended to talk to the cops, to others, and would have prepared. I have to factor all of that in.'

'You're right. I don't like it.' He shoved up, circled the room. 'But the fact so many people are dead outweighs that. What now?'

'I want to go by the lab, see if there's anything new, give Dickhead a push if I have to.'

'A bribe, you're meaning.'

'I better not have to bribe him for this. But if I do, it's nice to have my deep pockets with me.' She stood. 'I want to talk to Shelby Carstein because I'm going to be giving the hard eye to anybody who walked out of that bar before the infection. Then I need to think. I want to check in with Morris on the way.'

'I'll drive.'

'Figured.' She pulled out her 'link to contact Morris as they headed down to the garage.

Dick Berenski, chief lab tech, hunched over his station with its series of comps like a gargoyle. His egg-shaped head rose over the shoulders of the lab coat he'd tossed over a screaming orange shirt and plum-colored skin-pants. She sincerely wished she'd lived her entire life without seeing Dickhead in skin-pants.

He sported a gold hoop in his ear – a new touch, and fancy, textured shoes that matched the pants.

He gave her a sour look. 'I was at a club. Salsa.'

She made a new wish, that she would never in her lifetime observe him doing salsa. 'Gee, sorry for the inconvenience. I bet the eighty-three dead people are a little put out, too.'

'I'm just saying. I've been to that bar, you know. They have a good happy hour.'

'Not today.'

'Guess not. Tox screen's over the roof, every one of 'em we've processed. You got that already.'

'Give me more.'

'Sent a runner over to get samples from the survivors so we'd have a mixed group. Had to consider those who made it handled the substance different, or the substance reacts different if your brain's still functioning, your heart's still beating or whatnot.'

'Okay. And?'

'Same deal. It's quick. In and out. Most drugs are going to give you a longer buzz – I mean, what's the point in a twelve-minute ride?'

'Twelve minutes is confirmed?'

'That's how long the effects last. Twelve minutes – give or take a minute depending on the size, weight, age of the vic, and how much alcohol or medication, illegals, food consumed. So it's an eleven-to-fifteen-minute window, but average time is twelve.'

He scooted on his stool, played his long, skinny fingers over a screen. 'What I did was mock up the substance. Got pretty damn close. I'm working on synthesizing a couple of the elements more exactly, but we've got the base here.'

'You can do that?'

He smirked. 'Ain't much I can't do. I tried comp reconstruction, but the real deal's going to give you more data. I put four micrograms together, infected a couple rats. Those fuckers went bat-shit. It wasn't pretty either. It was kind of funny for a second or two, then . . . it wasn't.'

'They killed each other.'

'They slaughtered each other. Tech I had assisting had to go puke. Mostly I'm going to rag their ass raw over that, but hell. It's bad shit, Dallas.'

'Explain the bad shit to me.'

'You got your lysergic acid diethylamide − the LSD − as the base. That's your hallucinogenic. Typically, you're going to take it orally or inject it.'

'I know what it is, Dickie.'

'Yeah, well, see this isn't typical. LSD's pretty potent shit, but this is mega, like, condensed. He, like, distilled it. Kinda genius in a way. Like, ah, LSD moonshine, you could say. Then he sweetened it with one of the synthetics we're still working on. With Zeus added to it, it's going to be ugly − hallucinations, delusions, and the energy and violence. Kick in the mushrooms − the ibotenic acid, again condensed. Double hallucinogenics. Add a touch of synthetic adrenaline to pump up the Zeus, condensed testosterone − see everything condensed for more punch. Then a trace of arsenic.'

'Poison?'

'Harpo hadn't started on the hair when we sent in the tox. She found arsenic in the hair tests. In small doses, and with these other factors, it can cause delusions. Mix it up, and you have bat-shit.

'You're going to be deluded, pissed off, panicked, strong −

for about twelve minutes. We averaged the effect time in humans from the rats. It would take maybe three or four minutes to start to feel the effects, go for twelve, then it would start fading.'

'That's more,' Eve murmured.

'The good news is, if you live through it, it's not going to cause brain damage, heart or kidney damage. Bad news, once it's in you, you've got to ride it out, unless you get clear.'

'Clear?'

'It's condensed, right, so if you get air – new air, fresh air. Get the hell outside, it's going to dissipate faster. I'm working on how fast, how much.'

'How about an antidote, or a blocker?'

'Can't say how you'd block it.'

'I thought you could do damn near anything.'

He scowled, then sulked, then considered. 'Maybe.'

'I bet he's got one.' There were bribes, and there were bribes, she thought. And a kick in the ego usually did the trick. 'A fucker who thinks this up would think up a way to keep from stabbing himself in the throat if he got a whiff, or contact. He'd need a lab.'

'Wouldn't hurt, but with a few beakers, tubes, a heat source? Hell, I could make this up in the freaking kitchen if I didn't mind the risk of blowing myself to hell. The LSD's a dicey choice. Finding the right combo, amounts – the recipe, say – that was the long, involved part. *That* was the genius. Putting it together, that's a snap once you've got it. I blocked and encrypted the formula, my eyes only. You're

75

going to want to keep a tight lid on the recipe, or it won't be safe to go to the goddamn corner deli.'

'He's right,' Eve said when she got back in the car. 'If the recipe for this insane stew leaks, somebody else – a lot of somebody elses – will cook it up.'

'There are viruses sealed up in government facilities on and off planet that could wipe out most of humanity.'

'That's not making me feel any better.'

'The point is, the world is never safe. Nowhere is, realistically speaking. No one is, as you know better than most. But we live day-by-day. Eat, shop, sleep, make love, make babies, and go on with it. It's what we have.'

'And sometimes what we have sucks. Let's spread the joy, and go talk to Shelby Carstein.'

Shelby Carstein's third-floor walk-up boasted a claustrophobic lobby and a stairwell that smelled, not unpleasantly, of roasted garlic. On the way up Eve heard a baby's fretful cry, the rolling laugh of a comedy on screen, and the weeping notes she thought came from a violin.

She noted the security light blinking red on apartment 3-C, and the lack of palm plate or camera.

'Security's not a top priority,' Eve commented.

'It's a decent enough neighborhood.'

'There was an illegals deal going down on the corner.'

'I said decent enough.' He smiled at her. 'You didn't bother to ruin the dealer's night.'

'Busting up a Zoner push isn't my top priority.' She knocked briskly, and was about to knock again when she saw the shadow pass over the Judas hole. 'NYPSD.' She held up her badge.

Locks clicked and clunked before the door opened.

Shelby Carstein looked like a woman who'd just rolled out of a very active bed. The robe she was still tying hit mid-thigh, and her bare feet sported toes painted pumpkin orange. Her hair, nearly the same color, tumbled around a face lax from sex.

She tugged the robe a little closer, but didn't cover the stubble burn down the right side of her throat.

'Is there a problem, Officer?' Her voice came out husky and thick as she looked from Eve to Roarke with a mix of annoyance and curiosity in sleepy green eyes.

'Ms Carstein?'

'Yes. What's this about?'

'I'm Lieutenant Dallas, and this is my consultant. We'd like to talk to you.'

'About what?'

'The incident this evening at On the Rocks.'

'The – oh for – look, so we had a fight. It's not like we threw things or broke up the place. And I didn't punch that stupid slut, even though I wanted to. I just told her to back off before I slugged her. And so I used harsh language, but I never laid a hand on her.'

'What stupid slut was that, Ms Carstein?'

'I don't know, just some big tits. Rocky said she was just

drunk and silly, but she came on to him. Right in front of my face.' Shelby pointed two fingers at her face, in case Eve missed its location. 'I don't have to take crap like that from some drunk big tits.'

'Ms Carstein, if we could come in.'

'Oh for God's sake.' She backed up, temper burning the sex haze off her face. 'Rocky! Rocky, you get out here. I've got cops at my door because of that blond bimbo from the bar.'

'Come on!' Exasperation colored the voice from a room off the smartly decorated living area. And articles of clothing — men's pants, shirt, a woman's skirt, jumbled shoes, littered their way toward that room.

Eve decided she didn't have to be a cop to detect the scenario.

A man, dark hair standing in spikes, a love bite on his bare shoulder, shuffled out, still adjusting cotton lounge pants.

So Rocky had closet and drawer space, Eve further deduced.

'What the hell, Shel?'

'Let's make this simple,' Eve decided. 'Your name?' she asked Rocky.

'Rockwell Detweiler.'

Seriously? she thought. *Rockwell?*

'You and Ms Carstein were in On the Rocks this evening. You left the bar at seventeen-twenty-nine.'

'Seventeen-twenty-nine? Jesus!' Shelby threw up her hands. 'What the fuck? Is this a military state now? I didn't do anything.'

'She didn't,' Rocky began.

'You thought it was funny.' She rounded on him, jabbed out a finger. 'That bimbo poured herself all over him when Rocky went up to the bar. He thought it was funny. Even when she wiggled her way over to our table, put her fricking number on the table, he thought it was funny.'

'Men have juvenile senses of humor,' Eve offered.

'We do,' Roarke agreed. 'It's part of our charm.'

'Charm my ass,' Shelby muttered.

'I didn't take it!' Rocky held out his hands in appeal. 'I didn't take her number.'

'You gave her that big, wiseass grin, didn't you? In my face!' Two fingers again noted the location of said face. 'Okay, so I told her where I'd put her number if she didn't back the hell off, and maybe I knocked my drink over so it splashed on her shoes. But, Jesus, it's not like I assaulted her. Or him.' Now she jerked a thumb at Rocky. 'I walked out!'

'We walked out, okay, Shel? Okay, it was stupid.' He appealed to everyone in the room. 'I did think it was funny – the girl was pretty drunk – and I confess – right, I confessed, Shel, it was a little flattering. But it was funny because you were there. I didn't do anything either. I love you, right? Didn't I tell you? When we went out and you told me I could suck it, and – well, and all the rest, didn't I come after you, Shel? Didn't I chase you for three freaking blocks to apologize. And to tell you I love you. I mean it hit me right there on Carmine Street. I love Shelby.'

'Oh, Rocky.' Temper died off into a gooey smile.

'Where did you go when you left the bar?' Eve asked.

'Here.' The gooey smile stayed in place. 'We came back here.'

'I take it you've remained in. Haven't watched any screen, used your 'links.'

'We've been kind of busy.' Rocky's smile matched Shelby's goo for goo. 'Listen, if there's a fine or something, I'll pay it.'

'There's no fine. I think you should sit down,' Eve told them. Because what she had to tell them would wipe that happy goo off their faces.

Nothing, she thought, putting her PPC and Peabody's notification report away as they drove through the gates. Nothing from those left behind but grief and confusion. She studied the house as they approached. All those warm, welcoming lights, she thought, in all those big windows. Roarke's fortress, a towering edifice of stone, style, and security.

Home. Too many people wouldn't go home tonight.

'Too late for interviews,' she murmured, 'after the Rocky and Shelby show.'

'It entertained. A bit of comic relief after a bloody horrible day.'

'Maybe – okay definitely – and it had to be done. But it ate up the clock. Not enough time for interviewing friends and coworkers tonight.'

'How much time do you think you have?'

She didn't misunderstand him. 'I can't say, and that's the bitch. I'm hoping we have a week, two is better. But if I were him – them – her – I'd hit within a couple days. Keep us running, get the city in full panic mode. Isn't that the point? Panic, fear, violence, death. I wouldn't wait very long. I have to think.'

She got out of the car, grateful for the jacket as the clear, hard sky had sucked up all the warmth of the day. Shorter days now, she mused.

Longer, darker nights.

'I have things to see to.' Roarke took her hand, and finding it chilled, rubbed his lips over it. 'I'll speak with Feeney once I've dealt with them.'

When they stepped inside, the scarecrow in black, Roarke's man about everything and her domestic ass pain, waited in the wide foyer. At his feet, the fat cat sat. Then Galahad padded over, wound between her legs, then Roarke's, then back again.

'I've heard the media reports,' Summerset began without preamble. Eve waited for the clever insult, and could only frown as he continued without one. 'They aren't detailed of course, as yet, but that many deaths in one place – contained in one place, and one you own,' he said to Roarke, 'is disturbing.'

'We're disturbed,' Eve responded and turned for the stairs.

Summerset kept his gaze on Roarke. 'Were you the target?'

'No.'

'The lieutenant disagrees.'

Now she had Summerset's eyes on her, and Roarke's. And

in Roarke's she clearly read the warning. 'I don't disagree. I'd say very unlikely.'

'Don't placate me. Either of you.'

'This wasn't about me.' Roarke raked his fingers through his hair, a sure sign of agitation. 'Eve says very unlikely only because she's a cop, isn't she? And she considers every possibility, however remote.'

'How did they die? I'll know soon enough in any case,' Summerset reminded Eve. 'The reports are starting to speculate about poison, or a chemical agent, a virus. Anonymous sources claim the bar looked like a battleground littered with corpses.'

'Shit' was all Eve said.

'It was all of that.' Roarke rounded on Eve as she cursed again. 'Don't be stupid. He will know soon enough, just as he said. And he's bloody well entitled to know.'

'I decide who's bloody well entitled to know on my case.'

'And your bloody case happened in my place, and a number of my employees are in the fucking morgue tonight, so I've some say in it.'

'You—'

'By the level of foolish bickering, I assume you haven't eaten,' Summerset interrupted, coldly calm. 'Either of you. Go in the dining room and sit down at the table like normal humans.'

He strode off, and after a flicker of hesitation, Galahad trotted after him.

'I'm going upstairs.'

'The hell you are. You'll be sitting your ass down in the dining room.' Roarke took her arm to steer her there.

She dug in her heels. 'I have work. Goddamn it, he doesn't run my life, and neither do you.'

'We'll sit, and we'll eat, because he asked it. When's the last time he asked you for anything? Anything?'

She started to snap back with an answer, but realized she didn't have one. 'I don't ask him for anything either.'

'But you've food to put in your belly when you remember to eat it, clean clothes, a house that runs smooth so neither of us have to give it a thought.'

'Why are you so *pissed* all of a sudden! Two seconds ago, you're kissing my hand, now you're in my face.'

'Because he's been waiting since he heard the first report, and I never let him know where I was, or what was happening. I never gave it a thought as I was wrapped up in the business of it, and in you.'

And that neglect shamed him.

'He would've made inquiries, of course, and would know we're both unharmed. But I should have spoken with him myself. So it's myself I'm so all of a sudden pissed at, and you're collateral damage. Now the both of us will do what he asked, and we'll sit down to eat. And we'll tell him what he can be told because, whether you like it or not, he's family.'

'Okay. All right. But it better be quick.'

She walked into the dining room where the fire was simmering, and candles put out a soft, pretty glow. Already there was a board with bread that smelled like heaven, a dish of butter, a tray of cheeses. Wineglasses sparkled, wide soup bowls gleamed on silver chargers.

A moment later, Summerset stepped in with a tureen on a tray.

'I should have spoken with you much earlier,' Roarke began.

'I believe you had a great deal on your mind.'

'Regardless, it was insensitive, and stupid.'

Summerset merely lifted his eyebrows. 'It was both.'

'I'm very sorry.'

'You're forgiven.' After lifting the lid on the tureen, Summerset ladled out soup. 'Eat your dinner.'

'This is yours. I'll get another setting. Please.'

Whatever passed between them, Eve thought, had Summerset nodding. 'As the only one in the house who's eaten is the cat, I wouldn't mind the soup.'

He sat; Roarke slipped out.

'I kept him pretty tied up,' Eve began.

'There's no need to explain. He tends to keep me informed, in general terms. He didn't, and as the reports were, as I said, disturbing, I had concerns. Eat your soup before it goes cold.'

Okay, it was odd, really odd, to sit there having dinner with Summerset. But the soup was good – warm and creamy and comforting.

When Roarke came back, set his place, filled his bowl, it wasn't quite as odd.

'Do your shopping or whatever you do online for the next

day or two,' Eve told Summerset. 'Until I get a handle on this.' As she spoke, she reached for the bread. Roarke's hand met hers, covered it, held briefly. And his eyes gave her simple gratitude.

'Was it terrorism?'

'I don't think so – not traditional – but I can't rule it out. A substance was released, by person or persons unknown, at the bar during the latter part of happy hour. Let's call it a super-hallucinogenic, airborne. People inhaled it into their systems and within a couple minutes became delusional, violent. The incident lasted approximately twelve minutes. There were eighty-nine people in the bar, including staff. We have six survivors.'

'You're saying they killed themselves.'

'Each other. The ME hasn't called suicide on any victim, as yet.'

He said nothing for a moment as Roarke poured wine for all of them. 'There were two incidents, similar, during the Urban Wars.'

Everything froze. 'This happened before?' Eve demanded.

'I can't say it's the same. I wasn't there, but I know someone who was at the first attack. He told me he was going to a café where some of the underground was known to meet, and where he hoped to have some personal time with a woman he had feelings for. He was young, no more than eighteen, I think. It was in London, South Kensington. Most of the main fighting was done there, at that time. He was a half block away when he heard the screaming, the crashing, the gunfire. He ran toward the sounds. Many were dead. The window of the café burst as he ran to it – by bullets, by bodies being heaved out. There were only perhaps twenty in the café at that time of day. All of them were dead or dying by the time he was able to get through.

'He assumed, as did others who'd come, it was an enemy attack, but all the dead and dying were known.'

'What caused it?'

He shook his head. 'The military came in, closed it off, and closed it down. It happened again in Rome a few weeks later. Our ears were to the ground for a repeat. "In the wine" was what we were told. Whoever hadn't had any was killed by those who had, and were maddened by it.'

'What was in the wine?'

'We were never able to learn. It never happened again, not that we heard. And we heard everything sooner or later. The military, the politicians, sealed it, and not even our considerable intelligence units could break through. I thought at the time that might be for the best.'

Eve picked up her wine. 'I bet you could find out now.'

5

As they started upstairs, Roarke took her hand again.

'That was good of you.'

'What was?'

'All of it. I know it cost you time.'

'Turns out he had useful information, so it didn't cost me time.'

Roarke paused on the landing, just looked at her. She tried to shrug it off, then sighed.

'Listen, like it or not, he's yours. I'm not going to kick at him when he's twisted up worried about you. I'll wait till he's untwisted, then kick at him.'

That made him laugh and give the hand he still held a little swing. 'Fair enough. You gave him a task. He's the sort who does better when he has a task.'

On impulse, she headed for the bedroom rather than her office. Might as well get comfortable before diving in again.

'He's still got his Urban Wars contacts. I want to see what he can dig up. I don't know if what happened downtown is connected to two attacks, in Europe, decades ago, but it'll be good to have the data. I'm no Urbans buff, but we had to study it in school. In the Academy we had lectures on tactics, riot control, chem and biological threats using the Urbans as a platform. I never heard of what Summerset talked about.'

'Nor have I, before this, and it sounds like the military shut the door on it. If any of it came here, or threatened to, Homeland would've had a part in that,' he added. 'Closing it, covering it. It's something they're good at.'

'We're not dealing with them yet.' She released her weapon harness, set it aside. 'If and when we do, the more we know, the better.' Sitting, she pulled off her boots. 'And if and when, if we find out they knew there was a formula, and what happened today was a possibility – and they just kept the lid on? I'm going to bury them.'

'You'll need two shovels as I'll want one of my own.'

If it came to it, she'd make sure he had an active part in exposing who and what in the agency played a part. Odds were, she mused, she wouldn't have to make sure of anything, and he'd see to it himself.

They'd have different reasons, and his would be payback. Then again, that was its own form of justice.

'I want a shower before I get to it.' She walked toward the bath, stopped. Gave him a look and crooked her finger.

He lifted his brows. 'Oh, really?'

'Up to you, ace, but in about thirty seconds, I'm going to be hot and wet. You're going to want to finish getting out of that suit.'

A round of water sports might be just the thing, he decided, to take both of them away from the ugliness of the day for a time.

Life needed to be lived.

As he suspected, steam billowed through the wide opening of the glass-walled shower. She had every jet pumping, and brutally hot at that. He wondered it didn't blister her skin.

But there she stood, long and sleek and glistening in the mists and the water, her face lifted, her short cap of hair glossy as a seal's coat.

He stepped in behind her, winced at the boiling punch of the waterfall. A small price to pay, he thought as he wrapped his arms around her, nuzzled his lips at the curve of her neck.

'Knew I could count on you.' She hooked her arm around his neck, leaned back into him. 'Feels good.'

'You do.' To prove it, he slid his hands up her body, glided them over her breasts. 'I won't speak of the lobster boil of the water.'

'We're burning out toxins.'

'Is that the way of it?'

'That's my story.' She turned, slippery and quick, to lock herself to him, to fix her mouth to his, drowning them both in the fast-rising flood of need.

His mind emptied but for her, the hungry mouth, the urgent press of her body. Steam rose up, swirled around them as he took his hands over all those lovely, familiar places. Made her gasp and moan and reach.

He spun her around, pressed her to the wall and gave himself the pleasure of her back. The line of it, the tough cut of muscle under smooth skin.

He tapped a tile then filled his hands with fragrant soap. Slowly at first, slowly running it over her in a slick foam. Back and shoulders, hips and thighs, belly and breasts, until her breath was deep and uneven, until the scent swirled like the steam.

Hands and mouth, only hands and mouth — still slow, lulling and seducing so his cop, his warrior, his wife trembled.

As did his own heart.

His fingers found her, teased, a featherlight torture.

Lost in him. Her hands fisted against the dripping wall as her system churned, yearned. She wanted to turn to him, take him in. Take him. But he'd trapped her, and used her, undid her.

Inch by inch he took her up, and held her, somehow held her back from that last reach so she quaked and writhed, steeped in pleasure, and just short of release.

'I can't.'

'You can.' Once again he pressed his lips to the curve of her throat.

Release crawled through the madness of sensation. She couldn't breathe without feeling. So much, so much. It rolled through her, a wave that built and built as it rose. Pleasure and relief blurred together, dizzying, glorious.

He turned her. She saw only the wild blue of his eyes, then his mouth was on hers again, ravaging, wrecking even as he drove into her.

Now the slap of wet flesh with the pounding drum of water, and the glory of mindless mating. He took her stroke by powerful stroke, stealing every thought, filling every void.

She fisted her hands in his hair, drew him back. She wanted his face in her eyes as well as her mind.

'You. Just you.'

The words, the magic of them struck his heart. Then for the last time he pressed his lips to the curve of her neck, and breathing her, let go.

They held each other up. Eve figured she'd get her breath back in a day or two. It might take up to a week before she got any strength back in her legs.

Otherwise, all good.

She'd figured they'd have a quick, stress-reducing bang, and instead, they'd come together in a way that left her both unwound and energized. If she didn't count her still-weak knees.

'I think we need to get out of here,' she managed.

'Not yet.'

'I'm pretty sure I can crawl.'

'We'll do better. Decrease jet temp to eighty-six degrees.'

'Wait—' The water poured cool considering what it had been. She squealed, cursed, struggled, but he held her snug to the wall.

Laughing, he snuggled her closer. 'It'll wake you up, and it's the same temperature as the pool. Hardly an ice bath.'

It felt like one to her. 'Jets off! Off, off, fucking off!'

When they shut down, she shoved her dripping hair out of her eyes, scorched him with a look.

He only gave her the most pleasant of smiles in return.

Hadn't she said men had juvenile senses of humor? 'You think that was funny?'

'I do, yes. And refreshing. And I bet you can walk under your own power now.'

Because she certainly could – and not to prove him right – she strode straight into the drying tube, letting out a relieved breath when the warm air swirled.

Through the glass she watched him select a towel. He sent her a grin as he dried off, then slung the towel over his hips and walked back to the bedroom.

He'd pulled on jeans and a T-shirt by the time she came out, so she did the same.

She gave one brief thought to the fact most people were in bed, or at least thinking about getting there at this time of night.

Cops weren't most people.

'I'm going to get started,' she told him.

'As am I.' He walked out with her. 'I'll give you whatever help I can once I've sorted some things out.'

They separated to their adjoining offices.

She set up her board first, lining up the faces of the dead, those who lived, and those who connected to them.

In her little kitchen, she programmed coffee, took it to her desk. There she sat a few minutes, feet up, eyes on the board. Let her thoughts wander.

Controlled. Callous – didn't care who died. Even if it had been target specific on one or more vics, the collateral damage didn't bother him, them.

Potentially that was the point. Kill as many as possible.

Political agenda unlikely. If there'd been one, credit would've been taken. That made it personal, but not intimate.

Not sexual. No monetary gain – none that showed, she amended.

Playing God – that's what Mira had said, and that fit best.

She turned to the computer and began to run probabilities. She wrote a report on the interview with Carstein and Detweiler, checked her incoming, added what her teams had finished into the report.

Until she knew more about the Urban War connection, should there be one, she left it out of the reports. If the feds or Homeland came on board, they'd demand copies of all files.

When Roarke came in, she'd poured more coffee and was up, circling the board.

'What can I do?'

'The notifications are complete, in person or via 'link for those outside of New York. Interviews with next of kin give us a few things to check out. Bad breakups, troubled marriages or relationships, family or employment tensions. We've got two vics who fairly recently filed for restraining orders – both on spouses citing abuse, and in one case spousal rape.'

'You don't think it's anything like that. A jealous boyfriend, an abusive husband, an angry sister or daughter.'

'Probability's low, but everyone has to be checked out. The whole thing could have been a cover for a single target.'

Who would do that? she wondered. Kill dozens for the one?

Then shaking her head, she answered her own question. 'People are fucked up, Roarke. Your spouse leaves you, or has you tossed in jail for smacking her around? Go big. Take her out, and take her friends or her new lover out, too. Take a shitload of people out, and more, you've got a way to make them do it to themselves.'

'Striking or raping your mate doesn't say controlled to me.'

'Sure, it can be. My father was controlled, in his way. He kept me isolated and afraid for the first eight years of my life. He did whatever he wanted to me.'

'You were a child.'

'Not the point. It's not,' she insisted. 'He controlled Stella, too, again in his way. Convincing her to get pregnant, give birth, deal with me. If Mira were to profile him, he'd fit this pretty well. Except there's no payday here – not that I can see, and that was the driving force with him.'

'He's on your mind,' Roarke stated. 'Him, McQueen, Stella.'

'Not up front. They destroyed lives, and these are a lot of lives destroyed. So . . . I thought of Cassandra, too, how that group targeted New York landmarks, taking out innocent lives in the bargain. That was obsession as much as terrorism. And this doesn't strike me the same.'

Understanding how she worked, Roarke gave her a springboard. 'How is it different?'

'He wants blood, but he doesn't want to get bloody. He

wants death, but doesn't want to kill – not directly. He doesn't need to watch the lights go out, to smell the fear, to taste the pain. Playing God, yeah, but playing God with science.'

'The two aren't mutually exclusive.'

'No, but some insist they are. Like God's all, *zip, pow,* and creates an orangutan out of thin air.'

'I simply adore your mind.'

'Well, that's the nutshell from one side, and the other far end's all, no, uh-uh. No higher power out there. What happened was basically a giant fart in space, and boom.'

'Absolutely adore it,' Roarke repeated. 'A space fart to orangutans?'

'Eventually. But there's a big middle ground who mostly figure God and science can coexist just fine. Like maybe he even created it. So it's fun to play God with science. That's what a formula is, right? Science. That's how they came up with stuff like LSD. Science. So . . . '

She did another circle around the board. 'Does he have some background in science, or some connection to someone who does? And what's the trigger? Why that place at that time? Why now? It's a big statement. So there's a reason he made it now, made it there.'

'If it's connected to the Urban incidents, he may be military, or have been. Or works, has worked, for whatever agencies have the files.'

'Yeah, I've got that, but it doesn't *feel* military. Cassandra, that felt military – or para. Big target, threats, taking credit, issuing warnings. This is personal. It's people, not things. Not symbols. There's something personal about this, and that's what I have to find.'

She rocked on her heels. 'One step – rule out money as motive, or don't. We check financials, see if any of the vics had a big, fat insurance policy, or bank account. And if so, who gets it? Another kind of gain. Power or position. A lot of the vics had high-end careers, and were climbing the corporate ladder or worked for those who do and are. So who goes up a rung or two if their associate or competitor falls off the ladder?'

She turned to him. 'You can start with money, power, and position since that's your deal.'

'All right.'

'I'll take jealousy, personal gripes, and the rest.'

'Because that's your deal?'

She shrugged. 'If you cheated on me, I wouldn't kill a bar full of people. Just you,' she said with a big smile. 'And I'd do it myself because that's how much I care.'

'I'm touched.' He moved to her, cupped her face. 'Don't work yourself into a stupor. You have to take your own power and position at your eight o'clock briefing.'

'I'm good.'

'Stay that way.' He kissed her lightly before returning to his office.

Pumped with more coffee, she dug for spouses, cohabs, lovers – former and current. She pored over family members. She scanned for official complaints or civil suits, picked through for criminal records, cross-referenced with any education, experience or employment within the military or that had connections to drugs, labs, added in medical, practice or research.

Like slogging through knee-deep mud, she thought, aligning, realigning bytes of data.

Because she wanted the visual, she hauled in another board, filled it with her possible suspects, connected them with the specific victim or victims.

She had a contentious divorce with an equally contentious child custody battle. A former cohab charged with assault who'd done time. A vic who'd worked in corporate medicine, another whose brother was an internist, a mother who was a retired army colonel. Six civil suits filed for a variety of reasons, and a number of family members, cohabs, spouses, exes, and coworkers with criminal records.

Not as many as she'd feared, she thought, but still numerous. She sat again, put her feet up again, and studied the faces of her possibles. Lives to explore, questions to ask. Lines to tug.

Some may – should – connect to whoever Roarke found. Those she'd bounce to the head of the class. Two motives were better than one.

It would give the investigation, at least an arm of the investigation, a direction. If the direction was correct, one of those faces hid a calculating, psychotic nature.

Most people, however clever, however controlled, never hid it completely. There were chinks, clues, habits. At some point, the real person showed through the facade.

Most tended to live alone, live quietly, keep to themselves — as neighbors and coworkers routinely claimed after the killer among them was revealed.

But not this one, no, she didn't think this one stayed huddled in his space.

He frequented or worked in that bar. He knew how to socialize, how to make himself part of the fabric. He thought far too much of himself to live the quiet, unassuming life.

That's what her father had done, though he'd traveled from place to place, never staying too long. But he'd socialized while leaving her locked away. He'd made his deals, run his cons, played his games.

As Stella had. Morphing, absorbing herself into the role she played. But there'd been chinks, other than the ones the child had seen long before the worst of the nightmare began. Weaknesses for illegals, for sex, for money, and a pure love of destroying others on the way to the goal.

Annoyed, she pushed herself up straight. Why was she thinking about them? They had nothing to do with the case, no connection or correlation to it. Yet her thoughts kept drifting back to both of them, to Dallas, to all that pain.

Push it down, push it away, she ordered herself.

Though she understood it was likely a waste of time she ran fresh probabilities, and picked three possibles at random. She did deeper runs now, shifting through layers, looking for triggers, abnormalities, odd affiliations.

To switch her focus and keep sharp, she brought up a split

screen of crime scene images and the promotion image of the bar, before it was washed in blood.

She tried to imagine the killer. Had he served drinks or ordered them? Had he walked in that day with a smile on his face, alone, in company, or to take his shift?

Sat at the bar, or worked behind it?

Ventilation system was on, circulating the air. That's what carried the substance throughout.

The bar, she thought again, or near it. The bar's the hub. Not a big place, and everyone's moving or talking – grabbing food, ordering drinks while they're still on special.

Sit at the bar, your back's to the room, she thought. But you could angle your stool, or use the mirror behind the bar to keep an eye on things.

She put her feet up again, thinking position. And tried to put herself inside that noise, that movement – the smells, the sounds.

As the long day took its toll, and she began to drift, she imagined too well.

Voices bounced off the walls, cutlery clattered at tables while people dug into the nachos, potato skins, rice balls, and drank away the dregs of the workday.

She recognized them – CiCi Way, and Macie Snyder, the boyfriend, the blind date laughing around the table.

Joe Cattery at the bar with Nancy Weaver, Lewis Callaway, Stevenson Vann, the accountant sitting alone with his work waiting for the latte he'd never drink.

The bartender, working the stick and arguing sports with a man he'd soon try to kill.

Joe Cattery turned to her first.

'I'll be dead in a few minutes. Since you're here, why don't you stop it? I'd really like to see my wife and kids again.'

'Sorry. It's already done. I'm just here to figure it out.'

'I just wanted a couple drinks. I wasn't hurting anybody.'

'No, but you will.'

She watched Macie and CiCi get up, start toward the stairs leading down.

'We were going to have dinner,' Macie told Eve. 'I have a good boyfriend, and an okay job. I'm happy. Still, I'm nobody. I'm just not that important, you know?'

'You're important to me now.'

'But I had to die for that.'

'They all do, don't they.' Stella swiveled on a bar stool, a drink in her hand, blood dripping from the slice in her throat. 'You don't give a shit about anybody till they're bleeding on the ground.'

'I have a man I love. I have a partner and friends. I have a cat.'

'You've got nothing, because there's nothing inside you. You're broken in there so nothing holds long.' Lifting her glass in a toast, Stella shook back hair matted with blood. 'What you are is a killer.'

'I'm not. I'm a cop.'

'The badge just gives you an excuse. It's your free fucking pass. You killed him, didn't you? Hey, Richie.'

Her father turned on his stool. Blood poured out of countless holes in his body. Holes she'd put there as a battered, broken child of eight.

'Hi, little girl. Drink up! It's a family reunion.'

He'd been handsome once, she remembered, hard and handsome before too many drinks, too many cons had softened him, worn at him. They'd made an attractive couple once, she imagined. But what lived in each of them had rotted them – rotten from the inside out.

She couldn't be theirs. She wouldn't be theirs. 'You're not my family.'

'You wanna check that DNA again.' Her father winked at her, sipped a foamy brew. 'I'm your flesh and blood. I'm in your bones, in your guts, just like Stella here. And you killed me.'

'You were raping me. Again. Beating me, again. You broke my arm. You choked me. You pushed yourself into me and tore me. I was just a child.'

'I took care of you!' He threw the brew down, but no one stopped talking, stopped laughing. 'I can still take care of you. Don't you forget it.'

'You can't hurt me anymore.'

He smiled, with teeth gone shiny and sharp. 'Wanna bet?'

'She killed me, too,' Stella reminded him. 'What kind of sick bitch kills her own mother?'

'I didn't kill you. McQueen did.'

'You drove him to it. You tricked me, you used me. You think you can come back from that? You think you can just live your life after that?'

They could hurt her, she realized. Something hurt in her now. Deep in the center of her. 'I can. I will.'

101

'You're broken inside, and I'm inside you just like you were inside me. Live with that, bitch.'

'Hey, Stell. Show's starting.'

All around them people screamed, stabbed, clawed, and bit. Some fell, bleeding, to be crushed or beaten. Crazed laughter joined the screams as a woman spun by in mad pirouettes while the blood fountaining out of her throat spattered faces, walls, furniture.

'Want to play?' Richie asked Stella.

'We got twelve minutes.'

'Why wait?'

She shrugged, tossed back the rest of her drink. Together they turned to Eve.

'Time for some payback,' Stella said.

Eve pulled her weapon, stunned them, and again, but they kept coming.

'Can't kill what's dead. You have to live with it.' Stella, hands curled like claws, leaped first.

She fought for her life, for her sanity. Slipping on the bloody floor, kicking out, crying out when her arm twisted under her. The pain spiked. She could all but hear the bone snap as it had when she'd been a child.

Her mind screamed, Wake up! Wake up!

Then she heard him, calling to her. Felt him, soothing her. And turned her face into Roarke's chest.

'Come back now, all the way, Eve. I've got you. I'm here.'

'I'm okay. I'm all right.'

'You're not, but I have you.'

She kept her eyes closed. Just to smell him instead of the blood and Stella's heavy perfume. Clean and hers. Roarke.

'It got mixed up, that's all. I let it get mixed up.'

The cat bumped at her hip. More comfort. She made herself breathe until breathing no longer scored her lungs. And opening her eyes realized they were on the floor of her office, with Roarke cradling her in his lap.

'God. Did I hurt you?' She shoved back, panicked as she thought of how she'd clawed at him in Dallas in the throes of a violent nightmare.

'No. Don't worry. Here now, just rest easy a minute.'

'I let them in. I let it happen.' It infuriated her, disgusted her. Terrified her. 'I shouldn't be thinking about them.'

'Bollocks to that.' Now he drew her back, and she saw there was more than concern on his face. There was temper, ripe and ready. 'I can count the number of easy nights you've had since we got back from Dallas on my fingers. And it's getting worse, not better.'

'It was a hard day, and—'

'Bloody bullshit, Eve. It's enough. More than enough. It's past time you talked with Mira about this, and seriously.'

'I can deal with it.'

'How, and for Christ's sake why?'

'I don't know how.' She shoved away because she felt tears burning her eyes. She'd be damned if she'd cry now, like the weak, like the helpless. 'I did it before, with him. This had stopped. I made it stop. I can do it again.'

'And until, you'll suffer like this? For what purpose?'

'It's my mind, my problem. I told you I'd talk to her, but I'm not ready. Don't push me.'

'Then I'll ask. If you won't do this for yourself, do it for me.'

'Don't use my feelings to manipulate me.'

'It's what I have, and they're my own. I'm as honest and true as I've ever been with you, Eve, when I tell you this is killing me.'

Her belly, already raw, trembled. Because she saw, too clearly, he spoke the truth. 'I said I'd talk to her. I will.'

'When?'

'I can't get into this now.' Leave it alone. Push it back. 'Jesus, Roarke, look at those boards, at those faces.'

He took her shoulders. 'Look at me. And let me tell you what I'm looking at. You're pale and shadowed. You're still trembling. So look at me, Eve, and understand I love you beyond anything and everything there is. And I need this from you.'

She preferred the temper. Temper she could fight. But he defeated her with the restrained – although barely – calm. And the utter misery in his eyes.

'I'll talk to her.'

'Tomorrow.'

'I have to—'

'Tomorrow, Eve. I want your word on it. For me.' He laid his lips on her forehead. 'And for them,' he added, turning her to face her victim board.

He knew how to draw a weapon, and use it so skillfully

you barely felt the blow. She'd beaten the tears, but she couldn't beat him, not on this.

'All right. I'll talk to her tomorrow. My word on it.'

'Thank you.'

'Don't thank me. I'm a little pissed you maneuvered me into this.'

'All right, I won't thank you. I'm a little pissed I had to maneuver you into it. Let's go sleep it off. I'll have you up early enough,' he began as she started to protest. 'You can go over what you've got, and what I dug out for you well before the briefing. You'll need a booster if you don't get a few hours down. You hate taking them almost as much as you hate losing . . . let's call it a debate, with me.'

He had that right. 'Five-thirty should do it.'

'Five-thirty then.'

Without discussion, they walked to the bedroom. In silence they readied for bed. She slipped in, shut her eyes. And saw his face – the worry, the temper, the misery. Heard all that as she replayed his words to her.

'I know this is hard for you,' she said in the dark. 'I'm sorry.'

His arm came around her. 'I know it's hard for you to talk of it even to someone you trust as you trust Mira. I'm sorry.'

'Okay. But I'm still a little pissed.'

'It's all right. So am I.'

She turned to him, curled to him, and let herself sleep.

6

She woke to the scent of coffee, and wondered if that was how mornings in heaven smelled. She opened her eyes to soft light, and Roarke sitting on the side of the bed.

Definitely had earmarks of heaven.

'Your wake-up call, Lieutenant.'

She grunted, shoved up, reached for the coffee he held. He moved it out of reach.

'What makes you think this is yours?'

'Because you're you.'

'So I am.' He brushed at her hair, a light, easy touch, but his eyes took a deep and thorough study of her face. 'You slept well enough, I think.'

'Yeah.' Taking the coffee, she breathed in the scent like air, then drank. Then gave her mind a chance to catch up.

He'd dressed, though he'd yet to put on his jacket and tie. The cat ignored them both, sprawled on the foot of the bed like a lumpy blanket.

A glance at the clock showed her it was precisely five-thirty. She didn't know how he did it.

He watched her come around, watched the sleep glaze fade until her eyes were alert, focused.

'And now you're you,' he decided.

'If there wasn't coffee, the entire world would shuffle around like zombies.'

She moved quickly now, and by the time she'd dressed he had breakfast set up in the sitting area. She eyed the oatmeal suspiciously.

'It's what you need,' he said, anticipating her. Then trailed a finger down the shallow dent in her chin. 'Don't be a baby about it.'

'I'm an adult. I thought when you got to be an adult you could eat what you want.'

'You can, when your stomach also reaches maturity.'

Because arguing about it would waste time she didn't have, she sat, spooned some up. Since it was loaded with apples and cinnamon, she tried to think of it as a weird apple Danish.

'I've copied the data I compiled and sent it to your computer,' he began, 'but I can give you a summary.'

'Summarize away.'

'There are some life insurance policies large enough to be tempting.'

She loaded a piece of toast with some sort of jam. Enough jam, she thought, might disguise the weird apple Danish. 'You have a different level of what's tempting, monetarily, than the rest of the population.'

'It wasn't always so, was it?' He ate his own oatmeal with apparent contentment. And probably actually thought of it as oatmeal. 'While it's true a certain type will kill for loose change, that's not what you're after here. We have a couple of victims who stood to inherit family money, and some substantially. There's also the matter of salaries, pay scales, positions, bonuses. A large percentage of the victims were executives, junior executives, which means they certainly stood ahead of someone, or several someones on that corporate ladder.'

As he spoke he simply lifted a finger, and the cat – who'd been bellying over like some furry combatant, stopped.

Galahad stretched as if he'd had nothing more in mind.

'The admins, assistants – the support also takes a rung,' Roarke continued. 'And all these positions can earn bonuses – often hefty ones – for bringing in accounts, clients, reaching or exceeding sales goals or running a successful campaign. There's only so much bonus money to go around, so if someone's rewarded—'

'Somebody else gets a hearty handshake.'

'Basically. Or may lose out on a desired promotion when the someone else lands that major client or account, has a good run of sales.'

'People get pissed when they get passed over, or somebody else gets the plum on top.'

'Cherry. The cherry's on top. The plum's in the pie.'

'Sometimes you want the plum, the cherry, and the whole damn pie. It doesn't feel like greed, not simple, "I want it all" greed. But it may be a factor. Ambition, greed, envy – it's what starts wars. You want what the other guy has, so you fight to take it from him. It feels like a war. That's why Summerset's Urbans connection rings for me.'

'Not old-style, hand-to-hand or weapon-against-weapon,' Roarke put in. 'But the more dispassionate, distant style of dropping a bomb from a great height, or launching a missile – or, more accurately, the cold science of germ and biological warfare.'

'That's what it is – warfare. Cold, dispassionate, and distant. But to start a war, or wage a battle, you have to want something.'

'It's possible all he wanted was to kill, and to see if his method worked, and how well.'

'Another factor, but if that was it, that was all, I think he'd take credit or taunt. *I'm so smart, I'm so clever. Look what I did.* Instead we're into the next day, and there's no contact. My sense is there's a connection to the bar and/or somebody in it he doesn't want coming back on him.'

She pushed to her feet, strode over to strap on her weapon. 'Another high probability, according to the percentages: It's a strike against a business or corporation whose suits frequent the place. He didn't get that bonus or promotion, or more probable, got demoted or fired.'

'I've got most of that data as well – or will have by now as I left the search ongoing last night. By the time you compile all these names, you and your team are going to have more suspects—'

'Persons of interest – for now.'

'However you want to term it. It'll take a week to run them, interview them, analyze.'

'I'm going to cross them with mine. Anyone who pops on

both lists, that's priority. We'll work through elimination, go with the percentages. I'll get more manpower for the drone work. Whitney's going public, so that means we'll have the cracks and loonies buzzing us – but there may be something in what comes in. We'll sift through, follow up.'

She paused, pulled on a jacket. 'I need to see the data, and I need my boards. There's time to filter it down some before the briefing.'

'I'll give Feeney, and you if you want it, time when and where I can.' He laid a hand on her shoulder as they walked out together. 'You'll contact Mira, make arrangements to talk to her.'

She actually felt her hackles rise. 'I said I would.'

'Then I trust you will.'

Even as she walked into her office, Summerset stepped out of Roarke's. The man had some kind of spooky radar, or he'd found a way to plant tracking devices.

Either way, it was creepy.

'I have some information you may want.' He offered her a disc. 'There are names on there of people who trust me. Their identities must be protected.'

'Understood.'

'Some of the information can't be officially confirmed, as the files have been sealed if not destroyed.'

She lifted the disc. 'Is this speculation or fact?'

'The attacks are fact. There were witnesses, including the boy I spoke of last night – though he's no longer a boy. You have his name now, and his statement as he related it to me.

Others I spoke to, who were in the position to know or find out, state the initial investigation was able to identify most of the components of the substance used. The base was lysergic acid diethylamide, commonly called—'

'LSD. I know what it is.'

'The other components are on the disc, but as I said, can't be confirmed. I have a connection who was, during the time, in the King's Army. We weren't acquainted during the war, but met some years after. He states a suspect was apprehended after the second attack, taken into custody. The investigation was subsequently closed, and deemed an accident.'

'An accident?'

'Officially, yes. Speculation, as he related the rumors that ran through the ranks. The suspect was transported to an unknown location. My acquaintance believes he was executed, but that can't be verified. Others believe he was held and used to create an antidote, or still others say the military used him to create more of the substance, perhaps others.'

'No ID on the suspect then?'

'The theory was, and remains, he – or they – were part of the fringe element who believed society had to be destroyed before it could be rebuilt. The Purging, they called it. They were, thankfully, small groups who used any means to destroy homes, buildings, vehicles – hospitals were a favorite target, as were children.'

'Children?'

'They abducted them. Those they abducted they indoctrinated, or attempted to indoctrinate into their ideology.

Once they'd purged – people, culture, technology, finance – the children would repopulate and rebuild.'

'Why haven't I heard of this?'

'The Purging is documented, though whitewashed and diluted. Study your history, Lieutenant. Past is prologue.'

'Shit.' She turned to her board. 'Maybe this is some fringe group of terrorists, and I'm going in the wrong direction.'

'Has there been any contact with authorities? Any claim for credit?'

'No. And damn it, this type of group *wants* the credit.'

'I agree. Any attack during the Urbans initiated by these fringe groups was immediately followed by a message sent to the nearest military or police authority. It was always the same message: "Behold a Red Horse."'

'Horse? What the hell does a horse have to do with it?'

'I remember this,' Roarke added. 'I've read of this, of them. They didn't have a specific leader or figurehead, and were for the most part scattered and disorganized. But fervent all the same. They believed the wars, and the social and economic upheaval before them, signaled the end-time. And they not only welcomed it, but sought to help it along to their own ends.'

'Great.' She shoved the disc in her pocket, then a hand through her hair. 'Add possible whacked religious fanatic to the mix. What's with the horse?'

'The Second Horseman of the Apocalypse,' Summerset told her. '"And when he had opened the second seal I heard the second beast say: Come and See."'

'"And there went out another horse that was red: and

power was given to him that sat thereon to take peace from the earth, and that they should kill one another: and there was given unto him a great sword."'

'Jesus Christ.'

'Don't blame him,' Roarke said. 'He didn't actually write it.'

'The red horse is often interpreted to represent war,' Summerset added. 'And so they used that symbol, and that passage to symbolize their beliefs, and justify their murder of innocents.' Summerset studied her boards. 'I don't know if it's what you have now.'

'It's a hell of a long time to wait between attacks, but I have to follow this up. I appreciate the information.'

'Of course.'

Roarke looked after him when he left. 'Difficult memories for him. You understand difficult memories.'

'Yeah, I do. And it's worse if they decide to make a replay. That horse thing's from the Bible?'

'Revelation.'

'I'll need to take a look at it, and at your data. Maybe there's another connection, personal grievance, greed, and bastardized religion. Abducted kids. We don't have that. Possibly the killer was an abducted kid – toddler gets snatched, raised in Crazy Town, grows up and decides to saddle the red horse.'

She shook her head. 'I have to work through this.'

'I'll leave you to it.' He took her shoulders, drew her in for a kiss. 'I'll come into Central later if I can.'

113

She went to her desk, called up Roarke's data. She gauged her time, hit the highlights, ordered the cross to run, and the results to copy to both home and office comps.

While it ran, she read Summerset's data, picked through it, wrote up her own notes. Somewhere, she mused, there'd be a file on known members of this Red Horse cult. Sealed and buried maybe, but they'd be somewhere.

Once she'd organized for the briefing, she decided she'd program Revelation to audio on her vehicle computer. Save time.

She hauled up everything she needed, snagged her coat on the way out.

She intended to bypass her office, head straight to the conference room to update the board, program the new images. And spotted Nadine Furst, Channel 75's top screen reporter, best-selling author, and dogged crime beat investigator pacing the corridor outside her bullpen.

They may have been friends, but at the moment, the always camera-ready, sharp-eyed Nadine was the last thing she wanted to deal with.

Nadine's power-red toothpick heels clicked, and the glossy pink bakery box she carried swung back and forth with her movements. Eve wondered why, of all days, her men hadn't snatched the baked goods and given Nadine a pass into her office.

Couldn't get past her, Eve calculated, and into the conference room where even Nadine didn't have the balls to intrude.

Eve moved forward, recognizing by those clicking heels and the swinging box Nadine was steamed.

'Getting an early start today,' Eve commented on Nadine's return trip.

Those cat-green eyes fired. 'You don't return my half dozen contacts, and Jenkinson – *Jenkinson*, for God's sake – turns down three dozen handmade pastries and tells me I have to wait out here or in the lounge. I get nothing but spin and double-speak from the media liaison. I deserve better than this, Dallas. Goddamn it.'

'I haven't returned your contacts or any from the media. We're Code Blue until the media conference later today.' Eve shot up a hand before Nadine could snarl a response. 'My men, including Jenkinson, have more on their minds than pastries. Whatever you think you deserve, Nadine, there are times you just have to wait.'

'If you don't trust me after all this—'

'It's not a matter of trust. It's about time and priorities. I can give you five minutes, and that's all.' She turned into the bullpen, held out her hand for the bakery box. Jaw tight, Nadine shoved it at her. 'Go on into my office. I'll be right there.'

Leaving Nadine to go or stay, she crossed to Jenkinson's desk.

'Sorry, LT. I couldn't order her out of the building, but—'

'No problem.' She dropped her bag on his desk. 'The minute Peabody gets in, give that to her, tell her to start setting up in the conference room. She'll figure it out.'

'You got it.'

Eve plopped the big pink box beside the bag. 'Fuel up. It's going to be a long one.'

His tired face brightened. 'Yes, sir!'

She heard, as she started toward her office, the stampede as detectives and uniforms surged Jenkinson.

Rather than taking the undeniably uncomfortable visitor's chair, Nadine stood at Eve's skinny window, arms folded.

'What group is responsible for the attack on the bar? Has Homeland or any government anti-terrorist organization joined this investigation? How many individuals infiltrated the bar, and do you have any in custody? Will you confirm a biological agent was used in this attack? There are sources that claim some of the victims were induced to injure or even kill others. Can you confirm?'

While Nadine rolled out questions, Eve rested her hip on the corner of her desk, waited.

'You just wasted a chunk of your five. You can be quiet, listen to what I can and will tell you, or you can keep wasting your time.'

'This is bullshit, Dallas.'

'No, it's not bullshit, not when over eighty people are dead. Not when families, friends, neighbors are reeling from the shock of that loss. Not when the handful of survivors is struggling with intense physical and emotional trauma.'

'I spent time with some of those families and friends yesterday. I know what they're dealing with. You're not giving them any answers.'

'I can't. Not yet. The reason you're in this office, and I'm talking to you isn't because we're friends. We've both got jobs to do, and we're both damn good at our jobs. You're in here because you're the best I know, and because I know whatever I tell you to hold, you'll hold. I don't doubt that, and I don't have to ask for your word. That's not friendship either, it's knowing what you do isn't just a job to you, any more than mine is to me. So be quiet, and listen, or let me get back to what I have to do.'

Nadine took a long breath, rolled her shoulders, shook back her streaky blond hair. Then she moved to the visitor's chair, sat.

'Okay. I'm listening.'

'I don't know what Whitney plans to say in the media conference. I haven't had time to connect with the liaison. Whatever I tell you that isn't part of that statement, part of what the NYPSD released to the public, has to hold.'

'All right. I want to record—'

'You can't. Take notes if you need to in that weird code of yours. Your eyes only.'

'You're starting to spook me,' Nadine said as she dug out a notebook.

'I haven't even started. We've identified a chemical substance that was released in the bar. Hallucinogenic base that causes paranoid delusions and violent behavior. It acts quickly, only lasts a short amount of time, but long enough. It's airborne, and as far as we know, these effects are also limited in area.'

117

'Like the bar, with the doors and windows closed, the air circulation helping disperse it.'

At least she didn't have to cross every 'T' with Nadine. She gave her what she could, what seemed enough to set Nadine's reporter's instincts humming.

'Nobody's taken credit or issued a political statement, so you believe an individual or individuals are responsible.'

'It's most probable,' Eve confirmed. 'However, I have some information from a source.' And this, Eve thought, was where Nadine and her research chops would serve.

She outlined, briefly, Red Horse, The Purging. 'I've only begun to dig into that angle,' she continued. 'I'm going to assign men to follow that up. You could look into that, dig into that, but whoever you use can't know it may be connected to this investigation.'

'Got it. I don't know much about that group, and history class was a long time ago, but didn't they take kids – for brainwashing? I haven't heard anything about child abductions.'

'No. It's a lead, an angle, with enough similarities to warrant a good, careful look.

'That's all I can give you, and I've got a briefing.'

Nadine got to her feet. 'I'm going to want more.'

'What I can, when I can. I can't promise.'

'You didn't need my word, I don't need your promise. It's professional respect, yes, but you're wrong, Dallas. It's also friendship.'

She started out, paused, smiled a little. 'I hate to admit this, but Jenkinson hurt my feelings when he turned down my pastries.'

'It was harder on him, believe me, than you.'

'I'm soft on him, on all of them. Good hunting, Dallas,' she added, and walked out on her power shoes.

Since she was there, Eve programmed a cup of coffee, and carried it with her to the conference room.

The reliable Peabody was updating the board.

'I'm putting up the current crop of persons of interest on a separate board,' she told Eve. 'Otherwise, the visual gets complicated to the eye.'

As she'd done exactly the same in her home office, Eve nodded. 'We'll need a third board. I have another angle I pulled out before I handed it off to Jenkinson. What do you know about the Urban Wars-era cult Red Horse?'

'Hard-line religious cult. Doctrine based on specific interpretations of Revelation. They were fanatics, dedicated to preparing for the end-time, which they believed had begun with the upheaval leading up to the Urban Wars. In their skewed vision, they saw themselves as servants or followers of the second horse – the red horse, of the Four Horsemen of the Apocalypse, which represents war, or general violence. Small, scattered groups attacked, bombed, set fires as part of their mission, and abducted children – no older than eight – as they believed their minds and souls were still pure enough to be indoctrinated. When the general population was destroyed, they would inherit the earth and repopulate it with true believers. They called this The Purging.'

Eve stared at her with narrowed eyes. 'How the hell do you know all that?'

Just a bit smug, Peabody buffed her nails on her cranberry-colored jacket. 'We studied it in school.'

'I thought Free-Agers studied herbs and flowers and fluffy woodland creatures, and how to weave blankets.'

'That – and a bunch of stuff. They also teach about wars, history, religious intolerance. You know, the ills of society and stuff. So you get the knowledge, the big pictures, and are free to choose your own path.'

'Huh. Have you read Revelation?'

'Some of it. It's really scary.' Smug died off in a shudder. 'It gave me nightmares.'

'Killer angels, pestilence, fiery pits, and death. I can't imagine why. When we get to that part of the briefing, you summarize, just like you did for me.'

'This was Red Horse?'

'You were doing so well, now you're jumping to conclusions. Detectives detect, they don't jump. Plus it's a stupid name for a murderous cult. It sounds like they should be frolicking in a meadow.'

'Maybe that was the point.'

'Maybe so.'

'They killed families, Dallas, sick people, old people, doctors. They took the kids, unless they were nine or ten or teenagers. Then they killed them, too. There weren't any kids in the bar.'

'I'll explain the possible connection. Just set up the third board.' She handed over a folder with attached disc. 'I need a few minutes. Nadine waylaid me.'

She sat at the conference table, pulled out her PPC to review her notes. Moments later, Mira came in.

'I'm early, I know, but I wanted to look over the . . . ' She trailed off as she saw the boards. 'That's considerable progress.'

'It's a hell of a lot more names, faces, possibles, and angles. I haven't decided if that's progress.'

'Motives. Money, power, jealousy, revenge.'

'Line up the usual suspects.'

'And religious fanaticism,' Mira added with fresh interest. 'The Red Horse cult? They were broken before the end of the Urbans. Do you believe they've reformed?'

'I doubt it, but fanatics find like minds.'

'I don't see the connection.'

'I'll explain.'

'They were greatly feared for the few years they purged. I had friends in Europe, where they were most prevalent.'

'I'd like your opinion on this angle once I brief the team.' Her promise to Roarke gnawed at her. 'I'd like some time today, if you have it.'

'I've cleared my day to focus on this. Any time you need.'

'Ah, this is mostly personal, so—'

'Of course.' Mira's eyes met hers. 'I'll be available when you need me.'

Get it over with, Eve told herself, *like a dose of nasty medicine*. 'Maybe we could take a few minutes after the briefing. That way it'll be off both our plates.'

'All right.'

They began to filter in, the detectives, the uniforms, the e-team. The room buzzed with voices, scraping chair legs, shuffling feet.

She took her place, waited a beat. 'Before you each give your own reports, I'm going to give you a fresh overview. As you can see we've added a selection of persons of interest.'

She ran them through it, focusing on the twelve people who'd come up in the cross-match search.

'We're going to add another factor to the scans. Connections to the Urban-era cult Red Horse, or any connection to cults or fringe religious or political groups. Peabody, give the team summary of Red Horse.'

'We didn't have much out of them in New York,' Feeney commented when Peabody finished. 'Had a couple hits, I remember they took credit for. They didn't last long here. People fight back, and fight dirty when you go after their kids.'

'My source has verified that there were two incidents in Europe, credited to Red Horse. Cafés where the substance we're dealing with – one with the same elements we've identified, and with the same results – was employed. The same substance,' she repeated, 'that the investigators identified. Before the government shut down the investigation, then closed and covered it. The cover-up included the apprehension of a suspect whose identity is unknown. Where he was taken is unknown. Whether he was executed, imprisoned or used to develop the substance or other chemical and biological weapons is unknown.'

She let the conversation on politics, cover-ups, the feds run its course.

'There's a connection,' Eve continued. 'And we need to find it. I trust Mira's profile. This isn't about politics or grand agendas. But the UNSUB has some connection to Red Horse or the cover-up or the original creator of the chemical.

'Feeney, I'd like to use Detective Callendar, and whoever you feel is your best in this area to dig for that connection. We need solid e-skills on this. Records were spottily kept during the Urbans.'

'You'll work with Nickson,' Feeney told Callendar.

'I'm all over it.'

'Anything to add from EDD, Feeney?'

'We don't have much, and nothing that adds at this point.'

'Baxter?'

'Stewart, Adam. You've got him up there. Sister, Amie Stewart's one of the vics.'

'Trust fund babies.' Eve flipped through her list of victims. 'She was in-house legal for Dynamo. And he's currently unemployed, and borrowing heavily from the trust.'

'We got some of that,' Baxter continued. 'Plus he buzzed. He's got something going. He's off, Dallas. And he was jittery, trying to pull off the grieving sib, comfort the parents. It didn't play. We earmarked him, too.'

'Bring him in. Toast him some.'

He gave her two more, another of which crossed with hers.

She called on Jenkinson and Reineke, got four with three crosses.

'Prioritize the board, Peabody. Stewart, Adam – connect to Stewart, Amie. Berkowitz, Ivan – connect to Quinz, Cherie. Callaway, Lewis – connect to Cattery, Joseph. Burke, Analisa – connect to Burke, John. McBride, Sean, connect to Garrison, Paul. Add Lester, Devon, manager of the bar, and Lester, Christopher, his brother, a chemist.

'These are the next wave of interviews. Work them. Dig in for a connection to the Red Horse cult, the cover-up. I want their financials and electronics gone over in detail. Peabody and I will take the Lesters.'

She handed out other assignments, legwork, drone work, to uniforms, scheduled a briefing at four.

Whitney stood. 'We'll issue a statement to the media this morning, and hold a media conference at thirteen hundred. I'll need you to meet with the liaison, Lieutenant, in an hour.'

'Yes, sir.'

'Handpick two more uniforms or detectives to assist in the search for sources of the chemicals and illegals. You're cleared for it.'

'I'd like Detective Strong from Illegals, Commander, if she's up for it.'

'Make it happen. You'll need more to run the tip line after the media breaks this. One hour, Lieutenant.'

'Yes, sir. Get moving,' she told the team. 'Peabody, contact Lester, Devon. Ask him to come in. Just a follow-up.'

'And the brother?'

'Not until Devon's in the house. We'll send a couple of stern-faced uniforms to bring him in. I need to reconnect with Morris, with Dickhead. And I want to go back to the scene. Get Devon in here asap, and we'll take him after I meet the liaison, shift to the brother, then go out in the field.'

'On it.'

Eve turned back to the board, started toward it.

'Eve.' Mira moved to her. 'You have an hour now. Why don't we go to my office?'

'I really should—' Get it over with, she reminded herself. 'Sure. I'll be there in five.'

7

Eve approached the dragon who guarded Mira's office expecting her to sniff in disapproval and tell her to wait. Instead the woman spared Eve a brief nod.

'The doctor's expecting you. Go right in.'

With no choice, no reasonable excuse, Eve stepped into Mira's sunny, comfortable office.

'You're very prompt.' Mira stood by her little AutoChef. 'I'm just getting tea. Sit down, relax a minute.'

'I'm kind of pressed.'

'I know. I'm going to look over the data you sent me, and your notes, and see if I can be of any more help. But meanwhile . . .'

In her quiet, easy way, Mira handed Eve floral-scented tea in a delicate china cup, then took her own. She settled in one of her set of blue scoop-chairs, sipped in silence until Eve felt obligated to sit.

Shrinks, she thought, knew the value of silence, just like a cop in Interview.

'You look well,' Mira said conversationally. 'How's your arm?'

'It's fine.' She rolled her shoulder, got a flash of pain memory. 'I heal fast.'

'You're a physical woman in excellent shape.'

'Meaning the body heals fast.'

Mira merely watched her with those quiet blue eyes. 'How do you feel otherwise?'

'I'm good. I'm mostly good. That should be enough. Nobody gets through perfect. There's always something, some ding, some cloud, some shit. And cops have more of all of that than most. So.'

'But you said this was personal, not work-related.'

'There's not much distance between the two for me. Sometimes none at all. I'm okay with that, too. I'm good with that.'

Stalling, Mira thought. So reluctant to be here. 'You've found a way to blend them very well. Will you tell me what's troubling you?'

'It's not me. It's Roarke.'

'I see.'

'Look, I've always had vivid dreams.' Eve set the tea aside. She wasn't in the mood to pretend to drink it. 'Ever since I can remember. They're not always pretty. Why would they be? Where I came from, what I do and see every day now. Maybe they were an escape when I was a kid. I could go somewhere else if I tried hard enough, and even if that place wasn't all warm and cozy, it was better than the reality. And the nightmares, the flashbacks, with my father, I'd beaten them back. I'd worked through it. I'd finished it.'

Mira just waited her out, waited for the pause. 'And now?'

'They're not as bad as before, but okay, I'm having some issues since Dallas.'

Small wonder, Mira thought, but nodded. 'That manifest in nightmares?'

'Not as bad,' Eve insisted. 'And I know I'm dreaming. I'm in it, but I know it's not real. They're nothing as bad as the one I had when I couldn't get out, and I hurt Roarke. I won't ever let that happen again.'

She couldn't sit. How did people talk about internal horrors sitting down? Pushing up, she let herself move. 'Maybe last night was a little more intense, but I'd had a damn vicious day. It's not surprising I mixed it all together.'

'Mixed what together?'

'The bar, the victims, the whole mess of it.'

She told herself to stay calm, just report. Ordered herself to stay fucking calm.

'I can put myself in a scene. It's part of being a cop. Seeing what happened, how, and maybe that takes you to why and who. I can see it, smell it, almost touch it. And Jesus, it was on my mind, wasn't it?'

She heard it, that pissy bite in her tone, worked to smooth it out again. 'So I went back to the bar, in my head, in the dream. But they were there, too. Stella, sitting at the bar. Her throat's open, the way it was when McQueen finished her. When I found her on the floor of his place. She comes back first when I dream now, sometimes without him. She blames me, always blames me, just like she always did.'

'Do you?'

'I didn't kill her.'

'That's not what I asked.'

'He'd have killed her eventually. That was pattern for McQueen. Maybe I speeded it up.'

'How?'

'How?' Eve stopped, confused. 'I caught her, arrested her. Hell, I put her in the hospital where I put the fear of God in her trying to get her to flip on McQueen.'

'Let me qualify.' With her elegant cup of fragrant tea perfectly balanced, Mira studied Eve. 'You caught her and arrested her. Doing so, as she ran, involved a vehicular chase during which she wrecked the van — the van she and McQueen had used in their abduction of Melinda Jones and thirteen-year-old Darlie Morgansten. She put herself in the hospital, where you did your job — again — pressuring her to tell you where McQueen was holding the woman and the child. Is that accurate?'

'Yes.'

'Did you aid in her escape from the hospital? Help her kill the guard, injure the nurse? Did you help her steal a car so she could run to McQueen to warn him you were closing in?'

'Of course not, but—'

'Then how did you speed her death?'

Eve sat again. 'It feels like I did. Maybe it's not accurate. It just feels that way.'

'Do you feel that way, here and now?'

'You mean do I feel guilty or responsible? Not guilty,' Eve

said. 'Not when I look at it, step by step. Responsible, yeah, to an extent. The same as I'd be if she'd been anyone. I was in charge. I took her in, and I pushed her hard. But she was what she was, did what she did. I'm not responsible for that.'

'She's not anyone. She was your biological mother.'

'I'm not responsible for that, either.'

'No.' Mira smiled, gently, and for the first time. 'You're not.'

'She didn't know who I was. In reality. When she was alive and looking right at me, she didn't know who I was. I was just a fucking cop who'd screwed things up for her. But in the dreams, she knows.'

'Did you want her to recognize you, before she died?'

'No.'

'So sure?'

'Absolutely.' Saying it, knowing it was true, settled her a little. 'I didn't have a lot of time to think about it while it happened. Everything moved so fast, and it rocked me, I admit, when I saw her face-to-face. And I knew. If she'd known me, somehow, it would have been a living nightmare. She could, and I know would, have done everything to ruin me, to ruin Roarke. To try to extort money. My life would have been hell if she'd known me, and lived.'

She took a breath, a long one, as she understood more fully what traveled in her own head. 'But there's the fact she didn't. She carried me inside her. Maybe she hated me for it, but she made me inside her, and at least for a few years, she lived with me. She must've fed me and changed me, at least sometimes. And she didn't know me. I don't know why she would, after so long, and I thank God she didn't, even for a minute. So, I'm glad she didn't, but I think she should have. It doesn't make sense.'

'Of course it makes sense. You have her recognize you, in the dreams, and deal with her blame, her anger, her vitriol.'

'Why? She's gone. She's done. She can't *do* anything to me now.'

'She abandoned you. You never had the chance to confront her, as the child she abused and left with another abuser. Nor, on that personal level, as the woman who survived it. What would you do, what would you say to her, if you could?'

'I'd want to know where she came from, what made her what she was. Is it just in the blood, or was she made – the way they wanted to make me – into something miserable. I'd want to know how she could feel so much contempt for the child she made, something innocent and defenseless. Her answers don't matter,' Eve added.

'No?' Mira arched her eyebrows. 'Why not?'

'Because everything about her was a lie. Everything about her was self-serving so no matter what I asked, her answers would be shaded with that. Why would I believe her?'

'And still?'

'Okay, and still part of me – maybe a lot of me is sorry I didn't get a chance to look her in the face, to ask those questions even if the answers didn't matter. Then to tell her she's nothing. She's *nothing*.'

131

The hell with calm, she decided on a rise of fury. *The hell with all of it.*

'They tried to make me nothing – no name, no home, no comfort or companions. All fear and pain. All cold and dark. I want to look her in the face and tell her no matter what she did, no matter how she hurt me, how she degraded me, she couldn't make me nothing. She couldn't make me her.'

Her breath came out in a shudder, and she felt tears on her cheeks. 'Shit.' Impatient, she swiped them away. 'It's stupid. It hurts to think about it. Why think about it?'

'Because when you try to block it out, it comes at you in your dreams where you're vulnerable.'

She rose again, still restless. 'I can live with the nightmares. I can beat them. I did it before, and they were worse. But Roarke . . . I don't know why, but I think it's harder on him now. Harder to deal with them, with me.'

'He couldn't confront her either. And he lived through this experience in Dallas with you. He loves, Eve, and those who love suffer when who they love suffers.'

'I know it. I see it. I'm here because I know it, I see it. And it pisses me off she's causing me more trouble dead than she did alive. I have faces of so many dead in my head. I can live with them. I did my best by every one of them when they came to me. I can live with her, too. But I don't want her to have this power, to make me weak.'

And there, Mira thought. 'Do you think having nightmares makes you weak?'

'It does. You said it yourself.'

132

'I said vulnerable. There's a difference, a considerable difference. Without vulnerabilities, you'd be brittle, inflexible, cold. You're not. You're human.'

'I don't want to be vulnerable to her.'

'She's dead, Eve.'

'God.' A little sick, she pressed her hands to her face. 'I know it. I know it. I stood over her body. I examined it, determined cause and time of death. I worked it. And yes, she's still . . . ' She searched for the term. ' . . . viable. Enough so when I dream about her, I'm afraid, and angry. She looks at me, she knows me, and something clutches in my gut.

'I'm part of her. That's how it works, isn't it? What a woman eats, whatever she puts in her body goes into what's growing inside her. What's in her blood. They're attached until the cord's cut. She was broken, so wouldn't something be broken in me?'

'Do you think every child born inherits all the flaws and virtues of the mother?'

'No. I don't know.'

'Sit a moment. Sit.'

When she did, Mira reached over, took Eve's hand so their eyes stayed level. 'You aren't broken, Eve. You're bruised, and still healing, but you're not broken. I'm a professional. You can trust me.'

Though it made Eve laugh a little, she shook her head.

'They did break you, all those years ago when you were only a child – innocent, as you said, defenseless. And you took what was broken and put it back together, made it strong, gave it purpose. And you let it love. You're more your own woman than any I've ever known – that's a personal and professional observation.'

'I need to end her. I know I need to end her. I won't have Stella in my head, and I won't have her bringing my father back.'

'Coming here? You've taken steps to doing just that. Tell me, I asked you once before if you knew why you called her Stella, and him your father. Do you know the answer now?'

'I thought about it, after you said something. I didn't real-ize I was doing it. But I think . . . What he did to me, what he did to a child – his own child? I think he was an evil man. I don't like using that word because it's sort of clichéd, but he was. But . . .'

Because her throat was dry, Eve gave in, picked up the tea, and drank.

'I was hungry a lot, but I never starved. I was cold a lot, but I always had clothes. I learned to walk, to talk – I don't remember, but he must've done that. It wasn't because he cared. I don't think he was capable of genuine feelings. But he didn't hate me. I was a commodity to him, a tool he could use and abuse, one he hoped to train to bring in money. I was with him until I killed him. He raped me and fed me, he beat me and he put clothes on my back. He terrorized me and put a roof, of some sort, over my head. He wasn't my father the way Leonardo is to Belle, or Mr Mira is to your children, or Feeney or any normal man is. But he was my father, and I accept that.'

'You've come to terms with it.'

'I guess. She left me with him, without a thought. And my memories of her are less detailed, less clear. But the ones I have are of her hurting me, in small, sneaky ways. Ugly ways. Slaps and pinches, shoving me into a closet in the dark, not feeding me and saying she had. And her looking at me with naked hate. She was capable of feelings. They might have been selfish and twisted, but she had feelings, emotions. And for me, there was hate.

'If he'd been the one to leave, she'd have killed me. Smothered me or locked me up to starve. She was capable of that, because she had feelings. She was my mother, that's a fact. But I won't call her that. Maybe it's some small way, some little step toward trying to end her.'

'Good,' Mira assured her. 'That's good.'

'I've been thinking about them, both of them, a lot the last few days. I should've known something was building up. I just wanted to work it out on my own some more first, but I should've come to you before.'

'You came when you were ready.'

'Roarke was ready,' Eve replied, and made Mira laugh.

'You might have come for him, but you wouldn't have talked to me the way you did if you weren't ready, too.'

'It's annoying that I feel better. Because he boxed me into this,' she explained. 'That makes him right. I have to report to Whitney.'

'You've a little time left.'

'I think time's going to be a problem. I don't think this

maniac's going to wait until my psyche's all nice and cozy again.'

'Cozy your psyche's never been. Whoever's responsible for all those deaths will find your psyche very formidable. You know you can contact me here or at home, any time, when you need to talk again. You won't resolve all this in an hour, or a day. But I promise you, you will resolve it.'

'And you're a professional, so I can trust you.'

'Exactly.'

'Thanks,' Eve said as she got to her feet again.

'I have one suggestion. A kind of experiment.'

'It doesn't involve pressure syringes or "you're getting sleepy"?'

'No. You have a strong mind, a flexible subconscious. I wonder if the next time you dream of Stella, you'll think of me.'

'Why?'

'As I said, an experiment.' Mira lifted a hand, briefly brushed Eve's cheek. 'I'd be interested in the results.'

'Okay, I can try. But I'm hoping I vented her out some. I've got a mass murderer to catch.'

'I'll send you my thoughts once I've reviewed everything.'

'I appreciate it.' Eve paused at the door, glanced back. 'I really do.'

She went to her office first. No point touching base with Morris, she decided after checking her incomings. He'd sent her another batch of reports, and after a quick read she found nothing new, not from him or the reports from the lab.

She did deeper runs to familiarize herself with the Lester brothers before the interviews, then headed up to Whitney's office.

She hated the media circus, so was relieved, even a little pleased to find Kyung with Whitney. The media liaison, and Chief of Police Tibble's top spinner, wasn't – as she'd told him after their first meeting – an asshole.

He wore a dove gray suit with a deeper gray shirt and a flash of red in the tie. Perfectly tailored, she noted, to his tall, fit body. His smile added charm to his smoothly handsome face.

'Lieutenant, a pleasure to see you again. It seems we have another difficult situation.'

'Yeah, upwards of eighty people dead is a situation.'

'One that must be carefully handled with the media. There's already been speculation regarding a terrorist attack. That we want to deflect and defuse.'

'It might have been one.'

'*Might* isn't a word we like to use in conjunction with terrorist and attack.'

'No. Agreed.'

'Commander Whitney will read a statement, and he'll take questions for a brief period. Chief Tibble has opted not to attend, as by so choosing he was able to convince the mayor to leave this to the NYPSD – for the moment.'

Keep the politics out. 'Good.'

'You won't take questions.'

'Even better.'

'The commander will simply acknowledge that you head an experienced investigative team, all of whom prioritized this incident. You're already working several leads, conducting interviews, examining evidence – and so forth.'

'What are we telling them about the difficult situation?'

He smiled again, gently. 'The NYPSD has recovered and identified a substance which was dispersed by an individual or individuals. Contact with this substance caused violent behavior.'

'That's pretty straightforward.'

'Too many leaks have already sprung regarding the substance, the aftermath. It will be your job to stick to the statement when and if questioned by any reporter.'

'That's no problem. Except I've already spoken with Nadine Furst, and used my own judgment.'

She noted Kyung's mild look of pain, plowed on. 'She'll hold the information I told her to hold until I clear it, but with it she'll be able to gather information that may be relevant regarding the Red Horse cult, and any connection to this investigation.'

'How much did you give her?' Whitney demanded.

'Enough so she'll dig into – confidentially – the cult, and anyone suspected or confirmed to have been a part of it.'

'I realize you and Nadine have a personal dynamic,' Kyung began.

'It's not a matter of our dynamics. It's a matter of her ethics. She agreed not to use the information I gave her until

I cleared it. She won't. There's a connection,' Eve continued, addressing both men. 'She'll keep digging until she finds it – unless I find it first.'

'Nadine's given me no reason to doubt her word or her ethics,' Whitney commented. 'If the Red Horse angle leaks . . .'

'It won't have come from her, or from my team. If it leaks, it's a damn sure bet it came from the killer. Sir?'

'Go ahead, Lieutenant.'

'We handle this, media-wise, in a straightforward fashion. Keep the details lean, but don't cover up the fact something was done to these people. I think that's exactly the right way to go. Going on the theory we have one guy, or a guy with a partner or partners. He'll enjoy the attention. The fast spurt of questions, the careful answers. But it won't be enough. The commander is a calm, and okay, commanding presence. While our guy'd enjoy the fact the NYPSD's commander is leading the charge, he's probably going to be irked he didn't get the mayor to come out and dance. Then he's going to bask awhile as the reporters get their stories on. But it won't be enough,' she repeated.

'You're saying he'll be compelled to repeat the experience.'

'Kyung, he's going to hit again unless we catch him first however we play it. Nobody goes to this much trouble, this much planning, achieves a whopping success, then dusts his hands off and moves on.'

'That's . . .' Kyung searched for the proper word. 'Unsettling.'

'Oh yeah. And if we go by the other theory, whacked religious cult picking up where they left off during the Urbans, same deal. This type needs to feed, and the appetite's voracious. For the thrill and satisfaction of the kill, from the glow and ego of the aftermath. Everybody's talking about him. They'll be talking about all the memorials for all the dead. All that grief's like chocolate sauce. It just sweetens the meal.'

'You're telling me to prepare for another statement, more briefings.'

'Don't plan a vacation. Sir, I've got an interview coming in.'

'Go. If you're in Interview or following up a viable lead, don't come in for the media conference. The media, and the public,' Whitney continued before Kyung could protest, 'will be satisfied the lead investigator is working the case.'

'Thank you, sir.' She beat feet before he could change his mind.

Eve moved through the buzz of Homicide. Cops who weren't out in the field or in Interview worked their 'links and comps. The smell of bad coffee swirled so thickly she could have bathed in it.

'Dallas.' Peabody intercepted her. 'I've got Devon Lester in Interview B. He came right in.'

'Cooperative.'

'Baxter and Trueheart have Adam Stewart in A. I don't know the status. I'm having Christopher Lester brought in, and hooked C for him. The uniforms are going to signal me when he's tucked in.'

'Okay. Quick overview. The Lester boys are tight. Christopher's five years older, big IQ, did the fast track through school. Some big, fancy degrees in chemistry, biology, nanotech. He heads his own department at Amalgom, developing and testing new vaccines.'

'Kind of tailor-made for brewing up a psychedelic stew.'

'He'd know how, or could find out. I didn't come up with a connection to Red Horse. Neither brother has any religious affiliation. Devon, average student, got an undergrad degree in business and management. Christopher's married, twelve years, two sons. Devon's divorced once, currently in three-year same-sex marriage.'

'I looked at criminal on Christopher,' Peabody told her. 'Traffic violations. He likes to drive fast. But that's it.'

'Their finances diverge like the education,' Eve continued. 'Chris pulls in about four times what his brother makes. But Devon stood as his brother's best man, is godfather to one son. Interesting bit. Before Roarke bought the property, Devon was looking to secure a loan to buy it himself.'

'I can't have it, I'll kill everybody in it, in a really spectacular way. Then maybe I can get it cheap?' Peabody pursed her lips. 'It could play.'

'Let's go try it out. Look busy,' Eve added, 'a little harried.'

'I already do.'

'Play it soft, sympathetic.'

Peabody sighed. 'What else is new?'

Eve breezed into Interview where Devon sat at the table,

hands clasped together. A long-sleeved black tee fit snug over his chest.

'Record on. Dallas, Lieutenant Eve, and Peabody, Detective Delia, entering Interview with Lester, Devon, on the matter of Case Number H–3597-D. Mr Lester, thanks for coming in.'

'I'm glad to do it, to do anything I can.'

'We're recording this follow-up. As you can imagine, we're taking statements and follow-ups from a lot of people.' She sat, rubbed the back of her neck as if it troubled her. 'When we have people in like this, we routinely read them their rights. It's for your protection, and it keeps everything clean.'

He paled a little under the explosion of red dreads, but nodded. 'Sure. Okay.'

She read off the Revised Miranda. 'So, do you understand your rights and obligations?'

'Yeah, sure. I keep thinking about my guys. D.B. and Evie, and all of them. Drew's still in a coma. Is there any more you can tell me? Anything?'

'We're shifting through a lot of evidence, Mr Lester.'

'Devon, okay? I know you're doing everything you can, but all those people . . . We went to see the rest of the crew, Quirk and me. He's been a rock, but it was the worst thing I've ever done, and I couldn't tell them why or how. I couldn't really tell them anything.'

'It's hard,' Peabody said gently, 'to lose someone, then to be the one responsible for telling others they've lost someone, too.'

'I didn't know how hard. Every time we told one of the guys, it was like it happened all over again.'

'Let's try to sort it out,' Eve began. 'You know the setup better than anyone.'

'Yeah, well, D.B. had it down. Really the whole crew.'

'Still, you're the manager.'

'I don't know how I can go back there. I don't know how anyone can. I don't know what Roarke's going to do with the place now.' He closed his eyes. 'I don't know what any-body's going to do.'

'Why don't you take me through the routine? Who opens, who closes, who has access to what.'

'Okay.' He took a long breath. 'Either D.B. or me are there. Either of us could open or close, or both depending.'

'No one else?'

'We were the only ones with the codes. Well, I mean Roarke would have them, and Bidot. But on the day-to-day, just me and D.B. One of us would be the first one in, last one out. You check the drawer. We don't do much cash business, but you gotta keep some. You check the night's receipts. The office isn't locked, but nobody goes in but me or D.B. And the comp and drawer are locked, and passcoded. That's SOP. You gotta check supplies,' he continued, moving through the opening procedure, then through the closing.

'Could D.B. have lent his codes to anyone?'

'No way. No way he'd do that.'

'And you?'

'Lieutenant. Ma'am. A manager's got to be responsible.

Trustworthy. You can't play fast and loose and keep your job. I trust my crew, but nobody but me and D.B. could open or close, or access the receipts.'

'You didn't share that information, not with your partner, your brother?'

'No. What would they want it for?' He leaned forward. 'You think somebody got in, planted whatever it was? I don't know how. It would've showed on security. It would've triggered the alarm.'

'Not if they had the codes. Easy to get by the alarm, then change the security disc out. You're sure, Devon. No doubt?'

'No doubt.' He sat back again, chopping a hand through the air. 'But hey, they could've jammed it, or cloned the codes, something. You see that stuff on screen. It could be that way. They could've put it on a timer or something, like a boomer. I think they did it to take a hit at Roarke.'

'Do you?'

'I've been thinking. Can't think about anything else. It doesn't make sense to kill all those people, people you couldn't even know. Everybody knows Roarke, right? It's his place. This happened in his place, and maybe he's not going to open it up again. He takes the loss. And he feels it, too, because it was his place. Some people are just sick. Some people are just sick enough to kill all those people just to take a hit at Roarke.'

'Something to think about. Still, he hasn't owned it long, and it's one of his smaller businesses. You were thinking about buying it, weren't you, Devon?'

He flushed a little, shifted a little. 'I took a look. Out of my reach, what with the capital, and the taxes and all that. I thought how it would be something to have my own place. Now, I guess I'm glad I didn't try it. Something like this? I don't know how you come back from it.'

'It's rough. Thinking about that, maybe somebody who wanted their own place, found it out of reach, might find a way to bring the price down to a bargain. It wouldn't be hard for somebody who knew the place, how it works, how it's set up. Somebody with access to everything, anytime. And somebody, say, whose brother's a chemist. Like yours, Devon.'

8

He stared at her with his shadowed, bloodshot eyes. Said nothing at all.

'Your brother's a big-shot chemist, right, Devon? Dr Christopher Lester, with a bunch of letters after his name. A really smart guy,' she added, opening a file, nodding as she scanned it. 'A scientist.'

'What?'

'Is your brother a chemist who specializes in the development and testing of medicines and drugs?'

'He – yeah. What's that got to do with any of this?'

'Put it together. You couldn't afford the place, so you have to work for somebody else. Somebody with more money, more connections. Somebody, like you said yourself, everybody knows. That's a pisser, I bet.'

'No – it's—'

'Your brother's got access to all kinds of drugs, chemicals, and the knowledge to put them together.' Eyes on Devon, she slapped the file closed. 'A substance is released in the bar you run, Devon, and when it's your day off. Boy, that's handy. People die, it's a massacre. And a scandal. Property value plummets. Like you said, maybe Roarke's not going to open again. Maybe he'll sell it. Maybe, again like you said yourself, somebody did this to take a hit at Roarke, and to bring the cost of the property down.'

'You – you think I did this? To my own people? My own place?'

'Roarke's place.'

Fury rose up until his face matched his dreads. 'He owns it; I run it.' Devon slammed a fist on his chest. 'I run it! I know every single one of the people who work there, and all the regulars, too. I know a lot of the people who died yesterday. They *mattered* to me. I come in here to try to help, because I want to find out what happened, who did this. And you accuse me?'

'No one's accusing you, Devon. It's a scenario.'

'It's bullshit. You're saying I could've made this happen. And worse, God, you're trying to pull my brother into it? Chris is a hero. You get that? A hero. He works to save lives, to make lives better, to *help* people. You've got no right to say anything bad about my brother.'

'We have to ask questions.' Peabody put on the calm as Devon's outrage spun through the room, sharp as whirling blades. 'We have to consider different possibilities before we can eliminate them and move on in the investigation.'

'You want to look at me, you look. Inside, outside, back and forward. Give me a truth test, stick a fucking probe up my ass. I've got nothing to hide. But you lay off my brother, right? You lay off Chris.'

'Let me ask you this, Devon.' Eve leaned back a little. 'If

Roarke sells, and the price is in your reach, would you buy the place?'

'In a heartbeat.' He folded his arms over his chest. 'Make something of it.'

'If you wanted the place, still want it, why didn't you ask your brother for a loan, or to make an investment? He could afford it.'

'If I can't make it myself, it's not mine, is it? I don't tap Chris when I want money. He's my brother, not a frigging bank. I've got nothing more to say about it. Unless you're charging me with something, I'm leaving.'

'We're not charging you with anything. You're certainly free to go.'

He shoved back, scraping the chair on the floor. At the door, he turned. 'I'd hate to be somebody who's always looking for the worst in people.'

When the door shut, Peabody lifted her shoulders in a hunch. 'He kinda made me feel guilty.'

'You're a cop. You're paid to look for the worst in people.'

'I like to think of it more as hunting down the worst people.'

This time she rubbed the back of her neck because it did trouble her. 'Do you want to count the number of times we've had somebody in that chair who looked like a nice guy who turned out to be a stone killer?'

'I don't have enough fingers.'

'Exactly. Let's talk to the brother.'

*

Christopher Lester shared his brother's coloring and build. Rather than dreads, he wore his red hair short, straight, styled like a Roman centurion. He wore a well-tailored suit and perfectly knotted tie, both in deep, bronzy brown.

His wrist unit winked gold in the overhead light.

'Dr Lester,' Eve began. 'Thanks for coming in.'

'I'm happy to cooperate. I assume this has to do with the murders at On the Rocks yesterday. My brother's devastated.'

'You've spoken to him.'

'Of course. I contacted him as soon as I heard there'd been trouble. If he'd been there . . .'

'I understand. We'd like to record this interview.' Eve ordered record on, read in the data. 'I'm going to read you your rights. It's routine.'

Chris lifted his eyebrows. 'Is it?'

'It's standard, and for your protection.' She recited the Revised Miranda. 'Do you understand your rights and obligations, Dr Lester?'

'Yes, I do.' His hands, big like his brother's and perfectly manicured, folded on the table. 'What I don't understand is what you think I can tell you, or what possible help I can be.'

'You never know. Yesterday, the day of the incident, was your brother's day off.'

'Thank God. That may be selfish, but he's my brother.'

'You contacted him, you said.'

'A friend heard the bulletin, told me. She knew Devon managed On the Rocks as I'd taken her there for drinks. I contacted him.'

149

'Where were you?'

'I was still at the lab. Actually about to leave. I tried his 'link immediately. I can't tell you how relieved I was when he answered.'

'You weren't aware of his work schedule?'

'No. It changes often, as does my own. When I reached him, he was at the bar. Not inside as they — the police — wouldn't let him go in. He said he was coming in here, to try to find out what happened. When we spoke later, he said he and his partner would visit the rest of his staff this morning to tell them.'

He looked away a moment. 'My brother is a strong man, a good manager. To be a good manager he has to know how to handle problems – small and large – with equanimity. And he does. I've never heard or seen him so broken. I hope to never hear or see him broken like this again.'

He looked back, straight into Eve's eyes. 'So I came in to speak with you, as requested. And I'll answer these questions fully understanding you suspect him. I'll answer them, Lieutenant, so you'll understand Devon is a strong man, with equally strong senses of loyalty and compassion. He not only loves his work, he cared, very much, for every single person who worked under him. He could tell you their names, the names of family members, pets, boyfriends, girlfriends. They are – were – family to him.'

'He wanted to buy the bar.'

'I'm aware. His partner, Quirk, told me Devon had looked into buying it some months back, but didn't have the funds.'

'You have them.'

'Yes. I would've lent him the money, and offered knowing full well he'd refuse. We're stiff-necked, you could say. Pride is a Lester family trait – or flaw, depending. I can also tell you Devon was pleased when Roarke purchased the property as it gave him confidence it would be well-funded, and marketed.'

'Price should be going down after this.'

He shot Eve a look of pained amusement. 'Lieutenant, do you seriously think a man like Devon would bring about the horror of what happened at On the Rocks so he'd lower the market value of the property into line with his own finances? He'd never deliberately cause anyone harm, and in addition, simply lacks the means. He wouldn't know how to . . . Ah.'

Now Chris sat back, nodding slowly. 'I would have the know-how. The reports haven't been very specific, but it was a biological or chemical agent, something that infected the people inside the bar. So Devon and I plotted this out, and I gave him the agent.'

'He wanted the bar, you have the means. It's a theory.'

'My brother isn't a wealthy man, not monetarily. Did you know he's planning a memorial, for everyone who was killed? Using his own funds. People mean more to Devon than money, and always have. You don't have to take my word. Talk to anyone who knows him.'

'You work with hallucinogenics, with psychedelic drugs?'

'Yes, I have.'

'Recently? Currently?'

'If you clear it with the board, I'd have no objections to discussing my projects – past, present, and pending. But I can't give you information on them without that clearance, not even to eliminate myself, even my brother, from a suspect list.'

'All right. Thank you again for coming in. Interview end.'

'That's it?'

'Yes, for now.'

He rose. 'Even if he weren't my brother, I'd tell you Devon is the best man I know. It's as simple as that. I hope you find who's responsible, Lieutenant. I don't believe Devon will begin to heal until you do.'

'Start working on getting a warrant for Dr Lester's records,' Eve told Peabody when they were alone.

'Okay.'

'Problem?'

'It's just ... The way each of them took up for the other, the way each one of them talked about the other. I'm not being soft,' Peabody insisted. 'But it's hard to reconcile that kind of love, affection, and respect with two people who'd plot a mass murder.'

'Do you have enough fingers to count the number of partners who had affection and respect, possibly love for each other who murdered, raped, stole, tortured, and committed other assorted crimes?'

'I guess not.'

'We follow through, Peabody, every detail, every angle –

even when the odds are they're not going to lead us any-where.'

'You don't think the two of them are involved?'

'No, but I can't prove it. If I thought they were involved, I couldn't prove it. Let's get data.'

Eve glanced at the time. 'Aw, gee, I missed the media con-ference. That's a shame.'

'That statement hits the red zone on the lie-o-meter.'

'But it feels good. I want thirty minutes in my office to check incomings and status, then we're going back to the crime scene.'

'Do you think they're not involved – the Lester brothers – for the same reasons as me?'

'Probably not.' Eve headed out, moving fast so Peabody had to hustle to keep pace. 'Devon's not stupid. Roarke doesn't have stupid people managing any of his interests. But when I push him on buying the place – would he if he could – he's all pissed off, damn straight. Smarter to say it's tainted, his friends died there. Smarter, too, to go straight to pissed or shocked when I led him to our looking at him and his brother. Instead he's just confused at first. He didn't have an answer for everything. He didn't have the right answers for everything. If he had, I wouldn't bump him down the list.

'The brother's smart, real smart, and a lot more cynical. He caught on fast. I want to look at his research, his experiments, I want a feel for what he does and how he does it. But it would be stupid for him to kill a whole bunch of people in his brother's bar. If he were going to do it, he'd have done it somewhere else, not so readily connected.'

'Part of your reasoning's like mine. It's the kind of people they are – the stand-up-for-your-brother people.'

'Half a point.'

'Three-quarters.'

'Three-quarters because I'm too busy to argue.'

'Yay!' Peabody said as Eve swung off and into her office.

She'd barely started on the first report when Baxter came to her door.

'Need a minute.'

'Take it,' she told him.

'Adam Stewart. We just finished up with him. He's alibied for the time line, and I've got nothing that puts him in that bar yesterday, or at fucking all.'

'But?'

'He's a bad bastard, Dallas, and he's cagey. Bad and cagey fits whoever did this.'

She saw his eyes flick toward her AutoChef. Under the circumstances, she thought, what the hell. 'Go ahead, but don't spread it around you got coffee in here.'

'To the grave.' He moved quickly before she could change her mind, programmed a mug for each of them. Knowing its miseries, he sat on the edge of her visitor's chair.

'But,' Eve prompted again.

'With him being a bad bastard and a cagey son of a bitch, I figure he's capable of doing this. But I don't think he had the means or opportunity. Plus, poking around, the sister –

that's Amie Stewart – didn't go in there routinely. Now and then, sure, but she wasn't a regular. How'd he know she'd be there? They weren't close, didn't hang out together, or make regular contact. But . . . '

Baxter let it hang a moment while he drank coffee. 'He's sweaty in Interview. He's evasive, and not doing such a hot job of pretending to be sorry his sister's dead. I had Trueheart drill down into his financials, and they don't add up. It looks like he found a way to siphon off some funds from the trust deal, so with a little work we could get him there.'

'We don't have time to poke at some bad bastard for embezzlement right now.'

'I get that, but there's more. The trustee who oversees all that stuff went missing two weeks ago. Being a detective, I detect two ways, the trustee was in on it with Stewart and went on the lam, or the trustee found out what Stewart was up to, and Stewart made him disappear. Either way . . . '

'Yeah.' She calculated. 'Do you have any problem turning this over to Carmichael and Sanchez?'

Baxter winced, comforted himself with coffee. 'I gotta say, I want to see it through. The fucker's dirty, and he just makes my ass twitch. But I can live with passing it on, at least until we clear this case.'

'Do that, and move to the next.'

'That'd be Callaway, then Weaver. They've been in meetings all morning, but we're going over to the offices, corner them, separately, try to follow up with some of the others. That place lost five people.'

He rose, set aside the empty mug. 'I wish it was Stewart, because he needs to go away.'

She made a note to stay on top of Stewart, then toggled back to continue with the reports, read Strong's, and saw the Illegals detective currently pushed on a lead on sources for large or regular purchases of LSD.

Back to the beginning, Eve decided, and returned to the bullpen. 'Peabody, with me. Unless otherwise notified, I want everybody in that briefing at sixteen hundred. I'm in the field.'

'I went to Reo for the warrant,' Peabody told her on the way to the garage. 'She doesn't see a problem getting it, and quick. Everybody's on full alert on this one.'

'I want at least two men on that, with experience and knowledge in Lester's field. Send in a request to Whitney.'

'Dickhead would have people.'

Eve sighed. 'Yeah, he would. Copy him on the request, further requesting Dickhead handpick two of his people to examine Lester's records, his lab – and I want reports on same in plain English.'

'I talked to McNab for a minute.'

'I don't want to hear your perverted sex chats,' Eve warned as they got into the car.

'We only spent like ten seconds on that part. They've about finished with the 'links. They got a couple more who were on when they were infected, and a couple more who made calls directly after becoming infected. It's ripping, he said, listening to it. They've been going over any and all recovered electronics. Memo books, notebooks, PPCs. Some of them were in use, too. It doesn't look as if they've got anything that's going to help. Nothing that pops as a communication with or from the perpetrator. But it shows, again, how fast and how strong the vics were affected.'

'How about the door surveillance?'

'They went back forty-eight hours. There's no break in the time scan, no anomalies. They ID'd some of the vics – I guess regulars – who went in and out the day before approximately the same time frame, and they're working on a search for any of the people who connect to vics or survivors to see if any showed up within the last couple days. They'll have those for you at the briefing. Some coworkers. The after-hours activity is just what you'd expect. Staff leaving, either alone or in groups. Last one out the two nights before the incident was Devon Lester, and that coincides with the work schedule for the week.'

Normal day-to-day, Eve thought. Until the world ends.

'Whoever's responsible knew about the door cam, which means anybody as it's right there in plain sight. If they didn't jam it, then they just walked in as staff or customer, and left the same way.'

'McNab says no jamming. They've run it through every analysis, including Roarke's. Feeney's also put a couple of his uniforms on listening detail. They're monitoring sites globally, and off-planet. Listening for any chatter on the incident. Any hint of any individual or person with prior knowledge, or claiming credit. Lots more chatter – it's the big buzz – but nothing that stands out.'

'He/they? There's going to be a reaction to the media conference. Lots of chatter and buzz, but Whitney's statement, and his delivery? It's going to strike as a challenge. Whitney's confident, stoic, steady. He might let some of the anger show, but that's just juice for this type.'

'You think he'll make some sort of contact.'

'That's what I'm hoping for.' But not what she feared.

When they got to the bar, Eve broke the seal, then took a moment to clear her mind. She stepped in, scanned the dimly lit space.

The ugly and all too familiar scent of blood and chemicals, of death and sweepers' dust, clung to the air. She cleared her mind of that, too.

'Lights on full,' she ordered, and imagined what it would have looked like at opening. Rather than broken chairs and tables, shattered glass, floors and walls stained with blood and gore, there would have been the shine and clean of closing mopping.

'Devon took us through the opening routine,' she said to Peabody. 'Be Devon. Walk through it.'

'Office first, check receipts and drawer.'

'Temp controls first,' Eve corrected.

'Right.'

While Peabody ran through the checklist, Eve stood back, watched.

Whoever opened moved through every area of the space – office, kitchen, storeroom, restrooms, behind the bar.

'He sees what he sees every day,' Eve said out loud.

'Sometimes people miss, in a routine, don't see what they don't expect to see. But Devon Lester's meticulous. He thinks of this as his place. I'd say the bartender followed suit, or he wouldn't stick as assistant manager.'

'No criminal on the bartender,' Peabody told her. 'I talked to the fiancée. Tough one. She said he thought of the bar as his home away from home as much as a job.'

'I saw the report.' And she'd read Roarke's background checks on the bartender, and the other employees. Nobody popped out.

'The substance or device had to be handy if it was used by a customer,' she considered. 'If it was staff, there aren't that many hidey-holes Lester, the bartender, or one of the other staff wouldn't see at some point during the day.'

'They're open for lunch,' Peabody pointed out.

'Yeah. Why risk leaving a dangerous substance on the premises, where it can be found or accidentally triggered before you're ready? You bring it with you, keep it with you.'

She moved to the bar, behind it, crouched, rose again.

'Not suicide.'

'Why?' Peabody wondered.

'All the next of kin have been notified. A good chunk of friends and coworkers have been interviewed. It's taking time, but vics' residences and places of employment are being searched. This was a big statement.'

She saw it again, like a film over the room. The blood, the bodies, the battlefield.

'If you're using it to self-terminate and take a bunch of

people with you, where's your announcement, your statement in your words? Suicides typically want people to know. And murder/suicides? They're not just depressed, they're pissed off. It's not impulse, so where's the mission statement?

'No,' Eve repeated, 'not suicide. He's out there. He came in.'

She moved back to the door, imagined the noise, the color and movement, the tables of people, the crowded bar. 'He's been here before, knows the place. He doesn't particularly stand out. He's one of the type who comes here after work, before heading home. Wears a suit, carries a briefcase or a file bag, a purse. Something normal, and it serves to carry the substance.

'He's not alone.'

'But—'

'You stand out more alone,' Eve said before Peabody could finish. 'He's got to figure there's a good probability there'll be at least a couple survivors. Maybe more. This is the first, so he can't be absolutely sure. Stop off for a drink with friends from the office, or meet a client, grab a table or a seat at the bar, order drinks. Get some finger food, talk shop, talk business. Blend in.'

'Pretty damn cold.'

'Cold, sure. But cool, too. Cool-headed. Controlled, detail-oriented. He's excited, has to be. He talks to the bartender or the waitress, maybe both. And he thinks, "'Soon you'll be dead. I'll kill you soon and I won't so much as smear the shine on my shoes. Today I'm God.'"

'Oh, man,' Peabody mumbled.

'And the same with the people he works with every day. You're not going into the office tomorrow, he thinks, or coming in for your shift. You'll never get that raise or promotion you've been busting your ass for. And I'm the reason. I'm the power here.

'His pulse may be racing at the thought of it, but it doesn't show. Not enough. He looks around at all the people – the suits, the drones, the eager beavers, the overworked. It ends for them here, over half-priced drinks and free salsa.'

'God,' Peabody breathed, because she could see it, too.

'It's so fucking funny when you think about it, and he thinks about it. But he doesn't laugh. He just has his drink, talks shop, eats a spring roll, bitches about the workload or the client or the boss – whatever the topic of the day might be.'

She wandered, glanced up, over. 'At the bar or a table close to it. This area, most likely. He wants to cover as much ground as he can – this space, the kitchen, down to the restroom. Ventilation's right overhead here.'

She studied the bar, pictured the nearby tables.

'Purse or briefcase or bag on the lap, take out the substance, the container. What does he do? What does he do? Under the chair, the table, the barstool? Drop something, bend down to pick it up. Set it down? Who'd notice? Could have your hand sealed, coated with it. Shake someone's hand, friendly slap on the back, whatever – spread it around some.'

'If it started spreading wouldn't he be infected?'

'That's the sticky,' Eve muttered. 'It works fast, so he'd have to get out fairly quick. Into the air. Or if he concocted this, he could've concocted an antidote, a preventative. But either way, he can't hang around and see how it goes.'

'Gotta go. See you tomorrow. I'll e-mail you that file when I'm finished. Easy-breezy, and out the door.'

She walked to it, opened it. Stepped out.

Traffic, noise, movement again. More of it when the killer had stepped outside. Slide right into the flood of people heading home, to other bars, to shops.

'Offices,' she said to Peabody, looking up at the towers with countless windows. 'But apartments, too. A lot of people like to live close to work. They can walk in the good weather. Plenty of buildings with a good view of the bar. He can't stay inside, can't risk planting a camera, but wouldn't it be fun to stand at one of those windows, look down here and know what was happening inside? Timing it, waiting for it, watching throngs of people walk right by the door, unaware, oblivious to the fact that you're committing murder right *now*.'

'I'll start a cross-search for anyone with a residence in eye-line with the crime scene.'

'Worth a shot,' Eve agreed.

'There are a couple cafés, street level, with street views. He could've walked across the street, sat down, and watched from there.'

'Start some uniforms on a canvass, showing photos of everyone who's marked for another round of interviews to whatever waitperson had window tables during that shift.

Yeah, he might've enjoyed having a bite to eat or a fancy coffee right across the street, watching the whole damn aftermath. All those cops swarming the place, checking out his work. He might.'

While Eve stood on the sidewalk, considering a killer's entertainment, the lunch rush at Café West was in full swing. They served good, simple food with table and counter service. Customers sat ass to elbow, talking over the clatter of dishes.

The air carried the appealing scent of fall with today's pumpkin soup. Most of the crowd looked for a quick, easy meal that didn't consume the entire lunch hour, so they could pop out again to handle an errand, or linger over coffee before scrambling back to offices and cubes.

Lydia McMeara picked at her tiny, undressed salad between sips of spring water. She was on a diet – again. She nibbled hungrily at lettuce, struggling not to hate Cellie for her perpetually svelte figure. Then there was Brenda who couldn't claim svelte but owned smoking.

Plus they both juggled men like tennis balls while she herself was in a two-year rut with dull, earnest Bob.

Even his name was dull and earnest.

Things would be different once she got in shape. And it would be easier if she could afford some body sculpting rather than starving herself on rabbit food.

The money she saved walking the eight blocks to work and back every day would add up, she assured herself. And God knew she spent nearly nothing on food anymore.

What she wouldn't give for a couple bubbling slices of pizza with the works and a calorically prohibitive beer.

'Here, Lydia.' Cellie with her perfect cupid's bow mouth smiled sympathetically. 'Have half my sandwich. Half doesn't count.'

'I'm fine.'

'You should join my health club.' The smoldering, smoking Brenda had a salad, too. A huge one with an ocean of creamy dressing, seasoned croutons, and golden slivers of cheese.

At that moment, Lydia hated her.

'I don't have time, and I don't have the money. Anyway, I'm not hungry.'

'I wish you wouldn't do this to yourself, Lydia.' Cellie, big brown eyes radiating sincerity, rubbed a hand up and down Lydia's arm. 'You're beautiful.'

'I'm fat,' Lydia said flatly. She hated herself, hated Cellie and Brenda. She wanted to slap the stupid, tasteless salad right in Cellie's face.

'I look fat, feel fat, am fat. And I'm going to fix it.' Annoyed, Lydia shoved the salad away. 'I'm not hungry,' she repeated, 'and it's too noisy in here. I feel a headache coming on. I'm going to walk for a while.'

'I'll go with you,' Cellie began.

'No. Stay. Eat. Eat, eat, eat. I'm in a bad mood, and I want to be alone.'

She stomped toward the door, squeezing through the spaces between tables while her temper spurted up like a black, oily fountain.

Oh yeah, midday headache from starving myself half to damn death, she thought.

She reached the door, yanked it open. Glanced back.

Her eyes met Brenda's, just for an instant. In them she saw the same vile dislike she felt, the ugly truth of it.

She always knew Brenda was a bitch. Always knew it.

For a moment she wanted to turn around, stomp back, and punch smoldering bitch Brenda in the face. Then claw her nails down it. Draw blood. Drink blood.

Instead, she slammed out the door, shoving her way down the sidewalk.

And lived.

9

They were under five blocks away when Dispatch notified Eve. She hit the lights and sirens.

'Run the owner,' she ordered Peabody. 'Now.' And soared up to vertical to skim over vehicles with no respect for a cop running hot.

She took a right, hard, blasted the horn as a clutch of pedestrians swarmed the sidewalk. They scattered like ants, and as she bored through, a woman in needle-heeled boots and towering blond hair took the opportunity to flip her the finger.

And thanks for your support, Eve thought.

'Privately owned,' Peabody called out, voice cracking only a little as Eve skinned by a loaded maxibus. 'Greenbaum Family LLC.'

'Building, too.'

Eve slammed the brakes, fishtailing as she squealed to a stop. She jumped out, and into pandemonium.

She spotted two uniforms and a beat droid scrambling to secure the scene, tape off the area from the crowd. People shouted, pushed. A couple of guys wrestled and rolled on the ground, trying to land punches. She saw a woman huddled on the sidewalk, weeping hysterically as another woman tried to comfort her. A man lay flat out while another administered CPR.

Several stood or sat, bleeding, eyes dazed.

Through the open door she saw the heaps and tangles of bodies – including the one facedown half in, half out of the café.

'Get that barricade up. Peabody, call for MTs.'

'We got them coming,' one of the uniforms shouted. 'We called for more backup, Lieutenant.'

'For Christ's sake.' She grabbed one wrestling man by the shirt collar, dodged a flailing fist, didn't quite dodge a jabbing elbow to the ribs. 'Peabody, goddamn it!' She managed to get a boot on the chest of the second man, rocked as he bucked. 'Stop! Cut it out or I swear to God I'll knock your empty heads together.'

She ignored the expected versions of 'He started it'.

'Make a move, and you're in restraints and headed for a holding tank. One move. Don't test me.'

Ribs throbbing, she turned. 'Listen up! I said, *listen up!*' Laying a hand on the butt of her weapon, she raised her voice over the din of the crowd. 'I'm Lieutenant Dallas, NYPSD. You will not cross the barricade. You will cease and desist any attempt to interfere with these officers or you will be arrested and charged with hampering an investigation, creating a public nuisance, obstruction of justice and anything else I can toss in to screw up the rest of your day.'

'People are hurt!' someone screamed.

'Medicals are on the way.'

'Fucking cops stunned unarmed people. I saw it. I recorded it.' He waved his 'link like a trophy.

'And I'm here to determine what happened. My partner will take your statement.'

'Then cover it up. Fucking cops.'

Enough, Eve decided, and stared hard into the bystander's eyes. 'Pal, I've got people bleeding on the ground and officers in harm's way. Record this.' She held up her badge. 'That's Dallas, Lieutenant Eve. Get the badge number? This fucking cop is telling you to clam it until my partner takes your statement. If you continue to attempt to incite a riot you'll be restrained and charged, and transported to Central.'

When he opened his mouth again, her eyes went to ice. 'Go ahead, say something. Once you do, get ready to tag a lawyer.'

She waited until he broke eye contact and stared at the ground.

'Officers will take statements, but anyone who's a doctor or medical professional please step forward, and this officer will enlist your aid for any wounded. Call in the rest of the team. Start talking to people,' she told Peabody. 'Get statements, keep them talking, and make sure you confiscate that asshole's 'link for evidence.'

'Yes, sir, and won't that be a joy.'

'Who owns the damn building?'

'Not Roarke.'

'Small blessings. Keep that line secured,' she ordered the

droid. 'And you' – she gestured toward the second uniform – 'report.'

'We were on patrol and observed several individuals running from this location. One ran into our vehicle as we pulled to a stop. He stated people were killing each other inside Café West. We called it in, approached the scene.'

He took a breath.

'Lieutenant, when we opened the door it was crazy. People were lying on the floor getting trampled while other people were fighting. Bare hands, knives – Jesus – forks, broken glasses. People screaming, howling like animals. Some of them laughing like mental defectives.

'We called out warnings. Some of them came at us. That guy didn't lie, sir. Some of them weren't armed, but they were coming at us, and still going at each other. We had to deploy stunners.'

'Is there going to be anything on that asshole's 'link vid you can't stand up to, Officer?'

'No, sir, Lieutenant. No, sir.'

'Then don't worry about it. Continue.'

'Okay. They'd go down, and more would come at us. I don't know how many we stunned before we got some control, because some of them didn't go down on the first stream. By the time we did, we had a riot brewing out here, with people who'd seen, some who'd started to go inside and got attacked before they managed to get out again.'

He nodded toward the black-and-whites that pulled up. 'There's backup. And the MTs.'

'What time did you stop at this location. Be precise.'

'Logged the stop at thirteen-eleven, sir.'

Fourteen minutes. Odds were they'd be clear.

'All right. Work with Detective Peabody. Get statements, names, contacts.'

She moved toward the arriving uniforms, snapped out orders.

'You—' She pointed at a pair of MTs. 'I need you to start moving the wounded out. Seal up first. With me.'

She stepped inside, noted cracks and breaks in the entrance door. Might've saved some lives, she thought.

Beside her the MT sucked in his breath. 'We're going to need more transpo.'

'Get it.' She sealed up herself, moved carefully through the café, around bodies, crouching now and again to check for vitals.

She began to mark the dead as she had at the bar.

As she worked the moans began, and the weeping. A hard sound, she thought, and still, it meant life.

'Reineke and Jenkinson are on scene,' Peabody said as she came in. 'They're getting statements. I logged Mr Costanza's 'link into evidence. Watched it with him first. He sort of changed his tune when he viewed it with me. It clearly shows the officers under attack.'

'I'm not worried about that. Does it show anything we can use?'

'Not much. It's from outside, on the sidewalk, but you can see people fighting inside, the movements, hear the scream-ing.'

She had to swallow. 'It's pretty awful.'

Peabody crouched as Eve had when someone reached up to her. 'Help's coming,' she comforted. 'You're going to be okay. We've got you now. They've got about a dozen wounded out, Dallas.'

'Smaller place, not as many people. Somebody smashed the glass in the front door. It may have helped dilute some of the agent.'

'Might be why so many people out there were ready to rumble.'

'That's just New York. Forty-one dead. Start getting IDs, TOD, COD.'

She moved outside again. 'Baxter, Trueheart, with Peabody.' She spotted McNab — a celery stick in his green cargos — ducking under the tape. 'Inside,' she told him. 'Start bagging electronics.'

She walked over to the comfortably rumpled Feeney. 'Not as bad as the first. Smaller place, and they got outside air from the broken door, more when the cops broke in. I didn't spot any cams inside. One on the front door, another on the alley exit, but I haven't checked them.'

'We'll take it.'

As Feeney glanced around, Eve noticed the dried blood smeared on the cuff of his trench coat. From yesterday, she realized. Only yesterday.

'I didn't figure he'd hit again so fast,' Feeney said.

'And I figured when he hit again, he'd go bigger. So he goes faster and smaller. But he's sticking to the same general

171

area. Places he knows. People he knows?' she speculated. 'Heavy on the business crowd again. Lots of dead suits in there.'

'Happy hour rush, lunch rush.' His basset hound eyes went grim. 'He's hitting prime times.'

'We haven't got a line on him, Feeney. He's scored over a hundred and twenty dead, and we haven't got a line.'

'Start at the top, work it through again. There's always something there, kid.'

'Yeah.' She let her gaze skim over the heads of the crowd to the buildings. *Somewhere around here*, she thought. *You're somewhere around here, you fuck.*

Reineke jogged over. 'Lieutenant, there's somebody over here you're going to want to talk to.'

She walked through the busy medicals to where Jenkinson stood with a plump blonde. Tears and tissues had smeared her eye makeup into black and lavender bruises. She wore New York black – jacket, sweater, pants, with short-heeled boots, and trembled as she bit at her nails.

'Lydia, this is Lieutenant Dallas.' Jenkinson used his trusted uncle tone. 'I want you to tell her what you told me. Okay?'

'I'm – I'm looking for Cellie and Brenda. We were having lunch.'

'In Café West?'

Fresh tears swam in terrified brown eyes, spilling through the makeup bruises. 'Yeah. In there. We were in there.'

Not a mark on her, Eve observed. 'What time did you leave the café?'

'I'm not exactly sure. A little after one, I guess. We were having lunch.'

'What time did you get there?'

'I – we – Well, we left the office about twelve-thirty, but the elevator was really slow, so that took forever. But it's only a little walk, maybe five minutes. And we got a table, 'cause they go fast. Then we went up to the counter to order. It's faster that way. I got a salad, just a plain salad. A little one because I'm on a diet. I was in a bad mood because I was hungry, I guess. I was really bitchy with them, even when Cellie said I could have half her sandwich. I was bitchy, and I left.'

'They stayed to have lunch, and you left, just a little after one. Did you have a headache, Lydia?'

'How did you know? I started to get a headache, and I just wanted to leave. It was crowded and noisy, and I was hungry, and my head started to hurt. I walked out, and walked around. I felt kind of sick, then I felt better. I felt bad, you know, because I'd been so bitchy. I thought I should come back. Tell them I was sorry, walk back to the office with them. But the police were here, and people were yelling. People were hurt and crying, and I can't find my friends.'

'We'll look for them. You come here a lot, on your lunch hour?'

'Sure. It's close, and the food's good. But you have to get here before one, or you're not going to get a table.'

'How did everything seem when you left?'

'Like usual, I guess.' Her eyes shifted, lowered, shifted again. 'Except . . .'

'Except?'

'I looked back when I got to the door, and Brenda was looking at me, really mean. She's not mean. I've never seen her look at anybody like that. It just made me so mad. I almost went back to the table. I wanted to punch her. I've never punched anybody. Now I can't find her.'

'Reineke, get the full names of Lydia's friends so we can find them.'

She signaled to Jenkinson, pulled him over. 'I want her examined. Get her to the hospital, have them run a tox, examine her nasal passages, her throat. She won't want to go. Convince her.'

'I'll take care of it. How many, LT?'

'Forty-one. It looks like sixteen survivors, at this point. We may find more, like Lydia, who got out before it took a strong hold. Get her examined,' Eve repeated, and moved fast to find Feeney.

'I've got a time line,' she told him. 'We got a wit who was in there with friends, but left – felt a headache coming on as she walked out. They got there approximately twelve-forty, and she left just after one. First on scene pulled up at thirteen-eleven. The vics inside were still infected.'

'It hit about the time your wit left. We'll focus on twelve-thirty to one-fifteen, to cover it. Cams were operational. I'll run the discs back at the house.'

'Run it with face recognition, using the faces we have

leaving the bar or connected to vics.' She pushed at her hair. 'We'll bump the briefing until eighteen hundred.'

She scanned the street, the buildings. 'He was here, Feeney. But he had to know about the cams. How could he risk popping on the security disc in both places? Can't. He found another way to get it in this location – or both. Or there's more than one of them, and they took turns. He had to leave about the same time the wit did. Hefty blonde, black pants and jacket. I want to see everyone coming and going about five minutes before up to five minutes after the wit.'

'I'm heading back now. Do you want to keep McNab?'

'If he's got the electronics, take him with you. Otherwise I'll send him in as soon as he has them all bagged.'

Baxter met her on her way back in. 'They're loading up the last of the survivors. We have fourteen from inside.'

'I counted sixteen.'

'Two didn't make it. I peeled off to talk to a couple of them who were lucid enough. It's running like the bar, Dallas. Having lunch, serving it or cooking it, headache, hallucinations, most with feelings of anger or fear along with the headache.'

'We've got one who got out, left with the headache.'

'Good.' He glanced toward the café, the blood on the sidewalk. 'She's lucky.'

He rooted in the pocket of his snazzy top coat – always the smart dresser, that Baxter. And came up with a PowerBar. 'Want half?'

'No. Maybe. What kind is it?'

'Yogurt Crunch.'

'That's a no.'

With a shrug he unwrapped it, bit in. 'I've had worse. McNab and two e-geeks have most of the electronics. We've got IDs on the survivors, and about half the DBs so far.'

'Take Trueheart and what you've got, go back and start running the names. I want lists of anyone with employment at any of the businesses involved in the first incident. There's going to be some cross. Another crossing the connections.'

It was going to come down to relationships and geography, she concluded. Who he knew and where he knew them.

'This is his comfort zone, his place. People tend to eat and shop in the same area, especially when they're on a schedule. Look for businesses between the two crime scenes. Use a two-block radius on both ends, list who lives in that sector who's connected to any survivor, any vic, or who we pin leaving either scene before the hit.'

Baxter took another bite of the bar, chewed thoughtfully. 'It won't be fast.'

'Get started. Briefing rescheduled for eighteen hundred.'

'LT.' Jenkinson hustled up. 'Lydia'll go in for exam, but I had to tell her Reineke and I would take her.'

'Get it done. Start interviewing survivors while you're there. Briefing's now at eighteen hundred. Don't waste time.'

Taking her own advice, she moved fast, walked back into the building, and spotted Morris kneeling beside one of the dead.

'You didn't have to come in,' she told him.

'You'll want confirmation as quickly as possible you're dealing with the same COD. There are tests I can run here.'

'And?'

'The same. I can give you solid confirmation within the hour, but it reads the same.'

She crouched down beside him. 'We're going to try to keep a lid on how and what. We won't, not for long, but do what you can.'

'Depend on it.'

'I am.' Still crouched, she scanned the room. 'Was it already planned? Both hits? Bang-bang. He went smaller. Impulse or planning? He's not impulsive, so ... Why this place?' She tracked the bodies. 'Who in this place?'

As he understood she was thinking out loud, Morris remained silent.

'Is he a familiar face, a regular? I bet he is. Pleasant enough guy, knows how to interact, but it's all surface. Probably speaks to the counter guy or the waitress whenever he comes in. Just a "How ya doing?" kind of thing. He *wants* attention, to be noticed, remembered. But he's just one of the many. Really just another customer here, and back at the bar. One of the many where he works? It's not enough. Not nearly fucking enough, not for him, not with his brains, his potential. He's not just one of the many. The suits and drones, the people who trudge through the workday. Goddamn it, he's special. They're beneath him, all of them. None of them matter, and still ...'

She shook her head, continued to study the room.

'Someone in here or something that happened in here mattered enough for this. Because it's not random.'

'He's going to need to brag,' she decided. '*You think the NYPSD worries me? Look what I can do, whenever I damn well please.*' She pushed to her feet. 'He'll need us to know that.'

By the time she'd finished, rounded up Peabody, and gone back to Central, she had a new batch of photos for her board.

'Post these,' she told Peabody, 'then check in with the lab.'

She moved straight into the bullpen, to Baxter's desk.

'Still working on it,' he said before she could speak. 'You were right. We've already found some vics who worked at the same places previous vics worked. Crossing survivors, too. There's a decent percentage, so far, who live in the area you designated.'

'Any connections between the vics in the two locations? Personal connections.'

'Still working on it.'

'Bring in a couple of e-men Feeney picks to help you run it. And tell him I'm heading up to talk to Callendar.'

She went straight up. Easier to go to, she calculated, then to send for.

She pushed into the color and chaos of EDD, scanned the neons and patterns, the busy movements for Callendar. When she didn't see her, Eve turned toward Feeney's office.

One of the e-geeks jogged by her. 'He's in the lab.'

She veered out again, turned toward the e-lab. She saw Feeney hunkered at a station on one end of the big, glass-walled area, and Callendar standing, doing some sort of dance, in front of another.

'Yo, Dallas. Got some bits and pieces.' Callendar stopped dancing, gestured toward a screen. 'Putting it together.'

'Anything I should know now?'

'Other than the Red Horse cult was full of crazy sick-heads? Not so much, but I'm working on it. I dug up a handful of names – abducted kids who got out or were recovered. Moving on it.'

'Keep moving.'

Taking her literally, Callendar went back to dancing.

'What do you see?' she asked Feeney.

'Something that might be interesting.' He, too, gestured to a screen.

'See for yourself.'

She watched him play back the door security disc, noted the time stamp. The busy sidewalk, people moving, moving, moving. Then the woman – brown and brown, early twenties, in a Café West shirt, unzipped navy jacket – came into the frame. She stopped, grinned at someone to the left; her mouth moved as she called out something. And she waved as she walked inside.

'Time's right,' Eve murmured.

'Yeah. It's fourteen minutes, thirty-nine seconds after the wit and the two with her went in. Wit leaves . . . ' He ran it forward, and Eve watched Lydia, her teeth clenched, her face rigid with fury, stomp out.

'Five minutes, fifty-eight seconds after the woman in the

Café West shirt goes in. Gets bitchy, gets headache, gets out. Yeah, the time's right.'

'I'm guessing if the wit had stayed inside another ten, twenty seconds, she wouldn't be a wit.'

'Her lucky day. Go back to the woman going in. What's she saying? Did you translate?'

'We don't have her full face, but the program reads her lips at eighty-five percent probability.'

He ordered it up.

No prob. I'll put it in for you.

'Okay. Do we have an ID on her?'

He toggled over to an ID shot. 'Jeni Curve, twenty-one. Part-time delivery girl, part-time student. No priors, no shaky known associates. Shares an apartment with two other females. And she's one of the vics. I checked.'

'She doesn't look suicidal,' Eve speculated. 'Doesn't look homicidal. Not nervous, not gathering her courage.'

'I've got others. Nothing's popping. Some in, some out, some alone, most with somebody. But your wit's the last out before this.'

He ran it forward six minutes. Eve watched the café door shudder, and the spiderweb spread over the glass. Most people on the street just kept going, one or two flicked the door a glance.

And one man bustled up, working his PPC as he pulled open the door. Distracted, he started to step in, stopped, goggled, stumbled back out of camera range.

'He's the one who called it in,' Feeney told her. 'Now

you've got this guy, paying less attention, pulls the door open, goes on in. See the door there?'

'Yeah. Looks like he tried getting the hell out again. He didn't make it.'

'Not his lucky day,' Feeney commented.

'Jeni Curve.' Eve stood, studying the ID shot. 'I'll look into it. Did you ID the people who left between Curve going in, Lydia coming out? We may get something from them.'

'Shot the data down to your unit. I ran them – standard – nothing pops there either.'

'I'll add them all to Baxter's cross. I'll put it in for you,' she repeated. 'Curve doesn't look crazy.'

'A lot of people who don't are.'

'Ain't that the fucking truth? Maybe. Maybe. I'll dig down.'

Halfway on the route between EDD and Homicide, her comm signaled. 'Dallas.'

'Lieutenant,' Whitney's admin spoke briskly, 'the commander needs you in his office, immediately.'

'On my way.'

She backtracked, grabbed an up-glide. Idly studied a couple of women with battered faces she made as street LCs. To her way of thinking their line of work was nearly as dicey as hers. You just never knew when some asshole would decide to punch you in the face.

In Whitney's outer office, the admin merely signaled Eve to go straight in. Still she knocked briefly before stepping inside.

Whitney sat at his desk, his hands folded. Chief of Police Tibble, his long frame suited in black with subtle chalk stripes, stood at the window.

She didn't know the third person, but made her as federal as quickly as she'd made the LCs on the glide.

She thought: *Fuck*, then settled into resignation.

It had to happen.

'Lieutenant Dallas,' Whitney began, 'Agent Teasdale, HSO.'

'Agent.'

'Lieutenant.'

In the three or four beats of silence, they sized each other up.

Teasdale, a slight, delicate woman, wore her long, black hair slicked back in a tail. The forgettable black suit covered a compact body. Low-heeled black boots gleamed like mirrors. Her dark brown eyes tipped up slightly at the corners. The eyes and the porcelain complexion had Eve pegging her as mixed race, leaning Asian.

'The HSO, through Agent Teasdale, requests to be brought up to speed on the two incidents you're investigating.'

'Requests?' Eve repeated.

'Requests,' Teasdale confirmed in a quiet voice. 'Respectfully.' She spread her hands. 'May we sit?'

'I like standing.'

'Very well. I understand you have reason to distrust, even resent HSO due to the events that occurred in the fall of last year.'

'Your assistant director was a traitor. Your Agent Bissel a murderer. Yeah, might be some lingering distrust.'

'As I said, this is understood. I have explained to your superiors the operatives and handlers who were involved in that unfortunate incident have been incarcerated. We have conducted a full and complete internal investigation.'

'Good for you.'

Teasdale's placid expression never changed. 'The NYPSD has also had some difficulties. Lieutenant Renee Oberman ran illegal activities, including murder, out of her department for many years before she was discovered, arrested, and incarcerated, along with the officers involved. Their dishonor doesn't destroy the honor and purpose of the NYPSD.'

'I know who I'm working with here. I don't know you.'

'A valid point. I've worked for the HSO for nine years. I was recruited while in graduate school. I specialize in domestic terrorism, and for the last four years have been based here in New York.'

'That's great. We don't believe we're dealing with any individual or group with a political agenda. I'll let you know when and if that changes.'

Teasdale smiled softly. 'Politics isn't the only basis for terrorist activities. The indiscriminate murder of multiple people in public settings is a kind of terrorism as well as homicide. I believe I can help you identify the person or persons responsible, and aid in your capture of same.'

'I have a solid team, Agent Teasdale.'

'Do you count among them a terrorist specialist with nine years of training? With nine years of field and laboratory experience? Who also holds advanced degrees in chemistry and who serves Homeland Security as an expert on chemical and biological warfare? You're welcome to check my bona fides, Lieutenant, as I have yours. I'm useful.'

'Useful to the HSO.'

'Yes, and that doesn't preclude my usefulness to you, your department, and your investigation. The request at this time is to consult and assist, not to overtake.'

'I can check your bona fides, but who do you work with, report to? And how long does "at this time" run?'

'I'll be working alone, as far as HSO contacts, and will report to, and only to, the head of the New York branch, Director Hurtz. You may or may not be aware that Director Hurtz, who moved into the position after the events of last fall, has been most directly responsible for the internal investigation that has led to several arrests and reassignments. I believe Chief Tibble and Director Hurtz are acquainted.'

'Yes.' Tibble spoke for the first time, his face as carefully schooled as Teasdale's. 'His personal request to me, and my acquaintance with him is the reason you're here, Agent Teasdale. And as I related to Director Hurtz, your clearance to consult will be the lieutenant's call.'

He held up a hand, in that quietly unarguable way he had to cut off her response. 'I'm perfectly aware the HSO and the director can, by law and procedure, attach themselves to the investigation, or take it over. As I'm sure you're aware, as is your director, that doing so will generate considerable difficulties with relations between the NYPSD and HSO, and in the media.'

'Yes, sir, that's very clear.'

'HSO has not endeared itself to the NYPSD, or anyone in this room save perhaps yourself. If not for my respect for Director Hurtz, I wouldn't have taken Lieutenant Dallas's valuable time for this discussion. It's your call, Lieutenant. You're free to take as much time as you need to make that call.'

'Can we have the room, sir?'

He lifted his eyebrows. 'Agent Teasdale. If you'll excuse us.'

'Of course.'

She exited as quiet as smoke.

'Permission to speak frankly, sir.'

'Weren't you?'

He had her there. 'If Teasdale's bona fides are as she states, and it would be monumentally stupid to lie, she'd be useful. I don't like HSO. Some of that's personal, some professional, and some because they're pushy, arrogant, and tangled in so much red tape investigations are often strangled. I don't trust them for all the same reasons, and more because they've shown that at the end of the day, the public results and opinions are more important than the victims and basic morality.'

She paused a moment, weighed it all. 'But I trust you, sir. I trust both of you without question or hesitation. If you tell me you believe this Hurtz is clean, that you believe he'll not only keep his focus on finding justice for those involved but also stay the hell out of my way – I'll take her on.'

'I've known Chad Hurtz for fifteen years, and know him to be a man focused on securing the safety of the country, and I know him to be a man of his word. He's playing this well, offering us one of his top people – and I've already checked her credentials. He'll keep their involvement low-key, as long as possible.

'If you agree, he and I will remain in contact, and will share information, and consult on a point-by-point basis if this consultation and dual investigation has merit.'

She nodded, glanced at Whitney. 'Commander?'

'If you refuse the assistance, I'll back your decision. If you accept, I'll make certain the terms remain as agreed upon.'

'Then she's in. I'll want to inform my team of the addition and the agreement. I need to get back to it.'

'You're dismissed.'

Eve went to the door, opened it. 'Briefing at eighteen hundred, conference room one, Homicide Division.'

Teasdale inclined her head. 'Thank you. I'll be there.'

'Screw it up, you're gone. No second chances for feds.'

Teasdale smiled again. 'I've never needed a second chance.'

'Let's hope you keep your record going,' Eve said briskly, and walked away.

10

Eve strode into her bullpen and the wall of noise from voices, comps, 'links. A quick scan showed her Detectives Sanchez and Carmichael were among the missing. They'd be out in the field, she assumed, scrambling to handle the cases dumped on them as she'd formed her team.

Before long, she calculated, they'd have more than they could handle. She'd need to consider pulling in from other divisions, other precincts.

'Listen up! We're taking on a consultant from HSO.'

She let the objections, bitching, disgust roll over her. She didn't blame her men as she'd had the same reaction herself.

'It remains our case, our investigation. Agent Teasdale is a domestic terrorist specialist, and she has qualifications I believe we can use. This is my call, so suck it up.'

She waited a beat. 'If, at any time, any of you have a problem – a legitimate problem with Teasdale, come to me. If it's a problem, I'll kick her ass. If it's bullshit, I'll kick yours.'

'You know how the feds work, LT.' Jenkinson brooded at his desk. 'Let us do all the legwork, put in the hours, bust down the doors, then come in and take it over when we've got it plated up like dinner.'

'If they get greedy, they have to get through me, then Whitney, then Tibble. As for this team? Over a hundred and twenty people are dead, so there will be no petty power plays, no whining and griping. Have your reports ready for the briefing.'

She walked out again, paused briefly when she was out of sight. She listened to the whining and griping. Let them get it out of their system, she decided, and headed to the conference room.

She expected to find Peabody, and came up short when she found Roarke working with her partner. She hadn't expected to deal with this, with him, quite so soon.

Marriage, she thought. Every bit as complicated and slippery as cop work.

'Another difficult day.' He looked at her as he spoke, carefully.

The man, she knew, saw damn near everything.

'Yeah.'

'I can't be of much use just now in EDD, so when you weren't in your office, I offered Peabody a hand. A lot of faces to go up, again.'

'Too many. Peabody, take a break.'

'We're almost – oh,' she said when she caught the look. 'I'll go check, see if we've got anything new in from the lab.'

Roarke waited until Peabody went out and discreetly shut the door.

'What is it?'

'You're not going to like what I have to tell you. It wasn't an easy call to make, but it was my call. And it's the right one — for them.' She nodded toward the boards.

'What call would that be?'

'We're taking on an agent for HSO as a consultant.'

His eyes went cool, very cool before he turned and walked to the AutoChef. Though he performed the everyday task of programming coffee, Eve knew when he walked away his anger was fierce.

'If we're going to fight about it, we have to fight later. There's no time now. But I need to tell you ... Roarke, I need to tell you I know what you did for me last year when you stepped back from taking retribution against the people in HSO who listened and did nothing while my — while Richard Troy beat and raped me. I know what it cost you to do that. I know you did it for me. You put me first. You put us first. I don't forget it. I won't ever forget it.'

'And yet,' he said softly.

'I can't put me, or us, ahead of them, all those faces. I can't, I just won't, let what happened to me years ago determine how I do my job, for them. It's already caused us both too much grief and pain. It has to stop. Maybe you'd have made a different call, but—'

'Yes, because I think more of you than you do.'

She couldn't fight it, couldn't find the fight, only the heart he filled with those simple words. 'No one's ever thought of me the way you do. I don't forget that either. And I knew when I made the decision it would upset you. You have every right and reason to be upset. I'm sorry.'

He set aside the coffee he didn't want. 'And yet,' he repeated.

'Her name is Teasdale. Miyu Teasdale. She's a domestic terrorist specialist, nine years in. She has advanced degrees in chemistry and biology. She'll be reporting only to Director Hurtz. Tibble knows him, personally, vouches for him. You look at them. Dig into them, use any means you want. I don't need to know. After you do, if you find they aren't as clean as Tibble and Whitney say, if you find anything that causes you to doubt I did the right thing, I'll break it off. I'll find a way.'

'Oh, I'll look. Believe me.'

'I didn't agree easily, and I wouldn't have agreed except . . . a hundred and twenty-six dead.'

'A hundred and twenty-seven. Another died in hospital shortly ago.' And because he saw that instant of sorrow on her face, he picked up the coffee, handed it to her.

'I need help. Maybe she'll just be deadweight, or worse an annoyance or distraction. But maybe she'll make a difference. Or there'll be more dead, Roarke, and we won't have enough boards for their faces.'

'If I look and find something, you'll end the consultation?'

'Yes. My word on it.'

He nodded, then took time to think, to settle, by getting coffee for himself. 'It doesn't sit well, does it?'

'No. But I'm afraid he's just getting started, and she'll have a fresh eye, a supposedly expert eye. And additional resources. Before you say it, I know I could ask you for anything and anyone. Someone equally qualified.'

'Yes,' he agreed, 'and that would sit better.'

'Probably with both of us. But this agreement keeps HSO's involvement minimal. It keeps me in charge. They could have moved in, tried to muscle away the whole shot. And while we were playing tug-of-war . . . ' Her eyes went to the boards again.

He said nothing for a moment, only drank some coffee. Then frowned at the mug. 'Why won't you stock your regular in this thing? It's not as if you don't have an unlimited supply of bloody coffee. Word is you married me for it.'

And with that, she understood the crisis had been averted. 'I don't want to spoil my men.'

'You'd rather burn all our stomach linings away.'

'Cops' guts are tougher than that.' She smiled. 'Civilians' may be more delicate.'

He stepped to her, flicked a finger down the shallow dent in her chin. 'Then you'll perfectly understand why I've ordered food in for the briefing.'

'You—'

'Have you eaten since breakfast? I thought not,' he said when she only frowned at him. 'I'll drink your deplorable cop coffee, you'll eat my food. And we'll get on.'

'We'll get on if it's pizza.'

'I know my cop.'

Yes, he did, she thought. 'I talked to Mira.'

He took her hand now, held it.

'I don't like the way you maneuvered me into it, even if you were right.'

He laughed at that, kissed the hand he held. 'I love you, Eve. Every contrary inch.'

'I'm working it out, and I don't want you to worry. I feel . . . lighter,' she decided. 'I can't talk about it now.'

'No need. Feeling lighter is enough.'

'I just want you to know, I'm getting a grip on it. I've got to put it away, get back to this.' She took a breath. 'And I'm going to keep doing that. Putting it away, where it belongs, and getting on with who I am, what I am, what we are. You need to do the same.'

'I'm with you, Lieutenant.'

'Then I'll bring Peabody back.' She reached for her comm just as the knock sounded on the door.

'That's probably the food. I'll take care of it.' Roarke walked to the door.

When it came to food, she thought, cops had noses like bloodhounds. She put her comm away, watched Peabody trot in behind the delivery team.

Then Jenkinson, Baxter, Reineke.

'Let them set it up, for Christ's sake, before you swarm it like locusts. And leave some for the rest. Peabody.'

Looking mildly concerned she might qualify as 'the rest,' and miss out, Peabody hurried over. 'Most of us missed lunch.'

'I'm aware. We have an addition to the team,' Eve began, and laid it out.

Peabody's face settled into stubborn lines that slid into a sulk. 'I don't like her.'

'You haven't laid eyes on her.'

'I don't care, and Teasdale's a pussy name. A prissy pussy name.'

'Really? And Peabody's a name that makes bad guys shiver in fear?'

'If they know what's good for them. Besides, she's HSO, and that makes her a prissy pussy in a bad black suit.'

Well, Eve thought, her partner had the suit right. 'Deal with it, and her. Now grab a slice, then finish the board.'

She started to grab one herself but moved off when someone called her away. Instead, she found a reasonably quiet corner and began her run on Jeni Curve.

She saw Teasdale come in, take her time crossing the room. The HSO agent would have to weather the flat, suspicious looks.

'Agent Teasdale. You're welcome to fight for a slice of the pie.'

'Thank you. I've eaten.'

'Suit yourself. Have a seat.'

When Whitney and Tibble came in, the noise level dropped by half.

'We'll start in a few minutes, Chief, Commander. Most of the team didn't manage lunch today.'

'I didn't manage it myself,' Tibble told her. 'It smells good.'

'Please, help yourselves.'

As they did just that, Eve turned and nearly walked into Teasdale. The woman moved like a cat, one with considerably less bulk than Galahad.

'Problem?' Eve asked her.

'No. I wondered if your AutoChef is stocked with tea, and if so, if I might impose.'

'There's some herbal crap in there. Dr Mira prefers it.'

'Doctor Charlotte Mira.' Interest kindled on Teasdale's face. 'I've studied much of her work. I'm looking forward to meeting her.'

'She'll be here. And Teasdale?'

'Yes, Lieutenant.'

'If you're working in the room, whatever's in the AC's up for grabs. You don't have to ask.'

'Thank you.'

Teasdale moved away. The cops in the room evaded and avoided, aimed suspicious stares at her back.

'It seems I'm not the only one who has an issue with HSO.'

Roarke was another who moved like a cat. Eve merely shrugged. 'They'll suck it up.'

When Strong from Illegals stepped in, Eve crossed to her. 'It's good to see you, Detective.'

'I appreciate the assignment. I've been on light duty long enough.'

'You still favor the leg,' Eve pointed out.

'Some, but it holds.'

She'd lost weight as well since her injuries. A header down a glide while being chased by a fellow cop who planned to kill you tended to screw up the appetite. 'Your new LT working out?'

'He's good. Anything's an improvement over Oberman, may she rot in her cage for the rest of her miserable life. But he's good. Solid. The squad feels like a squad now that we swept the dirt out.'

'Grab some pizza and a chair. We'll get started.'

She waited until she had the full team in the room, noted that Teasdale introduced herself to Mira, and took a seat beside the doctor. And that, as was his habit, Roarke opted to lean against the wall rather than sit.

'As you've been informed,' Eve began, 'we have a consultant from HSO. Agent Teasdale will be given access to all case files, reports, and data, and will share any data she acquires during the course of her consult.

'Between twelve-fifty-five and thirteen hundred this afternoon the occupants of Café West were exposed to the same chemical substance identified at On the Rocks. The ME and lab have confirmed. There are forty-four additional dead. The smaller venue, and the quick response by patrol officers resulted in more survivors. Jenkinson, Reineke.'

'We talked to some survivors and wits on scene,' Jenkinson began. 'The uniforms stunned anybody who advanced, and that kept them breathing. Most of them were dazed, not yet lucid. Some of the injuries were severe, and we lost a couple more as a result.'

'We talked to some of the injured at the hospital.' Reineke picked up the report. 'The ones who were able to remember mentioned the onset of a headache followed by hallucinations, anger, fear. It's a replay, LT.'

'We got Lydia McMeara examined, as ordered,' Jenkinson told her. 'She's got mild inflammation, nose and throat. They ran her blood. She's got some trace of the chemical. She was jittery, Dallas, but it's hard to tell if that's the chemical or shock. One of the women she was with, Brenda Deitz, is in the morgue. The other's in the hospital, in critical.'

'We got two survivors . . . ' Reineke gestured to the board, got Eve's nod. He rose, walked to the board with IDs of survivors.

'Patricia Beckel and Zack Phips. Each stated they'd known someone who was killed yesterday. On further questioning, Beckel identified her neighbor Allison Nighly, and Phips a coworker, Macie Snyder. We pursued with five more survivors. Three of those knew a total of seven of the dead or injured from the bar. The remaining four survivors were in surgery or unable to be questioned. We'll follow that up.'

'So out of the eight survivors you were able to question on this point, five had a connection to one or more victims from the first incident.'

'Yeah, that's more'n half, Loo. I call bullshit on coincidence.'

'I second that bullshit. Keep on it. Following that theme. Baxter?'

'We've been doing the cross, employment, relations, residence. Survivors, vics, wits, persons of interest. Our boy Trueheart made a graph.'

'It's more of a spreadsheet.' Trueheart, young and built in his uniform, flushed a little. 'There's a lot of cross, Lieutenant, like you figured. I programmed it so it's easier to see. Peabody loaded it if you want it on screen.'

'I do. Peabody.'

When it flashed on, Eve rocked back on her heels as she scanned. 'Run the numbers, Trueheart.'

'Sir?'

'Run it through. Explain.'

He looked a little ill, but he rose, took the laser pointer she handed him. 'We've grouped them by type – DB, wit, survivor, POI. We cross that with places of employment and residence. An additional cross with relations. We highlighted areas of connection – blue for employment, green for residence, yellow for relationships.'

'It's colorful,' Eve commented.

'Yes, sir. We anticipated considerable employment connections as both scenes catered to the offices in that area. And as you suggested, there's also additional matches with residences. The numbers drop off with relationships, but as you can see there are crosses there, too. The highest percentage of connections involve Stevenson and Reede for place of business, excluding the crime scenes themselves, sir. For residence, the highest percentage of connection ranges along this block of Franklin. A probability scan has a sixty-eight-point-three the target or targets and/or perpetrator or perpetrators work or worked in, um, the highlighted triangulation.'

He cleared his throat. 'With more time, I think I can eliminate some of the connections and refine the results.'

'Do that.' Geography, she thought again. Geography and relationships. 'Give Feeney a copy. I want this transferred to a board we can work on. That's good work, Trueheart, Baxter. Feeney, will you run the EDD report?'

She stepped away, pulled out her 'link when it signaled, then slipped out of the room.

When she came back, Feeney had several ID shots on screen.

'We don't need all of them,' she told him. 'Just her. Just Jeni Curve.'

Feeney's eyes narrowed. 'You got something.'

'She's the source. I asked Morris to do a secondary exam on her and the others you've got up there. Curve's tox levels were significantly higher than the other vics, the inflammation more pronounced. At this time forensics is testing her clothing, and the minute pieces of glass recovered from her jacket pocket.

'Morris has also determined that Macie Snyder, a vic from the first incident, exhibits those same elevated levels. Her clothing is also being examined at this time. She was the source on the first.

'Peabody, bring up Trueheart's chart again.'

'Yes, sir. There's no connection between them,' Peabody said when the data was on screen.

'Yeah, there is. It's just not highlighted yet. We'll use red for the killer. It fits. Replay Curve's security image. Walking into work. Stops, smiles, waves, calls out what lip-reading program makes out as *No prob. I'll put it in for you.*

He gave her the substance – a vial, a little bottle. Or slipped it into her pocket without her noticing. Either way, she didn't have a clue. Maybe he asks her to order him a sandwich, a bowl of soup, whatever. Has to run next door or across the street for a minute. She knows him, she's served his lunch plenty of times. *No prob. I'll put it in for you.*'

'But CiCi Way, the friend who survived the first attack, didn't say anything about Snyder being approached,' Peabody began. 'Wait. Bumped into someone at the bar. She said Macie bumped into somebody at the bar.'

'Crowded, talking, bump – easy to drop it into her pocket. He's ballsy,' Eve observed. 'He's plenty ballsy. Unseal or open the container, drop it into a pocket, walk away. The couple minutes he's exposed in the bar – if that long – doesn't worry him.'

She lifted her eyebrows when Teasdale raised her hand. 'Agent?'

'I would like to know the nature of the substance. Has your lab fully identified it, or—'

'We have it. Peabody, put up the lab report.'

When it came up – all those long, strange scientific names, all the odd symbols, Teasdale folded her hands in her lap, studied and nodded.

'I see. Concentrated, and with the synthetic . . . But it would require . . . Hmm. Yes, I believe I see. I'd like to have a copy of this formula, and any data pertaining to it. I assume you've verified my security clearance.'

'You assume correctly. Peabody, copy the nerd file for Agent Teasdale. No offense.'

Again, that slight smile. 'Absolutely none taken. As you appear to be both efficient and thorough, I assume you know the genesis of this formula.'

'Revelation, Six,' Eve said coolly. 'So HSO is aware.'

'I can't verify this formula is in HSO's files, but can verify a substance containing much of these elements, and some which were not identified at the time it was discovered, has been documented. I've studied what was available to me.'

'Care to share with the rest of the class?'

'Red Horse. Hard data on the cult, and the man suspected of using this substance has been classified. Above my clearance. I am, however, well versed in the history and culture of the cult. To believe the use in these two incidents of the same formula used in the name of Red Horse during the Urban Wars is coincidence would be, as Detective Reineke succinctly put, bullshit. Therefore, there must be a connection between these incidents and those. Though the details are buried, and most — again to my knowledge — were destroyed before the end of the war.'

'We agree on the bullshit.'

'I can and will request authorization to access more data.'

'Do that. Meanwhile, Detective Callendar's been looking for that connection.'

'I've got names,' Callendar reported. 'Names of people known to be or suspected to be members or associated with

Red Horse. Names of children reported abducted. Names of those recovered, and those unrecovered. I'm working on crossing those names with our vics, wits, and those connections. It's not finding the needle in the haystack, Lieutenant, it's finding the right sliver of hay in the stack.'

'Here I could help,' Teasdale stated. 'Authorization will take time, even with Director Hurtz's backing. But on this I can be useful now. If Detective Callendar is agreeable.'

Callendar glanced at Dallas, got the nod. 'Yeah, sure.'

'What about chatter?'

'We're monitoring that,' Callendar told Eve. 'We've got some excitement from the sickos, but nothing that mentions Red Horse, nothing that claims credit.'

'Keep at it. Detective Strong, progress?'

'It's the mix,' Strong began. 'The peyote, the mushrooms. They're natural substances and easy to come by. And they're old school so not a lot of dealers bother with them. In the mix, it's the LSD and the Zeus that have the better potential to track. I'm tugging some lines, poked at a couple of my weasels. A significant buy of LSD would pop. It's not a popular illegal. None of my sources know anything about a major buy. I think he's cooking it.'

'If so,' Teasdale commented, 'he'd need equipment; a safe, private area, preferably a lab, and a strong knowledge of chemistry. It's a dangerous recipe.'

'If he got his hands on the formula, he doesn't have to know much chemistry,' Strong argued. 'No more than your average chem cook. But the ingredients mean he needs funding and contacts. He'd need ergotamine tartrate – according to my research. That would flag, too – unless he sourced it outside the US Belize is a popular source, and one of the lines I'm tugging.'

'He'd require reagents, solvents, hydrazine—'

'Tugging those lines,' Strong repeated. 'Maybe he's a chemist, or works in a lab. But if the recipe for the substance was passed on, the recipe for LSD could have been passed on, too.'

'Could you make it?' Eve asked Teasdale.

'Yes, but I have an advanced degree in organic chemistry.'

'Degree or not, he's got motivation. We'll cross-check our names with chemistry degrees, or education. Doctor Mira, do you have anything to add to the profile?'

'I find it interesting that in both cases the killer chose a woman as delivery vessel. If, as seems most probable, neither woman knew his intentions, he used women as both dupe and weapon. She's the means, and as first exposed, the first infected. It would follow she'd be the first to attack.'

'Probability would be high,' Eve added, 'she'd be one of the first to die.'

'Logically, yes. He enjoys using women. If he's in a relationship she would be subservient to him, the one assigned to do the menial chores. It's unlikely he's abusive physically. His violence is internal, even intellectual. In his work, he would resent women who are in positions of authority. He connives rather than confronts.'

'And treats females under him as tools?' Eve suggested.

"Hey, honey, would you mind getting me some coffee? I didn't get to the dry cleaner. Take an extra ten for lunch and pick up my suits."

'Yes. Jeni Curve smiled at him – a genuine, easy smile. He coats his demands with charm. He may reward with little gifts, large tips. I'd look for someone whose mother or mother figure was quiescent, a professional mother with no outside career, or a low-level job. Whose father or father figure was dominant, ambitious, very likely ruthless in his career. There's no political, social, or religious agenda here, or he – or the group he represents – would have issued a statement. This is a personal mission.'

She spread her hands. 'His connection to Red Horse may be through family. A parent or grandparent in the military, or who belonged to the cult at one time.'

'All right. Factor in the family background on your runs and searches. Look for wits and coworkers with the female guardian as professional mother. Let's make use of Trueheart's method,' Eve decided. 'Highlight this element in – what color do we have left – orange.

'The subject is most likely male. He works in that sector, lives in that sector. He eats and shops in that sector. He's known in both target locations. Re-interview. Look for someone who's cooperative, concerned. He'll ask questions as well as answer them. Somewhere in his background is a connection to Red Horse. Find it, find him. Keep digging on the drugs. He's got a dealer or a source. Find it. If he sticks to pattern, he'll hit again within twenty-four hours.

Callendar, make a place for Agent Teasdale in the EDD lab. McNab, get me that chart thing asap. Peabody, make sure Agent Teasdale has a copy of all files. I'm on twenty-four/seven until he's down. Anything pops, I hear about it. Let's go.'

11

When the room cleared she went to the board, removed the photos of Snyder and Curve, repositioned them together.

'These two,' she murmured.

'You're convinced neither was part of it?' Roarke handed her a fresh cup of coffee.

'CiCi Way, Snyder's friend, coworker, described how it played out. Having drinks with the boyfriend and his coworker, talk about stretching it out to dinner. Women head down to the bathroom. On the way, passing the bar, Snyder bumps into someone. Gets bitchy to her good pal when they're done in the john. Says she's got a headache. Head back, and Snyder shoves some guy out of her way . . .'

'At the bar,' Eve remembered. 'In her way. Could it be the same guy she bumped into? Could he have waited that long, wanted to see if it worked?'

'Risky,' Roarke commented.

'Calculated. He'd know he had about four minutes. If she isn't back, he leaves. But it would be so chill to see her, see the change in her face. Happy going down, pissed coming back. Maybe.'

She set it into a file in her mind. 'Snyder's just the tool, doesn't know a thing except she's got a headache and she's pissed off. About the time Way feels a headache coming on, Snyder picks up her fork and stabs her boyfriend in the eye. Hell ensues.

'Plus nothing rings on Snyder. Just like Curve. We'll look deeper, but it fits they were dupes. He didn't even know Snyder, the way this plays. Maybe he'd seen her before; she'd seen him before. The way you do when you frequent the same bar, when you work in the same area. She may have worked in his offices, or the same building.'

'Trueheart's famous chart indicates,' Roarke said.

'Yeah. That was good, creative work. So with Curve, I'm going with a customer. She's delivery. I'm betting she delivered to his residence. He lives close enough.'

She glanced back at the clutter of empty pizza boxes. 'To his offices, maybe. Can't get out for lunch, call in a delivery. Working through dinner, call delivery. He knew the routine. He hung around close enough to the café to watch. If not her, one of the waitresses, or a coworker going in. Luck of the draw, both times. It's a good plan because it's no one specific, no one in particular. No real link back to him.'

'And he may not have factored in you'd identify the sources. All those bodies, all those injuries, the chaos of it. It's a detail easily missed.'

'I want to take this home. Can you do the board thing with the Trueheart graph?'

'I can do that.'

'Dallas.' Peabody poked in the door. 'Sorry. Christopher Lester's here, wants to see you.'

'Does he?' She looked back at the board, considered. 'Put him in Interview, same box as before if it's free.'

'Okay. I thought you'd all but eliminated him and Devon.'

'All but. If Strong's right, this guy's cooking up his own drugs, not just the mix. If Teasdale's right, he'd need experience and equipment. Lester's got both. And he's here. I'll see what he has to say.'

'Why don't I gather up your files while you do?'

'Appreciate it.' She started out, pulling her 'link when it signaled. 'Dallas.'

'Lieutenant, Nancy Weaver.'

'Ms Weaver.'

'We heard about what happened at Café West.'

'You know the place?'

'Yes. A lot of us eat there, or get food from there. Lieutenant, we've lost more people. Three of my people who went out for lunch never came back. I can't reach them. I've checked with other departments, and there are more people who never came back from lunch.'

'I can't give you details.'

'Please. Lew and Steve are here with me. We've been helping plan a memorial for Joe. When we heard—'

Her voice wavered, went thick. 'We're at the offices. Is there any way you can come here or we'll come to you. If you could just tell us what happened. We knew people who worked there, at Café West. We might be able to help.'

'I'll be there within the hour.'

'Thank you so much. I'll tell night security to expect you.'

Interesting, she thought as she walked toward the interview room. Wasn't it interesting?

'Do you want me in there?' Peabody asked her.

'Yeah. When we're done, find out whatever you can about the Lester brothers' family. That includes their parents, and this one's wife. Take a good look at Devon's spouse's family background. You can do it from home, but on the way, go by their residence, talk to neighbors until you get a picture of their relationships, their movements.'

'Got it.'

'Nancy Weaver just contacted me, wants to chat. She's with Callaway and Vann.'

'Interesting.'

'That's what I thought.' Eve entered Interview, started the record.

And she thought Christopher Lester looked a great deal wearier and less spiffy than he had the day before.

'You don't have to read my rights again,' he said, 'as you already have, and yes, I understand them.'

'Good. Saves time. What can I do for you?'

'We heard about Café West. My brother ... it's another very hard blow. We sometimes met there for lunch.'

'You two didn't like the food at the bar?'

'He liked to get out. He knows the day manager, and

hasn't been able to reach her. Her name's Kimberly Fruicki. I knew her, too. She came to parties at Devon's. He and Quirk went to her wedding last year. Lieutenant, he's frantic. He's tried the hospital. They won't tell him anything, even if she's there, as he's not family. If I could tell him she's all right ...'

'I can't release the names of the victims until the next of kin's been notified.'

'She's ...' He looked away, rubbed his hands over his face. 'God.'

Eve gave Peabody a signal. 'Detective Peabody exiting Interview. How often did you eat at the Café?'

'I'd say once or twice a month – with Devon, or Devon and Quirk. Lieutenant.' He leaned forward, eyes direct, earnest. 'You brought me in before because I'm a scientist, a chemist. I realize you have resources, but I doubt they reach the level of my experience, my skill, or my facilities. I know the police department sometimes enlists civilian consultants. I want to help.'

'That's generous of you.'

'Yesterday I thought it was a terrible accident. Someone experimenting, and having it go horribly wrong. I was upset, disturbed, even angry. But today I know it wasn't an accident, an experiment. And today I'm afraid. I've sent my family away to our home in Oyster Bay. I don't want them in the city. I want to help find this maniac, or maniacs. I want my family to be safe.'

'I appreciate the offer, Doctor Lester. However, we have a

very qualified chemist consulting, and at this time I wouldn't feel comfortable involving a civilian.'

'You have a police chemist. I can't believe he'd have the qualifications or facilities I can offer. Perhaps I can work with him.'

'I'll consider that. But at this time, we're on it. Your wife was able to leave her work?'

'What? Oh, my wife is very involved in charity work. She can do whatever she needs to do from Long Island. It upsets her to leave, to take the children out of school, but of course she wants them to be safe. And knows I won't worry with them out of the city.'

'I bet you've got a home lab, too.'

'Yes.'

'You'd keep it well secured with kids in the house.'

'Of course, but my children know not to go into my work space.'

'Good for them. I need to get back to work. Interview end.'

'Please, if there's anything I can do, any question I might answer, contact me.'

'Count on it.'

Peabody came back in, whispered in Eve's ear.

'You can tell your brother his friend is in Tribeca Health Center in serious but stable condition.'

'She's alive.'

'Yes.'

'Thank God. This is going to mean so much to Devon and Quirk. Thank you. I'm going to let them know right away.' Even as he walked off, he pulled out his 'link.

'Let's take a look at this Kimberly Fruicki. Maybe she's doing the nasty with Chris.'

'Threatens to tell the wife.'

'Isn't it always the way. Those sidepieces never keep their mouths shut. Today's target didn't go as well as yesterday, what with the cops on scene and stunning people before they could kill each other. Maybe he wants to know if he managed to kill his focus point.'

'He looked shaken up to me.'

'Not so smooth as the first time.' Eve lifted her shoulders. 'We check it out. He's the only one, so far, who's pushing to horn in on the investigation. I'll go see what Weaver, Callaway, and Vann have to say.'

She saw Roarke striding down the hall with a pair of file bags. 'Roarke. With me.'

'Man,' Peabody breathed. 'I wish I could say that. Just once.'

'Once would be all before I stabbed out your eyes with an ice pick.'

'Ouch. Might be worth it.'

'A dull ice pick,' Eve added just as Roarke joined them. 'Scram.'

'Good night, Peabody.' He sent her a smile that made her think, *Still worth it.*

'Dull ice pick?' he said as they continued toward the glides.

'Girl talk.' She took one of the file bags, slung it over her shoulder. 'Taking you in's going to throw this trio off some.

That's good. I want impressions. I haven't met the one, Stevenson Vann, but I'll fill you in on all three of them. You drive; I'll talk.'

'I have a few words of my own.'

'Teasdale?'

'We'll talk in the car.'

She worried – marriage so often had some little pocket of worry – he'd found enough to push on ditching the fed. Shaking off Teasdale wouldn't be a snap, but . . .

As the elevator opened, a human tank wearing restraints and sporting a massive erection under his flopping trench coat charged out. He upended cops like bowling pins as two uniforms scrambled out in pursuit.

'Never a dull moment,' Roarke commented just before Eve danced to the side, stuck out her foot. The tank, his long blond wig askew, went airborne.

He shouted, 'Woo-hoo!'

He hit the floor with a bone-rattling thud, skidded – taking out another line of bystanders, then smacked the wall with an audible crack.

He lay, eyes glassy, erection spearing up like a monument.

'For Christ's sake, cover that thing up,' Eve ordered. 'He could put somebody's eye out.'

In the ensuing rush, she nipped onto the elevator, ordered the garage as Roarke stepped in beside her.

'Nice,' she decided. 'You hardly ever get an empty car to the garage.'

'We owe it all to a three-hundred-pound flasher.'

'More like two-eighty, but yeah.' She rolled her shoulders. 'Anyway, it gave me a little boost.'

'It would as kicking ass is your drug of choice.'

'Maybe, but I only tripped him. No time to kick a naked flasher's ass right now.'

'There'll be others, darling.'

'Something to look forward to.'

She got off the elevator, headed straight to her vehicle slot. 'You talk first.'

'All right then.' He slid behind the wheel, spared her a quick look before he wound his way out of the garage, punched out into traffic. 'Teasdale has an impressive background. Her father was US Air Force, retired as a major general. Her mother served as an assistant Secretary of State. She traveled considerably as a child, speaks several languages, excelled in her schooling. She was recruited by HSO while at university, but didn't officially join until she'd completed her advanced degrees.'

'Officially?'

'Officially,' he confirmed. 'She was an operative at the tender age of twenty-three – unofficially. And she's quietly, steadily risen up the ranks. She worked with Hurtz on the investigation of Bissel, and in fact, gathered the lion's share of intel and evidence against him and others involved – though her part in that business was, again, what we'll call unofficial.'

'Okay. Just give me your take on her.'

'She's brilliant, dedicated, ambitious, and though your styles appear to be polar opposites, she's quite like you. In that she doesn't give up, can't be bought, and appears to believe in both the rule and the spirit of law.'

'You're okay with her.'

'I don't know that I'll ever be okay with anyone associated with HSO, but I can deal with her. You believe she had no prior knowledge of the formula.'

'Yeah. I do.'

'She's a trained liar.'

'So am I. It rang true, Roarke. And it *feels* true that when and if HSO got anything on this back during the Urbans, they covered and/or destroyed. Made it disappear.'

She sat in silence a moment. 'But we don't have to be okay with HSO. Why should we? Maybe they've cleaned house, maybe they have. Good, fine. But we don't have to be okay with what they did, not back in Dallas years ago, not here in New York last year. They can bite me.'

She took a long breath. 'But I can work with Teasdale, at least for now, at least until I get a better sense of her. If you're good with that, I'm good with it.'

Roarke took his hand off the wheel, covered hers. 'Then we're good.'

'Okay. Moving on. I've got to consider the Lesters. Too many connections, too many elements not to.' She ran through the high points of the interview quickly.

'Mass murderers want attention. They need to be important. Shock and awe, that's the deal. Christopher Lester's used to certain levels of attention, but he's still a relatively small fish, right? No big, shiny international prizes. He makes piles of money, gets kudos from his peers, but he's still, basically, a lab rat. Taking out over a hundred people in two days, with this method? That's big and shiny. It's the sort of thing that lives in, you know, infamy.'

'Wouldn't he reach for the big and shiny with an antidote to the infection? Discovery, in his area.'

'Depends on how pissed off he is. Besides, nobody's going to care much about the cure if they haven't experienced or heard about the infection. If that's not news, the cure isn't news.'

'That's a point.'

'The missing link is Red Horse, or a military source. I'm not going to buy he just stumbled on the same exact substance while dicking around in his lab.'

'Odds are a bit long on that.'

'And now we have the S&R trio. Weaver, Callaway, and Vann. Whistler looks clear – so far?'

'Whistler. Refresh me.'

'The suit who left the bar at the same time as Callaway – same company, different department. He's Sales. I've read his statement. Left with an oncoming headache, went home, and that's verified, to his wife and six-month-old baby. He's three weeks into a big, fat raise and promotion. He doesn't fit for me.'

'Lucky for Whistler, and likely his mother?'

'What? Why?'

'Weak joke. So back to your corporate trio.'

'Right. S&R lost people in both incidents, a chunk of

them in Weaver's department. And, so far, they're the only ones from those offices who've contacted me directly – twice now for two of them – and asked for a meeting.'

'A way to get information and attention.'

'Four suits walk into a bar.'

'And what's your punch line?'

She angled toward Roarke. 'Only three walk out. The thing is, if I'm one of the four, the target's more likely to be Vann. He's rich and connected. He breezes in while the others put in years. But he's the one who walks out. If the statements were accurate, they all knew he'd only be there for a short time. So, if Cattery – the dead suit – was the, or even a, target – why? What do the other three – or one of them, possibly two of them – have to gain by offing Cattery? None of them could be sure any of their other coworkers would be there at the right time.'

'It may very well have been random. You know that.'

'I don't like random.' She scowled out the window. 'Random pisses me off.' She continued to frown as he turned into a lot. 'You could've grabbed some curb. I can put the On Duty light on.'

'A short walk won't hurt either of us.'

More time to think, she decided when she got out of the car. 'I'm going to spend some time with Joseph Cattery tonight. See what I see.'

'Spend a moment with me now.' He pulled her in for a kiss, laughing when she nudged him back. 'Your On Duty light isn't on, Lieutenant.'

'It just doesn't show.'

She studied the towering steel and glass building as they walked, and the way it caught the red gleam of the lowering sun.

'A long way to the top,' she considered. 'Lots of rungs to climb, hours to put in, hands to shake and palms to grease.'

'So it is in the world of business.'

'That's why you're handy to have along. You know the ins and outs, the slippery corners. They're marketing people, right? So they're always selling something.'

'Including themselves,' he agreed. 'It's not only selling the product, showing it in the best and most creative light, but hyping themselves as the ones with the best ideas, the freshest angles, the most muscular follow-through.'

'I get it, as a theory anyway. They're coworkers, and there's a pecking order. But they're competitors, too. It's not just other firms they compete against.'

'Exactly. There'd be accounts, prestige, and bonuses at stake. A daily race.'

'Could be one of them decided to narrow the field. But it's not that simple.' She argued with herself, struggling to focus the picture. 'There are easier ways to do that. This is ego, anger, cruelty, and a complete disregard for humanity – more for people he sees every day.'

They went inside, crossed the wide lobby to the security desk.

'Lieutenant Dallas,' Eve said, holding up her badge, 'and consultant, for Weaver, Callaway, and Vann – Stevenson and Reede.'

'You've been cleared, Lieutenant. Ms Weaver's expecting you. Elevators to the right. Forty-three West. I'll let them know you're on your way.'

With Roarke, Eve stepped into the elevator. 'Forty-three West,' she ordered. 'He didn't ask for your ID. Weaver told him to expect me and a partner. She's assuming Peabody.'

'I'll try to be half as charming.'

'No charm, pal. You're aloof. You're not just a boss, you're a mega-boss. People like this aren't worth your notice. I'm doing my duty. Follow-ups are routine. I intro you as consultant, but it's clear you're just here because we're on our way home. You're bored.'

Enjoying her, he smiled. 'Am I?'

'You have planets to buy, minions to intimidate.'

'Well, now I am bored. I've already done all that today.'

'Then it won't be hard to pretend to do it all again. Be scary Roarke-lite.'

'Excuse me?'

'You know what I mean. I don't want them to piss themselves. I just want them off balance. Here we go.'

Nancy Weaver stepped forward as the elevator doors opened, then stopped short, eyes widening on Roarke.

Eve thought: *Perfect*. 'Ms Weaver, my expert consultant, civilian, in this matter, Roarke.'

'Yes, of course. Thank you for coming, and so quickly.' She offered her hand to Roarke. 'I was expecting the other detective.'

'Detective Peabody is handling another area of the investigation at this time,' Eve said as Roarke offered Weaver a cool nod and handshake. 'You said Mr Vann is also present for this follow-up.'

'Yes, Steve and Lew are waiting in the small conference room. Just this way.'

Weaver wore black, Eve noted – except for the flashy red soles on her towering heels. She'd drawn her hair back. The severe style accented the shadowed eyes and strain lines around them. Her voice carried the rough edge of someone who'd slept too little and talked too much.

'I sent all my people home,' she began as she led the way through a reception area as flashy and red as her soles. Sparkling white lights studded spirals of silver whirling from the ceiling. Weaver's heels clicked over the dizzying pattern of floor tiles.

Glass doors whisked open at their approach.

'A number of people – companywide – have put in for leave,' she continued. 'The CEO will issue a statement in the morning. Right now, everyone's in shock. Everyone's scared. So am I.'

'It's understandable,' Eve said, and kept it at that as they moved down a wide, silent corridor.

'Steve and Lew and I thought, since we were at the bar before ... before it happened, and as we had people at the café when ... I got word an hour ago that Carly Fisher didn't make it. She went to the café on her lunch break. She was one of mine. I trained her. She was my intern when she was in college, and I hired her as an assistant. I just promoted her.'

Weaver paused, voice shaking, eyes swimming. 'I saw her on her way out to lunch, and I asked her to bring me a salad and a skinny latte. She never came back.'

Her voice broke as she pressed a hand to her mouth. 'I got busy, and didn't notice. She never came back. Then we heard about the café.'

'I'm sorry for your loss.'

'I keep thinking, if I hadn't held her up, hadn't asked her to take the time to get my lunch, maybe she'd have been out before it started. Maybe she wouldn't have been there when it happened.'

'There's no way of knowing.'

'That's the worst part.'

Weaver opened double pocket doors. Inside Lewis Callaway stood beside the tall, slick-looking man Eve recognized as Vann from his ID shot.

Vann wore a power suit, a black armband, and a rich man's golden tan.

The 'small' conference room spread wider than the one she habitually used at Central. She wondered fleetingly how much acreage their large conference room took up. Windows ribboned two walls so New York shimmered outside the glass.

The long, glossy table dominated, surrounded by cushy, high-backed chairs. The wall of screens was currently blank, but the black counter held two AutoChefs, silver water pitchers, glasses, and a bowl of fresh fruit.

She took in the space and its fancy touches while she watched the men react to Roarke.

Shoulders went back, chins lifted – and while both men started forward, Vann moved just a hair faster, and reached Roarke first.

'An unexpected pleasure, even under the circumstances.' He offered his hand for a brisk, businesslike shake. 'Stevenson Vann,' he added. 'And this must be your lovely wife.'

'This is Lieutenant Dallas,' Roarke responded, with just a hint of cool, before Eve could answer herself. 'She's in charge here.'

'Of course. Lieutenant, thank you for meeting with us. It's been a horrible two days.'

'You spent part of them out of town.'

'Yes. I shuttled back right after my presentation. Lew contacted me to tell me about Joe. I was at dinner with the client. We were both so shocked. It still doesn't seem quite real. And now this new nightmare. Please, won't you both sit. We're so anxious to hear anything you can tell us, anything at all.'

'Actually, I'd like to speak with you alone first.'

He looked blank. 'I'm sorry?'

'I haven't interviewed you as yet, Mr Vann. We'll take care of that now. Here, if we can have the room. Or your office might be easier.'

'Oh, but couldn't you just—' Weaver broke off, then simply sat down. 'I'm sorry. I wish I could handle this better.

I'm good in a crisis. I keep my head. But this . . . Can't you tell us something?'

'I'll tell you what I can once I've gotten Mr Vann's statement. Let's take it to your office,' she decided. 'Roarke? With me.'

She walked to the door, paused while the three exchanged looks.

'No problem.' Salesman smile back in place, Vann crossed to the door. 'It's just down the hall.'

As they walked, Roarke pulled out his PPC, gave it his attention. Rude, Eve thought. Just what she'd wanted.

Eve noted nameplates: Callaway's office, Cattery's, a large area of cubes and assistants' desks, then Vann's – a corner deal easily three times the size of hers at Central.

'I didn't notice Ms Weaver's office,' Eve commented.

'Oh, she's on the other side of the department. Can I get you anything? Coffee?'

'I'm good. Have a seat.' She gestured to one of the two visitor's chairs facing the desk, gave Roarke a subtle signal.

'You don't mind, do you?' Roarke asked even as he sat at Vann's desk.

'No.' Obviously nonplussed, Vann spread his hands. 'Help yourself.'

'I'll be recording this, and I'm going to read you your rights.'

'What? Why?'

'It's routine, and for your protection.' She rattled off the Revised Miranda. 'Do you understand your rights and obligations?'

'Yes, of course, but—'

'It's just standard procedure. Why don't you tell me about yesterday, before you left for your shuttle?'

'I'm sure Nancy and Lew told you that we – and Joe – had been working on a major campaign for some weeks.'

'Your campaign. You were on point.'

'Yes. I actually pulled in the account, so I headed up the project. I was due to give the presentation first thing this morning, and traveled yesterday evening to have dinner with the client, talk it up. As I said, I was at dinner when Lew called to tell me about Joe.'

'You all went to the bar together.'

'That's right. We knocked off a little early as we'd finished the project. We all wanted to celebrate, just have a drink – and talk it through again.'

'Whose idea was it to go have a drink, and at that particular bar?'

'I . . . I'm not sure. It was more or less a group decision. It's the usual watering hole for the company. It's so close, and it's a nice spot. Joe may have suggested the drink, and we'd all just assumed that's where. We left together, arrived together. Grabbed bar seats. Actually, it was already crowded, and I stood at the bar. I couldn't stay long. I left a few minutes after five, took the car service to the transpo station.'

'You must have had your presentation, your overnight, briefcase.'

'In the car. I'd given all but my briefcase to the driver.'

223

'Did anything strike you as odd or unusual at the bar?'

'Nothing. It seemed like the typical happy hour crowd. I saw a few people from the office spread around.'

'You go there a lot?'

'Once or twice a week, yes. With coworkers, or with a client.'

'So you see a lot of the same faces.'

'Yeah. People you don't know necessarily.'

'And how did Joe get along with the rest of you, the others in the office?'

'Joe? He was a go-to guy. If you needed an answer, an opinion, a little help, you could count on him.'

'No problem with you coming in, snagging a corner office?'

'Joe wasn't like that.' He spread his hands. His wrist unit – platinum, she'd bet her ass – winked. 'Listen, some people might think I got a leg up, but the fact is I'm good at what I do. I've proven myself.' He leaned forward now, exuding sincerity. 'I don't flaunt my connection with the top. I don't have to.'

'This major campaign, no problems with you taking point? Making the presentation solo.'

'Like I said, I brought in the client. I don't look for special treatment, but I don't step back when I've earned something. I don't understand what this has to do with what happened to Joe.'

'Just getting a feel for the dynamics around here,' she said easily. 'You'd understand that, getting a feel for how people work – alone and together. What they look for, what they want, how they work to get it.'

His smile came back. 'I'm in the wrong business if I don't. It's competitive, that's the nature of the beast and what keeps things vital and fresh. But we know how to work together to create the best tools for the client.'

'No friction?'

'There's always a certain amount of friction. It's part of being competitive.' He glanced toward Roarke. 'We're one of the top marketing firms in New York for a reason. I'm sure Roarke would agree that a certain amount of friction brings the fire needed to create and satisfy.'

Roarke spared Vann the briefest glance, said, 'Hmmm.'

'Were you and Joe friendly outside work?'

'We didn't really travel in the same circles, but we got along well. Our boys are about the same age, so we had that in common. His kid . . . ' He trailed off a moment, looked away. 'He's got good kids. A nice place in Brooklyn. I took my son, Chase, to a cookout there last summer. The boys hit it off. God.'

'And Carly Fisher?'

'Nancy's girl.' He looked down at his hands. 'I didn't really know her. To speak to, of course, but she'd just been promoted, and we hadn't worked together yet. Nancy's just sick about what happened to her.'

'Anyone else you're friendly with here – outside the office?'

'If you mean romantically, that's sticky. I try to avoid tangling work with relationships.'

'Okay.' Eve got to her feet. 'We'll finish up in the conference room.'

'I hope I was helpful. I want to help – anything. All of us
want to help.'

Eve kept her eyes level with his. 'I'm sure you do.'

12

Weaver and Callaway had their heads together when Eve walked back in. They each gave a quick, guilty start, then shifted in their chairs.

'Don't get up.' Eve flicked a hand, then chose a seat at their end of the table. 'A couple of questions. Was it Joseph Cattery's habit to stay later at the bar, alone?'

'I . . . Not that I know of,' Weaver began, glanced to Callaway.

'We grabbed after-work drinks there now and then,' Callaway stated. 'Sometimes he stayed on, sometimes we left together. He was friendly with some of the regulars, so he might stay, hang with someone else.'

'You left last, Mr Callaway. Was he with anyone else, or talking to anyone else?'

'The bartender. They always got into sports. But I didn't notice him "with" anyone, if that's what you mean. We blew off some steam. I left. I was beat. I think I told you yesterday, he wanted another drink, made some noises about going for food, but I just wanted to get home and crash. I wish I'd taken him up on the dinner idea. We wouldn't be here now.'

'There was nothing odd in his behavior when you left him?'

'No.' He shook his head, picked up a glass of water but didn't drink. 'I've thought and thought about those last few minutes, trying to remember all the little details. It was just usual, just another day. It was all small talk and shop talk. He was tired, too, but he just wasn't ready to go home.'

She reached in her file bag, pulled out Macie Snyder's photo.

'Did you see this woman at the bar?'

'I don't . . .' His brows knitted together. 'I'm not sure. She looks familiar.'

'I saw her.' Weaver took the photo. 'I've seen her in the bar a few times. I'm sure I saw her in there yesterday.'

'Must be why she looks familiar.'

Vann angled his head. 'Oh yeah. She was at a table with another woman and a couple of guys. Lots of laughing and flirting going on.'

'Okay. How about this woman?'

She offered the photo of Jeni Curve.

'Jeni,' Nancy said immediately. 'She delivers for Café West. She's up here nearly every day for someone. Was she—'

'Yes, I'm sorry.'

'God.' Breath hitching, Weaver squeezed her eyes shut. 'Dear God.'

'Do both of you know her as well?' Eve asked the men.

'Everybody knows Jeni,' Callaway said. 'She's a sweetheart,

always ready to take the extra step, always cheerful. Steve had the flirt on with her.'

'She's dead,' Vann murmured staring at the photo. 'We just got lunch from her a couple days ago. Locked in on the campaign, and she brought in our lunch order. Extra soy fries because she knows I like them. She's dead.'

He rose, walked over, poured water. 'Sorry. It just hits. I got take-out from there one night last week, walked out just as she did – off her shift. I walked her home before I caught a cab. I walked her home, and I thought about talking my way up to her place. I think she'd have been open to it. But I had to work, so I let it go. She's dead.'

'You were interested in her?'

'She's beautiful and bright. Was. Yeah, I thought about it that night. Long day, take-out food because it's going to be a long night of work. And here's this bright, beautiful woman giving me all the right signals. I thought, well, why not. An impulse thing,' he said. 'But the campaign.'

'So the two of you never connected that way.'

'No. I figured, plenty of time if the mood strikes again. That's what you think,' he said as his grieving eyes met Eve's. 'There's always plenty of time. Time for bright, beautiful women, or for another drink with a friend from work. Plenty of time to get your boys together at the park one Saturday. Goddamn it.'

Saying nothing, Weaver rose, opened a glossy cabinet and took out a decanter. She poured two fingers of rich amber liquid, took it to Steve.

'Thanks. Thanks, Nancy. I'm sorry,' he said to Eve. 'It's just hitting me. It's real. It happened.'

'No apology necessary. What about you, Mr Callaway? How well did you know Jeni?'

'I liked her. Everybody did. I never hit on her, if that's what you mean. She was the delivery girl, and I liked her, but that's it.'

'Tell me about Carly Fisher.'

Callaway looked mildly surprised by the request. 'Another bright girl. Nancy's protégée. Creative, hardworking.'

'I'm going to have a drink, too.' Weaver went back to the decanter. 'Anyone else?'

'On duty,' Eve said simply.

'Oh, right. Lew?'

'No. Thanks.'

'Would you say Carly was competitive?' Eve asked Lew.

'Sure. You can't make it in this business without an edge. She had one. She wanted to move up.'

'Always eager to work,' Weaver added. 'She'd take on anything. She liked to be busy. She pitched in with both of you.'

'Yeah.' Vann sipped his drink, stared out the window.

'And you?' Eve prompted Callaway.

'If you asked her to get something done, she got it done. Nancy trained her, so she had a strong work ethic and plenty of ambition.'

'She was going places,' Nancy said quietly. 'I used to tell her she'd be running the department in ten years. Please, can't you tell us the status? Isn't there something you can tell us, or something we can do?'

'I can tell you we're pursuing every angle, avenue, and lead. That this investigation is my priority, and the priority of the team of police officers under my command.'

'What leads?' Callaway demanded. 'You're asking us how well we knew the café's delivery girl. Was she involved? And the other woman you showed us. Is she a suspect?'

'I can't answer questions specific to the ongoing investigation.'

'We're not just being nosy. We were at that bar, sitting with Joe. Sitting right there with . . . I left him there,' Callaway said, with a hint of bitterness. 'I left him.'

'Oh, Lew.' Nancy reached out to lay a hand on his arm.

'I'll never forget I left him there. Like you'll never forget you asked Carly to get you a latte. We worked with people who died. Any one of us might have been in the café today. And what about tomorrow? I live in this neighborhood. I work here, eat here, shop here. It makes us a part of this.'

Callaway glanced at his coworkers for confirmation. 'It puts us in a position where we might be able to help, if we just knew the questions that need answering.'

'I've asked you the questions I need answered at this time.'

'But you won't answer ours,' Weaver pointed out. 'It's just as Lew said. You asked about Jeni, specifically. We all knew her, all interacted with her, often daily. If she was somehow involved . . . She moved freely through these offices. Does that mean something could happen here? Right here?'

'Jeni Curve died this afternoon,' Eve reminded her. 'I will tell you security cameras verify she went into the café very shortly before the incident. Due to the timing, we'll pursue a possible connection, and will thoroughly investigate.'

'Lieutenant.' Callaway, brows knit again, rubbed at the back of his neck. 'I understand you have an excellent reputation within the NYPSD, and you have resources,' he added with a sidelong glance at Roarke. 'But it feels as though you're conducting this as if you're dealing with a standard homicide.'

'There are no standard homicides.'

'I'm sorry.' Again, he spread his hands. 'I don't mean to make light of what you do. But this is obviously some kind of terrorism. Nancy and I were just discussing that while you were talking to Steve. She – that is we – wondered how much experience you have in that area.'

'You might ask those associated with the group formerly known as Cassandra.' Roarke spoke off-handedly, without looking up from his PPC.

Eve spared him an annoyed glance, shifted her attention back to Callaway. 'I can assure you that I and my team are well trained, and with the assistance of the HSO—'

'The HSO is involved?' Nancy broke in. Eve allowed herself a brief wince.

'Their involvement in this matter is not, at this time, a matter of public record. I'd appreciate your discretion. If the perpetrators learn of this new direction, it may impede the investigation.'

She got to her feet. 'This is all I can or will tell you at this time. If you think of or remember anything – any detail, however small – contact me. Your input will be given all due consideration. Otherwise, let us do our job.'

'Lieutenant.' Weaver rose as well. 'The public has a right to know. Innocent people are dead, and more could die. Some warning—'

'What warning would you suggest?' Eve snapped back. 'Lock yourselves in your homes? Flee the city? Expect the building where you live may be the next target. And don't go out for any supplies before you leave or lock down because the store where you shop could be the next target? Panic's exactly what these people want, and attention feeds them like candy. We're going to do everything we can to avoid both. Unless and until you have something viable to offer to the investigation, I can't give you more of my time.'

Roarke walked to the door, timed it so he opened it just as Eve reached it in a dismissive stride. Purposefully he left the doors open as they continued toward the reception area.

'You spend too much time placating people.'

'Part of the job,' she snapped out.

'A tedious one.' He paused at the glass doors. 'I know you're frustrated with the HSO involvement, but the additional resource might give you time to sleep, which you've barely done since this began.'

'I'll sleep when we've got the bastards.' She shoved through, called for the elevator, then shoved her hands in her pockets.

They didn't speak again until they'd reached the sidewalk.

233

'"You might ask those associated with the group formerly known as Cassandra."' She used a haughty tone, then gave Roarke a friendly elbow jab. 'Good one.'

'I thought it might give you the opening to slip the HSO business in. You did want to.'

'If all, or any of them, are involved, it'll give them something to think about.'

'And knowing they have HSO's attention may satisfy for now, give a breather between incidents.'

'Slim chance, but I'd rather take it than not. Something's up with those three. Together, separately, I can't figure. But they've all got something going on. What the hell were you doing on that toy of yours the whole time?'

'This and that. Did you know Nancy Weaver broke off an engagement, at the age of twenty-three, only weeks before the wedding?'

'People change their minds. And twenty-three's pretty young.'

'The breakup coincided with a change of firms – and a promotion. She did the same when she came aboard in this firm. Broke an engagement, took a new position. According to my source, she was involved with the man who held her current position. In this case, he's the one who left. Transferred to London, and she stepped into the job.'

Now it was getting interesting. 'Who's the source?'

'I know people who know people – and part of the this and that was tugging those lines.' He opened the car door for her, smiled.

'Using sex or relationships to advance doesn't make her a killer.'

'No, but it does make her a bit callous, doesn't it?' He walked around the car, slid behind the wheel. 'She defers, on some level, to her male subordinates. Lets them see her as female, softer – and yet she's the one who's climbed to the top of her department. I'd say a bit callous, certainly cagey.'

'She's emotional and nervous, or wants to be perceived that way right now,' Eve agreed. 'And she's slept with Vann. Not serious, from my take, but they've banged. I saw it on her face when he talked about Jeni Curve.'

'He has a reputation for not-so-serious banging, according to my source.'

'He put himself next to Curve, closer than either of the other two. Made it personal.'

'He's used to getting what he wants. He's good at what he does – knows how to think in marketing terms, knows how to connect. And he's not interested in climbing rungs, working his way up. The basics don't interest him. He likes the shine, the corner office. But he wouldn't want Weaver's job. It's too demanding.'

'Your source?'

'My personal observation.'

'Nice that it meshes with mine.' She settled back as he drove. 'He wants to be out front – the fancy business lunches, the travel, the wining and dining of high-dollar clients, with the occasional not-so-serious banging. And his relationship with the head of the firm gives him that opening over the others. Even Weaver, who outranks him. Pisser.'

'So she sleeps with him, hedging her bets, you could say.'

'You could say. Both Weaver and Vann make Macie Snyder right away – with Vann even elaborating – sitting at a table with another woman, two men. Laughing. Callaway's more vague. Both men refer to Carly Fisher as a girl – a small thing, maybe, but it shows an innate lack of respect for females in the workplace. You perceive them as girls. Callaway referred to Curve the same way.'

'I have to point out Feeney refers to his e-geeks as boys.'

'That's affection. He calls them all boys even when they have tits. This was different, knee-jerk. Something going on there,' she repeated, picking at it. 'Something. Two key players in their department dead. Cattery and Fisher. Cattery – the go-to guy, Fisher, Weaver's "girl", an up-and-comer who dug into any job that came her way.'

'If Weaver wanted either of them out, she could find a way to fire them.'

'Yeah. It's harder to fire somebody who maybe knows something you don't want them to know. Five people – that we know of – worked on this major campaign. Two of them are dead. It makes you wonder.'

'It's a damn complicated and callous way to get rid of a competitor or a blackmailer – or inconvenience.'

'I don't know. Business is dog eat cat, right?'

'Dog.'

'I said dog.'

He chuckled, sent her a look of amused affection. 'Dog eat dog.'

'That's just stupid. Dogs eat cats. Everybody knows that.'

'I stand corrected. Business is dog eat cat.'

'Like I said. So. Factor in Mira's profile. Not getting the attention he wants, craves, no conscience, a need for power and control. Add in both times a woman – say, girl – was used as the vessel. He's pissed off. It's time for a goddamn statement. But he doesn't have the balls to kill direct, to get his hands bloody. Let the girl do it. The girl's beneath him anyway. Delivery girl – menial – the girl at the bar – just some unimportant drone.'

For a moment or two she tapped her fingers on her knees. 'So, if it's one of them, it's not Weaver.'

'She'd have used a man.'

'Bull's-eye. Using men is what she's used to. And if, again, it's one of them and Cattery was a target, she would have used him as the vessel. Just slip the vial in his pocket, walk out. Same with Fisher. Plenty of opportunities for her to plant the substance on Fisher. Say she ran into her, like she said, on Fisher's way out. She could've walked out with her, told Fisher to go on in, get them a table. Just have to run over to the wherever for a minute.'

'Yes, it's simpler. Why complicate it?'

'And Weaver's not a loner, not by nature. Engaged twice. Maybe she can't commit, but she makes personal connections. She's a team player, just one who wants to captain the team.'

Time well spent, Eve considered. The meeting at S&R had been time well spent.

'I'm going to look at Fisher's financials, run her hard, just in case. But until I see different, she was Weaver's protégée. Someone she was training and molding to rise. And that rise would be a feather in her pocket, right?'

'I hesitate to say, but that would be cap. And yes, it would be.' He drove through the gates, wound up the drive. 'Who is it then? Vann or Callaway?'

'I don't know if it's either of them. Maybe Scientist Lester. Maybe somebody I haven't looked at hard enough yet. We still haven't nailed down any connection to Red Horse, and that's key.'

He got out of the car with her, looked at her in the brisk, breezy fall evening. 'But you're leaning toward one.'

'I'm thinking about leaning toward one. What I'd like to do is think about leaning toward one with a glass of wine and a clear head.'

'Why don't we arrange that?'

'Why don't we?' She held out a hand for his. 'You were aloof, superior, and just a little rude.'

'And it comes so naturally.'

'Yeah, it does.'

He laughed, leaned in to kiss her. And bit her lightly on the bottom lip. 'And here I was considering arranging spaghetti and meatballs with that wine.'

'I take it all back. You had to put on an Oscar-winning performance to pull off the aloof, superior, and just a little rude.'

'Now you're just pandering. Speaking of Oscars, the premiere for Nadine's vid is only a few weeks away.'

'Please, don't remind me.' She walked inside where Summerset stood in the foyer. Before she could formulate an opening insult, he stepped forward. 'I have a name. Guiseppi Menzini.'

'Who is he?'

'Was he. He was a scientist, reputed to be the leader of one of the Red Horse factions. He was apprehended in Corsica, two weeks after the incident in Rome.'

'He was responsible?'

'One moment,' Roarke interrupted. 'We'll go sit down in the parlor. Eve wants a glass of wine, and you look as if you could use one.'

'Yes, I could. I'll get it.'

Roarke laid a hand on Summerset's arm. 'Come in, sit. I'll get the wine. Have you eaten?' Roarke asked as he crossed to a japanned cabinet.

'Tending to me now?'

'You look tired.'

Eve stood for a moment, hands in pockets. 'I was thinking you look even more dead than usual.'

That got the slightest ghost of a smile as the cat rubbed against his legs. 'The day's been long.'

So they should get to it, Eve decided, and sat on a plush ottoman as rich as rubies. 'Guiseppi Menzini. What do you know?'

'Born in Rome, 1988, the son of a defrocked priest and

one of his faithful. My information indicates Salvador Menzini's literal interpretation of the Bible meant women were to bear children in pain and blood. Guiseppi's mother died a few weeks after his birth from complications in child-birth, attended only by Salvador.'

'Rough start.'

'Indeed. Thank you,' Summerset said when Roarke handed him a glass of wine. 'Salvador raised the boy alone, educated him. They traveled across Europe, Salvador preach-ing. He may have fathered more children as part of his doctrine held that man was obligated to populate the Earth, and women were created to subjugate themselves to a man's will, his needs, his desires. There was no rape in Salvador's teachings as he claimed it was a man's God-given right to take any women he pleased, over the age of fourteen.'

'Handy for him.'

'The law, however, disagrees. He was arrested in London for sexual assault. Guiseppi would have been twelve, if records are correct.'

'Close enough,' Eve told him.

'The boy evaded child protection. One of Salvador's wealthy followers posted his bail and he went into hiding. There isn't much information on either of them for the next several years, but the Red Horse cult was born during that period, or at least the seeds of it were planted. In 2012 Salvador was shot and killed by the father of a fifteen-year-old girl during an attempted abduction.'

'And the son?' Eve prompted.

'He came to the attention of the CIA, MI6 and various other covert organizations two years later. He had an aptitude for chemistry.'

Eve looked into her wine, thought: *Click*. 'I bet he did.'

'It's believed he must have studied under an assumed name, but I can't find any confirmation. Between 2012 and 2016, and the dawn of the Urban Wars in Europe, he developed biological weapons for various terrorists groups. He had no particular allegiance, even to Red Horse, though it's believed he stood as leader of a faction of that group. He had fortifications in at least three locations in England, Italy, and France.'

'Not here?' Eve interrupted. 'Not in the US?'

'Nothing on record, no. He enjoyed Europe, and preferred cities over the country, as had his father. While the Urban Wars raged and spread, he supplied the highest bidder with munitions, explosives, and his specialty – bioweapons.

'He had no children on record,' Summerset continued, 'but witness reports – including those of recovered children his sect and others abducted, state he had many – though it's not verified if they were biological offspring, or abductees he'd taken as his own. There were others like him, and others with more followers, more power. He wasn't considered a top priority, though there were attempts to capture or assassinate. Again, according to reports – reports that were and are carefully buried, one of the assassination attempts resulted in the deaths of five children. Two months after that, the café outside of London was attacked. He became a top priority.'

'Sometimes late's as bad as never.'

Summerset studied Eve as he sipped his wine. 'To say the world was in disarray is the least of it. Looting, burning, bombing, indiscriminate killings, rapes. At first it seemed the police and the military would quell it, all would right again. People locked themselves in their homes or fled to the countryside to wait it out. But they didn't quell it, and it didn't right again, not for a very long time. It became a tidal wave of rage and violence that wouldn't be stopped.'

Summerset paused a moment, sipped his wine. 'I'm told he was a small man – a gnat as it were – compared to others who sought to destroy.'

'Gnats need to be swatted.'

'I agree, but there were so many more, so much more organized. There are always those who wait and plan for just such a thing. There were armies that attacked strategically – military bases, communications, food and water supplies – much more so than Menzini or other Red Horse sects. They thought they would win, but in the end, they too were engulfed in that wave. What you've seen these last two days? Imagine it everywhere, the bodies and blood, the waste, the fear and panic. The law broke under it. There weren't many like you who stood between the guilty and the innocent – and neither were easy to recognize for a time. For too long a time. You're too young, both of you, to have known it. Be grateful.'

'I know some who stood, like you. They rarely, if ever, talk about it.'

'There aren't words.' He looked thinner, if possible, as he spoke, Eve thought. Paler. Bad memories, she knew, could carve you out.

'What they teach, what they wrote? It's pale and soft compared to the reality of it. What you've seen the last two days? There are some of us who were there at the beginning of it, those of us who remember. I remember,' he murmured, 'and I'm afraid.'

She hadn't expected him to say it, hadn't expected to see it. She spoke to him now as she would to a victim. 'This isn't a movement or a war. It's a man with a weapon who wants your fear, your attention. I think I know him, that I've spoken to him, that I've looked in his eyes. I'm going to stop him.'

'I believe you will. I have to believe it.' He took a slow breath, sipped again. 'The details of his apprehension after the attack in Rome aren't just buried. Much of the data was destroyed. What I learned can't be confirmed. Menzini created the substance, but did not, in fact, deliver it personally. He created it, selected the two targets, gave the order, but he used two women – girls. His own children, if you will, sent by him on a suicide mission. Each took a vial of the substance into the location, released it, and under his orders remained so they were also infected.'

'Girls. You're sure?'

'It can't be confirmed.'

'You know if it's true?'

'I believe it to be true.'

'That's good enough for me.'

'You said you knew him. What is his name?'

'I said I think,' she corrected. 'I have three suspects, viable to me – if I'm pursuing the right angle. Even if I'm right, I can't prove it. I'm missing essential connections.'

'You know which of the three. I want to know his name. I want his name in my head so I can say it when you stop him.'

'His name's Lewis Callaway, but—'

'That's good enough for me.'

He tossed her own response back at her so casually, she couldn't think what to say. When her pocket 'link signaled, she considered it a reprieve.

'It's Nadine. I need to take this upstairs. Dallas,' she said in answer. 'Wait.' She thought of what she probably should say. 'Lewis Callaway,' she repeated. 'He's a coward. It used to surprise me how many killers are cowards. We're going to stop him. Everything you told me yesterday, everything you told me now is going to help us make the connection, make the case that's going to put him away for every minute he has left in his sick, cowardly life. So you can forget him. Macie Snyder, Jeni Curve. Those are the two women he used to do his killing, and not under his orders. They didn't even know. If you need to have a name in your head, put theirs in it. They're the ones who matter.'

She turned, switching her 'link off HOLD as she went. 'Nadine. Go.'

Roarke rose, topped off Summerset's wine. 'This may be a record.'

'What would be a record?'

'You and Eve having an actual conversation without sniping at each other, two days running.'

'Ah well.' Summerset let out a sigh. 'I expect the lieutenant and I will be back to normal shortly – to our mutual relief.'

'You need food and rest.'

'I believe I do. I'll get both shortly. I believe I'll have the cat as well for a while. I could use his company. Go, see that your wife eats a meal. I'm surprised she didn't starve to death before she had you putting food under her nose.'

'It pleases me to do it.'

'I know it does. You were an interesting boy, always so bright and clever, so thirsty for more – of everything. You made yourself an interesting and clever man. She's made you a better one.'

'She's made me more than I ever thought I could be.'

'Go feed her. I expect the pair of you will work late tonight.'

Alone, he sat with the cat sprawled over his feet, the wine in his hand. A fire simmered in the hearth of the beautiful room of gleaming wood, sparkling crystal, rich fabrics, and art. The room where the pain, the loss, the fear of long ago tried to haunt him.

Macie Snyder, he thought, Jeni Curve. Yes, he'd remember those names. The lieutenant was right. The innocent mattered.

13

Roarke found Eve in her office, circling her board.

'Nadine's pretty damn good,' she told him. 'She came up with some of the same data Summerset gave us. Not as much detail – she's not *that* good – but enough I'll have two sources when I hit Teasdale with questions on Menzini. And between Nadine, Callendar, and Teasdale, I've got a good long list of abductees from back in the day. Separated into recovered, and not recovered.'

'What does that tell you?'

'Can't be sure. Callaway's too young to have been taken during the Urbans. But one of his parents? Grandparents somehow involved? Possible. Gotta dig into that. Fucker's not a scientist so there has to be a connection, a way he got his hands on the formula.'

Roarke handed her the wine she'd left downstairs. 'You never had this.'

'Right.'

'Or food.'

She looked back at her board.

'You can talk it through while we eat. I'm under orders to feed my wife.'

Her shoulders hunched, then released again. 'He's okay?'

'It's hard — as you'd know better than most — to go back, look close at traumatic past events. He said more tonight about the horrors of his experiences than he has to me in all the years we've been together. I don't know, not really, who he was before he saved me, took me in.'

'You never looked. You never looked at my past either, until I asked you to.'

'No. Love without trust? It's not love at all.'

It upset him, she knew, worried him to see Summerset so frail, so tired. 'I'll get the food. We'll eat.'

He ran a hand down her hair, brushed a kiss on her lips. 'I'll get it. Orders.'

She looked at the board again, sighed, then walked to the kitchen while Roarke programmed the meal. 'Roarke? Whoever he was before, he was the kind of man who'd take in a young boy, tend to him, give him what he needed. He's still a pain in the ass, but that matters.'

'I'm not sure, not at all, I'd have lived to be a man without him. I expect my father might have done for me, as he did for my mother, however slippery and clever I might have been. I'm not sure, had I lived, what manner of man I'd have been without him. So it matters, yes. It matters.'

She sat with him by the window at the little table, the spaghetti and meatballs she had a weakness for heaped on her plate like comfort.

Would they be here now, together like this, if Summerset had made another choice the day he'd found the young boy, beaten half to death by his own father? If he'd walked on, as some would, or had dumped Roarke in an ER, would they be here, sharing wine and pasta?

Roarke would say yes, they were meant to be. But she didn't have his faith in fate and destiny.

All the steps and choices made life an intricate maze with endless solutions and endings.

'You're quiet,' Roarke commented.

'He wanted something else for you. You're his, and he wanted something – someone else for you. He deals with me now, we deal with each other. But he had a kind of vision for you. That's what parents do, right?'

'Whatever he envisioned, under it he wanted me happy. He knows I am. And he knows, as he told me before I came upstairs, you've made me a better man.'

For an instant she was, sincerely, speechless. 'He must really be feeling off.'

When Roarke simply shook his head, sipped at his wine, she wound pasta around her fork. 'It just made me think, wind it through my head.' She held up her fork. 'Like pasta.' She ate, wound again. 'The abductees. They wanted kids under a certain age, when it's likely they're more malleable, more defenseless. Most of Red Horse would be, by the popular term, bat-shit crazy. But not all. It's never all. There'd be kids there, too – sucked in or swept along. And women who felt they had no choice – scared. Men too weak-spined or weak-minded to do anything but go along.'

'Add the world was going to hell in a handbasket.'

'What does that mean? What's a handbasket? If it's a basket, you need your hands to carry it, so it's a given.'

'It might be a bushel basket. You'd need your arms.'

'How much is a bushel?'

'Four pecks.'

Her eyes narrowed. 'Now you're messing with me. Peck's what chickens do.'

He laughed. 'I stand corrected.'

'What I was saying, before handbaskets, is some people would, given human nature, feel protective of the kids. And maybe bond with them, especially kids who were kept for a good chunk of time. They'd have to assign people to take care of them. The babies, say.'

'And there'd be that bonding. Yes, I can see that.'

'With the bonding comes the vision, the wants for the kid. The kid has to depend on you, for food, shelter, protection. Mira asked me questions today that made me think about that. I was afraid of Troy, and even as a kid, hated him on some level. But I depended on him. Not on her. I never depended on her.'

Was there a twinge of pain there? Eve wondered. Maybe – maybe just a twinge.

'I think that's one of the reasons I remember him much more clearly. It's not just that he had me longer, but that he was the one who brought in the food, that sort of thing. He couldn't turn me. Maybe I was stronger than either of us knew, or he wasn't as smart as he thought he was. But it's not hard to turn a kid – even an adult – pain and reward, pain and reward, deprivation, fear, repetition. You can even turn them with kindness, if you're smart about it.'

'I agree, but as you said, Callaway's too young to have been an abductee.'

'If his father was, Callaway might've been raised in the doctrine. Or he could know someone who was. I'm going to fine-tune those lists of abductees.'

'Why Callaway? Specifically.'

'It's little things. They start to add up. He's the first to come forward – with Weaver. Come in, show concern for their pal and coworker. He admits to being at the bar, and that's the ground zero area, from what I can piece together. Vann left too early. Weaver's already in charge, and like I said, she'd have used a man.'

'Then why not go after Weaver, or Vann for that matter? Weaver's a woman, in charge. Vann's got the family connections, the shine.'

'Maybe he's working his way up. Eliminating direct competition first. Maybe he's just hitting indiscriminately, and he got lucky. In ratio, his office lost more than any other in the two attacks. Relationships. He lives and works in that sector. Weaver and Vann live on the edges of it, but Callaway's right in the middle. Geography. And he's pushing, and pushing Weaver to push for information.

'He's single,' she went on. 'Has no long-term relationships that I've found.'

'And Vann's been married, has a child. Weaver's had two engagements.'

250

'You could say Weaver and Vann don't ace it on commitment, but they each gave it a shot. Nothing shows where Callaway did. And though it was kind of a toss out, Weaver mentioned her mother, Vann his son. Callaway?'

'No one,' Roarke finished.

'It adds up,' she repeated. 'He lives alone, and he's spinning in middle management. Of the three of them he was the most controlled tonight. Careful what he said. It felt as if he took his lead from them – didn't want to stand out, not in this situation. He wanted to let me think about the other two, respond primarily to them. Until closer to the end of it. He wasn't getting everything he wanted, so he had to insert himself instead of relying on the other two to pull out the information he was after.'

She sat back, hissed out a breath. 'And it's all a feel, a read. I don't even have enough to pull the manpower to watch him.'

'Then we'll have to find enough.'

'If I'm right, there's going to be something, something buried in his background. His education, family history. And there has to be a trigger. He didn't just wake up one morning and decide to kill a bunch of people. Something set him off, or gave him permission.'

'The campaign seems to have been their focus for the last several weeks. It's interesting that the first attack came the night they'd completed it, and Vann left for the client presentation.'

'Maybe you know somebody who knows somebody who

could arrange for me to talk to the client on the QT. Get impressions.'

'Why don't you leave that to me? The client's more likely to talk to me about business than to a cop about a murder suspect.'

'Okay, if you deal with that—'

'In the morning.'

Her brows drew together. 'Why not now? I don't want to waste time on this.'

'During business hours,' Roarke insisted. 'If I approach this now, it's going to make the client wonder. A contact during regular business hours – then it's regular business.'

'I guess you'd know,' she grudgingly agreed.

'I guess I would. And it frees me to help otherwise. Abductees or background?'

She considered. 'Go ahead with the background. Teasdale's probably looking at abductees. Not the way I'm going to. But I can jump off her data.'

'Will you tell her what you're doing?'

'After I do it, sure. It's my case,' Eve reminded him when he smiled. 'She's consulting. She's probably clean, especially after you microscoped her and think so. But I don't know what she's made of. She'll get what I've got at tomorrow's briefing, just like the rest of the team. Unless one of us strikes gold and we can move tonight.'

'Then I'll get started being nosy. And since I fed you, you can deal with the dishes.'

'There's always a catch.'

'The way of the world, darling.'

She couldn't argue with that. Plus the spaghetti had hit just the right spot. She felt fueled and ready. All she needed was coffee to top it off.

By the time she'd finished, had a pot on her desk, she'd aligned her strategy. She'd start with the unrecovered.

Seventy-eight children who'd never been located – alive or dead. Most, she noted with a quick scan, had families, though there were war orphans and fosters scattered through. Easier prey, she decided. And without a parent searching for them, easier to indoctrinate.

She'd start with those, working her way from youngest to oldest.

The first, a female infant – three months – snatched in a raid of a makeshift orphanage in London. Mother dead, father unknown. She'd been one of eight children abducted. No DNA on file, but a small birthmark, like a blurry heart on the back of the left knee.

She called up the records, studied the search patterns, the statements from witnesses. Three women had died trying to protect the kids. Two survivors – male and female – had described the raid, the men and women who'd attacked the location.

The oldest, an eleven-year-old boy, managed to escape with two others. Smart kid, she thought as she read. His father had been a soldier, had taught him how to track, how to evade pursuit. He'd lead his two friends to a base camp, given the location where they'd been kept.

As a result, two more of the kids had been recovered – and the remains of another. Only the infant – who'd been named Amanda – and a two-year-old boy – Niles – were left. Whereabouts unknown.

She ordered the computer to perform an age-approximation image on both Amanda and Niles, studied the faces as the computer portrayed them today. Split-screened those images with those of the ID shots of Callaway's mother and father, his paternal aunt, his uncle by marriage, even his grandparents, though that was stretching it.

No distinguishing marks listed on IDs for the women, she noted. But such things could be removed or covered up. Still she found no resemblance at all between the two lost children and any member of Callaway's family.

She wondered if either child still lived, and if so where, how, with whom? Then she let it go. If she thought about each young innocent, she'd drown in depression.

So she moved on, inching her way through photos, descriptions, witness accounts, interviews with recovered kids, family members, interrogations of prisoners.

An ugly time, she thought, and as with any ugly time the innocents suffered and paid more than those who incited the ugliness.

More than lives lost, but lives fractured, or damaged beyond all understanding.

By the time she'd worked her way through half the list of lost children, she had a solid handle on how Red Horse had worked. Their leadership, their individual missions, credos, disciplines, even communications may have been loose, but their methods ran along a common line.

Use females to infiltrate camps, hospitals, child centers, gather intel on routines, security, numbers, then raid. Often, very often, she noted, sacrificing the female or female infiltrators in the process.

Take the kids, kill the rest – or as many as possible. Secure the kids, transport – scatter.

If kids died during the operations, well, there were always more kids.

She took a much needed break and carried her coffee to the door of Roarke's office.

'I've got considerable,' he told her without looking up, 'and some fairly interesting. I'm not quite done.'

'No, I just needed to step away from it a minute. It's harsh.'

Now he stopped, looked at her. He'd seen her stand over the dead countless times, mutilated bodies, and take the blood and gore with her. So this was more.

'Tell me.'

She did, because it helped.

'After they scattered, regrouped, they'd begin indoctrinations on the kids who survived the raid. The younger ones, under four, they'd draw in with reward. Candy, sweets, toys. The older ones, or the stubborn ones, they broke down with pain or deprivation. No food, no light, whippings. A few escaped – very few. Some died, not so few. I've been reading old interviews with recovered kids that detail abuse – physical, emotional, psychological, sexual, off-balanced by care and comfort, then back to abuse if the kid didn't renounce his family or swear allegiance to Red Horse – learn the doctrines, toe the line.'

'They tortured children.'

'All in the name of some vengeful God they'd decided to worship.'

'God has nothing to do with it. Man created torture.'

'Yeah, we're good with inventing ways to screw each other up. If the kid had family, they threatened to kill his mother or father if he didn't cooperate. Or they'd say his family was already dead. Or tell him, again and again, his family didn't care about him, no one was coming for him.'

'Methods used throughout history to demoralize and break POWs, and to turn them when possible into assets.'

'It's worse than what happened to me.'

She wanted to pace, to steam off the angry energy. Because she needed all the energy she could get, from whatever source, she continued to stand, rocking on her heels.

'These kids lost families who loved them, or were taken from them, then systematically tortured and brainwashed. The older ones, the stronger ones were used as labor – and if a girl was old enough, they forced her to have sex with one of the boys. They had freaking ceremonies, Roarke, and watched. Like a celebration.'

'Sit down, Eve.'

'No, I'm okay. Working through being pissed. It's harder to work clean pissed off. I've got records of over thirty live births through abducted kids. The youngest on record was twelve. Twelve, for God's sake. They took the babies from the girls. Impregnated them again when possible. I have one who was fifteen when recovered. She'd had three babies. She self-terminated six months after recovery. She's not the only one. Self-termination rates among the abductees is estimated at fifteen percent, before the age of eighteen.'

She took a long breath. 'Most of the data on pregnancies and suicides came from Callendar and Teasdale. Nadine didn't dig it up, because it's classified. I'm not sure Summerset's sources knew all of it or told him.'

'No, he'd have told us if he knew.'

'Why isn't this public knowledge? Why wasn't it screamed from fucking rooftops?'

Difficult for anyone to think of children being tortured and raped, he thought. But when you've been a child who'd been tortured and raped, it hit harder, and it hit closer.

'I think a combination of factors.' He rose to go to her, ran his hands up and down her arms to soothe them both. 'The massive confusion during that era, the desperation of governments to cover up some of the worst. And the needs of the victims, their families, to put it all behind them.'

'It's never behind you. It's always in front of you.'

'Would you consider going public with what happened to you?'

'It's my personal business. It's not . . . ' She breathed again. 'Okay, I get that. Or at least some of it. But burying it – not just here, but in Europe, everywhere it happened. That took work and purpose and a hell of a lot of money.'

'The authorities didn't, or couldn't, protect the most vulnerable, and from a radical cult, one that wasn't well funded or organized. Such things are worth the work and money to many.'

'HSO was practically running things, at least in the States back then.'

'And the power may have slipped away during the post-war rebuild if this had been public knowledge. I don't know, Eve.'

'They're giving me the data now, or some of it.'

'It appears Teasdale's superior genuinely intends to run a clean house, or as clean as such houses can be.'

'Then he's got a lot of dirt to sweep.' Not her job, she reminded herself. 'I need to get back to it.'

'Why don't we take a look at some of Callaway's background first?'

'You're not finished.'

'Enough to start.'

'I can't let this get personal. And I can't stop it from being personal.'

'If you could stop it, you wouldn't be the woman or the cop you are.'

'I hope that's true.'

'I know it is. Here, let's have some of this.' He put his arms around her. 'For both of us.'

She held on. He'd given her someone to hold on to. A gift she never wanted to take for granted. She thought she'd known what darkness was, and despair and terror. Now she knew there were people who lived and worked and slept and ate who'd known far, far worse.

She hoped they had someone to hold on to.

'Okay.' She drew back, laid her hands on his face briefly. 'Callaway.'

'You know the basics. Born in a small town in Pennsylvania. His father did three years military service, as a medic.' They walked back to Eve's office as he spoke. 'He worked as a physician assistant after his enlistment was up. After he married, had the son, they moved six times in as many years.'

'Interesting.'

'Mother – professional mother status. They live in rural Arkansas now. They farm. Callaway was homeschooled until the age of fourteen. They moved twice more during his teenage years. He attended three different high schools. His record is slightly above average, no particular disciplinary trouble – on record.'

'Which means?'

'I found some reports. There was concern, initially, about antisocial behavior. Not a troublemaker, but not one to join in, not one to form friendships. He did what he was told, no more. He was encouraged to participate in extracurricular activities, and finally settled on tennis.'

'No team sports.'

'Again, he was slightly better than average, but it's noted he had a fierce sense of competition, and had to be reminded, regularly, about good sportsmanship. No fights, no violence.'

'That fits, too.'

'He attended a local college for two years, then managed to get into NYU, by the skin of his teeth. He studied marketing and business. He showed aptitude there, for ideas and big pictures. He didn't do as well at presentations or again, team projects. Not initially. He improved, and eventually joined Stevenson and Reede. His reviews give him solid ratings on work ethic, ideas, and less stellar marks on social skills, presentations, client relations. He's moved up, based on his work, and it's been a slower climb than it might have been as he has no real skill in articulating the product to clients or, basically, showing them a good time.

'Just as a contrast,' Roarke continued, 'Joseph Cattery's reviews praise his client skills, and his ability to team think. While Vann may have the corner office, Cattery recently received a hefty bonus and was in line for a promotion and pay hike. The bonus was due to his work on a project he shared with Callaway. Callaway's bonus for the project was considerably smaller.'

'Smells like motive for Cattery. But not for a bar full of people.' She paced around her board. 'It's not some twisted religion with him. It's not about Revelation and using kids. But there's still some elements of Red Horse. The use of women to do the dirty work, the utter disregard for innocents, and the use of the substance to mass murder. He cherry-picks. And it's still not enough.'

'One interesting point. It's been his habit, since college, to travel to see his parents once a year.'

'That would be duty, not affection. Right?'

'I'd say so. However, this year he's traveled to Arkansas four times. Neither of his parents have anything on their medical to indicate an illness or condition. No particular change in their financials.'

'He's going back for something.' Eve shoved at her hair. 'Something he needs, wants, something he found, something he's looking for. I need more on the parents.'

'I've done the father. He was nearly forty when he married Callaway's mother. She was twenty-two.'

'Big age gap. Could be interesting.'

'He was doing some private nursing at that time, and came in to help her care for her father. The father had fought in the Urbans, had been wounded, and was suffering from complications of those wounds as well as depression. His wife was killed in a vehicular accident about six months before Russell Callaway met the then Audrey Hubbard. They married a few weeks after the father's death.'

Eve went to her computer to check. 'I don't have a Hubbard on my list of kids – recovered or not.'

'I've just started on the mother. I'll be able to give you more shortly.'

'What about the father's war record?'

'He retired an army captain. He saw considerable combat, but there's no record of him being involved in any of the Red Horse operations. I don't know if there would be.'

'The mother's mother.'

'Barely started there. Give me some time. I'm picking through decades here, and all matter of records.'

'And I'm holding you up. It's good data. It fills in some blanks. Callaway's an insular man, a loner by nature. Competitive. His mother married a much older man at a difficult point in her life and chose professional mother status, homeschooled her son. Kept him close. Lots of moving, no real chance to form outside bonds. Father's likely the dominant. Changing jobs, uprooting the family when it suits him. Maternal grandparents dead, and he hasn't maintained close ties with his parents as an adult. But now he goes to them several times in a few months. It's good data to chew on. Get me more.'

'I live to serve, Lieutenant.'

She went back to it and sent Roarke's data to Mira with a request for an eval asap. She moved through more names, let her mind circle.

On impulse she called up Callaway's parents' ID photos, studied them. And began the slow, painstaking process of pulling up abductee photos, aging them.

She got more coffee, considered, then rejected, a booster when the caffeine didn't eliminate the growing fatigue.

Then . . .

'Wait a minute.'

'Eve.'

'Wait. Wait. I think I've got something.'

'So do I.'

'Look at this. Give me your take.'

He came around to study the screen and the images on it. The first he recognized now as Callaway's mother; split-screened beside it was a computer-generated image.

'They appear to be the same woman, or very close. Different hair color and style, but the face is the same.'

'The aged image is of Karleen MacMillon, an abductee at the age of eighteen months. Never recovered. But she was recovered and raised by the Hubbards as Audrey, because there she fucking is.'

'The record of Audrey Hubbard's live birth is fake. It's a good one, but it's fake.'

'Because she wasn't born to the Hubbards. She was one of the taken. But never listed as recovered.'

'Hubbard retired from the army and moved from England to the US with his wife and four-year-old daughter. His wife had a half-sister. Gina MacMillon. I'm still digging there.'

'Gina and William MacMillon, listed as Karleen's parents, both killed in the raid where the kid was abducted. It's the link. It links him to Menzini and Red Horse. Not enough for an arrest, but enough to put a tail on him.'

She walked to the board. 'He found out his mother was an abductee, and it set something off. But how did a four-year-old kid get the formula, or have knowledge? Maybe Hubbard was in on the raid that took Menzini down, or in on interrogations. They have something – or had it – and Callaway kept going back to find it, to find everything he could, or interrogate his mother. I need to talk to her.'

'Are we going to Arkansas?'

'No, my turf. Teasdale's got the HSO muscles to get the mother here. She told Callaway what she knows. Now she's going to tell us.'

'You need to sleep. I'll put the run on the half-sister on auto. We'll both catch a few hours. You've done what you set out to do tonight,' he told her when she hesitated. 'You'll want to gear up for tomorrow.'

'You're not wrong. I want to get this data to Whitney, get a couple men on Callaway tonight. I don't want him hitting some twenty-four/seven while I'm sleeping.'

'Fair enough. Get it done, and I'll put what I have together for your briefing tomorrow. Then we'll go to bed.'

'That's a deal.'

14

In the dream she knew for a dream, the world exploded. Fire plumes of murderous reds, virulent orange, greasy black lit the night sky to the east as blasts shook the ground and punched like fists through the smoke-stung air.

She heard the boom of explosives, the *crack, crack, crack* of what she recognized as gunfire. There'd been a time, too long a time, she thought, when people had lived and died by guns.

Now they found other ways to kill. But she wasn't in the now.

The canyons and towers of New York thundered with the sounds of war. The Urbans.

A dream, she thought, just a dream. Still, she made her way carefully, weapon drawn, down the deserted street. Maybe dreams couldn't kill, but they could damn sure hurt. She'd woken far too often with phantom pain screaming to travel unarmed, even in her own subconscious.

But sometimes dreams showed you what you needed to know and didn't recognize in the busy business of the day.

So she'd look, she'd listen.

She stopped by a body sprawled over the sidewalk,

crouched to check for a pulse. And found the bloody slice across his throat. Barely more than a boy, she judged. They'd taken his shoes, and likely his jacket if he'd had one – and not long before as his body still held some warmth.

She left him where he was – no choice, just a dream. But checked her weapon. And saw it wasn't her police issue but a .38 automatic. She recognized the style from Roarke's gun collection, checked to make certain it was loaded, tested the weight.

Moved on.

She passed windows and doors, dark and boarded, burned out husks of cars her subconscious must have fashioned out of memories of vids from the period.

Chained fences barred the entrance to a subway station. Uptown train, she noted and skirted its black maw carefully. Streetlights – those that weren't broken stood dark. Traffic lights blinked red, red, red, and made her think of the room in Dallas where she'd killed Richard Troy.

It's not about that, she reminded herself. It wasn't about the child she'd been, but who she was now. What she did now.

She came to a street sign, Leonard and Worth, and realized she wasn't far from the first crime scene.

Maybe the answer lurked there.

She started to cross, heard the gunfire – closer now – the screams. She changed directions, ran toward the sounds.

She saw the truck – military, armored, and the man at the machine gun on the roof. She heard more gunfire from inside the building the truck guarded, and the cries and screams. Children, she realized. They'd come for the children.

She didn't hesitate, but took her stance, took aim at the man on the truck. He'd be wearing body armor, she calculated, and aimed higher. Took the head shot.

As he fell she raced forward, ducked into shadows as two men and two women dragged out struggling, screaming children. She sucked in her breath, held it. Fired.

She took both men out, credited either the target shooting she did with Roarke or the luck of dreams. The women fled, one with a wailing baby in her arms.

No, Eve thought, not even one, not even in dreams. She ran in pursuit, barely pausing at the huddle of terrified children.

'Get back inside, block the door. Wait for me.'

And ran on.

The women split up, so she ran after the one with the baby.

'NYPSD! Halt! Halt, goddamn it or I'll shoot you in the fucking back. I swear to Christ.'

The woman stopped, turned slowly. 'That would be just like you.'

She stared into her mother's face, watched the blood run in thin rivers from the gaping wound across her throat.

'You're already dead.'

'I just look that way. How many times do you have to kill me before you're happy?'

'McQueen killed you. I'd've put you in a cage, but you'd still be breathing.'

'I'd be alive if you'd minded your own.'

She had been minding her own, Eve realized. But why explain? Even in dreams Stella would never comprehend.

'That's an old tune, Stella. I'm bored with it. Put the kid down.'

'Why should I? You know what this little bitch is worth to the right people? I've got to get by, don't I? You don't know what it's like now, here. It's hell here. I lived through it. What do you think made me what I am?'

'I lived through it.' Mira stood beside Eve, spoke quietly. 'So many of us did. She made her choices, Eve, just as I did, just as you did. You know that. Nothing made her. She made herself.'

'What the hell does she know? Fucking shrink with her fancy clothes, fancy ways. She just wants to fuck you over, like everyone else. I'm the one who carried you inside me. I *made* you.'

Mira barely spared Stella a glance. 'You know the truth, and you know the lie. You always have. Say it to me, say the truth.'

'I made myself.'

'Yes. Yes, you made yourself, and did it despite her. She never controlled you, not where it matters. Why do you let her control you now, even here?'

'I can't. It has to stop.'

'Make it stop,' Mira urged her. 'Make it end. Make a choice.'

'Put the kid down, Stella, and walk away. Stay away.'

'You can't stop me. Put a bullet in me, go ahead. I'll just come back. And maybe I'll snap her neck first. It's easy, all those soft bones. I thought about snapping yours. Whining, crying brat, just like this one.'

'You left me with him instead, so he could beat me, rape me, torment me. But I got through it.'

'By killing. The blood's still on your hands. Richie's blood. My blood.'

'I can live with it.' That was the answer, wasn't it? She could live with it. 'Put her down.'

'What do you care?' Stella closed a hand over the soft, tiny neck.

Eve started forward, to end it, and the baby cried out.

'Das!'

Bella. Mavis's Bella, with tears streaming, her arms held out.

On a hot spurt of fury, Eve pressed the barrel of the gun to Stella's forehead. 'Let her go, you bitch, or I'll splatter your brains on the sidewalk.'

'She's nothing to you.'

'They're all something to me. Mira, take the kid.'

'Of course. There now, sweetheart.' Sliding Belle from Stella's grip, Mira nuzzled her. 'Everything's all right. Eve won't let anything happen to you.'

'She's just another brat. Plenty more where she came from.'

'Not for you. You're finished.'

Stella's eyes gleamed. 'What? You're going to shoot me

now?' She held up her hands. 'You're going to shoot me when I'm unarmed?'

'No, I don't have to kill what's already dead.' Eve holstered her weapon, watched Stella's smile spread. And rammed her fist, with all her force – her anger, her despair – into that smiling face. 'But I think I've needed to do that for a long time.'

Stella lay on the sidewalk, as she'd laid on the floor of McQueen's apartment. The blood pooled around her, a black lake in the shadowed dark.

'You can come back. I'll just kick your ass again.'

'Well done,' Mira commented.

'Where's Bella? Where's the kid?'

'She's safe. They're all safe tonight. You just needed to put a face on the innocent. It's easier for you to stand for them than it is for yourself. Tonight you did both. I'm proud of you.'

'I punched a dead woman. That makes you proud?'

'So literal.'

'She'll come back.'

'And you'll beat her back again. You're stronger than she is. You always were.' Mira took Eve's hand, looked toward the fire in the sky. 'These were terrible times. Out of terrible times, perhaps more than ordinary ones, heroes and villains spring. Sometimes there's little difference between them but a choice, and the choice made defines them. Look at the choices.'

'Whose?'

'It started here, didn't it? It's time to go.'

She woke in the dark, steady and warm. No shakes or unloosed screams in her head. So she lay for a moment, still. She'd dreamed quiet, she decided, as Roarke slept undisturbed beside her. And she felt the considerable weight of the cat, heavy across her feet.

Not quite a nightmare, not quite a dream – and not quite a solution, she thought. But progress. She'd have to think about it, about choices, and about the fact it had felt so damn liberating to punch the image of her dead mother in the face.

She wasn't entirely sure what that said about her, but she figured she'd be okay with it.

In fact, she felt pretty much okay now. Sort of happy, definitely energized.

She shifted, propped up a little as her eyes adjusted. She hardly ever got to watch Roarke sleep. Most of the time he rose before she did. And sleep for her tended to be wandering in lucid, often disturbing dreams, or an absolute exhausted void.

He looked peaceful, and God, so beautiful. How did genes decide to mix themselves up, combine and create such serious beauty? It didn't seem quite fair to the rest of the population.

Then again, all that serious beauty belonged to her.

Screw the rest of the population.

'There now.' He murmured it, reaching for her. 'Ssh. I'm right here.'

Could he hear her think now? she wondered, but went with it when he drew her close.

'Did you have a nightmare?'

'Sort of.'

'It's all right.' He stroked her back, brushed a kiss over her hair. 'It's all right now.'

Look at him, she thought, comforting her. So ready to soothe and hold. Could she be any luckier?

'I'm okay.'

'Are you cold? I'll light the fire.'

Love simply swamped her. 'I'm not cold. Not now.' She rolled over, onto him, laid her lips on his. 'How are you?'

She saw his eyes, the dazzle of them close to her own. 'Curious at the moment.'

'I had a dream. I'll tell you about it.' But now she swept kisses over his face. 'Then I woke up, and it was good. You were sleeping, and the cat was weighing down my feet. And it was all so good. The world's so fucked up, Roarke, but right here? It's all just exactly right.'

He trailed his fingers over the back of her legs, along her hips. 'It feels just exactly right.'

'You're probably tired. That's okay. You can go back to sleep, and I'll take care of this.'

'Oh, I think I can manage to stay awake, with the proper motivation.' He rolled her over, pressed center to center. 'And there it is.'

'At times like this, I like that men are so easy.'

'Handily, I feel the same. It's easy enough when I have my wife under me, warm and soft.'

'Maybe.' She hooked his legs with hers, reversed positions again. 'But I like having my man under me, hot and hard.'

'That must've been some dream.'

She laughed, nipped at his jaw. 'Not that kind. Besides, I like this better when it's real.' She levered up, lifted off the nightshirt she'd pulled on, tossed it aside.

His hands slid up her torso to her breasts. 'Again, we agree.'

She pressed her hands to his, closed her eyes as pleasure, easy as breath, wound through her. His hands, his skin, his body, taut and chiseled, under hers. Oh yes, so much better than dreams.

He rose to her, wrapped around her as their mouths met. Deep and slow. Their bodies pressed close, a single shadow in the quiet dark as her hands combed through his hair, tangled there.

He stroked the length of her, his fascinating, complicated Eve, and the muscles he too often found tense and knotted moved warm and loose. He found the pulse in her throat with his lips, relished the life there in that tender curve.

He let her ease him back, but caught her hands and drew her down to him. He so much wanted her mouth, wanted that most simple, most basic of matings before the heat and the hurry.

She gave, thrilled to be wanted, and to want. All but felt her skin shimmer under the glide of his hands. While she shimmered she tasted. The strong line of his throat, the sculpted lines of his torso, the spread of his shoulders.

Not a dream, but dreamy as they moved together, touched,

savored. Neither of them heard the solid thump of the cat as he leaped down from the bed, undoubtedly in disgust.

Soft sighs, the whisper of sheets, a sudden catch of breath, and the world centered in that wide pool of bed even as the sky window over it bloomed with the first pale lights of dawn.

In its pearly glow she rose over him again. And took him in with a shudder, shudder of gluttonous pleasure. All and more, she thought as the need squeezed her heart. Together they were all and more.

While she rode him he watched her in that breaking light, her eyes gold and fierce, her long, lean body gleaming. With her hair like a tousled crown, her head fell back as the climax took her. Then even her image blurred as she whipped him to the edge of control. As she snapped it like a single thin thread.

As he broke, he reached for her, and held her close on the long fall.

When she got her breath back, they were still tangled together. And the cat had climbed back onto the bed to stare at them, his bicolored eyes unblinking.

'What's his problem?' she asked.

'I expect we disturbed his beauty sleep.'

'He gets so much sleep he ought to be the Roarke of cats.'

'The what?'

'I was thinking, before your telepathy woke you up, how pretty you are. Then, since you woke up, I figured I might as well take advantage of you.'

'It's appreciated.'

'You were probably almost ready to get up anyway, to slink off and start the first stage of your daily world domination.'

He glanced toward the clock. 'Ah well, I'll have to get a late start on that today.'

'I'd better get started on my daily hunt for bad guys.'

'Let's have coffee in bed first.'

She liked the sound of it. 'Who gets up to get it?'

'That's a question. Rock, paper, scissors?'

'You'll cheat.'

'How?'

'It's the telepathy.'

'Ah yes. Then you might as well get it, as you'll lose anyway.'

'Maybe, maybe not.' She shifted enough to hold out a fist. He held out his in turn. Counted to three.

'Damn it,' she mumbled as his paper covered her rock.

She rolled out of bed, fed the cat as she programmed the coffee.

'Tell me about the dream.'

'It was weird. Mixed up. All this digging into the Urbans. That's where I was, here in New York.'

She brought the coffee back, told him.

'I was so pissed, but not . . . I don't know. Upset? I don't know if that's the word. But I kept looking at her, listening to her. Bitch, bitch, bitch. Blame, blame, blame. And there's Mira, so calm. Unshakable, the way she can be. Part of my head's thinking, look how different they are. Like opposite

275

sides. And Mira had some bad shit in her life, but it didn't turn her into some monster. I didn't let Stella turn me. So what has she got? She's got nothing but what I let her have. I know it. I always did. But . . . '

'What happened in Dallas was vicious. You had to work through it.'

'I know it took a piece out of you, too. And I know the time since hasn't been easy for you. It's going to be better.'

'I can see it.'

'She wasn't going to walk off with that kid, or hurt her. Then when I saw it was Bella. Jesus. Over my dead body, you worthless cunt.' Eve took a breath. 'She wanted me to shoot her. It's weird, right? Even though it's my dream, my inner whatever running the show, *she* wanted me to shoot her, then it's like I killed her. I guess there was some stupid little seed of guilt in there I had to dig out and crush. Punching her felt so damn good. Mira'd probably have something to say about that.'

'I believe she'd say, *Brava.*'

'It's going to be like it was with Troy, when I worked through that. She may come back, but she can't hurt me anymore. That's done.'

He lowered his forehead to hers. 'I can't tell you what it means to me.'

'You don't have to. There's probably some crap in here that still needs shoveling, but everybody's got crap, right? It's what you do about it. Choices. I've got to take a good look at mine, at some point. And now, I've got to start looking at choices people made in the Urbans that helped build the maze that led to the choices Callaway's made.'

'As I said, some dream.'

'You got telepathy, I've got dreams. And I'm going to use them to kick some ass.'

She compiled the notes, the data, the images, shuffling them together for the morning briefing. She rose just as Roarke stepped into her office.

'I've got to get in, start setting this up.'

'Before you do. Gina MacMillon.' He offered her a disc. 'You may want to familiarize yourself on the way in. I've copied the files to your office comp.'

'Thanks. Interesting?'

'Very,' he said as she pocketed the disc. 'She was married to a William MacMillon, and while he was listed as the father on the birth record – that record wasn't recorded until the child was more than six months old.'

'That is interesting.'

'Also interesting. William MacMillon had filed for divorce, ultimately citing desertion. He filed eight months before the birth of the child, and the claim on the old documents states she'd abandoned him and the family home six months previously.'

'Fourteen months? If he was telling the truth, it's either the longest gestation on record, or the kid wasn't his. I'm going with the second option.'

'Better. I dug up a deposition where MacMillon states his

wife had become involved with a religious cult, specifically names Menzini as an influence.'

Eve's eyes sharpened as she turned to her board. 'The wife takes off with Menzini's group, gets knocked up. Somewhere in there has a change of heart – or re-engages her brain. Goes back to the husband – with a kid. He forgives her, takes responsibility for the kid.'

She paused a moment. 'I've got some problems with that unless MacMillon is registered as a saint, but the time line reads like that.'

'It does. Love, if love it was, makes saints or sinners out of men.'

'I think mostly people are just born that way. So, the bio father maybe comes for the kid, and Karleen MacMillon's now listed as an abductee.'

'And both Gina and William listed as dead, killed during the home invasion where the child was taken.'

'And eventually Gina's half-sister finds the kid, takes her as her own – changing the name. Protect the kid.'

'It reads that way.'

'I'd like some verification instead of speculation, but I can push on it. Maybe there's family or somebody in the know still alive. I'll put some work into finding out.'

'I have one more,' Roarke told her. 'I had a quick word with Crystal Kelly.'

'Who?'

'CEO of New Harbor, Callaway's client.'

'Is it business hours?'

278

'Close enough for those of us trying to wrangle world domination. She'd heard about the incident here, of course, and knew Cattery. She was cooperative, and sounded sincerely fond of Cattery. She was, as he stated, at dinner with Vann when Callaway contacted him to tell him Cattery was dead.'

'Right on the spot. Handy.'

'It was, yes. She says Vann was stunned. Both of them were stunned and upset. They considered postponing the presentation, but then agreed to get it done and over. Joe, as she said, had worked hard on it.'

'And Callaway.'

'She claimed she didn't know him as well as Vann, Cattery or Weaver. Hadn't really connected with him, and considered him a more behind-the-scenes type. She didn't really have any specific impression of him, which made one on me.'

'Yeah, he's invisible to her – and that would grate.'

'More, Vann specifically – before he knew of the death – credited Cattery with two key points in the campaign, and Weaver for her flexibility. She doesn't recall him mentioning Callaway except as part of the team.'

'Still doing what he's told, and no more – sounds like. And pissed off that someone like Cattery, the family man, the soccer coach, the nice guy is passing him by.'

'It's not much more than you had.'

'Little things, adding up.' To a clearer picture, she thought. 'I appreciate it.'

'I'm a bit crowded today, but I can look into it sometime late this afternoon if there's still a need.'

'I'll keep that in reserve.' She stepped closer. 'But don't screw with your work and time for this. I'm covered, and you've already done more than your part.'

'Over a hundred and twenty people are dead. I'll make time if I'm needed.'

'I'll let you know. Thanks for this.' She patted her pocket. 'I'll bone up on the way to Central.'

'It's a dangerous world out there. Take care of my cop.'

'Don't worry.'

Wishing he could give her what she asked, he watched her walk out.

With her mind on steps, angles, she hurried downstairs to find Summerset in the foyer. He held out her long leather coat.

'It's been fitted with the body armor lining, as in your jacket,' he told her.

'Yeah?' Roarke, she thought, never a miss. She took the coat, tested the weight, studied the flexible, protective lining.

He might tell her to take care of his cop, but he often beat her to it.

'A cold front moved in,' Summerset said simply. 'We've had a hard frost, and there's a bitter wind this morning.'

'Okay.' She hesitated, knowing very well they were both aware he rarely greeted her in the morning, much less with a weather forecast. 'I can't give you all the details, but we found a link between the suspect and Red Horse. I have to tighten it, but it's a connection, maybe – probably – an important one.'

'I could be useful.'

'Be useful to him.' She glanced upstairs. 'He's let too much slide the last couple months. I've got this.'

'Then I wish you a very productive day.'

She stepped outside, found Summerset's description of the wind exactly on target. The bitter blew straight into her bones before she jumped into the vehicle – heater already running – at the base of the steps.

She plugged in the disc Roarke had given her, started to order it on audio. Then gave herself permission to deal with personal business first.

A sleepy-eyed, slurry-voiced Mavis came up on her in-dash screen.

'Hey. Guess I woke you up.'

'Not so much. We're all having a snuggle. We put in a late night, and Belle woke up early.'

'Okay. Sorry I haven't been able to get back to you. You texted you were all in Florida. Still?'

'Miami. We zipped down a couple days ago. I had a two-night gig, and Leonardo's meeting with some totally-too-tanned clients while we're here. We're good.'

'Why don't you stay down there until I get back to you?'

There was a rustle, baby-voiced babbling, and a low rumble that must have been Leonardo. 'That's affirmative.' Mavis shook back her hair, a cotton-candy pink froth sparkling with some sort of silvery overlay. 'Weather's mag, and we got a place with our own pool. Bellarina's our little mermaid. We got the skinny off screen. What the you-know-what, Dallas.'

'I can't give you the details, but we're working it. I'll be in touch as soon as I can.'

'There's lots of buzz about terrorism.'

'It's not, but it's messy. Just stay sunny.'

'Totally, but – okay, sweet potato. Bella hears your voice. Hang a mo.'

'Das!' Belle's pretty face popped on screen. Eve had a flash of that pretty face, with tears streaming.

'Hey, kid.'

'Das, Das, Das,' she repeated, and bouncing launched into a long, incomprehensible babble, ending with, 'Kay? Kay, Das?'

'Ah, sounds good. You do that.'

'Say bye, Belle. Bye-bye.'

'Bye, bye, Das! Bye slooch!'

Lips pursed, Belle pecked kisses at the screen. Sliding her gaze right and left – in case any other driver might catch a glimpse – Eve gave a single peck back. 'See ya.'

'Ya!'

'She wants you to watch her swim,' Mavis said.

'How do you know that?'

'I'm multilingual-like. I speak Belle.'

'If you say so. Gotta go.'

'Stay chilly, stay safe.'

'That's the plan. Talk later.'

Satisfied, oddly relieved, Eve ordered the disc to audio. She listened to data on the MacMillons the rest of the way to Central.

She tagged Peabody the minute she'd parked in the garage. 'Where are you?'

'Walking into Central.'

'Grab me a coffee – real coffee from my office, then meet me in the conference room. I need to fill you in.'

'On that.'

Time to fill her in, Eve decided as she muscled onto the packed elevator. On a lot of levels.

15

Eve worked the board, running through data, connections, time lines as she added them.

Callaway to Hubbard to MacMillon to Menzini. How many turns, decisions, mistakes made in that chain? she wondered. All of them leading to this.

And how long had Callaway simmered, stewed, planned? How long had some suit whose purpose was to sell products — half of which people didn't need in the first place — dreamed of murder?

And how long had he known murder was his legacy?

She thought of her recent dreams. Murder and misery could have been her legacy, if she'd reached for it, if she'd opened that door instead of another.

So now she stood here, studying murder — the victims, the killer, the whys, the hows. Another path, another choice, she might have been up on a board like this, with someone else doing the studying, the wondering.

Mira was right, she determined, in reality and dreams. It always came down to choices.

She heard Peabody's clumping footsteps, then caught the scent of coffee.

'Long night,' Peabody said. 'I worked with McNab, and we've got everything there is to know on Macie Snyder and Jeni Curve, plus we have deep data on five of the abductees who settled in New York.'

She paused, scanned the new data on the board. 'Wow. Long night for you, too.'

'Did you read the data I sent you on Guiseppi Menzini?'

'Twice. Bad guy, chemist, religious crazy – and the primary suspect in two attacks, using the agent we've identified was used in our attacks. Captured and erased.'

'Callaway's linked to Menzini through his mother, an abductee.'

'Callaway.' Peabody's eyes narrowed on the board. 'I took him for a lightweight. I don't remember any Audrey Hubbard on the list.'

'Because there wasn't. She was born Karleen MacMillon to Gina MacMillon – Tessa Hubbard's half-sister – and an unknown father. The MacMillons were reported killed during the home invasion. Hubbard recovered the kid, changed her name, got a fresh birth certificate, and moved with her husband to New York.'

Eve grabbed the coffee. 'There's more. I want the images programmed as I've outlined while I fill you in.'

She ran it through while Peabody set up the programming.

'I've got two men on him. Roarke dug into the mother – Gina MacMillon. There's more there, but we'll pass that to Feeney.'

'With all the angles, all the data to sort through, I never

285

thought we'd zero in this fast.' As Eve had, Peabody turned to the victim board. 'I went to bed last night thinking we'd have to go into another scene like the bar and the café. I didn't get a lot of sleep thinking it.'

'We won't give him a chance to add to this board.'

'I'll sleep a hell of a lot better tonight then. Are we picking Callaway up this morning?'

'I want to see what he does this morning, where he goes. But yeah, we'll be talking to him. I want to interview the Hubbards, and I'm damned if I'm going to Arkansas. I figure Teasdale has the pull to bring them here. Maybe enough pull to get a warrant to search their place while they're out of it.'

'Do you think there's something there, something with his parents? Jesus, Dallas, do you think they know?'

'I think there's something there.' Eve stepped back from the board, drinking coffee as she scanned. 'I can't say what they know, but there's a direct link from Red Horse, Menzini to Lewis Callaway. It's biological, and there's nothing here that comes close to proving he knew his own biology, or cared, or has any information on the substance used.'

'Maybe not, but we've got a lot of key pieces.'

'Now we need the whole picture. We need that to show means. There's no clear motive. Was there a specific target – Cattery, Fisher – or were the attacks broad based? If target specific, why Cattery and Fisher? We've got opportunity. He was in the bar, and he lives and works within spitting distance of the café, and has admitted to frequenting same.'

She sat on the edge of the conference table, scanning, scanning. 'We need more. We need to prove he had knowledge, had access to the formula. We need motive, specific or broad based. To sew him up tight, we need it all.'

'You've got enough to sweat him,' Peabody pointed out.

'Yeah, I can sweat him, and I will. I'd like more in my pocket before I do.'

She went back to her notes as cops trickled into the room. Then her head came up. She scented baked goods seconds before the wolf pack circled Feeney.

'Listen, the wife made this coffee cake thing from her cooking class deal. It's probably not half bad.'

As if it mattered, Eve thought. She let them have the next couple minutes to tear in, devour while she finished off her coffee.

'Fall in,' she ordered. 'And wipe the crumbs off your faces, for Christ's sake. In case any of you have maintained some minor interest in the current investigation, we've connected Callaway to Red Horse.'

That shut them up. Attention zeroed in on the boards as cops grabbed chairs.

She waited one more beat, nodded to Peabody. 'Gina MacMillon,' she began as the image came on screen. 'This is Lewis Callaway's biological grandmother. She is twenty-three in this ID, issued before, according to statements and documents, she abandoned her husband and joined an unnamed cult. During her association with the cult, she gave birth to a female. The certificate of birth lists her husband as father, and was issued when the infant was six months old. The infant was named Karleen MacMillon, listed as an abductee at the age of eighteen months, and never recovered. However—'

The next image slid on.

'This is Karleen MacMillon's computer-aged image at the age of twenty-one. And this is Audrey Hubbard Callaway's ID photo at the same age. Audrey Hubbard's certificate of birth is fake, and issued to Gina MacMillon's half-sister Tessa and her husband, Edward, who left England when the child was approximately four years of age, and settled in Johnstown, Ohio. Audrey Hubbard married Russell Callaway, and sub-sequently gave birth to a son, Lewis.'

'The dots connect,' Baxter commented.

'Yeah, they do. William MacMillon's petition for divorce, and his deposition, cite abandonment, a cult, and specifically names Menzini. Unless MacMillon was lying, the date of the deposition and the date listed as the kid's birth make it impos-sible for him to be the biological father.'

'He took her back,' Baxter said, 'and took the kid as his? What is he, an apostle or something?'

'Find out. You and Trueheart find out everything you can, find me somebody who knew him, knew them. He's listed as killed, along with Gina, in the raid that took the kid. I want the dirt on the marriage – people always know the dirt, and they remember it.'

'Reineke, Jenkinson, I want the same on the Hubbards. Why did they change the kid's name, fake a birth certificate, move to another country?'

'Could be the sperm donor was trouble,' Reineke speculated. 'They wanted to keep the kid from him. Or hell, they just wanted a fresh start.'

'I like the first, that's my push on it. They could've legally adopted the kid, or applied for guardianship. I can't find anything that says they went that route. Why not? Hubbard was military, retired a captain. She was the kid's closest blood relation, except for the grandparents. Her father, Gina's mother. The grandmother's still alive, in England. Get me the story.'

'I think Detective Callendar and I might have something.' Teasdale glanced toward Callendar, got the nod. 'We have considerable data on Red Horse, though much of it is anecdotal, speculative or unsubstantiated. We focused most directly, for obvious reasons, on Menzini once you passed his name to us, and were able to find a few reports, and images – all dating prior to his apprehension.'

'I've got the data, if I can use the auxiliary,' Callendar said.

'Go ahead. While she's setting that up, further search showed Callaway's habit of visiting his parents – now in Arkansas, an average of once a year, until a few months ago. He's traveled there several times this year. And in reading the employee reviews, we found Cattery received a much larger bonus than Callaway on a recent project – initiated by Callaway, completed by Cattery. Cattery was also in line for a promotion. Money and position may be motive.'

'I've got it, Lieutenant.'

'Run it,' Eve ordered Callendar.

'The images were grainy, indistinct. I cleaned them up, and

I can clean them more. This is a photo run on the Daily Mail blog, out of London. It identifies Menzini, preaching to a group after a firefight in the East End. The woman to his right is identified only as his companion.'

'Magnify her.' Eve moved closer to the screen. 'Dyed her hair red – that fits – and it's longer – but that's Gina MacMillon.'

'There's another.' Callendar switched images. 'Leaving some kind of revival. She looks knocked up to me.'

'And right beside Menzini again. Run the image against her ID, make sure we've got a match.'

'There are very few photos of him during the Urbans,' Teasdale commented. 'It's interesting that two of the few have this woman at his side.'

'It's going to be more interesting if he's the biological father.'

'Yes.' Teasdale smiled serenely. 'It will.'

'His DNA is on record somewhere. HSO would have it.'

'I'll do what I can.'

'The birth mother and the half-sister are dead, but there might be DNA records there. And the grandmother's still alive. I need Menzini's. Make it happen, Teasdale. And while you're at it, I want the suspect's parents brought to New York for questioning.'

'I believe that can be arranged.'

'Arrange it, and asap.' She pulled out her 'link, read the incoming text. 'The suspect is leaving his apartment building – dressed for work, carrying a briefcase. He'll be kept under surveillance. I want to interview the parents before we bring him in.'

'Then I'll begin arrangements.'

'I want to search their house once they're en route.'

Teasdale lifted her eyebrows. 'As you know, what we have is compelling, but there is no hard evidence, and securing a search warrant on civilians, who even with this compelling data show no association with Red Horse, or any involvement in the murders, may prove difficult.'

'There's a reason he went back there multiple times in the last few months.'

'Agreed. But the residence in question is one belonging to two, apparently, law-abiding citizens. I'll do what I can to persuade my superior and the appropriate judge that the warrant is vital to public safety.'

'Fine. Feeney, everything Roarke has on Gina MacMillon's on disc. He ran out of time.'

'I'll pick up where he left off, get more.'

'Let's all get more. I want to know everything there is to know about this cast of characters, including their freaking shoe size, by midday. Move on it.

'Stone, any updates on the illegals?'

'I found a fresh source for Zeus that's going to make my lieutenant happy, but it doesn't look like it connects to this. The LSD's running cold, but I'm still pulling on it. I poked, and can tell you there haven't been any on-record requisitions from Christopher Lester or his lab for the ingredients necessary to create the agent. Not in the last two years I was able to access.'

'All right, keep pulling.'

'Lieutenant? I think he's got a legit source. I mean, a lab or chemical distributor. Some way to access the synthetics, the LSD off the street. I think he's got a connection.'

Strong shifted as Eve waited for her to elaborate. 'This guy? He's not a street guy. He's a suit. Nothing in his background shows he used, has or had any street connections. Some suit tries to make a buy like he'd have to for this? It should pop out. Going underground, overseas, even off-planet. There's not even a whiff. There should be.'

'I agree,' Teasdale put in. 'Added to it, he has no experience in this kind of chemistry. While he may follow the formula, I believe he'd need someone to show him how to set up, what he'd need, how to handle the elements. This is advanced work, and I don't think a novice could accomplish it without guidance.'

'So, back to a chemist. Stone, have a talk with Christopher Lester. See if he has any ideas on where Callaway could access the synthetics. What labs in the area – because it's going to be in New York – routinely handle that sort of thing. There's a connection. Find it.'

'Yes, sir.'

'Russell Callaway's a medic, now into farming. Maybe he's got a chemical source, or has some experience there. Farms use chemicals. Callendar, see what you can find out, see if the Callaways bought any strange chemicals in the last few months.'

'On that.'

'Doctor Mira, if I could have a minute. Peabody, take a deeper dig on the Callaways' financials. See if there's any indication they've gotten any scratch from the grandmother out of England, or made any unusual purchases from a chemical distributor.'

She waited till the room cleared. 'There are a lot of ifs,' she told Mira. 'I need you to work with them. Let's start with if Audrey Hubbard knew where she came from, knew her own story and passed that onto her son, does his background data give any indication?'

'It would depend, of course, how the information was related. All indications are Callaway had a reasonably normal childhood, though he would have needed to adjust to several moves during his formative and teenage years. While he was a loner, he was also uprooted several times during those formative years, and this makes it difficult to form lasting relationships. His records show no discipline problems, no juvenile record.'

'Yeah, that's the thing. Normal, normal, but all those relocations. Did they relocate because of the father's itchy feet, or because there was something hinky with the kid?'

'Hinky?' Mira repeated.

'Yeah, hinky. He's acting up, or causing some sort of concern, so you pick up and move, start again. The Hubbards did that – only once, but they picked up, moved, started over. Let's try this.'

She stepped to the board, tapped Callaway's photo. 'He didn't know, either because his mother didn't know, or opted not to tell him. He finds out, comes across some sort of information, or somebody slips up and says something that makes him wonder. He goes back, hunts for the information.'

She tapped Audrey Hubbard's then Menzini's picture in turn.

'What's a loner by nature, with no solid or lasting relationships, who feels he's stuck on the promotion ladder because other people are getting the breaks going to do about that?'

'You think he found out Menzini was his grandfather, and this was his trigger, or his excuse, to kill.'

'His trigger or excuse to use his grandfather's method to make a statement, to punish, to advance himself, to use others to kill. To be important. And by doing so eliminate two coworkers, both of whom he could consider in his way. A violent nature suppressed for so long, given release. Given, in a way, permission. This is who I am, where I came from. At last I know.'

'He was raised, by all appearances, by two decent people.'

'I don't know that yet. What I have is an older, potentially dominant father. A mother who lived her life caring for others – her parents, then her child. He'd see that as weak.'

'Do you?'

'I see it as a choice – not one I'd make for damn sure, but a choice. Unless she's been pushed into it, which I intend to find out. I don't look at Callaway and see myself, if that's what you're worried about. Bad blood? I've got it, but it's not an excuse to live a crappy life. It sure as hell isn't an excuse to kill. Maybe I've got a violent nature, but I channel it. Mostly.' She shrugged. 'I need to bring him in before he decides to do it again. I have to keep him in, because if he walks out, he's going to do it again. He'll find a way. I have to know him, know where to drill. I need his trigger.'

'Until you've talked to the mother — and I'd also like to talk to her at some point — it's only speculation.'

'I may not have time to pull it out of the mother first, and I'll take your speculation over most people's absolutes.'

Mira drew in a breath, looked from Callaway to Audrey Hubbard to Menzini. 'Then, he knows. How he found out, I can't possibly say, but in my opinion, the knowledge didn't repulse him, didn't upset or concern. On the contrary, it freed him.'

'Okay.' She nodded. 'Okay. I can work with that.'

'He's nothing like you.'

'Damn right he's not.'

Mira turned away from the board, focused fully on Eve. 'You've come to some level of . . . is it peace?'

'I don't know about that. I've got a mass murderer to take down, and I don't feel peaceful about it.'

No, she realized, she felt revved. She felt ready. She felt right.

'But I'm good. Quick version — I had a dream, about this, about Stella. You made a cameo appearance. I finished it off punching Stella in the face. That violent nature, I guess. It felt right, just. It felt almost finished. Pretty much done. And I look at him?'

She turned to the board, again to Callaway. 'And I see, yeah, I could've gone another way. I didn't. And I like where I am. Most of the time I like who I am. That's got to be good enough.'

'It's very good.'

'I punched her in the face,' Eve repeated. 'Stella. What do you think about that?'

'I think congratulations are in order.'

The laugh surprised her. 'Is that like *brava*?'

'Yes, in fact, I'll say that. *Brava*.'

'Roarke nailed that one,' Eve murmured. 'So, anyway, I'm going to put a lid on it by telling Peabody what went down in Dallas. I've avoided that, just wasn't ready to spill it out. It's not right to hold back from a partner, so I'll get that over. And it's done. As done as I can make it.'

'If you need me, I'm here.'

'I know. I wouldn't have made it through this without you. It's not easy for me to say that, or to know that. But it's not as hard as it used to be.'

'That's also good enough. I'll leave you to work. When Agent Teasdale arranges for the Callaways to come in, as I have no doubt she will, I'd like to sit in. Or at least observe.'

'I'll save you a seat.'

She went directly to her office, noted her blinking incoming for data and for messages. She found the bulk of the messages from reporters trying to skip through channels for the story. She forwarded them on to Kyung, with a brief update.

The incoming data reminded her just how many dead lay in Morris's house, how much of them was even now being dissected, analyzed, studied in the lab.

Though she found nothing new, no game changer, she added the new data on each body processed to her murder book.

She checked on surveillance. Callaway was in his office. Unless he decided to cut loose in his own department, he was as secure as she could make him at the moment.

So she grabbed her coat, walked out to the bullpen.

'I'm not finding anything off on the financials,' Peabody told her. 'The Callaways live within their means, have a small, but steady nest egg. No major income or outlay in the last year. And no purchases of weird chemicals. They're organic farmers.'

'Let that go for now. I want to talk to Cattery's wife, get a feel. If there's time, we'll do the same with Fisher, talk to her roommate.'

'I'm all about it.' Peabody popped right up. 'I feel like I'm swimming in the data stream and getting nowhere. Hey, I talked to Mavis,' she added, pulling on her coat as they headed out. 'She couldn't reach you so she tagged me last night.'

'I talked to her this morning.'

'They've got Belle swimming.'

'I heard.'

'I talked to my parents, too.' Peabody jumped on the glide behind Eve. 'They're worried, you know, just getting all that

297

bullshit from the media. I told them enough to calm them down some, and to make sure they didn't decide to rev up the camper and drive to New York. They were out of the Urbans, you know.'

'I hadn't thought about it.'

'Well, they were young, really just getting started when all that went on. Just a couple of Free-Ager kids doing their commune thing. They made clothes, grew food for people who needed it, but they were never in the hot areas.'

'It's good they were.'

'My dad said he can't remember hearing about Red Horse at the time. It was after, like a history book footnote. A lot of people barely heard of them, or not at all. I bet everyone's heard of them now.'

Eve paused before they transferred to the garage elevator. 'That's a point, isn't it? It could, maybe should've been a major deal, but it not only got crushed, it got buried. Some footnotes for historians and researchers, but no big play. Until now.'

'Do you think that's what he's after?'

'I think he's a selfish, bastard coward, but it's a factor. His grandfather might have been up there with Hitler given more time, more exposure. The powers that be snatched away his infamy. Recognition's part of it.'

'Jeez, who'd want to be Hitler's grandson?'

'People who think white's right, lunatics, and selfish bastard cowards who want recognition.'

'Yeah, I guess there are those, but . . .'

'Your Free-Ager's showing, Peabody. A lot of people are no damn good, and a lot of those people are proud of it.'

She got in the car. Maybe that was an opening, she thought as she programmed Cattery's address.

'You should know what went down in Dallas.'

'With McQueen?'

'With McQueen's partner.' She drove out of the garage, concentrated on traffic. It might be easier to lay it out if she had to pay attention to the external. 'She was no damn good, and I'd say she was proud of it.'

'She was as fucked up as he is. Maybe more.'

'Yeah.' It tightened her belly to hear it, but she could live with it. That was the key, she reminded herself. Just living with it. 'When we were looking for his partner, running the list and images of women who'd visited him in prison, something about her — as Sister Suzan — kept pulling me back. I thought maybe I'd busted her sometime, or interviewed her. Same deal with her other IDs. Just something that tugged, but I couldn't put my finger on it.'

Curious, Peabody shifted toward Eve. 'Had you busted her?'

'No.'

'Maybe you just recognized the type. Instinct kicking in.'

'That's what I thought, but that wasn't it. Or not all of it. You read the reports. You know we had her and her place covered. We were right there when she walked out of that townhouse, going to meet up with McQueen. Bad luck. A kid on a bike, a little dog, oncoming car. She made us, took off.'

'I wish I'd been there. I probably wouldn't have at the time, flying down the streets after her van, crashing. You got banged up.'

'Not bad, it wasn't bad.' A little bloody, a little bruised, Eve thought. The bad came later.

'She got banged up more – no air bags, safety gel in that clunky van. And she hadn't taken time to hook her seat belt.'

'Good. She deserved to get banged up.'

'I was so pissed,' Eve continued. 'Afraid she'd been able to tag McQueen during the chase, knowing damn well, we'd lost the best chance to find him and get the kid and Melanie back safe. So fucking pissed.'

All that rage, Eve thought, gushing through her like an open wound. And then . . .

'I yanked her out of the van, got her blood on me. I spun her around. Stupid pink sunglasses, crooked on her face. Pulled them off her . . . I looked at her face, into her eyes. And I knew her.'

It was Eve's tone that had a chill working up Peabody's spine. She spoke carefully. 'You didn't put that in your report.'

'No. It didn't have anything to do with the case. It's personal. She went by Stella back then, where I remember her from. She'd changed her eyes, her hair, had some work done, but I knew her. I knew Stella. She was my mother.'

'Jesus.' Peabody laid her hand on Eve's arm, just a light touch though her fingers wanted to tremble. 'You're sure? I guess I thought she was dead. I mean, had been dead all along.'

'I had the blood. Hers, mine. I had Roarke run DNA to verify, but I knew. I don't remember much about her, she left me with him when I was about four or five. I'm not sure; it's vague. But I remember enough.'

'She left you with . . . did she know?' Even the thought of it had sickness coating Peabody's throat. 'Did she know what he did to you?'

'She had to know. She didn't care.'

'But . . .'

'There's no bittersweet aside here, Peabody. She didn't care and never had. I was a commodity, and the investment was taking too long, was too much trouble to suit her. That's what I figure.'

The sickness faded. In its place rose a vicious disgust, icy hot. 'Did she recognize you?'

'No. I wasn't that important. All she saw was the cop who'd fucked up her plans with McQueen, who put her in the hospital, who was going to put her in a cage. I'd've put her in a cage. Maybe I should've put two men on her.'

'Dallas, I read the reports. You had her restrained, and under guard. There were still cops in the hospital when she escaped.'

'She wouldn't tell me where McQueen was. I couldn't flip her, and I went at her hard. Maybe too hard.'

'Stop.' Peabody's voice roughened and firmed. 'You did the job. If you weren't sure you could do it, you'd have gotten somebody else to sweat her. But you did the job.'

It helped to hear it. She'd gone over every step, every

move, every decision countless times, and believed she'd done everything she could. But it helped to hear it. 'I was going to go back at her again. I'd bought some time, wanted to let her think about it, then go back at her. But she got out, went to McQueen, and he killed her.'

'And you found her.'

'She was still warm. We hadn't missed him by much.'

'You got Melinda Jones and Darlie Morgansten out, safe. I can't imagine what it was like for you.' Peabody took a quiet, unsteady breath. 'What it's been like since. You had Mira,' Peabody remembered. 'Thank God you had Roarke and Mira.'

For a long moment, Peabody stared out the side window. 'Dallas, you could've called me down. You shouldn't have had to work that alone. I'd've had your back.'

'I know it. I had to work it alone. And I've had to work through it. You deserve to know, but I had to work through it before I told you.'

'I read her file.' Voice strong and steady again, Peabody shifted back. 'I know who she was, what she was. Now I know she left you with an animal. It's good she's dead.'

Stunned, Eve turned her head, stared. 'That's not very Free-Ager.'

'Fuck that.' Peabody's eyes flashed like supernovas. 'Fuck tolerance and understanding. Yeah, you'd have put her in a cage for the rest of her pathetic, evil life. But maybe some- time during her rot, she'd have put it together. Maybe she'd have remembered you. She'd have used that on you; she'd have tried. Before you scared the piss out of her, if you could get to her before Roarke. If he could get there before me. And it's good she was such a selfish, pitiful excuse for a human being so she didn't remember you, didn't think about you all those years. She might've recognized you, especially after Roarke. She might've seen you on screen, and recognized you, caused you more grief and trouble. Dead's better.'

The rant was so unPeabody, Eve sat in silence. 'I'm not sure how to respond,' she decided.

'We should go get a goddamn drink. A whole shitload of goddamn drinks.'

'Jesus, don't cry.'

'I'll cry if I fucking want to.' She sniffled, swiped. 'Fucking bitch.'

'It's mean to call me a bitch when I've shared personal trauma.'

'I didn't mean you! I meant your — I meant McQueen's fucking bitch. I should've been there for you.'

And she'd know not to use the M word, not to say mother. That was very Peabody. 'Roarke sent for Mira after McQueen killed Stella. And he had Mira bring Galahad.'

Now the tears really rolled — big, fat drops until Peabody had to dig through her pockets to find an old tissue. 'I love him.'

'He's a pretty good cat.'

Wet laughter blew through the tissue. 'Sure he is, but you know I meant Roarke. I love him. And if something terrible happened to McNab, I'd fight you for him. And I've been practicing.'

'So warned.'

'You're okay?'

Eve thought it over. 'I'm okay. There's probably going to be some rough spots here and there, but I'm okay. Sperm and egg – that's what they were. For eight years, between the two of them, they made me a victim. They made me afraid and gave me pain. Now they're dead. I'm not a victim. I'm not afraid. And pain? Not much. They can't hurt me anymore, so what I have, it's just echoes. It'll pass.'

She pulled up in front of the little house in Brooklyn. 'Do something about your face. You're all splotchy.'

'Crap.' Peabody began lightly slapping her hands over her face.

'What does that do?'

'Makes it all red, distributes the blood. Maybe. It'll calm down in a few minutes. Just keep Mrs Cattery focused on you.'

'Christ. Stay behind me.'

Peabody got out, lifted her reddened face. 'It's really windy, and cold. It'll just look like I'm windburned.' She took a steadying breath. 'Did you tell me this when we were in the car and on our way to interview so I couldn't hug you?'

'It's a side benefit.'

'I'm going to hug you later. You won't know when it's coming.'

'The same goes for my boot up your ass.'

'That's a given. It's a daily surprise.'

'Settle down, and let's do this.'

'It's a nice house,' Peabody observed as they walked to the door. 'Nice neighborhood.'

'He was the only one on the team who did the campaign who didn't live within blocks of the office.'

'Wife and kids. Fenced yard. Dog.' She nodded toward the back. 'See, doghouse.'

'What's in a doghouse? Mini-screen, AutoChef?'

'Probably a ratty blanket and a collection of soup bones. How's my face?'

'I've seen worse.'

With that ringing endorsement, Peabody angled herself slightly behind her partner as Eve knocked on the door.

16

Eve pegged the woman who answered as a well-toned sixty-five. Her hair, a stylishly streaky sweep, swung around a tired face currently dominated by suspicious eyes.

'Can I help you?'

'Lieutenant Dallas, Detective Peabody, NYPSD. We—'

'Of course, I recognize you. Have you found the person responsible for Joe?'

'We're pursuing all leads. We'd like to speak to Mrs Cattery if she's available.'

'She's resting. Can you talk to me? I'm her mother. I'm Dana Forest. I don't want to disturb Elaine if there's nothing new. She's barely slept since—'

'I'm up, Mom.'

Eve caught a glimpse of the woman on the stairs. She wore a bulky sweater over blue and green sleep pants, thick red socks on her feet. Her hair, a deep, bark brown, hung in a lank tail down her back. Bruises of grief and exhaustion provided the only color in her face. If her mother looked tired, Elaine Cattery looked utterly depleted.

'Lainey, you need some rest.'

'Don't worry.' She came down, leaned against her mother in a way that made them a unit. 'Where are the kids?'

'Sam and Hannah took them to the park to let the dog run, just to get them out for a little while.'

'It's so cold.'

'Everyone's bundled up. Don't *you* worry.'

'I'm sorry. We're leaving you out in the wind. Please, come in.'

'How about some tea?' Dana kept her arm around her daughter. 'I'll make some tea.'

'That'd be great.' Elaine stepped away, moved into a living area with a bold-colored sofa, brightly striped chairs. A comfortable home, Eve thought, with cheerful colors, deep cushions, surfaces holding framed photos, flowers, pretty little bowls.

'Sit down, won't you? I didn't expect . . . I've already talked to the police.'

'I know. We're doing a follow-up. If you could answer some questions, Mrs Cattery.'

'Are you seeing everyone? There are so many. So many. I've stopped watching the news. Are there more? Has something else happened?'

'No, ma'am. Mrs Cattery, there are many, too many. And every one who died deserves our time and attention.'

'I wasn't here, you see. I'd taken the kids to see my mother and my brother. Now they're here, with us. But I wasn't home. Joe was working on that campaign. He worked so hard on it, so long, and I'd just finished up a project for work. I thought I'll get the kids out of his hair for a few days, they can keep up with school on screen, have a nice visit with my family. Everybody could just take a breath, I thought. So we weren't here, and he didn't come home. If I'd been here—'

'Mrs Cattery.' Peabody reached out, laid a hand on Elaine's. 'You can't think that, or wonder that.'

'That's what my mother says, and still . . . I'm pregnant.' On a choked sob, Elaine pressed her fingers to her lips. 'I found out, confirmed, while I was at Mom's. We weren't trying, weren't not trying. We said we were finished, then we both got this itch. Let's just see what happens, that's what Joe said. I never got the chance to tell him. I wanted to tell him when I got home, but it was too late. I don't know what to do now. I can't think of what I'm going to do.'

'I'm sorry,' Peabody murmured. 'I'm so sorry for your loss. We're going to do everything we can to find the person responsible.'

'Will it help? My brother, he's so angry, and he's so sure when you find who did this, put them away, it'll help. But Joe still won't be here. He won't watch his children grow up. He won't see this one born. So I don't know if it'll help.'

'It will,' Eve assured her. 'Maybe not right away, but it will. You'll know the person who did this won't ever be able to hurt anyone again. He won't ever take another father from his children.'

'Joe never hurt anyone. He's such a sweet man, so easy-going. Sometimes too easy, that's what I'd tell him. He never pushed at work, and the kids could always twist him around their fingers. He never hurt anyone.'

'He was up for a promotion.'

'Was he?' The faintest of smiles touched her lips. 'He didn't tell me.'

'He may not have known, but it was in his file. He put a lot of work into this last campaign.'

'Yes, he did. The whole team did.'

'You know the people he worked with.'

'Yes. Nancy – Nancy Weaver, his boss – she's been by. She's been wonderful. Steve and Lew, they both contacted me. Steve sent food. This huge ham with bread and ... things. For sandwiches.'

'And I wish you'd eat a little more of it.' Dana came in with a tray, set it down.

'I will. I promise.' Elaine took her mother's hand, drew her down.

'Sometimes when people work so closely together, on an important project, there's conflict,' Eve began. 'Was there any conflict within the team?'

'It's hard to fight with Joe,' Elaine said while her mother poured out the tea. 'He loves his job, and he's good at it. He likes being part of a team.'

'Was he aware Vann and Weaver had an affair?'

Again, that faint smile. 'Joe's a quiet man, and quiet types see things. He knew.'

'Did it bother him?'

'No. It bothered me, some. I thought – said – how Steve

covered all the bets. Family and sex, but Joe just laughed it off. And Steve did good work. He loves his boy. I guess that goes a long way with me – and with Joe. When a father loves his son, and it shows.'

'That leaves Callaway.'

'Lew?' Elaine curled up her legs, pretended to drink her tea. 'Another quiet type, but not as naturally outgoing or easygoing as Joe. Joe used to say Lew had to work at the grip and grin. He did better with ideas – big pictures. Joe liked to fiddle and finesse, dig in. I'd get annoyed sometimes when Joe worked out Lew's concepts, spent all the time to bring them in line, if you understand me. And most of the time, he wouldn't take credit for it. But I guess people noticed anyway. He was up for a promotion, Mom.'

'Nobody deserved it more.'

'So he never complained to you about his coworkers?'

'Well, he's not a saint. He'd gripe now and then, in his Joe way. Steve took another two-hour lunch, or left early for a hot date. Lew's on the broody train again.'

'Broody train?'

'Joe's expression. Lew'd get moody – kind of sulk, I guess, when his ideas got shot down or re-imagined. Stuff like that rolls off Joe's back, but I guess it stuck to Lew's.'

'Did you know Carly Fisher?'

'Not really. I met her, and I know Joe thought she was bright, and had a strong future. I hated hearing she'd been killed. She was Nancy's favorite.'

'Was she?'

'Absolutely. I think Nancy saw a lot of herself in Carly. Joe said he was looking at his next boss.'

'It didn't bother him?'

'Not Joe. He didn't want to be the boss. He wanted to be one of the team. That's what he was good at.'

After they'd left Elaine with her mother, Eve stood out in the wind for a moment. 'What did we learn?' she asked Peabody.

'That Joe Cattery was a nice guy who enjoyed his work. His wife loved him, and they'd built a nice life here.'

'And other than the eulogy?'

'But that's the thing, isn't it? Nice guy with a nice life. Not the big idea guy, not the driven guy, the flashy guy. But the nice guy who's working his way up because he likes his work and he's good at it, because he's a team player by nature. He's willing to help, to take the extra step without making a big deal out of it. And apparently the brass noticed. So he got the juicy bonus, and would've been promoted. Then there's Callaway. He's got the big ideas. He's driven. He's no team player but he pretends to be. Everybody's always fucking with his concepts, nudging him aside so somebody else can slide by him on the way up. So he sulks and the brass notices.'

'Now you're talking.'

'Can I talk in the car? It's freezing out here.'

'Clears the head.' But Eve opened the car door, slid behind the wheel. 'Big campaign, and Joe's out of the way. Promotion's up for grabs. Vann's already got the corner office. Callaway's got to think if somebody's going to get promoted, get fucking noticed it's going to be him now. Fisher's gone, too, so no teacher's pet's breathing down his neck. He showed them. Boy, he showed them. Fucking worker bees, buzzing in their hive. He can take them out any time. Whenever he wants, as many as he wants. And they did it to themselves, didn't they? He wasn't even there.'

'That's a little scary.'

'I'd say he's plenty scary, the fuck.'

'No, I mean you, being him. That's a little scary.'

'She gave me a nice picture of him and she doesn't much like him, that came through.'

'It did.'

Eve started the car, pulled away. 'No particular feeling for him, which tells me Joe likely didn't warm up to him either. She talked about Weaver coming out here, and there was emotion when she did. She talked about Vann and Callaway contacting her, and she was grateful. Vann sent a big-ass ham so she wouldn't have to think about food. It meant something to her.'

'People send food for death.'

'They do?'

'It's a line from a book, I can't think what book. But yeah, people send food for death, flowers for sickness. *To Kill a Mockingbird!* That's it. Score for me.'

'I'll make a note,' Eve said dryly. 'Weaver comes all the way out to Brooklyn to see the widow, and I'll bet they had a weep together. Vann contacts her, talks to her, and sends food. But Callaway, just the contact. He does what he has to do, and nothing more. That's why somebody like Joe wouldn't especially warm to him, and why his widow didn't either. Weaver doesn't like him either, or she'd have slept with him. He does a good job, he has some good ideas, but he doesn't shine for her. Carly Fisher did.'

'We should find out who else did. If we can't close him down, he's going to go after another.'

'You're right about that.' Eve tapped her fingers on the wheel as she drove. 'We'll talk to Fisher's roommate, find out who she hung with from work. And we'll bring him in. I want to talk to the parents, get a—'

She broke off when her 'link signaled, then switched it to her wrist unit. 'Dallas.'

'That is so iced,' Peabody murmured.

'Lieutenant, Agent Teasdale. I've arranged for the Callaways to be brought into New York. They should be at Central by fourteen hundred.'

'That'll work.'

'The search warrant proved more problematic. However, given the scope of the investigation, and the crime, I was able to persuade the appropriate judge to sign off. If you agree, a team from HSO will assist whoever you send to Arkansas.'

'That works, too. I'll get back to you on that. I've got some arranging of my own to do.' She clicked off, tagged Baxter.

'Get Trueheart, huddle with Teasdale. You're going to join an HSO team in Arkansas on a search of Callaway's parents' house.'

313

'Arkansas? Barbecue!'

'Glad I can bring a smile to your face. Look for mementos of the Urbans, letters, journals, photos, discs. Religious stuff, political stuff – anything personal Callaway might have left there. Anything from when he was a kid. Schoolwork, music, books. See if there's anything that shows he had an interest or aptitude for science.'

'I got it, Dallas. When do we leave?'

'Teasdale will let you know. And contact the locals, Baxter. HSO might shoulder them aside. Let's reach out there, cop to cop.'

'Got that, too. Are we using Roarke's transpo?'

'Forget it,' she said, and cut him off. 'Peabody, contact Callaway.'

'Me?'

'Don't squeak. Jesus. You tag him. The lieutenant would appreciate him coming down to Central, if he has the time.'

'So I'm polite.'

'Polite, even deferential. We could use his help. He's familiar with both attack locations, and knew several of the victims. You can let it slip we had a lead fizzle out, and we're backtracking. He wants to be involved, he wants to know what's going on and have some role in the investigation. I haven't given him much chance. Now I am. He's going to jump at it. He'll make noises about his schedule,' she speculated, 'but he'll come in. When he does, we'll take him in the conference room.'

'You want him to see the boards?'

314

'With a few adjustments. Ask him if he can come in about three, three-thirty.'

'After you've got his parents in.'

'And it'll give him time to plan what he wants to say, how he wants to behave. It'll also tip him away from any impulse he might have to hit some deli or sandwich shop at lunchtime.'

'Should I tag him now?'

'Yeah. We're in the field, the lead went south. I'm on the 'link with the commander. No, the chief. Let's take it to the top. We're scrambling. We're sweating. We don't know when or where he'll hit again.'

'Got it.'

Eve checked the time while Peabody made contact. She nodded at the frustration, and yes, deference in Peabody's tone. Just the right notes.

By the time Peabody finished, Eve managed to squeeze into a street-level spot a half a block from Fisher's apartment building.

'Just like you said,' Peabody reported. 'His schedule's very tight. Lots of work piled up. He's taken on some of Joe's out-standing projects. But, of course, he wants to do everything he can to help. He'll be there.'

'Okay, we're going to separate. Talk to the roommate, and whoever she gives you. I want a coworker she was friendly with, hung around with. Get the picture, like we got from the widow.'

'Okay. What are you doing?'

'I'm going back to Central, setting the stage. If you're not back by the time the Callaways are in, sit tight. Just signal me, and I'll let you know the play.'

'Take the car.'

'Sorry.' Lips pursed, Peabody tapped at her right ear. 'I think standing out in the wind before clogged up my ear. Did you say take the car?'

'Keep it up, you'll be the one hoofing it.'

'I don't wanna hoof it. But, Dallas, it's really cold.'

'I have my magic coat.' She opened it enough for Peabody to see the lining.

'Sweet! Like the jacket. Oooh, let me—'

Before Peabody could get her fingers on it, Eve tugged the coat back into place, got out of the car. 'If you get anything new, anything useful, pass it to me. Otherwise, just write it up.'

'You're not really going to walk all the way back, are you?'

'I know how to ride a subway.'

Her coat billowed in the wind as she strode off, and she pulled out her 'link to contact Mira, give her the time, the setup.

'I'll be there,' Mira assured her. 'Do you intend to bring in Agent Teasdale?'

'Why?'

'She's a steady, unshakable presence, and she's another woman. He wouldn't like being outnumbered by women, and at the same time would be supremely confident he can and will outwit and maneuver all of us.'

316

'That's a point. I'll ask if she wants in.' She hesitated at the steps down to the subway, considered the crowds, the noise, the smells. Considered the wind, the cold – and the fact a few thin flakes of snow began to fall.

Opted for the cold wind and the fifteen-minute walk. 'I'm on my way in. You can observe with the Callaways if you've got time, then I'll see you about three in the conference room.'

'Where are you?'

'Actually not far from the first crime scene.'

'On foot? It's miserable out. Take a cab.'

'I feel like the walk. Later.'

People moved fast, heads down. Busy, busy. She smelled the smoky scent of soy dogs, the heady grease of fries, the bitter edge of takeout coffee. She spotted a girl in high boots, a puffy purple coat, and a rainbow of scarves walking a pair of big white dogs. Or they walked her as she trotted to keep up with their manic prance. A sidewalk sleeper bundled in so many layers only his narrowed eyes showed. He hunched on a threadbare blanket against a building and sported a sign announcing the end of days.

She wondered if he heard any coins or credits thunk into his cup with such depressing billing.

She stopped, hunkered down. 'If the world's ending, what do you need money for?'

'Gotta eat, don't I? Gotta eat. I got a beggar's license inside my coat.'

'Which coat?' She dug in her pocket, tossed in some

317

change though she figured he'd spend it on brew rather than a bowl of soup. 'This your usual spot?'

'No. Buncha people killed right down there. People come to look, maybe they spare some change. Like you. 'Cept cops don't usually spare some change.'

'Cops don't usually have it to spare.' She got up, walked on. She passed the bar, resisted the urge to go in. Nothing new to see, she thought. But the sleeper was right. She watched a few people take pictures of the front, a couple more try to see in the window over the door.

Bloody murder always drew a crowd.

She snagged fries and a tube of Pepsi at the next cart – who could resist that smell? And ate her way back to Central as the thin, pretty flakes of snow turned to a bitter, wetter sleet.

She stopped by the bullpen first, noted Baxter's and Trueheart's absence, Jenkinson's and Reineke's empty desks. She walked over to Sanchez.

'Looks lonely in here.'

'Baxter and Trueheart headed out. Arkansas. Reineke and Jenkinson just left, going to tug a few lines.'

'You and Carmichael are picking up a lot of slack. Anything you need?'

'We've got it, LT.'

'Let me know if that changes.'

'The Stewart deal – brother of a vic? He's wrong, but it's not connected. We're sniffing him down on embezzlement, and maybe doing the missing accountant. He looks good for both. Thing is, the sister's death triggers an automatic inventory of the trust. Last thing he'd want. We don't like him for the bar.'

'Then get him on the rest.'

'It's looking good. I heard you were bringing the suspect in.'

'You heard right. With any luck we can close this up, get back to what passes for normal.'

He'd only been assigned to her for a few months, but he'd slipped right into the rhythm. She considered, angled her head.

'I bet you know who's stealing my candy.'

He gave her a blank cop's stare. 'What candy?'

'Yeah, that's what I thought you'd say.'

She went to her office, ditched her coat, sat to write up her report. While she had time, she walked out, into the conference room.

She turned the boards around, gathered the copies she wanted, began to arrange them. Connected some, wrote in time frames. Kept it all loose, a little scattered, a little vague.

Except for the board of vics. That one she covered with the images of the dead.

She studied the table, noted no one had tossed the box Feeney'd brought in that morning – though she didn't see even a single crumb inside.

That was fine. She left it there, tossed some files on the table, programmed shitty coffee, poured half of it out, set the mug on the table.

She hunted up more debris.

319

'Lieutenant, I heard you were back in the house.'

'Yeah.' She glanced over as Teasdale came in, noted the agent's slight frown at the conference table.

'It's like a play. It should look a little disorganized, and like we're spending lots of time here.'

'It does. You changed the board.'

'I'm bringing Callaway in here, make him feel like he's a kind of consultant. This is what I want him to see.'

'Hmmm.' Lips pursed now, Teasdale walked forward. 'All of the victims. Yes, that will please him. And only a handful of those we've connected to them – including himself. He'll enjoy that as well. The time line isn't quite right.'

'No, it's not. And there's no mention of Red Horse or Menzini. I'm saving those for a nice surprise. You want in?'

'On the "consult". Yes, I do, thank you. The Callaways are en route. They're slightly behind schedule, but should be here by thirteen-fifteen.'

'Let's go to my office, get some decent coffee, and I'll bring you up to date.'

In her office, Eve programmed two cups, offered one. 'Peabody's in the field, talking to Fisher's roommate and whoever else she can dig up. We—'

'Oh.' After a sip, Teasdale blinked, breathed out. Sipped again. 'This isn't what I'm used to.'

Eve remembered her own reaction the first time she'd tasted Roarke's blend. 'Nice, huh?'

'It's . . . very. May I sit? I feel this should be savored rather than gulped.'

'Take the desk chair; the other one's crap.' Eve settled for a corner of the desk. 'Peabody and I talked to Elaine Cattery,' Eve began, and ran it through.

'So, he remains in pattern,' Teasdale observed. 'If he knew Vann had sent food, he'd be compelled to do the same. And more. Something bigger, or more expensive.'

'You're right. Competition, standing out. Which makes me think Vann didn't tell him, and that makes me think more of Vann. He just did the good deed, and wasn't looking for acknowledgment.'

'Callaway must have acknowledgment. The lack, or perceived lack of it, burns in him. I believe, after a time, he'll contact you or the media. It won't be enough as it is.'

'Probably. But I don't want to give him that chance. I want to shut him down today.'

'You believe you'll get him to confess.'

'That's the plan.'

Maybe it was the coffee, but Teasdale leaned back in the chair, crossed her legs. Seemed to relax. 'I believe his sense of self-preservation will be stronger than his need for acknowledgment.'

'We'll find out.'

'There's no break, as yet, on a supplier for the illegals or the medicals elements. Knowing his source, pulling the source in, that would add weight and pressure.'

'How about using your power of persuasion to get us a search warrant on his place?'

Teasdale smiled into her coffee. 'I suspected you'd ask. I

have it. I was told I could liaise with APA Cher Reo. Between us we managed it. When would you like to move on it?'

'Before he leaves here. I want to bring Roarke in on that, if he's able. He's got a good nose for hidey-holes, and for dealing with encrypted data.'

'It must be satisfying to be married to someone who not only understands your work, but is willing and able to share in it.'

'Plus, coffee. Want another hit?'

'I would, but I'd better not. I'm not used to it. I like your office,' Teasdale said as she rose.

Mildly surprised, Eve glanced around. 'I think you're the first one who's ever said that.'

'It's small and efficient with few distractions. And it has this coffee in the AutoChef.' She set the empty cup aside. 'I'd like to say something to you.'

'Okay.'

'Your files with HSO have been redacted or removed. Some destroyed or . . . rather inexplicably deleted.'

'Is that so?'

'It is. But before that occurred I had occasion to familiarize myself with some of the data – during the early stages of our internal investigation. I want to say to you that I'm very sorry for what happened to you, and very sorry the organization I represent was culpable, was heartless. Was wrong.'

'It's done,' Eve said flatly.

'Yes, it's done. I wonder, should our positions have been

322

reversed would I have agreed to work with you. I don't know the answer.'

'You weren't part of it.'

'No, nor was the man I answer to. Director Hurtz is an honorable man. Our business is often secretive and fueled by deception, so I couldn't work for less than an honorable man. But you have no reason to know or believe that.'

'I know and I believe over a hundred and twenty people deserve justice. I'll use any tool, weapon, or means at my disposal to make certain they get it.'

'I'm determined to help you make certain.'

'Then we're good.'

She waited while Teasdale answered her 'link. 'Yes, thank you. Interview B, please. The Callaways are here,' she said to Eve.

'Then let's dig out the tools.'

17

The Callaways, Russell and Audrey, sat on opposite sides of the table in Interview. She looked nervous; he looked belligerent.

He'd have been in his seventies, but she could clearly see the man Audrey Hubbard had found attractive. Russell emanated strength, steadiness, and a no-bullshit toughness.

'Mr and Mrs Callaway.' Eve kept her tone and her step brisk as she moved to the table, sat. 'I'm Lieutenant Dallas, and this is Agent Teasdale. Thank you for coming.'

'Don't see we had much choice.' Russell gave her a hard stare out of faded blue eyes. 'Your people come onto the farm, right onto private property and say how we gotta go with them to New York City. Nobody tells us a damn thing, just get and go. We got squash to harvest.'

She could safely say it was the first time she'd heard that used as a complaint or excuse in Interview.

'And we'll try to get you back to that quickly. We're going to record this interview.'

'Can I get you anything before we begin?' Teasdale asked. 'Coffee, water, a soft drink?'

'We don't need anything.' Russell folded his arms, set his squared, weathered face into pugnacious lines.

'Record on,' Eve said. 'Dallas, Lieutenant Eve, and Teasdale, Agent Miyu, in Interview with Russell and Audrey Callaway. I'm going to read you your rights.'

'We haven't done anything. Russ.' Audrey reached across the table for her husband's hand.

He gave hers an impatient pat. 'Don't worry. They're just trying to scare us.'

'Why would I want to do that?' Eve read them both their rights, asked if they understood.

'We've got the right to mind our own business, too. And that's what we do.'

'I appreciate that, Mr Callaway. But in minding your own business, I suspect you've heard about the two incidents here in New York.'

'It's all over the screen night and day, isn't it?'

'I imagine so.'

'It's nothing to do with us.'

'No? Your son, Lewis Callaway, was in On the Rocks, the bar where the first incident took place. He left minutes before it happened.'

'Lew was there?' Audrey clutched at her throat and the small gold cross she wore there.

'You didn't know?' Eve leaned back, rocking slightly on the back legs of her chair. 'Reports on the incidents are all over the screen, you have a son who lives and works not only in New York, but within blocks of both locations. You didn't think to contact him, make sure he was okay?'

'I—'

'How are we supposed to know all this happened near his work or his place?' Russ demanded. 'We don't know the layout of New York. We've never been here before, and don't much like being here now.'

'You've never come up to visit your son?' Teasdale asked them, in the most pleasant and sympathetic of voices.

'He's the one moved to this godless place. We don't have the time or wherewithal to come hieing up here. He comes home to visit.'

'Is he all right?' Audrey asked. 'I tried to get a hold of him, but he didn't answer. He texted me back last night, just to say he was fine, and he was busy. But you said he was there, at that place where it happened.'

'That's right, with some coworkers. One of them died there.'

'Oh.' Again she closed her hand over her cross. 'Rest his soul.'

'He lost other coworkers there, and at the café where the second incident took place.'

'Oh, this is terrible. Russ, we have to go see him. He must be very upset.'

'Not upset enough to tell you he lost someone he'd worked with for years. Someone he'd just had a drink with.'

'He's got no cause to worry his mother.'

'Maybe not, Mr Callaway, but it strikes me his mother was already worried. That's why she tried to contact him. When's the last time you saw or spoke to him?'

'He came down a few weeks ago, stayed a couple days. Audrey, you stop fretting now.'

'I see he's come to see you several times in the last few

months.' Eve opened a file, scanned data. 'Yet previously, his visits were spaced much further apart. Once a year.'

'He's very busy.' Head down, Audrey spoke quietly. 'He has an important position in his firm. People depend on him. He has important clients, and a very demanding job.'

'Have you ever met any of his coworkers?'

'No.' Russell spoke before his wife could. 'We've got nothing to do with any of that.'

'I'm sure he's shared stories.' Teasdale spread her hands. 'About the people he works with, his friends, his work.'

'I said we've got nothing to do with it.'

'But an important man with such a demanding job, and all these recent visits. Surely he'd talk about his life here.'

'We don't really understand his work.' Audrey shot her husband a nervous glance.

'Why has he come home so often recently?' Eve demanded.

'It's restful. It's restful on the farm.'

'Restful 'cause you wait on him hand and foot. Up till all hours doing God knows what. Can't risk his soft hands on a good day's work.'

'Now, Russ.'

'The truth's the truth, but it's none of your business,' he said to Eve. 'What are you after here?'

'Oh, it isn't clear? Your son is a person of interest in this investigation.'

'What does that mean?' Audrey looked from Eve to her husband, back again. 'I don't understand what that means.'

'You mean you think he had something to do with it? With killing those people?'

'No. No. No.' Audrey covered her face with her hands, did her best to turn herself into a ball while Russell stared at Eve.

And she saw it in his eyes. Shock, yes. And a little fear. But not dismissal, not rejection of the idea.

'You moved a lot while he was growing up,' Eve commented.

'I went where the work was.'

'I don't think so. You were — are a trained medical, Mr Callaway, and someone with your qualifications and experience doesn't have to travel for work. He did things, didn't he? Got into trouble. Small things at first. Boys will be boys, right? But there was something, always something not quite right. The neighbors didn't much like him. The other kids didn't want to play with him. Then there were bigger things, things you had to deny or cover over. Best thing to do is move away, start again. He never made friends. Nothing was ever really enough, or satisfying to him, not for long.'

'He got picked on,' Audrey claimed. 'He was sensitive.'

'Broody,' she suggested, remembering Elaine's words. 'Moody, sulky. Holed up in his room. You schooled him from home. It was better that way, for him. You thought that because he didn't make friends, didn't like being told what to do and when to do it.'

'He just needed more attention. Some boys need more attention. He never hurt anyone.'

'He'd start rumors.' Teasdale sat in her quiet way. 'Tell the

328

boy next door what the girl down the block said about him, whether she did or not. He enjoyed stirring up trouble – maybe stealing things, then planting them on someone else. Watching others fight over the trouble he'd stirred.'

'He did the same to the two of you,' Eve continued. 'You especially, Mrs Callaway. Little lies, quiet little sabotage to cause conflict and friction between you. He still does it when he can. When he comes to visit you, there's always some upheaval, some new tension. It's such a relief when he's gone again.'

'That's not true, that's not true. He's our son. We love him.'

'Love's never been enough for him.' Eve saw it clearly in Audrey Callaway's eyes. 'When he comes you make his favorite meals, wash his clothes, wait on him like a servant. And still, he looks at you with contempt – or worse, boredom.

'But just recently, he's taken more of an interest. He's had questions. When did he find out Guiseppi Menzini was his grandfather?'

'Oh no. No.'

'Hush now, Audrey. Hush now.' Russell laid his big, hard hand over his wife's, but Eve saw a gentleness in the gesture this time. 'We're Christian people. We live our life, don't bother anybody.'

'I'm sure that's true.' Teasdale folded her hands neatly on the table. 'I'm sure you tried to be a credit to Edward and Tessa Hubbard, Mrs Callaway.'

'Of course.'

'When did you learn they weren't your biological parents?'

'Oh God. Russ.'

'Listen here, Audrey, she was raised by good people. She didn't know anything about Menzini until her father was dying. He thought she needed to know. It'd been better if he'd let it die with him, but he was sick and dying and afraid she'd find out when he wasn't there to explain how it was.'

'That man wasn't my father. Edward Hubbard was my father, and Tessa Hubbard was my mother. The woman who bore me, she strayed, she did bad things, but she repented. She redeemed herself. She died trying to protect me.'

'When did you tell him? When did you tell Lewis?'

'Russ—'

'If he did something, Audrey, it's our responsibility to say. He's our son, and we're the ones who have to say.'

'He couldn't do something like this.'

'Then you can help clear it up, put him off the list,' Eve prompted. 'What did he find? What did you tell him?'

'There were things – journals and essays and mementos, pictures. I'm not sure. I never really went through all of it. My mother boxed everything up. They talked about destroying it all, Dad said, but it didn't seem right. So they kept it all boxed up, put away, and my father told me about what had happened before he died.'

'What did he tell you?'

'Russ, I can't.'

He only nodded. 'I tended to Audrey's father while he was dying, and I guess he could see I cared for Audrey. And she

330

cared for me. So he told me everything, or everything he knew. Tessa's half-sister was wild. She married a good man, but she betrayed him, and ran away to join Menzini's cult. They used God's word, twisted and defiled it to prey on the weak. She lay with him, and had his child. She was one of them. But she came to realize she'd taken an evil path, came back to her husband with the child. She begged for forgiveness from him, from her family.'

'And William took her back,' Eve prompted. 'Took you as his own.'

'He was a good man,' Audrey said. 'And he forgave her. They were going to take me away from her, and she ran away with me, went home.'

'But this Menzini found them,' Russell continued. 'He killed them, took the child. Edward Hubbard was a soldier. He and his wife searched for the child, and finally found her. Menzini had vanished, but they feared for the child. They left their home, their friends and family, and came here to America. They changed her name, and raised her as theirs.'

'They loved me. They were good, and gave me a good life. I'm their daughter. Theirs.'

'Mrs Callaway, I don't believe in the sins of the father. I believe we make our choices, make ourselves. I believe Edward and Tessa Hubbard did the very best they could for you, and loved you, and that you were their daughter.'

'I was. I am.'

'Lewis found the boxes?'

'He came home. He was restless, and upset. Something at work. Someone stole one of his ideas.'

'Audrey.' Russell sighed.

'They didn't appreciate him or respect him enough,' she insisted, with an edge of desperation in her voice. 'That's what he said. I don't know why he went up in the attic. We were working outside. He found some things, and started to ask questions. We talked it over, and decided we should tell him. We should tell him what had happened all that time ago, and we should destroy everything. It isn't who we are.'

'But he didn't want you to destroy it.'

'He said it was his legacy, his right. That he should know his family tree, the truth of it. He seemed – not happy, but satisfied. He seemed calmer. As if, I thought, he'd always known something was different, and now that he knew the truth, it contented him.'

'He came back for more.'

'I had things of my mother's. My mother,' she said, laying a hand on her heart. 'And some things she'd kept from when she and her half-sister were young. Some I have in the house. My mother's dishes, and some of her jewelry. Not heirlooms, really,' she said as her hand covered the little cross again, 'but they matter. He was sure there was more, on Gina MacMillon, my mother's half-sister, on Menzini. He searched the attic, the basement, the outbuildings. He came back again, again, looking, asking the same questions.'

'You don't know what was in the boxes? You never went through them.'

'Not really. I looked, after my father died. I read some of Gina's journal entries, but they were upsetting – written when she'd run off with the cult – so I stopped. She died for me, so I couldn't throw her things away, but I didn't want to read what she'd written when she'd lost her faith.'

'But he wanted to. Lewis wanted to read the journals.'

'He said it was important to know. And he . . . '

'What?'

'Don't be angry,' she said to her husband. 'Please.'

'Did he hurt you?' Russell's fist balled on the table.

'No. No, he didn't.'

'Has he hurt you before?' Teasdale asked.

'It was a long time ago. He lost his temper.'

'He wanted shoes, some fancy shoes we couldn't afford. His mother caught him stealing money from her household bank. When she tried to stop him, he struck her. He struck her with his fist. He was sixteen, and though she tried to make excuses for him, I could see what he'd done. He came home with those damned shoes, and for the first time in his life, I laid hands on him. I struck him, my son, as he had struck his mother. I burned the shoes. He apologized, he made amends, and for a while . . . '

'It seemed better,' Teasdale prompted.

'But it wasn't, not underneath it all. We knew,' he said to his wife, and laid a hand over hers again. 'We knew.'

'We just couldn't make him happy. But he's a successful man now. He has a good job.'

Russell shook his head. 'He lies, Audrey, he's always lied

333

and sneaked around, and connived to cause trouble. What do you think he's done?' he asked Eve.

'I think he found information, and he's used that information, as his grandfather did. He's responsible for the deaths of more than a hundred and twenty people.'

'That can't be true. You're only saying that because you found out about Menzini. You're using that to accuse Lew. Russell, tell them!'

But he only sat, and to Eve's surprise, and pity, tears slid down his cheeks. 'He's our son. We wanted a child, so much. We did our best by him. We did everything we knew. You're saying he's evil. How do we believe that? How do we live with that?'

'They're wrong. They have to be wrong.'

'I can pray they're wrong. But we always knew.'

'You don't love him!'

'I wish I didn't.'

Audrey broke down, laid her head on the table, sobbed. Russell sat, head bowed, silent tears running down his face.

When they stepped outside the room, Teasdale glanced back. 'They'll grieve.'

'A lot of people will.' Eve pulled out her 'link, nodded. 'Peabody's back. I need to talk to her, and we need to keep the Callaways under wrap. He's going to be here any minute.'

Mira came out of Observation. 'I'd like to go in and speak with them now.'

'Could you give me some time first?' Teasdale asked. 'In this first wave of grief, they may tell me more.'

'Callaway's coming in soon,' Eve told Mira, 'and I need you in there. Why don't you observe for a few minutes, and if you think Teasdale's got in, come to the conference room. I'll signal you when we've got him set,' she told Teasdale. 'Here's how it's going to work.'

Once Eve laid it out, she went straight to Peabody in the conference room. 'Give me what you got, make it quick.'

'Boiled down, Fisher wasn't a Callaway fan. She bitched about him to the roommate. Main beef? He had her do some grunt work on one of his projects. She came up with a fresh angle, created an entire ad – tags, visuals, market projections. He took the credit.'

'Did she tell Weaver?'

'No. But the next time he dumped something on her, she dated and initialed all her work. And she ran it all by Weaver first, like she was looking for a second, more experienced opinion.'

'Smart. She got the credit, and he had to swallow it.'

'He never used her again. Plus she got a bonus, and got to head another, smaller project. Fisher was friends with one of the people she chose for the project team. I went to see her, too. She corroborated the roommate's story.'

'We've got the Callaways in Interview. Teasdale's doing a second pass.' She paused when Mira came in.

'Has Teasdale got it?'

'Yes, she's very good. I'll talk with them later.'

'I need to run this through for Peabody, and I'd like your opinion,' she told Mira. 'It's looking like they moved around a lot because Callaway got into trouble as a kid. He punched his mother in the face when she caught him stealing from the house bank.'

'Nice,' Peabody muttered.

'For shoes. The father tore him a new one, first physical discipline according to the father. Destroyed the shoes. The timing coordinates with them staying put, staying in one place, until he went to college.'

'Factoring in what else we know and believe, this incident taught him that authority, or those stronger than he, could punish or hurt him,' Mira said. 'He went under – that is, changed the face, the surface in order to blend. Violence brought violence on him.

'Their hearts are broken,' Mira added, 'because in those hearts they know he's capable of doing what he's done. And because they love him, and did the best they could.'

'He made his choice. It's not on them.'

'Parents always feel the pride, and the responsibility.'

'It's going to get tougher on them, so you'll help them there. A lot of stories are going to come out once we take him down. Things he did, trouble he caused, people he pissed off.' Eve checked the time, cutting it close. 'Additionally, he found out about his connection to Menzini a few months ago. The trigger.'

'Yes, I agree.'

'The mother kept documents, photos, journals – and I want a look at those. She had them stored away. Whatever's in there has to include the formula.'

'That not only gave him means,' Mira commented, 'but permission.'

'I'm sending a team over to his place. They'll find it, and that's the smoking gun. If the PA can't build a solid case from what we're stacking for him, he's useless. But I want Callaway to tell us. I want him to need to tell us. We're frustrated, missing pieces, basically nowhere, and under pressure from the media, from the brass.'

'We're a bunch of women,' Peabody put in, 'who need his help.'

'That's how we start it. Give me five to set up the search team. I'll bring him in when he gets here, so look busy and baffled.'

'Take off your jacket,' Mira told her.

'What?'

'Leave your jacket on the back of the chair. You'll appear more desk work-oriented, and it exposes your weapon. He'll resent the fact you have a weapon. You're an authority figure, capable of violence, yet he's smarter, so much more clever.'

'Got it.' Eve tugged it off, stood in a black sweater and shoulder harness. 'Teasdale's coming in after he's here. We don't like her.'

'Actually, I kind of do.'

'Peabody, catch on.'

'Oh, we *act* like we don't.'

'Five minutes,' Eve said and hurried out.

She contacted Jenkinson and Reineke first, ordered them

337

to coordinate with Cher Reo for the warrant and move on it immediately. As she contacted Roarke she grabbed one more cup of real coffee.

'I figured I'd get your admin,' she said when he came on himself.

'I happen to be free at the moment.'

'I've got Callaway coming in to help the inept females, and a search warrant for his place. He found docs his mother had stored away. I need them. Maybe he's got some docs on where he's getting the drugs, the fixings. I need his source. Jenkinson and Reineke are getting the warrant and implementing it. If you want in—'

'It sounds like fun.'

'If you're busy with—'

'Aren't I entitled to a bit of fun?'

'You're right. It's the least I can do for you. I'm going to see if Feeney can join in, or send McNab. I want all his electronics, and if he's not a complete idiot, he's got a hide in his place. Somewhere the cleaning people or a casual guest wouldn't stumble on his work. He has to cook up the substance somewhere.'

'Even more fun.'

'I'm going to get mine by twisting a confession out of him.'

'We'll plan to celebrate later.'

'How?'

He smiled, slow and wicked. 'I'll think of something. Kick his ass, Lieutenant.'

'Count on it.'

When she got the signal Callaway was on his way up, she strode back into the bullpen, caught Carmichael and Sanchez on their way out.

'We caught a fresh one,' Carmichael told her.

'Let it hold a minute. Give me grief.'

'Sorry, what?'

'Suspect's coming up. Give me grief, put on a show, storm out. Mostly you,' she said to Sanchez. 'He sees women as weak and expendable.'

'Is that so?' Carmichael muttered.

'What the hell do you expect?' Sanchez demanded, his voice bordering on a shout. 'I'm running this department, working damn near around the clock.'

'Hold it down, Detective,' Eve ordered, but wearily.

'I *am* holding it down. Holding it all down, while you're dancing with the feds, giving the media face time, and running in circles.'

'We are carrying a lot, Lieutenant.'

'We?' Sanchez rounded on his partner. 'I'm carrying you, sister, just like always. And while I am Dallas sucks up all the manpower, all the resources. Every case we've got, that you dumped on us, is backed up because the lab's put everything else on hold – on your authority.'

'I've got a mass murderer who could strike again at any time, anywhere in the city,' Eve began.

'Yeah, and you're nowhere. You'd rather see this department go to hell than step back and let the feds take it. Get

339

this, and get it straight, when you go down for screwing this up, I'm not going down with you.'

He strode out, bulling by Callaway. Carmichael hunched in. 'He hasn't had much sleep, Lieutenant.' With a last nervous look, she hurried out after Sanchez.

Eve let out a long sigh, dragged her hands through her hair as she turned. She jolted, wished she could pull off an embarrassed blush, but thought her expression accomplished the same thing.

'Mr Callaway, thanks for coming in.'

'Your detective made it sound important.' He glanced back in the direction Sanchez and Carmichael had taken, didn't quite mask the smirk before he sent Eve a sympathetic look. 'It must be a difficult situation for you.'

'Everyone's overworked and on edge. If you'll come with me, we're set up in a conference room.'

'I'm not sure what I can do,' he said as Eve led the way. 'How I can help.'

'You knew several of the victims, of both attacks. You're familiar with both locations – the layout, the employees, the neighborhood. My sense, when we talked before, is you're observant, and the fact you were actually in the first location may help.'

'Believe me, I've gone over that evening countless times.'

'We're hoping if we talk you through it again, you may remember some small detail. I'm not going to lie to you—'
Oh yeah, she thought, *I am*. 'We're in a bind.'

She opened the door to the conference room, blocking

the way for just a moment to make sure her voice carried in. 'I have to tell you what we discuss here, what you see here is confidential. I'm trusting you, Mr Callaway.'

'You can. Please, call me Lew.'

'Lew.' She tried for a relieved smile as she gestured him inside. 'Detective Peabody, my partner, and Doctor Mira, our profiler.'

Peabody nodded, continued to work on a computer while Mira rose, hand extended. 'Thank you for coming in to consult.'

'I consider it my duty.'

'If only more did.'

'Do you want some crappy coffee, something from Vending?' Eve asked him.

He gave her an easy smile. 'Crappy coffee's just fine.' He moved forward to the boards, shifted to study the victims. 'All of these people. I knew how many. The media's reported so much. But seeing them like this, all together. It's shocking.'

'Those responsible have a great deal to answer for,' Mira stated.

'You're looking for more than one person?'

'We've determined it's not possible for a single individual to pull this off.' Eve spoke briskly as she programmed a pot of coffee. 'It's too complex, involves too much risk, too much planning, too many steps.'

'At this time,' Mira put in, 'we feel it's most probable we're dealing with a group.' She gestured to the victim board again. 'In each case one of these people sacrificed themselves for the whole.'

'My God.' He took the coffee Eve offered, ignored her. 'But why?'

'We have a few theories, but foremost, if there's a group, there's a head.' Eve took a seat. 'Whoever that is, must be charismatic, dominant, and highly organized and intelligent. The target locations catered to businesses and offices like your own.'

'People who work and live in that area,' Mira continued, joining Eve at the table so Callaway stood in the position of dominance. 'We expected, and hoped, he would issue a statement, reveal his agenda or demands. The fact that he hasn't proves him canny and very, very dangerous. He understands the value of noninformation, of inciting fear and panic. Those who believe in him believe in that agenda. Without that information . . . ' She lifted her hands.

'Which is where you might be able to help,' Eve told him. 'We've been able to eliminate some of the victims, through background checks, interviews. We're taking a close look at survivors of the attacks.'

'Ah.' He nodded. 'Yes, that makes sense. Whoever the leader sent in would have the best chance of surviving — knowing what's coming, being able to take some sort of defense against it.'

'Exactly. It helps we don't have to spell everything out for you.'

'Just common sense again,' he said to Eve.

'Now the lab has been able to identify the most probable

source, and we've reconstructed the attack – again the most probable scenario given the data.'

'A reconstruction? It may jog something if I could see it.'

You'd love it, Eve thought. 'Let's hope we don't have to go there, Lew. Even computer-generated, it's gruesome.' She opened a file. 'This woman.' She tapped her finger on CiCi Way's photo. 'Do you recognize her?'

'She looks familiar.' He knitted his brows.

'She's one of the survivors.'

He took the photo, studied it carefully. 'Yes. Yes, I remember her. She was with the woman you asked us about yesterday evening. Sitting at a table with two men.'

'If you could think back carefully,' Mira urged him. 'Try to visualize the bar, your position, the movements, this woman.'

'I had my back to the room the majority of the time.'

'There was a mirror behind the bar,' Eve reminded him.

'And we tend to see things that don't really register at the time, but we can bring back.' Mira leaned forward. 'I'm trained in hypnotherapy. If you'll allow me, I might be able to help you remember.'

'Just give me a minute to think, to visualize.' When he closed his eyes, Eve exchanged a quick glance with Mira.

'I can see her at the table,' Callaway said slowly. 'She and the other three. A lot of laughter, drinking, eating. But she . . . I see her looking around, and checking the time. Yes, she's tracking the room, shifting in her chair.'

'As if she were nervous?' Mira asked.

'It strikes me that way. I didn't pay attention at the time.

Or I might've thought she was nervous to be on a kind of blind date.'

'Why do you think she was on a blind date?' Eve asked.

His eyes opened, stared into hers for a moment. 'I must've heard her say. I honestly don't – wait, yes, wait. She and the other woman got up. I think they must've gone down to the restroom. I can't be sure, but they left the table, passed right by us at the bar. In fact, I was standing up by then, starting to leave. She bumped into me. Didn't even apologize. I think she said something to the other woman about it being a blind date.'

'So, this woman didn't actually know the man she was with.'

'I don't believe so. But I had the sense the two women were friends. Good God, how could she do that to her friend, to someone who trusted her?'

'Trust is often a weapon,' Eve said. 'But we're not absolutely certain CiCi Way was a source.'

'You believe she was.' He shook his head as he studied her picture again. 'She's young. The young are often impressionable, easily swayed. Easily used.'

'Did you see them come back?'

'I was getting ready to leave, as I said, but Joe stalled me for a few minutes.' He lifted his face to the ceiling, eyes half shut. 'I hadn't had a full night's sleep in nearly a week. I was exhausted. Joe wanted me to stay. His wife was away with the kids, and he wasn't in the mood to go home to an empty house. But I wanted to get home, just crash for the night. I'd gotten up, yes, that's right. I was standing, telling Joe I'd see him in the morning, when they came back. Passed the bar again. They had to walk right by to get to their table.'

He lowered his face, widened his eyes at Eve. 'She wasn't watching where she was going.'

'No?'

'It was still crowded, and she was looking around again. She shoved at me. Shoved me out of her way as she went by as if she was in a hurry, and she said something rude. Something like, "Move your ass." I'd forgotten all about that. I've been so wrapped up in what happened to Joe, I'd forgotten about that. I walked to the door as they walked to the table. I know I looked back, she'd been so rude – and she . . . she took something out of her pocket as she sat down. She reached in her pocket.

'She's the one.' He laid his hand over the face in the photo. 'She has to be the one.'

As he spoke, the door opened and Teasdale walked in. She hesitated as she spotted Callaway, then sent Eve a hard stare. 'Lieutenant, I need to speak with you a moment. Privately.'

'We may just have caught a break,' Eve began.

'I prefer not to have this discussion in front of a civilian.'

Eve surged to her feet, stomped out.

'Looks like a power struggle,' Callaway said.

'You could say so.' Peabody looked up from her computer. 'While they're at it, let's go over those details again.'

18

'I've had the parents taken to a safe house. I persuaded them to tell me about a couple incidents in Callaway's childhood.'

'Feel free to use them,' Eve told her, 'if a door opens. But don't screw up my timing or the rhythm. We're working him. He thinks he owns the room. I led him to one of the survivors, tailoring her into the source. He took the bait and ran with it.'

'Once you take the bait, you're hooked. Running becomes problematic.'

'Whatever, he's adding a lot of details. Too many details.'

'Pride and pleasure cause people to elaborate as much as guilt.'

'I'm going to push him on Jeni Curve next. The conflict between you and me gives him the illusion of power. He's going to pride and pleasure himself right into a cage. So.' Eve hooked her thumbs in her belt loops. 'I think you're a pushy federal shill wrapped in red tape.'

Teasdale picked a minute piece of lint from her lapel. 'I see you as an incompetent, overly aggressive city employee.'

'That should do it.' Eve opened the door. 'It's still my case.'

'Not for long. I beg your pardon, Mr Callaway, but I have strong objections to involving a civilian in this highly sensitive investigation, particularly one with connections to several of the victims.'

'That connection's given us CiCi Way, and an angle to push, Agent Teasdale,' Eve reminded her. 'You and the HSO are secondary investigators in this matter. You're basically a consultant yourself until I hear different.'

Deliberately she turned her back on Teasdale, faced Callaway. 'I'd like to move on to the second location.'

'I wasn't there.'

'But you're familiar with the café, know several of those who were killed or injured. Let's try the visualization again.'

'For God's sake,' Teasdale muttered.

'Look, Agent, we might get the same line on Curve with this.'

'Jeni?' Shock registered on Callaway's face. 'You don't seriously suspect Jeni.'

'I don't want to influence your memories here. Let's just focus on yesterday. You stayed in for lunch?'

'Actually, I wanted some air, some head-clearing time, so I went out.'

'Do you remember what time you left the office? The building? If not, we can check logs and discs.'

'I think it was around twelve-fifteen. Near that time. I grabbed a pita – veggie and cheese, and a ginger ale from a cart about a block from the office. I'm not sure he'd remember me. He was busy.'

'Where did you go, what did you see? Take your time,' Eve encouraged. 'Try to see it again.'

'I was thinking about Joe. It's why I wanted the air, and some time to myself – out of the office. Thinking about him, his wife, his kids. I kept remembering how we'd sat at the bar just before ... I didn't want to say anything in front of Nancy, but Joe and I worked together quite a lot on the side. He often needed a little help on projects.'

'He'd come to you?'

'I was glad to help.' Callaway brushed that away, as if it didn't need mentioning. 'As I said, he has kids, and that long commute every day. A wife who, understandably, wanted his attention when he was home. Sometimes he had trouble keeping his head in the game – a spat with the wife, the kids acting up.'

'So he had trouble at home?' Eve asked, all attention.

'Oh, I wouldn't say that.' But his face clearly did. 'But that added pressure, and demands on this time, his attention, so I'd give him some input, another set of eyes, you could say.'

'I'm sure he appreciated it.'

'It wasn't a big deal,' Callaway said, glancing down in modesty. 'I'm sure he'd have done the same for me if I'd needed his help. In any case, I just wanted to walk, so I walked and ate lunch. Nancy's so emotional right now. She hasn't been able to get a handle on things. I'm happy to lend a shoulder or take on some extra work, but I needed a break.'

'I understand. Were you ever in sight of the café?'

'I walked by it, on the other side of the street. I actually thought about going over, getting a latte, but I didn't want to deal with the crowd, the noise. They're always busy at that hour.'

'Exactly.' Eve shot Teasdale a look. 'You'd know that as you'd had lunch there regularly.'

'Everybody at the office had, one time or another. I was just walking, trying to settle. I'd nearly gone the other way, to the bar, just to . . . but I couldn't.'

'You were walking,' Eve prompted.

'Yes.' He stared up at the ceiling. 'Just taking the air. It was brisk. Not as cold as today, and it felt good to be out, to be moving. There was so much on my mind. You can't imagine how many people in the office want to talk about it, ask questions, ask for details.'

'Because you were there, right there.'

'Yes. Something I'll never forget. Even if I could, people in the office, reporters, and of course, the police, ask questions, bring it all back.'

'Of you especially.' Eve tried to add a note of sympathy. 'Steve left early, then Weaver left. But you, you were there almost till it began.'

'Yes. Just minutes before. I . . . wait, wait. I saw Carly.'

'Carly Fisher?'

'It had to be her, going into the café. The red jacket she wears, with the floral scarf. I caught a glimpse of the jacket and scarf as she went in. I didn't really register, didn't really think about it. But now I wonder if that's another reason I didn't go in.'

'You didn't get along?'

'No, not that. Carly was very driven, very focused on advancing her career. She'd often pick my brain for an

349

assignment or project. That was fine.' He waved that away, a man burdened, but accepting the weight. 'But I wasn't in the mood yesterday. In fact, I remember now, seeing her made me decide to go back, just close myself into my office. But I saw her, poor Carly. I must've been one of the last people to see her alive.'

'Like Joe.'

'Yes. This is very upsetting. Could I have some water?'

'Absolutely.' Eve rose, got a bottle herself and offered it. 'Just take your time, Lew. What did you do next?'

'I might have walked just a little more, then I turned around, and . . .'

'You saw something.' Eve leaned toward him. 'What did you see?'

'Who,' he murmured. 'It's who I saw. I saw Jeni.'

Eve sat back, once again leveled a stare at Teasdale. 'You saw Jeni Curve. Where?'

'Across the street, maybe a half a block – less, I think, from the café. But I'm used to seeing her around. I didn't think about it, didn't even retain it – or so I thought.'

'What was she doing?'

He closed his eyes, balled his fists. 'She was talking to someone. A man. His back's to me. I don't see his face. He's taller than she is. Yes, taller, broader, and wearing a black coat. He – does he give her something? I think yes, yes, she puts what he gives her in her coat pocket.'

'What next? Think!'

'I – I hardly paid attention. He kissed her – lightly, on both cheeks. Like a salute. He walks away, and she walks toward the café. This doesn't seem real.'

'Did you see him with anyone else?' Eve demanded. 'Did you see where he went?'

'I only know he walked in the same direction I was, but across the street, ahead of me. I stopped to look in a shop window, just to stall going back to the office. I didn't see him again, or Jeni. Or any of them.'

'Lew, I want you to think and think hard. Did you ever see Jeni Curve with CiCi Way?'

She set both of their photos on the conference table. 'Do you ever remember seeing these women together?'

'I can't be sure. I'd see Jeni so often – in the offices when she made deliveries, or in the café when she picked something up. Even around the neighborhood. I can't be sure if I saw her with this other woman.'

'You can't link the two of them together,' Teasdale pointed out. 'You've got Curve walking into the place she worked, and Way at the bar – with friends. You've got nothing that ties them to this.'

'We push on Way again. We can take Lew in, let her see him, shake her up. Would you be willing to do that?' Eve asked him.

'Anything I can do to help.'

'Let's go back to Curve for a minute. You saw her talking to someone just before she went in. You said you'd see her around the neighborhood. Did you ever see her with someone? With this man?'

'I think . . . I think I may have. I wish I could be sure.'

'What about when she delivered to the office? Did she spend more time with certain people than with others?'

'Well, Steve flirted with her. He told you that himself. And she'd talk to Carly from time to time. They were close to the same age, I suppose.'

'Not with you, particularly.'

'No. She was just the delivery girl.'

'Yeah, just the delivery girl.'

'Do you think that's why this person – this leader – used her?' Callaway widened his eyes. 'She was young, susceptible. No one in particular, if you know what I mean. I imagine manipulating her, and this other woman, this CiCi, would have been easy for someone like him.'

'Like him?'

'As you said.' He turned to Mira. 'He's highly intelligent, organized, charismatic.'

'We could be talking about you,' Eve said.

He laughed, did the same wave away. 'That's flattering, but I don't think I qualify.'

'That's just the tip of the profile, isn't it, Doctor Mira?'

'Yes. I've also determined that he's a loner by nature with sociopathic tendencies. His violence is internal, rigidly suppressed. He uses others to carry out the violence.'

'He doesn't want to get his hands bloody,' Eve added. 'He's a coward, without the balls to kill face-to-face.'

'I don't want to tell you your business.' Though his face had gone stony, Callaway spread his hands, all affability. 'But it seems to me by staying above the fray, he's only demon-strating that intelligence. How will you find him if he doesn't actively participate in the murders, if he keeps himself removed from the actual killings?'

'He'll make a mistake. They always do. And look at how much more you've been able to tell us. We know more about him.'

'You can't tell a civilian details like that,' Teasdale began.

'Don't tell me what I can do,' Eve snapped back. 'We know his type, his needs. He lives alone. He has no genuine social circle and has never been able to develop or maintain a last-ing relationship. He may be, likely is, impotent sexually.'

She tossed that one in, for icing, watched a dull color stain Callaway's cheeks.

'He works and lives in the area he's targeted. See, that's a mistake right there. He should've spread out, but he took the easy route, targeting places and people he knew.'

Eve rose now, wandering to the board, thumbs hooked in her front pockets. 'No one particularly likes him, and the ones who pay attention see him as a fake, as a user with an inflated sense of entitlement.'

'You said he was charismatic.'

'That may be an overstatement. He adapts, morphs, blends, but he's weak on social skills. It's why he hasn't climbed as high as he feels he deserves in his career. You know the type I'm talking about, Lew. You work with people like that. Then there's people like your pal Joe. He had the social skills, and a willingness to go the extra mile, so he was making that climb. Slow, but steady. Or Carly Fisher. Bright, young, ambitious – more fast-tracking her way. But this guy? He's plateaued. He isn't moving up, getting the credit or the perks he wants. He's been brooding about it for a long time.'

'Again, this is your area, but I think you're underestimating him.'

'He'd think that. But the fact is, he's intelligent, sure. He's got a good brain, but he uses it more to manipulate and undermine than to produce. He's lazy. He didn't even come up with this plan, this agenda. Somebody else had already done all the hard work, already done it. He's just coattailing.'

Callaway turned aside, but not before Eve saw his jaw twitch, his mouth thin to a scissor blade. 'I'm surprised to hear you describe the person who accomplished this as lazy or weak. I'm not sure how you'd describe yourselves as he's outwitted you.'

'Outwit, hell. This guy's more of a lucky half-wit. He's the stupid using the vulnerable, and that's always full of pitfalls.'

On the broody train, Eve thought as Callaway turned his sulky face back to hers. 'How so?'

'Sooner or later, somebody figures out they're being used, and they turn. And you can count on the fact this guy's going to bite off more than he can swallow.'

'Chew,' Teasdale corrected automatically.

'You need to swallow after you chew, right?' Eve shrugged it off. 'The asshole's got delusions of power and glory, but he's nothing. He's nobody. Just a cheap copycat.'

354

'Nobody? The media's made him a star. No one's talking about anything or anyone else.'

'For now. That's how it works. Somebody else'll come along – probably smarter and more newsworthy, and—' She snapped her fingers. 'He's over.'

'You're wrong. People will *never* forget.'

'Come on, Lew. Once they know he's just some lunatic, worse some religious fanatic lunatic who stumbled onto a formula cooked up by another religious fanatic lunatic, they'll laugh.'

'I'm afraid they'll be laughing at you when you try to tie these accomplishments to some doomsday group like Red Horse.'

Eve smiled. 'I guess we'll find out. But it bears out what I said. Outside of this room, I'd bet eight out of ten people never heard of, or have barely heard of Red Horse – and less than that have heard of Guiseppi Menzini. Sure, we have, but it's our business to dig up arcane data like that. It's interesting that you know, Lew.'

'Know what?'

'About Red Horse.'

'I don't, not really. When you brought it up as being tied to this, I remembered hearing the name.'

'But I never mentioned Red Horse.' She sat on the edge of the table, still smiling at him. 'We can play the record back if you want.'

'I simply assumed you meant that particular cult.'

'That's a big assumption, but it's logical you'd make it.'

'I simply put two and two together, but I fail to see any religious overtones in this.'

'You're right. There aren't any. That was your grandfather's deal. It's not yours.'

'I don't know what you're talking about. And I've given you all the time I can spare for now.'

'If you try walking out that door, Lew,' Eve said mildly when he turned, 'I'm going to stop you. You won't like it.'

'I came here to do you a favor. I'm done.'

She laughed, not just because she wanted to, but to see that angry color deepen at the sound. 'You came here because you're an idiot. Now you're under arrest for first-degree murder, a hundred and twenty-seven counts thereof. Agent Teasdale will also charge you with domestic terrorism, but I get first crack. You can take a seat, and we'll talk this through, or I can cuff you and drag your ass into an interview box. You choose.'

His voice went cold, but the heat burned in his face. 'I can only conclude the pressure's gotten to you, and you've lost control of yourself. You can't arrest me. You've got no evidence.'

'You'd be surprised what I have. It's all about choices, Lew. Your next one is to sit down or try for the door. Personally, I hope you try for the door.'

'I'll be contacting my attorney, *and* your superiors. You can count on it.'

'Please,' Teasdale added as he started for the door again. 'Allow me.'

'You're the guest.'

Teasdale sprang up, fast and quiet. When Callaway tried to push her back, she slid in, fluid as water, used a foot to tangle his, bent her body like a flower on a delicate stalk to turn his own body weight to her advantage. In a kind of pretty, flowing dance she had him on the ground, her knee against his spine, his wrists clamped in her hands.

'Nice moves,' Eve commented.

'Thank you, and thank you for the opportunity.'

'No problem. Peabody, why don't you assist Agent Teasdale and secure the prisoner in Interview A?'

'I'll ruin you for this! Every one of you useless bitches.'

'Oh-oh, strong language. Golly, now I'm scared. Haul him out, Peabody. Let's give him a little time to cool off.'

'You're finished!' he shouted at Eve as Teasdale and Peabody perp-walked him out. 'You have no idea what I can do.'

'Yeah,' Eve murmured, turning back to the victim board, 'I do.'

'You did well,' Mira told her.

'I'll have to do better yet to get it to stick. I'm counting on the search team finding something we can hang on him. Right now, I have to use his own ego and cowardice to get him to confess.'

'You infuriated him. Switching from talking about him as intelligent, to weak, from being bogged down in the investigation to being confident. It confused him, but more it infuriated and insulted. He could control the violence he felt,

357

but not the resentment. He couldn't stand there and allow you to insult him, again and again.'

'I'm not sure a replay of that will work in Interview. I'm going to push him with Menzini, the backstory.'

'My sense is he finds the religious overtones absurd, even a little embarrassing.'

'Yeah. I can push there. His grandfather was a fuckhead. Maybe you should take him first. Tell him you convinced me he should have the opportunity to get in touch with his insane brat of an inner child or whatever. String him out awhile – can you do that?'

'I can do that.'

'It'll give the search team more time.' She checked her wrist unit, calculated. 'I'd like to trip him up with the parents, then kick him when he's off balance with something they've found. He's smart, smart enough to know when I lay it out I've got enough to cage him. He may want to wrangle a deal.'

'The PA will never deal on something like this, and HSO will come at him once you're done.'

'Yeah, but even some guy sliding off a cliff hopes he'll snag a handhold. Give them a couple minutes to settle him in. I want to put my boards back.'

'One thing I found particularly telling,' Mira said. 'He called two mass murders "accomplishments".'

'Yeah, I got that. Can you use it?'

'Definitely.'

'Me, too.'

While Eve put her boards back in order, the search team combed through Callaway's apartment.

Roarke found it too trendy, far too studied, and utterly impersonal. Black, white, and silver dominated the open living area and kitchen. Occasional blots or streaks of some bold color – a purple cushion, a red tabletop, only served to accent the starkness.

Sharp lines, he thought, cold lighting, and an array of stylish gadgets. It struck him like a photo of decor rather than a place to live.

'Do you want to start on the electronics out here?' Feeney asked him.

'Do you mind if I wander about a bit first, get a feel?'

'I got a feel.' Rumpled, Feeney looked around. 'Feels like a showroom display put together by somebody who's never taken a couch nap or watched a ballgame on screen.'

'But it doesn't feel like somewhere you plot mass murder.'

'What else you gonna do? Sit on one of those damn chairs for five minutes, your ass'll be numb for a week.' Feeney sniffed at them. 'Might as well kill somebody.'

'I'll be sure not to sit in one of the chairs. Just in case.'

'Yeah. You wander. I'll start on this 'link and comp.'

Roarke moved into the master bedroom where Reineke and Jenkinson were already systematically going through the closet, the bureau.

Callaway chose gray here, Roarke thought. Every shade of gray from palest smoke to deepest slate. He supposed Callaway read gray soothed, and was this season's hot color choice, when in reality, in this unrelieved palette, it depressed.

Might as well kill somebody, Roarke mused.

'Must be like sleeping in a fog bank,' Reineke commented. 'Can't see a guy getting lucky in here.'

'I'd say being fashionable is more important to him than getting laid,' Roarke suggested.

Reineke just shook his head. 'Sick fuck.'

Amused, Roarke moved toward the closet and Jenkinson.

'Got plenty of clothes. Shoes never been worn. Everything all nice and tidy.'

'Mmm.' Roarke studied the space, the walls, the floor, the ceiling. Then moved out again to roam into the master bath.

White here, oyster, snow, cream, ecru, ivory. A huge white urn of flowers in autumn shades added some color and texture, but like the rest, the room felt *done*. Coldly done.

As a boy, he remembered, in his B&E days, he'd enjoyed this part of the job. The wandering, the getting a sense of who lived in the space, how they lived. He'd learned a bit about how the wealthy lived – what they ate, drank, wore.

For a street rat with nothing, it had been a world of wonders over and above the take.

He learned how Callaway lived as he went, and wasn't surprised when Reineke announced, 'No sex toys or enhancements, no skin mag discs, no porn.'

'Sex isn't one of his interests.'

'Like I said, sick fuck.'

The bedroom was for sleeping, Roarke determined. For

dressing, undressing. Not for entertaining, not for work. For sleep and show should he have guests. Rarely guests here, Roarke mused as he moved out, and into the office.

'Here now,' he murmured.

This was the hub. Energetic colors to stimulate the senses. Too many, and the hues too harsh, but here was a feel of movement, of activity, of living.

An important desk of glossy black facing the privacy-screened windows, an important chair of bold orange leather mated to it.

The first-rate D&C center – yes, he'd have a look at that. The long, deep sofa in hard green, deep blue tabletops, a dizzying pattern on the rug, art in those same colors, splashed and streaked and framed in black.

Except for one, he noted. A moody and rather lovely painting of Rome. The Spanish Steps on a sun-washed afternoon.

As he found it the only really tasteful item he'd seen thus far, he walked over, examined it, looked behind it, checked the frame, the backing.

Finding nothing, he put it back on the wall.

Comfortable enough, Roarke decided. A mini AC and Friggie. He could settle in here, have what he needed.

He opened a double-doored closet, smiled. Shelves of office supplies, extra discs, even a small unit for washing dishes.

'A bit shallow, aren't you, and a fairly recent addition here?'

He crouched, studied the underside of the shelves, the

sides, then patiently removed some of the supplies. Gave the back wall a few knocks.

'Ah. Yes.'

He imagined Callaway considered himself cagey and clever to have installed the false wall, the shelves. And they might have fooled a casual observer, a cleaning crew or a very sloppy search. It took him under three minutes to find and access the mechanism. Released, the shelves pivoted out, opening the small room beyond.

And here, Roarke thought, *here, he'd brewed up death.*

Mushrooms sealed in jars, seeds, chemicals, powders, liquids – all meticulously labeled. While tiny, the lab appeared carefully laid out and supplied. For one purpose, Roarke thought. Burners, petri dishes, mixers, a microscope, and a small, powerful computer – all fairly new, he saw, all top of the line.

He found the old journal, its cover cracked and faded, paged through it. Crouched again, he opened the lid of a storage box, nudged through photos, more journals, clippings, a tattered Bible, and what he recognized as a manifesto – handwritten, and signed by Menzini.

He stepped out, walked across the hall. 'I think I've found what you're looking for.'

He got out of their way, went back into the living area.

'Nothing on this unit,' Feeney said. 'Bastard barely used it.'

'This area's for show. There's a small laboratory behind a false wall in the office closet.'

As Roarke spoke, Feeney's head came up like a wolf

scenting a bloodied sheep. 'If I remember the formula correctly, all the necessaries are there, as well as journals, the formula itself clearly written in one, and what appear to be more recent, handmade notes. There are photographs, and Menzini's personal manifesto. And a computer which will likely prove more interesting than that one.'

'Got the fucker.'

'It seems so. I'll call the lieutenant, let her know.'

'Tell her we'll bring everything in. She can start wrapping him up.' He started toward the office. 'When we close this down, I'll buy you a beer.'

'I'll hold you to it.' Roarke took out his 'link, waited for Eve to come on screen.

'Give me something good.'

'Would a small, secret lab with the ingredients contained in the substance, the formula for said substance, Menzini's journal, and a computer that likely holds pertinent data be something good?'

'Jesus. Jesus, you're going to get so much sex.'

'Jenkinson says: "Hoo-haw!"'

'For Christ's—'

'I'm winding you up, darling. I'm quite alone at the moment, and will happily take you up on so much sex. Do you have him in the house?'

'In restraints. He slipped up enough I've charged him, and I'm about to head in to work a confession out of him, with details. You just nailed it shut.'

'Feency said we'll bring everything in.'

'Give me some details so I can use them to cook him some.'

'The lab's behind a false wall, lined with shelves, in his office. The journal with the formula has a leather binding – it's faded brown leather and cracked with age, and there are notes that appear more recent and in another handwriting with the formula. There's a storage box holding more journals, an old Bible, and a manifesto handwritten by Menzini. It's titled *End of Days*.'

'That'll do it. Mira's messing with him now. I'll fill in Teasdale and Peabody, and we'll tie it up.'

'I'll see you soon then.'

'Yeah. What's wrong? There's a thing.'

'Nothing, really. This place. It's depressing. It's a good building, has character. It's a nice space, really, but it's lifeless and cold. The only place I think he's ever felt happy, perhaps ever felt normal – that is, felt himself – was that office, and that lab.'

'He had every chance, every choice. Don't feel sorry for him.'

'Not at all. But I can see him here, finding himself at last in the blood and death. It's depressing.'

'Get the goods, get out. We can get a little drunk before the so much sex.'

'Well now, that sounds promising. Soon, Lieutenant.' He clicked off, grinned at Reineke as the detective cleared his throat.

'Sorry, didn't mean to catch that.'

'No problem. Now you know I'm not a sick fuck.'

Reineke snorted out a laugh. 'Never figured it. So, Feeney thought you'd want to take a look at the comp. Says the data's encrypted.'

'Excellent. That should liven things up.'

'Ah, maybe you don't have to mention to the LT I happened to hear her say that business. The sex business.'

'I think we'll all be happier that way.'

19

Moving fast, Eve headed for Observation, contacting
Whitney on the fly. 'Put me through to the commander,' she
snapped when she reached his admin. 'Priority.'

'One moment, Lieutenant.'

She pushed through the doors where Peabody and Teasdale
watched Mira work Callaway. 'We got him.' She held up a
finger as Peabody started to speak. 'Commander, Callaway is
currently in Interview with Mira, charged with the murders.
The search team found his hole. They're bringing in his electronics, and journals, and chemicals. They got it all.'

'Wrap it up,' Whitney ordered. 'I'm on my way.'

'Interview A, sir,' she told him as Peabody punched her
fists into the air, and Teasdale yanked out her own 'link. 'I'm
about to go in, finish it. I'll contact the PA, get someone in
here.'

'Hold until I get there. Coming now.'

'Yes, sir.' She clicked off, shot a finger up in the air again,
then contacted Reo.

'Cher Reo.'

'We've got Callaway, Interview A, and enough evidence to
bury him on its way in.'

She watched the petite blonde scramble for her suit jacket. 'The boss is in court. I'll tag him now, head to you. Give me some details.'

'We tied him to Menzini. He has the formula, the chemicals, the works in his apartment. You want more, get here fast.'

She clicked off. 'Has he said anything I can use?' she demanded.

'He's claiming he's not related to Menzini, keeps asking to be allowed to contact his parents. How they'll worry about him. Mira's playing it soft, so he's trying to wheedle.' Peabody took a breath. 'Holy shit, Dallas. He really had everything in his apartment?'

'With some precautions. He never believed we'd make the connection. He wasn't worried.'

'I've contacted my superior.' Teasdale replaced her 'link. 'HSO will be filing federal charges. In addition to the murder charges, Lieutenant,' she added quickly. 'Not in lieu of.'

'Fine. I don't care which cage he lives out his miserable life in. Here's how it's going to work.'

She broke off as Whitney stepped in. 'Commander.'

He nodded, turned to study Callaway through the glass. 'He looks ordinary, doesn't he? An ordinary man in a well-cut suit.'

'That's his problem. He couldn't tolerate being ordinary. That's why he's in there, and that's why he'll confess.'

'If the formula and the items required to create the substance were in his possession,' Teasdale said, 'in addition to the statements of his parents, on record, the biological connection to Menzini, a confession may be superfluous.'

'Not for me. He's going to say what he did. He's going to look me in the eye and tell me what he did. Peabody, I want you to go in. Hard eye him, but don't talk to him, don't respond if he talks to you. Whisper to Mira we've got the evidence, and I'm coming in. She should keep going until I do. Go in now, stand against the wall, and look tough. It'll add some sweat.'

'Looking tough.' Peabody tightened her jaw, hardened her eyes as she went out.

'I'd like a shot at him myself,' Whitney stated.

'Commander, I'd like to keep the room unbalanced. All women, and him.'

'Understood.'

'I want to circle him awhile,' she said to Teasdale. 'He'll expect the direct hit, and he's prepared for that. I'm going to dribble out what we have on him, keep hacking at his ego. Follow me?'

'I do.'

'Commander, if you could direct APA Reo to come in as soon as she arrives? Another woman's going to piss him off. Ready?' she asked Teasdale.

'Very ready.'

Eve walked in first. 'Dallas, Lieutenant Eve, and Teasdale, Agent Miyu, entering Interview. Excuse me, Doctor Mira, we're going to have to cut you off. You're welcome to stay, of course.'

'This is bullshit.' Callaway jabbed a finger into the table. 'As I've been telling Doctor Mira, you've obviously got me confused with someone else. I've never heard of this Menzini person. My maternal grandfather was a decorated military officer, Captain Edward Gregory Hubbard. I can verify that. I demand to contact my parents. It's my right to have communication.'

'Not once you're charged with terrorism.' Eve shrugged as she sat. 'We can hold you for forty-eight hours without communication or representation. It sucks, but that's how it plays.'

'If there's been a mistake' – Mira lifted her hands – 'it would save time, and any additional stress to Mr Callaway if you arranged for his parents to come here. If you spoke with them to verify his parentage.'

'I won't have my family subjected to interrogation by incompetent police and witch-hunting government agents.' Callaway folded his arms. 'I'll wait. I have nothing to say for the next forty-eight hours.'

'Okay. You can just listen. We can and will run DNA tests to prove Menzini's your grandfather.'

'Go ahead! I welcome it.'

'And once we do that, you're not just cooked, you're served up with tasty side dishes. How did you know about Red Horse?'

Like a child, he turned his head away, stared at the wall.

'Because it's interesting you'd bring up Red Horse in connection with the killings as Menzini headed one of the sects during the Urbans. Menzini was a chemist, more self-taught

369

than educated. And completely bat-shit. He created a substance that caused violent delusions, extreme paranoia. The same substance you used at On the Rocks and Café West.'

She let it hang, said nothing. Silence ticked, ticked, ticked as she kept her gaze steady and cool on his averted face.

He shifted in his chair. 'I'm not a damn chemist. I can't make something like that even if I wanted to. Which I don't.'

'How did you know about Red Horse?'

'My grandfather served during the Urbans. I've heard stories.'

'He died before you were born.'

'They've been passed down. And I've familiarized myself with some of the battles he was in. He fought this Red Horse cult. When you mentioned religious fanatics, that came to mind. It's that simple.'

'But Menzini was never mentioned in this family history?'

'I've never heard the name before today.'

'That's pretty strange, Lew, seeing as he's your mother's biological father.'

'That's utter nonsense. If you had any brain at all, you'd have checked her birth records.'

'Oh, I had enough brain to do that. With enough left over to ask her face-to-face.'

Now his head came around, fast. 'What did you say?'

'It's really more what she said. I get you didn't want us to speak to her or your father, but, hey, I'm just bullheaded that way.'

'Obviously you frightened and intimidated her. She's not a strong woman. She's frail, emotionally. You coerced her.'

'That would be your method. Here's the thing – the break I'm going to give you right here and now. You can keep denying knowledge, figuring when the truth comes out, you stick to being unaware. Nobody ever told you.'

She waited a beat, gave him time to calculate. 'That's one way. Or you can admit you found out, discovered the documents your mother told me about. The shock of that sent you into a tailspin. Why, your family lied to you, and your grandfather, rather than being a decorated war hero turns out to be some homicidal lunatic mass murderer and child abductor. A religious looney on top of it. He might get mentally impaired out of that line, right, Doctor Mira?'

'The shock alone . . . ' Shaking her head, Mira trailed off.

'It could work to your advantage.'

'I want to speak with my mother.'

'Not going to happen, Lew.'

'A mother testifying against a son,' Teasdale said quietly. 'The weight of that testimony will be great.'

His jaw set. Eve imagined she heard his teeth grinding.

'She'll never agree to it.'

'She won't have a choice. And when we bring Menzini in—'

'He's dead!'

Eve angled her head. 'What makes you think that?'

'I – I assumed.'

Smiling, she wagged her finger. 'You shouldn't assume. He'll tell the whole story, about your biological grandmother, the abduction of your mother, her recovery. It's the sort of thing that might play for you, if you admit you knew – you found out and it screwed you up. APA's on the way. I want to wrap this up, get home, have a drink. The prosecutor's office wouldn't like me giving you this wiggle room, however slim. Make a choice, Lew. And fast.'

'I want to speak to someone in charge.'

'You are. Oh, you mean a man. That's not going to happen either. Make a choice. I know you found the box of documents. I know you learned Menzini was your grandfather. You found the formula. You've got a chance to come clean on that, help yourself. Or you can keep lying, and go down that way.'

'They did lie to me.' He turned – a deliberate move – to Mira. 'All my life. I could never understand why they couldn't love me, couldn't give me the affection a child needs. My father . . . He's a violent man. The secrets in that house . . . I can't speak of it.'

All sympathy, Mira leaned toward him. 'Your father abused you, physically.'

Callaway turned his head away, managed to nod. 'And in every way. She never stopped him, never tried to. My mother. But she couldn't help it. She's weak, and afraid.'

'He abused her as well.'

'She's terrified of him,' Callaway whispered. 'Of everything. We moved constantly when I was growing up. I never knew what it was to have a real home, friends, roots. Then I found that damn box, and knew why she'd never protected me. I was a constant reminder to her of what her mother had suffered – her real mother. I even look like him a little. The coloring, the build. I stepped into a nightmare.'

'I understand,' Mira said gently.

'How can you? How can anyone? To know that runs through you. I wanted to kill myself.'

'But you kept going back,' Eve interrupted. 'Hoping to find more.'

'Yes, yes. To find it all, to get rid of it. I brought it all back here, and I dumped it all in a recycler.'

'Oh please.' Eve rolled her eyes. 'How stupid are you? Nobody's going to buy that. You brought it back, and you re-created the substance. Admit it, for God's sake. Own it. The PA's going to push for consecutive life sentences in an off-planet cage. Hard as hard time gets. Lay it out, lay it all out and you might have a shot at a facility on-planet. You can write a goddamn book, do media interviews. You can *be* somebody. Find your balls, Lew.'

'I was going to kill myself. I was going to use what he made to destroy myself. I lost my mind for a while. I wasn't sure it would work, but I took it with me, into the bar. I was going to wait until it was nearly empty, but Joe wouldn't leave. I lost my nerve. I got up to go, and that woman bumped into me. She knocked the vial, and it fell. I panicked, and I got out.'

He covered his face with his hands. 'All those people.'

'You made the substance?' Eve repeated. 'You took it into the bar?'

'Yes. God help me, yes,' he said just as Reo stepped in.

'APA Reo, Cher, entering Interview. Pull up a chair. Lew's entertaining us with fairy tales.'

'How can you be so callous?' he demanded. 'So cold.'

'Me? You're the champ there. Lew's just confessed to creating the hallucinogenic and taking it into the bar.'

'I was traumatized! I meant to self-terminate.'

'There are easier ways,' Eve pointed out. 'Did you also mean to self-terminate when you took another vial of the hallucinogenic, palmed it off on Jeni Curve without her knowledge?'

'I don't remember any of that. There are blanks in my memory. The shock. The stress. I want to speak with your superior!'

'Fuck that.' Eve slammed her hands on the table, pushed up to lean into his face. 'You needed a vessel, she was handy. You made up some story about a man in black. You were the man, Lew. You. Do you know how many buildings on that street have security cams? Do you think you avoided all of them?'

'You idiot. I never went near camera range.'

'No? You're sure. Your memory's clear on that point?'

'I don't know. You're confusing me. I want to talk to your commanding officer. I don't want to talk to you.'

'You can talk to me,' Reo suggested. 'I'm Assistant Prosecuting Attorney Cher Reo.'

'Do you think I'm going to talk to an assistant? Some *secretary*?'

'That's telling her, Lew.' Eve circled him. 'Show her who's

in charge here. Who's the fucking boss. You murdered a hundred and twenty-seven people, for Christ's sake, without getting a drop of blood on you. And she sashays in here in her girly suit and sex-me-up shoes and expects you to give her the time of day?

'This is bullshit. Just bullshit. You put an entire city on notice, and you did it because you *could*, not for some crackpot end-of-days bullshit like your whacked-out grandfather. You've got book deals and vid deals coming. They'll be beating down your door, throwing money at you. And fame. Everybody's going to know your name, and fear it. That's what you want, isn't it? The attention, the respect you deserve.'

'That's right, and I'm not talking to a bunch of idiot women.'

'Come on, Lew, show us your balls. Give us a thrill. When the real PA gets here, he'll know he's dealing with a *man*. A man who demands respect. Not some weak sister like Joe Cattery. That bitch Weaver was going to promote him over you. It was time for a game changer. Time to level the field. And all those happy hour assholes, slurping up the half-priced drinks. I bet they made you sick. Plenty more out there just like them, but you – you're special. It's about damn time people treated you the way you should be treated.'

'Joe was nothing. A flunky.'

'That's right. That's right. It had to burn your ass when he got the big bonus.'

'*My* bonus. Weaver fucked me over.'

'That bitch.' Not controlled now, Eve thought. Cornered, furious, cracking. 'And it wasn't the money, not really. Right? It was the principle. What did you do, Lew? Impress me. You had the formula, you had the journal – all those secrets inside the faded brown cover. Sure, we found that.' She kept her eyes steady when he blinked. 'The men said you really put it together, Lew. All the time, the effort, the planning that went into building the lab, outfitting it. And the risk. Talk about balls. It's dangerous, cooking up LSD, mixing it, getting all the parts and pieces together. That takes brains and balls. It takes imagination. People are going to talk about Lewis Callaway for generations.'

'You admit it.' He jabbed a finger at her. 'You admit that.'

'I was messing with you before. Nobody's ever going to forget what you did, who you are. Jesus, Lew, you're in a league of your own. Tell me what you did. I'll never forget.'

He shook his head, turned away again, but his breathing was fast, his eyes calculating.

Nearly there, she thought.

'If you did this,' Teasdale put in. 'Can prove you did this, the agency will be very interested. They want people like you, Mr Callaway, working for them. High-level positions.'

'Wait just a damn minute,' Eve began.

'Lieutenant, we're talking about global security. My superiors – and this reaches the highest chambers – have authorized me to persuade Mr Callaway, should he prove himself, should he offer details that leave no room for doubt he perpetrated these events, to consider an offer.'

'Working for the HSO?'

'Menzini's talents have certainly been useful. My superiors are of the opinion yours will follow suit.'

'Some cushy job!' Eve rounded on Teasdale. 'Some big, covert government deal? For killing people? I should've known you'd play it this way. Let me do all the work, then grab the prize at the end.'

'Those with the skill and aptitude for such matters are more useful with us than not.' Teasdale merely shrugged. 'HSO values creativity and – as you so aptly stated – balls. But I can't discuss any of it any further without solid evidence, and Mr Callaway's statement.'

'My grandfather works for the HSO? He's alive and working for you?'

Teasdale pokered up. 'I'm not at liberty to say anything more on that matter at this time. I don't have that authority.'

'I should've known you'd screw me over,' Eve said bitterly.

'Priorities, Lieutenant. And power. The choice is yours, Mr Callaway.'

'You thought you had me.' He sneered at Eve. 'You don't know who you're dealing with. All my life I knew there was something more in me, something different. They tried to hold me back.'

'They?' Eve prompted.

'My parents. But I could always get what I wanted, make people do what I wanted – or pay. I knew I didn't get the more from them. They're nothing. Ordinary. And when . . . when I found out where I'd gotten it, I was happy. At last.

I've finished playing the game, pretending to give a shit. People needed to pay.'

'Joe Cattery, Carly Fisher.'

With a cagey smile, Callaway folded his arms. 'Immunity.'

'I can't authorize that.' Reo put a little squeak in her voice. 'My boss has to—'

'The HSO offer takes precedence over assistants,' Teasdale said, smugly. 'Once Mr Callaway has given me the information necessary, I'm authorized to make him that offer. People needed to pay,' she repeated to Callaway. 'And you had the means.'

'I had what I needed. Cattery, Fisher, they'd pushed the wrong buttons, hadn't they? Messed with the wrong person, and for the last time. That's what I can bring to the table,' he told Teasdale. 'I've got the means and the brains to make HSO the most powerful agency on- or off-planet.'

'I'm listening.'

'What's the offer? Spell it out.'

'That depends on what you tell me, and what can be proven. I can tell you HSO is very interested and intrigued by your – alleged – talents.'

'Bureaucratic bitch,' Eve muttered, and got a cool smile from Teasdale.

'You've been outmaneuvered, Lieutenant. If, of course, Mr Callaway elects to cooperate with us.'

'I'm going to have terms,' Callaway told Teasdale.

'We can certainly discuss terms, but we require proof you had not only the means, but did, in fact, execute these incidents.'

'They all did what I wanted, didn't they? What I made them do. Everyone in that bar, in that crappy café danced to *my* tune. That's what you'll get with me,' he told Teasdale. 'Someone who gets the job done.'

'What did you make them do, Mr Callaway?' Teasdale asked.

'Kill each other. Slaughter. Live their fears and die fighting. It was all there in the journals, my grandfather's papers. His crazy religious angle? You don't have to worry about that from me. I'm not crazy, and I don't believe in anything but myself.'

'That's important. My superiors will want to be assured of just that.'

'Idiot Joe, sitting there, moping for his wife and brats. And I thought, you won't mope much longer, asshole. I wanted Weaver, too, but she left, skipping out to have sex. I settled for Joe, and the rest of them. That fucking bartender, the bitch of a waitress, that *stupid* woman and her friends. All I had to do was put the vial in her pocket when she bumped into me. Already opened. It takes a few minutes to take effect, and I timed it right down to the heartbeat. That's how good I am. Got a little headache, but that's all. I was out in the air before it took hold. And I just kept walking.'

'You made the substance yourself?'

'It's tricky,' he said with a nod at Teasdale. 'Not that hard to come up with the ingredients, especially if you take your time. I had to build the lab. It's small. I wouldn't mind playing around with other ideas in a better lab. I've got a knack.' He tapped his chest with his thumb. 'I guess I got it from the old man.'

'I'll pass that on,' Teasdale replied.

'I think I can improve it, so it lasts longer, starts faster. The second hit would've been better if the effects had taken hold quicker. Once the cops got there, started stunning people, it cut down on the count.'

'How did you choose the second location?'

'For that bitch Fisher. She thought she was going to climb over my back? Her and Weaver, always plotting and planning out to hold me back.' He sliced his hands like an umpire calling the runner safe. 'That's done.'

'And the second accomplishment. How was it done?'

'I wasn't going to go in. It would give the cops a reason to look at me. See, I think things through, figure the angles. I just waited for the delivery girl. Dumb as a bag of hair, that one. I stopped her, asked her to order me a sandwich, grab me a table. Said I had to run into the drug store, but I'd be right there. Gave her a thank-you hug, stuck the open vial in her pocket. Done and finished. I grabbed that pita and strolled on back to the office.'

'Where were you hitting next?' Eve asked. 'Indulge me.'

'Why not? There's an Italian restaurant down from the office. Appetito. Weaver goes there a lot. All I'd have to do is check her book, see when she's taking some fuck there for foreplay. I made friends with one of the waitresses. I'd use her for delivery. With those three out, I'd move up, take over

380

for Weaver. Now they can suck me. Their loss is HSO's gain.'

'It is indeed,' Teasdale agreed.

'Is that enough, Reo?' Eve asked.

'Oh, I'd say that, served on a silver platter.'

'Peabody, get a couple of uniforms to help you take Lew through processing. I don't believe he's going to feel very cooperative.'

'Yes, sir.'

'Screw that.' He tipped back, smirked at Eve as Peabody slipped out. 'I'm not doing any time, even overnight. I'm with the HSO.'

'What you are, Callaway, is deeply stupid.'

'What you are, bitch, is fucked. When do I meet the head men, Agent?'

'I'm sorry, Mr Callaway, if I gave the impression the offer would precede you serving out your sentences. The HSO does believe you'll be very useful to us – should there be a medical miracle and you survive one hundred and twenty-seven life sentences. And we feel you'll be very useful serving approximately the same amount of additional time in a federal institution.'

'This is bullshit. You said—'

'I believe the record will show I gave no specific details on this offer. In any case, lying during Interview or interrogation is accepted – even encouraged. I believe, Mr Callaway, it's you who are fucked. I'm very happy to have played a small part in it.'

Eve braced when he surged to his feet. 'Please try it. My turn,' she said to Teasdale. But even as she spoke, Peabody came in with two uniforms.

'Oh well, maybe next time.'

'I want a deal.' He struggled against the vice grip on his arms.

'Sure. Ask me after, say, seventy of those life sentences.' Reo smiled at him like a raptor. 'We'll talk.'

'I want a lawyer!'

'Let him contact a rep after processing,' Eve told Peabody. 'Nice work, Agent.'

'The same, Lieutenant. He was proud of it. You were right about that.'

'Yeah, and ambitious. You were right with the HSO angle.'

'I'll report to my superior, handle the paperwork on my end.' Teasdale let out a long, windy breath. 'Then I'd like a very big drink.'

'I hear that. One thing. Is Menzini still alive?'

'My information is he died a few months ago.'

'Okay. I'll be around.' She turned to Reo. 'No deals, right?'

'What's to deal? He spelled it out. If he gets a decent lawyer, he'll try for insanity or mental defect.'

'He's not insane nor defective,' Mira said. 'I had a session with him right here, on record. He isn't legally insane, and was perfectly aware what he did was wrong, immoral, illegal. There won't be a health facility sentence here. It's his conscience, his morals that are defective, not his mind.'

'Good to hear. I'll have all the records for you within the hour,' she told Reo.

'I'll wait. By the way, sex-me-up shoes?'

'I was following a theme.'

'Well.' Reo turned her ankles, looked down. 'They are pretty fabulous.'

'They are,' Mira agreed.

'I was going to say the same about yours. What a terrific color.'

'Could we not talk about shoes in the box that still smells of evildoer?'

'You started it,' Reo reminded her before she turned back to Mira. 'Do you have time to run through your findings on him? I'll buy you a drink in the lounge.'

'That sounds good. Eve?'

'I'm going to deal with the paperwork.'

She stepped out behind them, spotted Roarke with her commander.

'Sir.'

'Good work, Lieutenant. Excellent work.'

'Thank you, sir. We had a good team who put a lot of hours into it, a lot of skill.'

'Agreed. I'll be addressing the team. We'll be making an announcement to the media, holding a brief conference within the hour. You'll need to be there.' He smiled at her, and for the first time in days, with a light in his eyes. 'I realize that feels like punishment, but it's important we inform the public, and you attend.'

'Yes, sir.'

'After which I suggest you go home and enjoy your evening. I'm going to.'

'I wonder if he means he's going to have so much sex,' Roarke commented when Whitney was out of earshot.

'Please. Don't put that image in my head. I need to see what you brought back from Callaway's.'

'Secured in your office, except for the electronics. Feeney's got them in EDD. I wanted to watch you work this one, so I came down for a bit. But I'll go back, give him some time. The bastard's encrypted everything. It's not overly complicated, but it's going to take a little time to get all his notes and so on.'

'Everything we can get adds to it, but I don't think there's a hurry. Still, I guess I'm going to be a couple hours.'

'Just let me know when you're ready to go. And we'll enjoy our evening.'

'I cracked that code,' she said as she split off to her office.

20

She stopped in the bullpen to speak to Sanchez and Carmichael. 'Nice job before, on the grief-giving. You could be in vids.'

Sanchez pinned her with a pointed stare. 'Did you think I was acting?'

She only lifted her eyebrows, pinned him in turn. 'That or asking for a thirty-day rip.'

Carmichael snorted. 'Told you not to try it. The LT always wins, Sanchez. It's why she's the LT.'

'Well, hell.' With a grin, Sanchez shrugged it off. 'Is he down?'

'Down and out. You can pass cases back to the others, just let me know who's on the board.'

'Can we give Baxter the bloater, cooking in his cat-infested apartment for eight days? I owe him some payback.'

'Fine with me.'

'Then it's all worth it.'

She left them for her office. Yeah, the new guy not only slid right in, she thought. He fit like he'd been there for years.

She considered a moment, then engaged her 'link.

'This is Nadine, make it quick. I'm in a production meeting.'

'You're going to want to step out for a minute.'

A flicker of annoyance came first, then cleared. 'I've got to take this. Keep going.'

Eve waited while Nadine walked out of the room, closing the door behind her. 'Tell me you made an arrest.'

'We made an arrest. Wait. There's going to be a statement and a media conference within the hour. I'm giving you a heads up on it. The data you dug up for me helped.'

'Give me a name, give me the official charges.'

'I'm not going to do that, Nadine. You know I can't. What you can do is get on air, do your breaking news thing. According to a source within the NYPSD, police have arrested and charged a suspect in the mass murders committed at On the Rocks and Café West. An official statement is imminent. Details to follow or whatever.'

'You're going to start writing my copy now?'

'It's the best I can do for you. Don't ask me for the one-on-one right now. I'll just say no because I'm fucking tired; I want to tie this up and go home. Ask me later.'

'Was he acting alone? Give me that?'

'At this time, we have no reason to believe otherwise. He confessed. That's big, Nadine. We apprehended, arrested, and charged an individual, and said individual confessed to perpetrating the incidents that led to the deaths of a hundred and twenty-seven people. You're going to want to postpone that meeting, get this out, and get your camera-ready ass to Central.'

'You can bet your mass-murderer-catching ass I will. Talk later.'

386

'A lot later,' Eve added when the screen went blank.

She hadn't lied about being tired, she thought. Now that it was done, every ounce of fatigue she'd shoved back since walking into On the Rocks wanted to push through and drop her like a stone.

It just had to wait, she decided. She wanted to write up the arrest report personally. And first, she wanted a look at the journals and papers the search team had secured and logged in.

She unsealed the box, initialed it, then sat to study the memorabilia of madness.

The religious rantings in the journal simply annoyed her. The way those thirsty for power, glory or the satisfaction of brow-beating others into their particular beliefs used God as a weapon of intimidation and fear perplexed her.

Not that they'd do it, but that anybody would listen.

If God actually took the time to go around smiting anyone, she'd like to see him start with the self-righteous pricks who inflated their own egos in his name.

But she supposed that was why God made cops.

Menzini had filled pages in tiny, crablike handwriting, pontificating about the chosen, detailing the ritual rapes of young girls, and calling them initiations or cleansings.

He rambled about his God-given mission to purge the unclean, sinners, the unworthy, his holy mission to prepare the way for the end of days. And his plans to repopulate the earth with the righteous after the purge.

He detailed his experiments, his frustrations with his lack

of success. One lack of success had resulted in an explosion that had killed one assistant and blinded another.

That, too, was apparently God's fault – or his will, anyway. And a test directed at Menzini, to help forge his determination.

'Yeah, it's all about you, asshole.'

She glanced up when Peabody stepped in.

'I just got to the part where Menzini's praising God for showing him the way to create the substance. He tested it on some prisoners, which included a sixteen-year-old boy. He dubbed the substance God's Wrath, and was damn proud of it.'

'Sounds like Callaway came by it naturally. Jesus.' Horror covered Peabody's face as it reddened. 'I'm sorry. I didn't think.'

'Don't worry about it. It doesn't bother me. He has this in him, but we've all got something. Even some daisy-sniffing Free-Ager like you has to have a rotted branch on the family tree somewhere. It's what we do with it, about it, despite it.'

'Yeah.' Peabody blew out a breath. 'I don't sniff daisies. They don't really smell. I like peonies, if you're taking notes on flowers to send me for a reward.'

'Sure, I'll mark that right down on my shopping list.'

'You don't have a shopping list.'

'Exactly. Did Callaway tap a lawyer?'

'Not yet. He clammed up, like total lockdown. He gave me a bad feeling, so I put him in solitary, and on suicide watch.'

'Good. We want him safe and secure. Whitney, or likely

Tibble will be making an official statement. We're expected to do the media conference deal.'

'I don't mind. It'll be good to let people know it's okay, we did the job. McNab's working on decrypting Callaway's electronics. I'm going to wait for him before knocking off anyway. The search team's back,' she added. 'There's talk about going out for some brew.'

'I'm going to skip it. I just want to ... enjoy an evening at home.'

'If you change your mind, they're hitting the Blue Line. Cops might as well celebrate a big win at a cop bar. Do you want me to do the five's?'

Tempting ... but no. 'I'm going to start on it now. Go ahead and get the records for Reo, and a copy of the log of everything taken from Callaway's apartment. We're going to want to send somebody in – with correct authorization – to confiscate his office electronics, toss his office.'

'I can tell Reo to take care of that.'

'That works. For now, get a uniform to get over there, seal it. Once the news hits, some big nose is bound to go in there and poke around.'

'I'm all over it. You know, it feels good, Dallas, but ... '
With a sad little shrug, Peabody looked down at the papers on Eve's desk.

'You wished it felt better. I'm betting there's a hit list on his comp, where he planned to target, who he'd earmarked to take out. Once you read that, think about all those people who can just go on living their lives, it will feel better.'

'Yeah. You know, thinking about that, it already does.'

'Then get out of here so I can work.'

She slogged her way through the arrest report, copied, filed, added it to her book. She considered the other journals. Not exactly light reading, she thought, but she wanted to know, to see.

She rose, intended to give herself a lift with another hit of coffee, and turned back to her signaling 'link.

'You're to report to the main media room, Lieutenant, along with Detective Peabody and any other officer you deem appropriate.'

'On my way.'

Coffee later, she promised herself. Better a nice cool glass of wine, or two. And that so much sex.

Then sleep. Lots and lots of sleep.

She stood, scanned the bullpen. 'Good work, all around. That includes Detectives Carmichael and Sanchez, and the other officers who took on the load so we could bag this fucker. Anyone who wants or needs some personal time or leave . . . Get real. We've got a lot of catching up to do.'

She appreciated the moans, the muttered curses. 'Commander Whitney's called for a media conference.' She appreciated the mild panic, the hunched shoulders as perfectly sane cops slid down in their chairs as if it would make them invisible.

'Peabody and I will take that as I have other assignments for the rest of you. When you've completed your current paperwork or at end of shift – whichever comes first – get the hell out of here and go have a beer.'

Baxter slapped his hands together. 'That's what I'm talking about! The Blue Line, Dallas. Bring Roarke.'

'So he can pick up the tab? I don't think so. I'm going home to the quiet.' She caught Reineke's eye roll to the ceiling.

'Problem, Reineke?'

'What?' He blinked at her, then averted his eyes. 'No, sir. No problem here.'

'Good. Peabody, with me.'

As she expected, the media prep room buzzed. Tibble, Whitney, Mira, Teasdale, and the ever-sharply dressed Kyung.

Tibble glanced up from his notes, pocketed them before crossing to her to extend a hand. 'Congratulations, Lieutenant, Detective. Solid work.'

'We had a solid team.'

'A show of all the officers who participated in the investigation would make a good visual,' Kyung commented.

'They need a break.'

'Of course. For myself, I know I'll sleep easier tonight knowing Lewis Callaway is behind bars.'

'I need a little more than that. Sir,' Eve said to Tibble. 'You know Director Hurtz. Agent Teasdale says he's an honorable man. There's a formula capable of killing masses of people. As Menzini has been in custody until his recent death, I have to believe that formula exists, and is buried somewhere deep in HSO's files.'

'I've never seen nor heard of this substance,' Teasdale insisted, 'until this case.'

'I believe you,' Eve told her. 'That doesn't mean it's not sealed up somewhere. There's also a copy in a journal secured in my office. Our chief lab tech is working on an antidote, and he'll probably come up with one – whether or not HSO already has. We need an agreement, Agent Teasdale, between your honorable man and mine. I'm not naive enough to believe your people will destroy all trace of said formula, but there has to be an agreement said formula will remain sealed and buried.'

'You'll have it.' Tibble looked from Eve to Teasdale and back again. 'My word.'

'Yes, sir.'

She believed he'd keep his word. As for Hurtz, she wanted to believe it. But . . . politics and positions changed. She'd have Roarke keep an eye on things on his unregistered equipment – and she had an ace reporter in the back pocket, should the time come to do that shouting from the rooftops.

'We'll all sleep better now.' She looked back at Kyung.

'I'm told you have Callaway's parents,' he said.

'I've had them transported to a safe house for tonight. Commander, I'd like to have them taken back to Arkansas in the morning, quick and quiet, and arrange for the locals to provide some protection until we see how that wind blows.'

'HSO will take care of that,' Teasdale told her.

'They'll need to issue a statement,' Kyung considered. 'I could help them with that if they're willing.'

'That would be good. They're decent people. It's going to be hard enough for them. Peabody, pave that road when we're done here.'

'We'd intended to wait for the mayor.' Kyung smiled. 'But he's been held up as the news of the arrest leaked.'

'Did it?'

His smile widened. 'Channel Seventy-five broke the story some thirty minutes ago. They're short on details, but it was enough to have reporters swarming the mayor's office. He'll link up with us from there. Now then, Chief Tibble will make a brief statement, followed by Commander Whitney. You and your investigative team will be acknowledged, as will Agent Teasdale and the HSO. Ah, APA Reo.'

'Sorry, I was delayed.' She hurried in, fluffing back her cloud of blond hair. 'The news broke as my boss was leaving court. He's dealing with reporters there. I'll represent the prosecutor's office here.'

'Perfect.' Kyung angled his head, gave them all a glowing smile. 'Five strong, beautiful women – all playing a part in securing the safety of the city. It's an excellent visual. Shall we go in?'

The room was packed, but she'd expected that, too. Cameras whirled and clicked, recorders blinked as Tibble stepped to the podium. Tall, lean, imposing, he stood in silence until the room quieted.

'Today, after an exhaustive and intense investigation, the New York City Police and Security Department, with cooperation from the HSO, arrested and charged the individual allegedly responsible for the deaths that occurred at On the Rocks and Café West. Faced with the preponderance of evidence gathered by the investigative team headed by Lieutenant Dallas, in consultation with Agent Teasdale of HSO, Lewis Callaway has confessed to the planning, the intent, and the execution of these crimes.'

Eve let it roll over her — Tibble's statement, Whitney's, then the questions that flew like crazed crows.

She wanted home, she realized, intensely. The quiet of it, the comfort, the indulgence of familiarity.

She answered questions when called on, and wondered — as she always did — why so many of them asked the same damn thing with slightly altered phrasing.

'Lieutenant, Lieutenant Dallas! Kobe Garnet with New York News. You interrogated Callaway.'

'I interviewed the suspect, along with Detective Peabody, Agent Teasdale, and Doctor Mira.'

'Did he tell you why? Why he did it?'

'Yes. I'm not authorized to relate the details of the interview or the suspect's confession that may deter from the prosecution's case, should this matter go to trial.'

'People want to know why.'

'Callaway's motives will be disclosed at the prosecutor's discretion. The why matters. It matters not only to this department in order to secure arrest and confession, to the prosecutor to secure a verdict, but to the survivors of the attacks, and the families of those who didn't survive. They should know it matters to us. More, and for now, they should know Lewis Callaway is behind bars. The NYPSD and the prosecuting attorney will do everything within their power to see he stays behind bars.'

She fielded more, as did the others, until she felt like a bone, picked clean to the marrow.

When her 'link vibrated in her pocket, she started to pull it out. Maybe she could use it as an excuse to step away, get out. But as she slid her hand into her pocket, Kyung stepped up to end the media torture.

Some reporters scrambled out, others continued – ever hopeful – to lob questions. Relieved, Eve walked out behind Whitney.

'Well done,' he told her. 'Go home, get some rest.'

'More than happy to, sir.'

She turned away, reached for her still vibrating 'link, noted Peabody doing the same.

Something in her guts churned.

Even as she pulled out her 'link, McNab – his own in his hand – burst in. 'Lieutenant, we need you in EDD, now.'

Whitney laid a hand on her shoulder to hold her in place. 'What is it, Detective?'

'Sir. We cracked the encryption. Callendar took the journal entries, and she's got entries detailing Callaway's meetings with his grandmother. Gina MacMillon. She's still alive.'

'Peabody, get me everything we've got on Gina MacMillon. Teasdale, get me more. When and where did they meet?' Eve demanded.

'I didn't get all the details. As soon as Callendar hit, she alerted Feeney. We tried to tag you, hoping we'd catch you before any release.'

'Too late. His name's out. Commander, I've got to get on this.'

'Go. I'll be there myself as soon as I can.'

'I've got her basic data,' Peabody said on the run. 'She was reported killed in the attack where her daughter – now Audrey Hubbard – was abducted. Her remains were cremated, per her wishes, and as was more usual in those circumstances.'

'Cause of death,' Eve snapped as she shoved onto an elevator. 'Who ID'd the body?'

'It's going to take longer to—'

'Gunshot to the face,' Teasdale stated, reading her PPC. 'Both William and Gina MacMillon were identified by a neighbor, an Anna Blicks, who died of natural causes in 2048.'

'Face blown away. Your neighbor IDs by body type, hair, clothes, jewelry, and because you're in the house, because who the fuck else would you be? Goddamn it. She started him up. That was the trigger. Not finding out about the grandfather, not initially. But the grandmother.'

'Why would she fake her own death?' Peabody demanded.

'Let me think. Let me think. Put extra guards on Callaway. Now!'

'Menzini might have arranged it,' Teasdale considered. 'He wanted her and the child back, located her, killed someone in her place so no one would look for her.'

396

'No. No. Women didn't matter that much. The kid – she's his blood, and part of the new world order, part of the new beginning. But not the mother. She did it. She went home for something, under Menzini's orders, had to convince her husband she was contrite – or she'd been brainwashed, abused. She's terrified, and there's this baby. He opens the door.'

'For all those months?' Teasdale began.

'Menzini needed someone on the outside, someone who could funnel him money, supplies, information. How the hell do I know, I wasn't there. Isn't that how it works – moles, sleepers, double fucking agents?'

She bulled off the elevator, tore toward EDD.

'In the lab, Dallas.' Fast on his feet, McNab passed her, led the way.

She spotted Feeney through the glass, pacing, his hair in wild silver and gray wires, and Callendar, her face grim in contrast to the sassy butt wiggle she performed in front of a swipe screen.

She didn't see Roarke until she'd pushed through the doors behind McNab. He huddled at a comp station, work- ing manually and by voice. The muttered Irish curses she caught meant he battled the work.

'I'm sorry, Lieutenant.' Callendar broke off the work and wiggle. 'If I'd been faster—'

'Forget that. Run it through.'

'Once we broke the code, I took the journal entries. I was taking my time because ... we had him. The first bit was just long, rambling bullshit about how he was special, different, important. It was just full of the E and the Go, and how now he knew why he'd always known it. Then he started talking about the grandmother. She set up a meeting, posing as a client, St. Regis Hotel bar. You should read it for yourself, Dallas.'

She ordered the segment on screen.

She was beautiful for a woman of her age. A strong face with piercing blue eyes. Her jewelry was understated, but good. I could see she was a woman of means and taste. She ordered a martini, and it suited her. I admit I found her fascinating even before I knew the truth. She kept her voice, strong like her face, low and intimate. I had to lean toward her to hear.

She asked me what I knew about my heritage. It seemed a strange question, but clients often ask strange questions, and she was picking up the tab. I told her of my grandfather – the war hero bit always impresses. How he and my grandmother had left England for America with my mother to start a new life.

Before I could begin on my parents – I always embellish there as they're tedious, ordinary people in reality – she told me everything I knew was a lie.

She told me her name – Gina MacMillon – not the name she'd given me to arrange the meeting. I had some vague recollection of that name, but didn't, right away, connect it to the woman I'd been told was my great-aunt who died in the Urbans.

She, this woman with the compelling eyes, told me she was my true grandmother. That my grandfather had been a great man. Not the soldier who'd done no more than follow the orders of other men, but a great man. A visionary, a leader, and a martyr.

I shouldn't have believed her, but I did. It explained so much. She and this great man had worked together, fought together, had been lovers. The child they'd created, my mother, had been stolen, and she herself, taken and kept prisoner by her former husband. She'd tried to escape, many times, with the child. Eventually, her captor beat her, left her for dead. Though she tried to find her way back to the child, back to my grandfather, the world was in pieces. She learned the government had captured my grandfather, and she had no choice but to go into hiding.

With a new name and identity, she'd struggled to survive. Eventually she'd married, and well, and used the resources gained there to try to find the child stolen from her. Years of searching led her to me. She understood now the daughter was lost to her. Women were weak — most women — but her grandson, so like the man she'd loved, was found.

I asked what she wanted from me. Nothing, she claimed. Instead she had much to give me, to tell me, to teach me. In me she saw the potential and the power taken from her and my grandfather.

His name was Guiseppi Menzini.

'There's more, Lieutenant,' Callendar told her. 'A lot more.'

'I need the name she's using, a description — where she's living.'

'He doesn't list any of that, at least not that I've found. I haven't gotten through it all, but I did searches. He refers to her as Gina or Grandmother. I've got that he started the journal because she told him Menzini kept journals, and he went on a hunt for them when she told him to. She said they were his legacy, and his gateway to power. And she knew his mother kept them.'

399

'She spun him a bunch of lies. Menzini's the hero, and MacMillon, who gave her forgiveness and took another man's kid for his, the villain. And she counted on sentiment and loyalty – her half-sister's for her, to keep her things, her papers, to believe she'd died trying to save the kid. Bitch. Peabody, get Baxter and Trueheart to the St. Regis bar, with a picture of Callaway. Maybe somebody remembers who he sat with on the date of the journal entry. It takes awhile to tell that story. Callendar, where else did they meet?'

'Her place. He doesn't say where it is. But he talks about her sending a limo to pick him up. Makes him feel like a BFD. The way he talked about it, driving along the river, the views from her place – totally fancied-out – it sounds Upper East Side. Doorman, big lobby, private elevator. So a condo. Oh, and he liked that she had droids – no live help.'

'So she's got money, or access to it. She sought him out. She's got an agenda. She made him important, exactly what he wanted. She knew that. She knew which notes to play.'

'She's been studying him,' Teasdale put in.

'It's why the banking for the drugs, the equipment didn't show on his financials. She's fronting all that. She may have gotten the makings for him, may have sources there Strong couldn't find. Out of the country, or deep down – some of her old contacts from Red Horse.'

'Why, after all these years?'

'Menzini died a few months ago, right? Maybe that *was* her trigger. I'll ask her when I find her. She coached him, taught him. She lit the match.' As she calculated, Eve's eyes narrowed, flattened. 'He's sitting down there now figuring out the best way to contact her. He's got to figure his rich grandmother will buy him top lawyers, get him off. He'll be thinking that.'

'But she won't,' Teasdale said.

'No, hell no. He's caught. No more use to her. Did Menzini's death start this?' Eve wondered. 'Is this some kind of revenge on her part? Or maybe a tribute. Fuck it.' She pushed her hands through her hair.

'We did an aging program,' Feeney told her. 'We've got what she should look like now, but—'

'She'd have changed her face,' Eve finished. 'A long time ago. She faked her own death, she can't keep the same face. She'll have heard we've got him. Will she worry he'll give her up?'

'Why didn't he?' Teasdale demanded, and for the first time since Eve met her, the agent looked mildly distressed. 'It would have given him a bargaining chip.'

'He's smart enough to know that, and to keep that chip in his pocket. If she doesn't come through for him, buy his way out, he'll roll on her.'

'She'll poof. Not your fault,' McNab said to Callendar. 'Just bad luck. But she's got the money and resources, so she'll blow.'

'Start running any and all private shuttles booked or alerted for flight prep since the media conference. Let's start running high-dollar condos, Upper East, riverview, fancy lobby, doorman.'

'With a terrace,' Callendar called out. 'I've got them having drinks on her terrace – facing east. He can see Roosevelt Island.'

'She can't help him,' Teasdale pointed out. 'If she tries, we'll have her. If she doesn't we still have him. HSO will certainly use all resources to locate her, but I don't understand the urgency.'

'She's got the formula.'

'I suspect she's had it all along, or enough of it with this much time, and the financial backing, she certainly could have created and used it before this.'

'We've just given her a reason to use it.'

'For him?' Teasdale shook her head. 'I don't believe she has that much sentiment in her.'

'Menzini's dead. The daughter's useless to her. Nothing to her. But the grandson? He's her legacy. He's shown her, twice, he has Menzini in him. She can't get to him, so she's going to want payback. Shit, shit!' Eve yanked out her 'link. 'Weaver and Vann. Maybe she'll want to finish what he started.'

She got Weaver's voice mail, left an urgent message, but managed to reach Vann.

'Lieutenant. We heard about Lew. I can't believe—'

'Where are you?' she demanded.

'At home. We closed the offices, and—'

'Stay there. Don't answer the door until my officers get there.'

'I don't understand.'

'You don't need to. Stay inside, door secure. Where's Weaver?'

'I'm not sure. She was upset, naturally. I assume she went home.'

'Stay inside,' she repeated, then tagged Jenkinson. 'Get over to Stevenson Vann's apartment. Keep it in lockdown until I say different. Nobody in, nobody out. Send Sanchez and Carmichael over to Nancy Weaver's. If she's home, keep her there. If she's not, I need to know. Go now.'

She went straight to Whitney when he came inside. 'I need Mira and Reo secured. As well as Chief Tibble and yourself, sir. Gina MacMillon may target the people who took down her grandson.'

'I'll take care of it.'

'What do we know about her?' Eve demanded. 'Attractive woman in her late seventies, early eighties. Wealthy. Patient. Jesus, she's like a spider. A trained soldier. More, a kind of operative. Could she have made contact with Menzini while he was alive?'

'I can't say.' Again, Teasdale looked mildly distressed. 'I would doubt it.'

'Why wasn't he executed? They still did that back then. He was a war criminal, a mass murderer, a child abductor, a rapist. Name it.'

'My guess? He was useful.'

'Making chemical and bio weapons?'

'It's possible. His mind was twisted, but he had brilliance in certain areas.'

403

'Enough he'd have found a way to get word to her. To keep the fire going. The world didn't end, but that doesn't mean you stop trying. Or shift focus. He made his living selling chem weapons. Maybe that's how she makes hers.'

Teasdale's face lit. 'I'll start a search for known dealers in her age span.'

'Bugger that.' Roarke sat back, pulled the tie out of his hair. 'I've got her.'

'How? Jesus.' Eve all but leaped on him. 'Let me see.'

'There was a painting in Callaway's office. The only piece of any taste or style in the whole place. It struck me at the time, but I didn't think much of it. It took me some time, but I found it. On screen.'

Eve frowned at the image of long, flower-decked steps, a fountain at their feet. They led to an old building, looked European to her.

'I don't get it.'

'It's the Spanish Steps, in Rome.'

'Menzini hit Rome, and was taken there.'

'So I recalled, a bit belatedly. This painting was done just prior to the war, by an Italian artist who died in Menzini's attack.'

'Too much coincidence, and coincidence is bogus.'

'So I thought. I've managed to track the owner through insurance. It's a very nice piece, and part of a collection. Owned by Gina M. Bellona. Bellona is the ancient Roman goddess of war. On screen.'

'There she is,' Eve murmured.

Attractive, yes. Strong bones, smoothly covered by olive skin, a sweep of dark hair liberally, artistically streaked with silver. It listed her as the widow of a Carlo Corelli.

'Find out what happened to Carlo Corelli,' she ordered Peabody when her partner came back in. 'And do it on the move. We've got a fucking New York address. Upper East Side – good call there, Callendar. Teasdale, I'd like you to stay back, monitor any transmissions Callaway requests to make. And use whatever magic you have to locate any private transportation she may have, and have gearing up. If she's trying to poof, let's block her.'

'I'll make sure of it. And have a biohazard team in place at her condo.'

'Set it up, but hold them back until we get there. You can freeze her accounts faster than we can. Do that.'

'Consider it done.'

'I'm ordering a SWAT team,' Whitney said. 'I want that building secure.'

'Yes, sir. I'm going to pull in Baxter and Trueheart. I think that's enough to take down one old lady.'

'You'll have one more. I'm with you, Lieutenant,' Roarke told her.

'You earned it. Let's move out.'

21

Eve worked as she went, her mind clicking through steps and strategies. 'Peabody, keep digging on Gina Bellona. I want to know if she has any other homes, properties, and if so, we want the locals there to obtain warrants for search and seizure. I want any and all vehicles – ground, air, water. I want relatives, employment or businesses. I want the names of her frigging pets.'

She pulled out her own 'link, grateful that for once the elevator had a little breathing room. 'Reo,' she began without preamble when the APA came on screen. 'Are you and Mira secured?'

'Yes, we're in the conference room. What—'

'Don't talk, listen. I need a warrant, now, for the homes, businesses, and vehicles of Gina Bellona, aka Gina MacMillon. We're on our way to her primary New York residence, and we're going in with or without the warrant. Make it clean, Reo. She's an imminent threat to the people and properties of New York. If she gets out of the city, she will be an imminent threat globally.'

'You'll have it.'

'Save time, use the conference room 'link. Put Mira on.'

'Eve,' Mira began when they switched 'links.

'Is Mr Mira at home?'

'He's teaching an evening class at Columbia. He—'

'I'll take care of it. Don't worry. I need you to go down to Callaway. I need you to keep him busy, talking, distracted. Say nothing about the grandmother. You know what to do, what to say. Just keep him occupied. I don't want him contacting or trying to contact MacMillon before, during, or after the bust.'

'I understand.' Mira's voice remained calm, but fear lived in her eyes. 'Do you think she would try to hurt my family?'

'She hasn't had time to do anything about it, but I'll make sure they're all protected. I promise you. She needs time and space to plan, to research. We're not going to give it to her. But we won't take chances. Get to Callaway.'

She clicked off, started to use her 'link again to order protection details. Roarke laid a hand on her arm.

'It's done.' He moved off the elevator with her into the garage. 'Private security, Mira's family, Peabody and McNab's apartment, Reo's, and so on.'

'It should be cops.' Then she took a breath. 'Thanks.'

'One less thing for you and the department to worry about.'

'Okay.' And she set it aside. 'Get me the layout of the condo – floor plan, exits, security. I'll drive, we're going hot until we're close, then we'll turn off the sirens.'

'Hot's my favorite thing.'

Peabody had a chance for one quick gulp before Eve tore out of the garage.

'Gina Bellona,' she began. 'In addition to her condo here, she has a home in London, a flat in Paris, and a villa in Sardinia. Her husband, deceased, was knighted for his contribution to science and humanitarian works.'

'Science,' Eve repeated while she punched vertical and zipped over a knot of traffic.

'Carlo Corelli – Brit mother, Italian father, dual citizenship, a scientist, primary work molecular chemistry. His father was one of the founders of Biotech Industries.'

'One of the leaders in the field,' Roarke told her while he worked. 'Innovations and development of synthetic organs, cancer vaccines, fertility, auto-immune research. They've built health centers in areas where medicine and health care was a luxury or simply nonexistent.'

'Pharmacology – lots of drug research.'

'No question.'

'Perfect for her. How'd he buy it, Peabody – Corelli?'

'Slipped in the shower seven months ago.'

'About the time Teasdale says Menzini died. I bet Corelli had help in the shower.'

'Death ruled accidental, but it looks like his first wife and his children made some noise about the widow. I can probably find some dish on it in the scandal sheets.'

'Marries him, gets rich, gets access to all the drugs she wants – and some expertise. Menzini dies, and she's done with Corelli. Wants this tribute, or revenge, or whatever the hell. She takes Corelli out, inherits, moves to New York.'

'Where she lives in a spacious, two-level condo,' Roarke

put in. 'Private elevator into a foyer. Secondary entrance/exit on south corner. Additional on second level, central. Video security, all entrances. There's also an interior elevator. Terraces off first and second levels, roof terrace on second level. She's on Fifty-two and Three, southeast corner.'

'What else is up there?'

'Three other units – one at each corner.' He continued to work quickly, coolly, while Eve drove like a lunatic. 'A central elevator, a maintenance/housekeeping area with service elevators. Three stairways – north and south and in the maintenance area.'

'Got it. Peabody, send Reo the info on MacMillon's properties.'

'She's also got a limo and town car here in New York, as well as a private shuttle.' A small '*Eek!*' escaped Peabody as the car threaded through snarled traffic. 'An all-terrain in Sardinia – and a yacht – town cars in London and Paris. Biotech's got a branch here, a complex on Long Island, and a facility on Park. Oh, another in Jersey City.'

'Get her all of it. Get warrants. Have her reach out to the European locals. She can add HSO's and Tibble's weight to get it moving. I want all her vehicles located and impounded.'

'Oh shit. Okay,' Peabody muttered prayers as they leapfrogged over a trio of Rapid Cabs. 'McNab's already located the shuttle, he's keeping me up. We're on that.'

'Box her in,' Eve stated, cutting the sirens, gliding the rest of the way.

'I think I just lost five pounds in fear sweat.' Peabody

mopped at her face. 'Now I want a cannoli. I don't know why.'

With a laugh, Roarke shifted to grin at her. 'I'll buy you a dozen, precious.'

'Cannolis, for God's sake.' Eve pulled into the loading zone in front of the building. The doorman, spiffy in red and gold, mistook the DLE for a piece of crap and hotfooted over.

'You can't—'

'I can.' Eve pulled out her badge as she pushed open the car door.

'What's this—'

'I ask; you answer. Gina Bellona. Is she in her condo?'

'Ms Bellona? She hasn't come out or ordered her car. What's—'

'How long have you been on the door today?'

'Going onto five hours. I'd've seen her if she'd come out. I opened the door for her myself about three hours ago when she came back from shopping.'

'Okay. The other tenants on her levels. Are they in?'

'The Cartwrights are in Africa, doing a safari thing. Mr Bennett hasn't come in yet, and Mrs Bennett and the boy went out about an hour ago. Mr Jasper just went up. His wife and kids are up there.'

'Which unit?'

'Fifty-two-oh-four.' His eyes widened as three black-and-whites and two SWAT vehicles roared up. 'What's the deal? Jesus.'

'Peabody, if you've finished dreaming of cannolis, have

Curtis here take you to the building manager, get this started.' She moved toward the SWAT commander. 'Lowenbaum.'

'Dallas. Cold night.'

'It's about to heat up.' She'd worked with him before, knew him to be steady and smart. Like his men, he wore black body armor, a helmet, and carried a long-range blaster. His eyes, a deceptively mild gray, scanned the building. 'Have you analyzed the floor plans?'

'Done and done.' He pulled out some gum – she remembered, for some reason, he preferred blueberry – offered it. When she shook her head he folded a piece into his mouth, then took out his tablet.

They huddled over the floor plans.

'My e-guy here's going to take out her security,' Eve told him. 'Once your team's secured the entrance, I need you to hold.'

She pulled out her 'link, printed out the warrant. 'We're a go there. There's a biohazard team en route, but I'm not waiting on them. Have your coordinator send them in, the minute they arrive.'

'We've got mouth-breathers. You want?'

'They leave a bad taste in my mouth.'

'Tell me.' He nodded, tapped his earpiece. 'My man says we're having trouble with eyes and ears. She's got it shielded.'

'Here's the deal, Lowenbaum. My team's going in, the team you select comes in behind us, helps us clear. She went in prior to the media report, and hasn't come out this way. If she's in there, we apprehend, incapacitate if necessary.'

She hesitated a moment. 'You know me, right?'

He grinned at her. 'Used to think maybe I'd know you better, but that didn't happen.' He turned his grin to Roarke. 'She wouldn't give me the green.'

Roarke grinned back at him.

'You could say I took my shot.'

'Jesus.' Eve shook her head. 'I'd like you on the clear team, and if I tell you to stun me and my people, do it.'

'That's ... unusual.'

'Maybe, but do it. Every room we go in, we open doors and windows. Blast them out if they're sealed. I'll get back to you.' She turned, moved fast to meet up with Baxter and Trueheart. 'They've got mouth-breathers. You may want.'

'You carry around that crappy aftertaste for hours,' Baxter complained.

'Your choice. We take the central elevator. Roarke, take down her private. Trueheart, you head to Five-two-oh-four, get the family inside out and down. Baxter, you and Peabody go in from Fifty-three, clear it, open all windows and doors. If she's up there, secure her, or take her down. Roarke and I go in on Fifty-two. Lowenbaum has men covering the terraces, moving now to secure all exits.'

'One old lady, right? A grandmother. Mine still makes the world's best apple pie.'

'She's nobody's pie-making granny. Let's go.'

Lowenbaum's men had the lobby secure, and empty. Roarke shut down elevators one by one as teams reported positions.

412

'You don't have body armor, LT.' Trueheart started to remove his own to give her.

'Keep it. I've got a magic coat.'

As Trueheart started to speak, Peabody nodded at him. 'Seriously. She does.'

'Okay, cut the chatter.' She stepped off with Trueheart and Roarke into a white and gold foyer, pointed at the ceiling before the doors shut on Peabody, Baxter, and the other men. Pointed Trueheart in the direction of 5204. She shook her head when a SWAT guy stepped forward with a battering ram, pointed to Roarke.

He studied the locks as he drew out his picks.

Lowenbaum grinned again when the locks quietly gave way.

Again she nodded at Roarke, then held up three fingers. Two. One.

They hit the door hard. She went low, Roarke high, splitting off as SWAT rushed in behind them. 'Get those terrace doors open!' She'd cleared the living area before she spotted the droid on the floor of a wide dining room.

She could smell the electrical burn in the air, noted the fried circuits spilling out of the back of the head of what had been a domestic droid.

Too late, she thought. They were too late. And she saw the proof of it when she, leading with her weapon, moved into a large kitchen done in soft green and golds.

She hadn't bothered to tidy up, Eve noted, but had left the burners and tubes, the conductors and jars in plain view.

She'd been cooking – and she hadn't made any damn pies.

She heard the calls of 'Clear!' ringing out. *Yeah, it's clear,* she thought. *She's cleared out, and taken her poison with her.*

Roarke came in behind her. 'I count two droids, both with their circuits destroyed. An empty safe, left open.'

'She left this out for us to find. A big fuck–you.' She shoved her weapon back in its holster. 'She's got money, fake ID, and I'm damn sure the means and contacts to change her face. She's either out of the city, or holed up until she can shift appearance and ID.'

'Maintenance exit,' Roarke concluded. 'She slipped out that way. Either undetected or she greased a palm or two on the way.'

'Her shuttle's locked down. She can't get out that way.' She yanked out her 'link. 'McNab, have you located MacMillon's other vehicles?'

'We have both locked, Dallas. What—'

'She's blown. Hold. Alert your security on the families and apartments,' Eve told Roarke. 'We're going to go over every inch of this place. McNab, I need men on all Biotech facilities in New York and New Jersey. Get e-men on it, check all security discs for any sighting of the suspect. She's to be considered armed and dangerous.'

She replaced her 'link. 'She didn't have much time here. I gave her more, just a little more by giving Nadine the heads up on an arrest. Damn it. Fuck it. How much did she make? Why? Why not just blow?'

She began to pace. 'She could've walked straight out the

front. She didn't. She wanted us to waste time, setting this up, assuming she was inside. But that cost her time. Time she couldn't spend getting on her shuttle and getting away. Now we've locked down her vehicles, frozen her accounts.'

'I suspect she has ready funds buried.'

'Yeah, but she took this time instead of running.'

'She's not ready to get out of New York.'

'She has a target. Something big. The mayor – she'd never get near Gracie Mansion, not today. Cop Central – same deal. She has to know security has her face.'

Peabody walked in. 'It looks like she might've packed a few things. Jewelry, I think. There's an empty safe in the master bedroom, and some signs she, or somebody, went through the closet in a hurry.'

'She figures on getting away. She took valuables, clothes. You don't bother with that unless you believe you'll need them.'

'It doesn't feel right she'd just leave her grandson,' Peabody said. 'Just take off, leave him swinging.'

'She doesn't give a rat's ass about him when push comes to bigger push. It's about the principle, the mission. About Menzini.'

'I think she does care about Callaway. She's got a picture of him framed on her dresser. And there's one of the two of them in the second bedroom – some men's clothes in there, too. Nice ones, new. They look like his size. It seems, I don't know, caring and sentimental.'

415

Eve pushed by, strode through the living room. 'Your men can stand down, Lowenbaum, but hold. Just hold.'

She took the stairs two at a time.

In the master, gold again with soft, almost watery greens and blues, Callaway's photo stood in a gold frame on an antique dresser. Facing the bed, Eve noted. She'd wanted to see him, see his face before she went to sleep.

'This was taken here.' She snatched it up, walked to the wide windows. 'On the terrace, probably. You can see the river behind him. Get me the other one,' she snapped at Peabody, and circled the room with the photograph.

'Caring, sentimental. I'm wrong here. Maybe, maybe. He's her blood – Menzini's blood. Male. Good-looking, fit, not stupid. And willing to kill. Willing to follow the path. Menzini dies, and what does she have left? Callaway. The daughter's nothing but the daughter provided the grandson. People put their hopes and dreams into their offspring.'

She grabbed the second photo when Peabody hurried back. It showed Callaway, wide smile, his arm around the waist of his grandmother. Was that pride in her eyes, Eve wondered. Affection? Ambition.

Maybe all of it.

'She gave him what she had,' Eve mused. 'The means to destroy. Let him start with his enemies, his competitors, those he considered in his way. No, that's not the mission, not the credo. That's personal. Indulgence. She lets him create panic and fear, for his own sake – not the big picture. Then they'd move on, together, to bigger and better. Is that it? Did she, along the way, develop feelings for him? Her grandson, her only worthy family. No, she's not going to leave him swinging.'

'What can she do?' Peabody asked. 'She can't get to him.'

'She's cooked up a hell of a bargaining chip, right down in her kitchen. She can finish what he started, what he'd planned to do next. Weaver. That restaurant. What was it? What – Appetito.'

Nancy Weaver hooked her arm through her date's as they strolled along the sidewalk. The night air, so cold and crisp, felt wonderful on her skin.

'Thanks, Marty.'

'For what?'

'For indulging me.'

He laughed, shifted so he could wrap an arm around her waist. 'I thought we indulged each other.'

'We did. I know I was a mess when I showed up at your door.'

'You've had a horrible couple of days. We all have, but you most of all.'

'It's been a nightmare, and I couldn't wake up. When I heard that Lew – Jesus, how could I have worked with him all this time and not known, not seen?'

'Don't they say it's often the people closest who don't see?'

'Maybe, but I'm trained to read people. Damn it, Marty, I'm good at it. Or I thought I was. I never read this in him. He can be difficult, moody, and annoyingly passive-aggressive, but,

417

Marty, he killed all those people. And our own. Our own Joe and Carly.'

'Thinking about it's only going to upset you again.'

'I can't stop thinking about it. Well, I did for a while.' She smiled up at him. 'And to think I nearly canceled our date tonight.'

'I'm glad you didn't – not only for the mutual, predinner indulgence, but because you shouldn't be alone.'

'I just walked out of work.' She tipped her head toward his shoulder. 'I couldn't be there. I just walked, and walked, and ended up at your door – two hours early. It was good for me, I admit it, but I have to think about everyone in the office. And, God, I still haven't turned my 'link back on.'

'Leave it off.' He gave her a comforting squeeze. 'Give yourself tonight. You can be there for everyone else tomorrow.'

'It feels selfish.'

'Speaking as the CEO of Stevenson and Reede's, I say it's not selfish but sane. You need some breathing room, Nancy. And so do I. The fallout on this is going to take weeks, months to dig out from under.'

'I need to contact Elaine – Joe's wife – tomorrow. See how she's doing. We need to do something for her, Marty, for her and Carly's family. For the other families. I don't know what yet. I can't think straight.'

He drew her a little closer. 'I promise you, we're working on just that. Take the breathing room. We'll have a nice bottle of wine, some dinner. You stay at my place tonight, and we'll talk it through.'

'If I hadn't had a date with you that night, that night we all went to the bar . . . '

He bent down to kiss the top of her head. 'Don't think about that either. You're safe. You're with me. And Lewis Callaway's in police custody. He'll never hurt anyone again.'

'Thank God for that.' She managed to smile at him as they reached the door. 'I'm glad you talked me into coming down, having dinner here after all. It's another kind of indulgence. I guess I need it.'

'We both do.'

They walked in to the sounds, the scents, the lights. Comfort, Weaver thought. She'd take all she could get, and try to put Lew and the nightmare away for another hour or two.

The maitre d' came toward her with hands outstretched. 'Ms Weaver, it's so good to see you. Don't worry about a thing. Your assistant called to confirm your reservation.'

'Oh, I didn't realize . . . '

'We have your favorite wine for you, with our compliments. We want you to relax. We want you to know we value you, and are happy you're safe and well.'

'Oh, Franco.' Her eyes welled. 'Thank you so much.'

'Now, you only relax and enjoy. Right this way.'

Weaver blinked at the tears, clutched Marty's hand. And didn't notice the attractive older woman at the bar, sipping a martini and watching her with hard blue eyes.

At the bar Gina slid a hand into her bag, trailed her fingers over the three vials she'd prepared – and the combat knife Menzini had given her a lifetime before.

Another life, she thought, coming full circle.

She would do this, here, tonight, for her grandson. The bitch who'd held him back from his happiness, his potential, would pay the price, while the police fumbled around in the apartment – if they'd gotten that far.

They'd freeze her accounts, too, no doubt. But she had more, she had plenty. Including the cash, the jewelry, the identification and passports now locked in the car she'd stolen.

She hadn't lost her touch there.

And once the city was again reeling toward panic, once this small bloodbath washed through, and this personal score was settled, she'd have the upper hand.

She would claim credit for all three incidents in the name of Red Horse. Guiseppi would be proud. She would demand the immediate release of Lewis Callaway or there would be another strike. More people would die.

If they remained stubborn, she'd strike again. They'd surrender, she knew it. The police, the government, were all weak, all shivered in the cold glare of public opinion.

She would level New York if need be to secure the release of her grandson, of her family. Of Menzini's legacy.

She had enough to make more, and only required a quiet place to do so.

She'd have to change her face, of course. But that was easily done, and wouldn't be the first time.

Once Lewis was free, she'd decide how to proceed. There were still people she could count on, threats she could make, havoc to be wreaked.

But payback first.

She considered waiting until Weaver went to the restroom. Idiot females such as she always went to the restroom to check their lip dye, their hair. Perhaps she'd just slit her throat. She could imagine it, all but feel the warm gush of blood on her hands.

It had been a very long time since she'd felt that warm flow of blood on her hands.

But that wasn't the way, however satisfying. She wanted Weaver to kill and be killed, to scream out her fear, her rage. To die Menzini's way.

But she had to know. She had to die knowing why and who. Yes, Lewis was owed that.

She uncrossed her legs, set down her glass. Elegant and predatory, she wound through the restaurant to Weaver's table, once again slipping a hand in her purse.

As she slid into the booth beside Weaver, she jabbed the point of the knife lightly against Weaver's side.

'I have a knife against this woman's guts,' she said conversationally to Marty. 'If you try anything, I'll carve those guts out before anyone can stop me. You're to smile, both of you. Smile at me, at each other.'

'What do you want?' Weaver tried to edge away, froze when the knife increased pressure.

'I want both of you to put your hands on the table. When

the waiter comes by, you're to ask for another glass for your old friend. Your good friend Gina. And smile.'

'Why are you doing this. Do you want money?' Marty demanded.

'People like you, people with petty powers always think of money. Your money means nothing and will mean less when the Red Horse rides again.'

'I don't understand.' On the table Weaver's hands trembled. She fought a bitter battle to steady them.

'I'm Lewis's grandmother. I'll gut you like a fish,' she murmured at Weaver's instinctive gasp. 'And cut off your balls,' she warned Marty. 'I'm very good with a knife, and very fast. Now smile. You're so happy to have run into an old friend.'

Weaver called on every ounce of control, forced her lips to curve as the waiter stopped at the table.

'Tony, would you get us another glass? My friend's going to join us.'

'Of course. Right away.'

'Good girl. I do feel like we're old friends. Lewis told me so much about you. How you've slept your way to power, and held him back at every turn. And this restaurant, your favorite. It made it easy to find you.'

'You called, said you were my assistant.'

'Lewis wouldn't sleep with you, so you've done everything possible to sabotage his career, to hold him back. So typical. So female.'

Under the table, Weaver pressed her foot to Marty's. 'He

frightened me – all that intelligence, his ideas, so innovative. You must be so proud of him.'

'Do you think you can play me, bitch?' She turned off the ferocity, turned on charm as the waiter brought her glass. 'Oh, thank you! This is just the most delightful chance, running into you tonight.' She beamed at the waiter as he poured wine into her glass. 'We must have a toast.'

'Gina.' Marty spoke quietly. 'Nancy was only following orders and directives. She had no choice. I'm the chief executive officer of Stevenson and Reede. If you need to blame someone, it should be me.'

'Marty—'

'Isn't that sweet – and revolting. He's trying to play the hero. Have a drink. Both of you. We're just three friends sharing a bottle of wine.' She picked up her own, sipped. '*Salute.*'

22

'I see her.' From across the street, Eve focused the field glasses through the narrow glass on the restaurant door. 'Rear booth, west corner. She's got Weaver boxed in. Male, brown and brown, late forties, seated on the other side of the booth.'

'Yeah, I got them.' Lowenbaum scanned, judging the crowd, the movement. He glanced left, right. Cops already worked to close off the block, reroute street and foot traffic. Satisfied, he closed his eyes a moment to feel the wind on his cheek, judge the direction and speed.

'Not much of a window,' Eve noted.

'It's much enough. It's a busy place. Maybe send a couple guys in, soft clothes, to plow the road. We do that right, we should be able to get off a clean shot.'

'She's got a weapon on Weaver. Can't see it, but has to be. Plus, she's got that shit with her. You drop her from here, she could take out Weaver before she goes down. And she could release the poison.'

Considering, Eve lowered the glasses. 'Maybe we get everybody out before it takes effect, or maybe we end up stunning a bunch of delusional civilians trying to kill each other over their ravioli. Or maybe she mixed up some other shit, and we can't be sure what the fuck it'll do.'

'That's a problem,' Lowenbaum said in his easy way as he pulled down his sniper goggles to look at Eve. 'Let's work the problem.'

'Straightforward. You wire me up. I go in, talk to her.'

'And if she's got a blaster under the table and takes you out?'

'I don't think so.' Eve could all but hear Roarke's furious objections behind her. He didn't have to voice them, the air sizzled with them. 'I get to the booth, sit, she knows we've got the place locked. She'll want to negotiate.'

'Rules of play, Dallas. We don't give her another hostage, much less a cop.'

'I know the rules of play, and sometimes they have to flex. Think of it as a showdown. A – what is it – Mexican stand-off.'

'Seriously? It's an Italian place, but this ain't gonna be a Roman holiday.'

He made her smile. 'Weaver's just a step for her, a slap. She's got bigger plans, and central is getting her boy out. She's got an emotional investment in him, and we can use that. I can use that. I get in, wired, you'll know what she's got on her. And I've got a better chance of taking her out, close up, without any hazard to civilians. Wire Mira in. She can help me with this.'

'We'll cover the exits, move in through the kitchen.'

'Yeah, I'm with you there. But somebody's got to get up

close and personal, draw her off Weaver and the man, keep her from releasing the agent.'

'I'm putting my best man – which would be me – on the target. She makes a wrong move, I'm giving myself the green. We got about seventy people in there – unknown number in the kitchen. If necessary, we'll do a broad range stun, make them all go nighty-night.'

'Let's see if we can avoid that.'

'She'd know your face.' She turned as Roarke spoke, and saw the hard anger in his eyes. 'If she's got a weapon, as she surely does, what stops her from using it on you while you're ten feet away?'

'I'm working on that. Peabody, take off those idiot boots.'

'My boots? But—'

'Do you really think a pair of pink cowboy boots disguises you?'

'It's just the start,' she told Roarke. 'Dig out those silly rainbow sunshades,' she told Peabody. 'And that scarf.' She tugged on Peabody's madly striped scarf. 'Wrap it around my head or something. Call out the Free-Ager.'

'A moment, Lieutenant.' Without waiting for assent, Roarke took her arm, pulled her aside. 'This is foolish.'

'It's not. I've got my magic coat.'

'It doesn't cover your hard head.'

'Okay, look, we can't see what she's got under that damn tablecloth. Maybe she got her hands on a blaster. It's more likely a knife. She could slice Weaver open any time, but again, it's more likely she'll hurt or disable Weaver enough to keep her in there, use the substance and get out. I can draw her attention off Weaver, get her talking. She'll bargain to get Callaway out. He's her legacy, her hope for the future.'

'The bargaining can be done from out here.'

'Roarke, there are kids in there. If she releases that shit, we don't know how fast it works on kids, but it'll be faster. They're smaller, lighter. I don't know, and I'm not risking standing out at a safe distance while kids get poisoned and maybe hack up Mommy's face with a pasta fork before we can control the situation.'

'Bloody fucking hell.'

'We can get some of them out. Her back's to the kitchen. We can move some of them out, quietly, while she's focused on me. I'm the game changer. Right now she thinks she's in charge. I change the balance, it throws her off. She has to rethink.'

'You go in, I go in.'

'Listen—'

He took her face in his hands. 'You go, I go. That's non-negotiable. If we're to get blasted to hell or poisoned into lunatics, we do it together.'

'Crap. Crap. You have to look less rich and gorgeous.'

God help him, she made him grin. 'I'll do what I can.'

'Wire him up, too,' she told Lowenbaum. 'Peabody, give me those stupid boots.'

'They're not going to fit you.'

'I'll manage.'

She stood while Lowenbaum's e-man fit her with mic and earbud. And shoving her feet into the pink boots learned

Peabody was right. They were miserably tight from toe to heel, awkwardly wide. She'd manage.

'Just enough to get me to the table,' she told her partner as Peabody began to wrap the scarf.

'You might as well look good. You're sure about this?'

'I'm sure the weird scarf and the shades will get me across the room.'

'Dallas.'

'I'm sure. I want you in the back, in the kitchen. We're going to move people out, and I need you to keep it smooth and quiet. And when I tell you, move in. Not before, Peabody. You, Baxter, Trueheart, move in on my go, and when Lowenbaum clears it. Not before.'

'Understood.'

She leaned in just a little, lowered her voice. 'Lowenbaum will stun me if he needs to. I'm counting on you to take care of Roarke.'

'Oh, jeez.'

'If it goes south, you take him down, get him out. That's not just an order, Peabody, it's a request from a friend. Get him down and out. Promise me.'

'I do. I will. And you, too.'

'Lowenbaum's men will come for the cop first. I'm not worried about it.'

Much, she thought as she stuck on the rainbow shades. 'How stupid do I look?'

'Actually, you look totally chill.' Peabody gave the trailing edge of the scarf a little flip. 'Sort of urban–bohemian chic.'

'God. Doctor Mira? Are you there?'

'Yes.' The voice, tight, tense, came through the earbud. 'And I feel this is an unnecessary risk.'

'A calculated one. I'm covered. There's a toddler in a damn booster seat smearing spaghetti sauce on his face ten feet away from the target. Once I get in position, feed me. Pull me back if I head in the wrong direction with her. I want to keep her engaged until we get as many civilians to safety as possible.'

'She's a soldier first. She'll sacrifice herself for her mission.'

'I'm counting on that mission priority being Callaway. Lowenbaum, are we set?'

'In position.'

She looked around. They'd worked fast, barricading the area. Already lookie-loos hugged the barricades, ready for some entertainment. Lowenbaum stretched over his shooting stand, weapon aimed. 'If you have to stun me, don't go for the body shot. The coat's lined with body armor.'

'No shit.'

'None. I'll show you later.'

'Lots of traffic inside,' he told Eve. 'Waitstaff moving by the booth. The table in front of it partially blocks the target. If you can move the interference, I'd appreciate it.'

'On the list.' She turned as Roarke came toward her, had to roll her eyes.

He'd ditched the suit jacket, the top coat for somebody's bunged-up fake leather jacket. He'd pulled his hair back in a tail, added a red, I ♥ NY ski cap.

'How much did you pay for that ridiculous hat?'

'Entirely too much.'

'Well, you don't look so rich anyway.' She took his hands. 'Let's go bag this bitch. On the move, Lowenbaum.'

'Copy that.'

'I bet the pasta's good here,' Roarke commented as they crossed the street.

'Maybe we'll get some to go when we're done. Clear visual on target from here,' she said when they'd reached the door. 'Entering building now.'

'Team Alpha, go.'

Into the kitchen, Eve thought as they entered the happy noise, the engaging scents. She slid her hand in her pocket as the cheerful-eyed maitre d' approached.

'Welcome.'

She turned up her badge before he could continue. 'Focus on me. What's your name?'

'I – Franco. Is there a problem?'

'There is, and I need you to keep on me, listen, and do exactly what I say. Are you a steady sort of guy, Franco?'

'I – yes, I think I am.'

'Stay steady. There are cops moving into the kitchen right now. They're going to get your staff to safety. No, keep looking at me. There's a woman in the booth – west corner, rear.'

'Ms Weaver, but—'

'The woman beside her. She's dangerous, probably armed. Steady, Franco. When we're at the booth, when I draw her attention, I want you to – quietly, very quietly, begin to move the people at the tables on her blind side out through the kitchen. One table at a time. You can tell them they've been chosen for some special deal, whatever it takes. Get them into the kitchen, and we'll take them from there. Do the same with your staff, one person at a time. Quietly. Can you do that, Franco?'

'Yes. But Ms Weaver—'

'I'll take care of her. Now, first thing. The table directly in front of the booth, the one with the kid with sauce all over him and the older kid pretending to eat his vegetables? Move them out now. You can make a fuss there. You have something special for the family in the kitchen. Something for the kids, right? Big smiles, big surprise. Got it?'

'Yes.'

'Do it now – happy face, Franco.'

His smile looked a little sick, but Eve thought it would pass. She let him reach the table. He actually clapped his hands – nice touch. Eve watched Gina's attention flick toward him, assess, then veer away.

'We're going in,' she said as the family – lots of kid excitement – rose from the table.

She wandered through, caught Gina's glance to and away. The minute the kitchen door closed behind the family, she zeroed for the booth.

'Nancy! Nancy Weaver, is that you!'

She let out a laugh, took advantage of Gina's momentary surprise and plopped down next to the man. 'Who'd've thought I'd run into you this way. How the hell are you?'

'I – I'm fine.' Weaver's eyes widened with recognition, but she held surprisingly steady. 'Just fine.'

'You look just fine,' she said as Roarke took a chair from the vacated table, angled it beside Eve.

'I'm sorry.' Gina spoke coldly. 'But this is a business meeting. You'll have to catch up another time.'

'Oh, don't be such a party pooper, Gina. I've got a weapon aimed at you under the table. Use yours on Nancy, make any wrong move, and I use it. Let's just talk.'

Out of the corner of her eye, she saw Franco murmur to the people at a side table out of Gina's range of vision. To keep attention focused, Eve pulled off the scarf, the shades. 'That's better.'

'I have enough Wrath of God on me to turn this place into Armageddon.'

'Then we all try to kill each other before the SWAT team stationed outside stuns us senseless. And where do we go from there? Let's avoid all that mess. Put your weapon on the table.'

'Not a chance. I'll cut her open like a ripe peach first.'

A knife then, better than a blaster.

'Nancy's not important,' Mira said in Eve's ear. 'Just a corporate shill.'

'You'd just be cutting open another corporate lackey. So what? And the minute you do, you're down. You're too smart to lose your leverage.'

Gina's sharply honed face held nothing but cold determination. 'I've got three vials of my leverage with me.'

'Show her respect,' Mira advised. 'Open negotiations.'

432

'You've got the hammer there. We want to avoid another incident. There are kids in here, Gina.'

And she smiled. 'That's right, and they're more susceptible. You won't be able to stop them fast enough. You'll stun them, open yourself up to outrage.'

'Got me there. What do you want?'

'I want this police state overturned. I want people like him—' She pointed to Roarke. 'I know who you are now. I want people like him on the street and all the money and material possessions he's so greedily grasped destroyed.'

'She's testing you,' Mira said. 'Draw her toward the grandson, the personal.'

'That's above my pay grade. Tell me something I can make happen. It's on the line for me, too, Gina. Let's be real. You hit this place, all these people, I look like a moron when I've just announced an arrest. Lew goes down, sure – and you – but so do I.'

'I want to speak to my grandson.'

'I may be able to arrange that, sure.'

'Here. Face-to-face. I want him brought here.'

'That'll take some time and doing. And what then? If I pull that off, he's in the hot zone, like the rest of us. Maybe you don't care about that, about infecting him.'

'I want to see him. Here. Then the two of us are going to walk out of here with the corporate lackey and the greedy bastard you married as shields.'

'Well, frankly, the corporate lackey's dispensable, but I'm pretty attached to the greedy bastard.'

433

'How can you say that?' Under the table, Weaver tapped Eve's foot twice, an acknowledgment. 'You're the police. You're supposed to protect me.'

'Grow up,' Gina snapped. 'Cops are cops, corrupt with power. Bring Lewis here, arrange for transportation to my shuttle – which will be clear – or I turn this place into a madhouse, complete with homicidal kids.'

'You should know how this works, Gina. Give a little to get a little. You're asking me to release a mass murderer – well, two counting you – give up two civilians, and what are you offering me?

'Let's start with a trade,' Eve suggested. She laid her weapon on the table. 'Mine for yours. Take mine, it's less lethal, but it'll get the job done. Give me the knife.'

'What the hell, Dallas,' Lowenbaum demanded.

'A show of cooperation and *trust*,' Eve said, eyes on Gina. 'I'd rather you didn't spill Nancy's blood all over the floor.'

When Gina reached for the weapon, Eve slapped her hand down on it. 'Let me see the knife.'

Eyes flat, but with a smirk playing around the corners of her mouth, Gina pulled the knife out from under the table. 'I've got the vials in my other hand,' she warned. 'Try anything, I toss them down, break them. That's no slow infection, and triple the usual dose. The children in here? They won't just kill, they'll die. The infection will kill them, or at the least cause brain damage.'

'How do I know you've got anything but bullshit in your other hand?'

434

Gina lifted it, twisted her wrist to show the three vials. 'If I drop them, you've got a bigger mess than this bitch's blood on your hands.'

'Okay.' To show cooperation, Eve raised both her hands – and gave Gina the opportunity to grab the weapon.

Gina rammed it against Weaver's throat. 'You know what this will do, on full, if I fire. She's dead.'

'You don't want to do that, Gina.' Eve let her voice waver a bit, stalling, stalling. 'That's no way to get Lew out.'

'Bring him *here*! And you.' She jutted her chin at Roarke. 'Stand up, move here, right here.'

'Do as she says,' Eve said quietly. 'She's got the advantage.'

'That's right.'

'He's blocking my shot,' Lowenbaum said when Roarke stood.

'It's okay. It's okay. We'll keep this under control. Trust me.'

'Trust you?' Gina laughed. 'Fuck you. Tell them to bring Lew. I want them to back off – all the fucking cops. I'm walking out of here with my grandson, this bitch, and your man.'

'Roarke.'

'It's all right.' He met Eve's eyes. 'I understand.'

'You understand nothing,' Gina hurled back, 'but you will.'

'Take me.' With a plea in his voice, Marty leaned forward. 'Let Nancy go, and take me. I'm in charge. She takes orders from me. I'm the one you want.'

'You want me to take you? You want to be the hero? Get out of the booth. You, cop, out and on your knees, hands

435

behind your head. Move your ass,' she ordered Weaver, sliding out to stand, shielded from the narrow glass door by Roarke.

'What are you doing, Eve?' Mira demanded. 'Tell her you'll start arrangements for the grandson.'

'I don't want anybody hurt. That's priority.' Slowly Eve eased out of the booth. 'That's why I had nearly everyone taken out of the restaurant. Look around, Gina. We've only got about twenty people left in here, and oops, they're heading out the front.'

'Then this is on you.' She pulled the trigger. Nancy let out a scream, then stared, open-mouthed.

'I guess I forgot to mention I disengaged that one.' Eve reached for the weapon in her pocket. 'But not this one.'

'Stun me!' Gina shrieked it. 'Go ahead, and these vials hit the floor. You'll turn that weapon against your own man.'

'It's done, Gina. Drop them and my buddies outside will see to it we all take an enforced nap. Not pleasant, but I can live with it.'

'Speak for yourself,' Roarke commented.

'Try it. See if it's fast enough. Try it! Stun me and find out who lives with it.'

Eve had a quick flash from her dream, of her mother's face, of that same vicious hate. 'I'm not going to stun you. Let's try this way.' She turned her weapon around, as if to offer it. In the instant Gina glanced down, Eve used her left – a quick, hard, bare-knuckled jab. And found it satisfying to see blood spurt from Gina's nose.

As she fell back, her hand opened. The vials slipped out. Braced for it, Roarke made the dive, caught them an inch from the floor.

'Just in case,' he said.

'Nice fielding.'

'Thanks. Now I have a bit of a headache. Kidding,' he said quickly when she swung her weapon in his direction. 'Just kidding.'

'Ha ha. Move in! Lowenbaum,' she continued as she stepped to Gina, rolled the dazed, moaning woman over to restrain her. 'Target's secured.'

'So I see. All teams, target's down and secure. Stand down.'

'Thanks for the assist, Doctor Mira.'

'You might've given me a clearer picture.'

'Some of it was spur. It was her eyes. I played off her eyes.' Eve turned Gina over again, hauled her up to sit. And looked in her eyes again. 'You're old, and you're slow – physically and mentally. You lost your way – maybe all those years of living off the fat – the fat you claim to despise. You'd have infected kids, and kids were the new hope, the foundation, the beginning. But you'd have infected them to get to your own. It was never about vengeful gods or Revelation with you. It was about the blood and the death, and your twisted revolution. You let me see that, and gave me the edge.'

'Your end-time will come.'

'Yeah, it will, but you won't be part of it. Odds are, given you've got about a half century on me, yours'll come first.

Whatever time you've got left, you'll spend in a cage. Just like your grandson. Just like Menzini's legacy.'

'There'll be others.'

'You keep thinking that. Baxter, you and Trueheart can take the old lady in.'

'Happy to serve.'

'She knows the formula,' Roarke murmured.

'Yeah, which is why Agent Teasdale and HSO will arrange for very special accommodations for her. I think Menzini left a vacancy.'

'Harsh.'

'I imagine it will be.'

'And what would you like me to do with these?' He held out the vials.

'Christ. Let's get that biohazard team in here, *asap*! Peabody, alert Teasdale re our new prisoner. The NYPSD gratefully passes her, and the processing of her properties, to HSO.'

'Got that, all over the place. But . . . can I have my boots back?'

Eve sat to pull them off. 'Ouch. I'm hungry,' she realized. 'Punching crazy old ladies makes me hungry.'

'I'll wager they have very nice cannolis.' Roarke smiled at Peabody as she pulled on her boots.

'Hot damn!'

'I'd like to buy you dinner.' Weaver sat, huddled against Marty, while an MT checked her out.

'Rain check. You were right about being good in a crisis, when it counts. You handled yourself, both of you.'

'I was terrified. I thought I was dead.'

'You're not, and you handled it. We'll need you to come in, make a statement. Tomorrow's soon enough.'

'We'll be there,' Marty assured her.

'Was Lew – was he always what we know he is now, or was it that woman? Did she make him what he is?'

'I'd say some of both. Go on home.' She left them to walk to Lowenbaum, shake hands – and take the boots he carried from him. 'Thanks.'

'I had the shot.'

'Too many civilians in potential harm's way, and I wanted to maneuver her so we had at least a chance of getting the vials.'

'Nice left jab.'

'It's a favorite.'

Someone called out, 'LT!' and both Eve and Lowenbaum turned.

'That one's mine,' Lowenbaum said.

'Guy back here wants to feed us. Is that a go?'

'What the hell. I could eat. Catch you next time, Dallas.'

Roarke moved to her, stroked a hand down her back. 'Which home are we headed to?'

'Central first. I need to tie this up, talk to Teasdale – and pay Lew a quick visit. I want to tell him, to his face, his granny won't be sending for him. It's petty, I know. But I deserve a little treat after all this.'

'Speaking of treats. I need a moment in the kitchen.'

'You're about to get a dozen cannolis,' Eve told Peabody when he walked off.

'Aww.' Peabody flexed her booted feet. 'I won't think about cannoli ass until tomorrow. Maybe not even then.'

'You called it right on her feelings for Callaway. Weak spot.'

'Most of us have them.' Peabody pushed to her feet. 'Ms Weaver, sir, I can arrange for an officer to take you home.'

'Thanks.' Weaver tipped her head to Marty's shoulder. 'I'm just going to sit here a minute until I'm sure my legs will carry me. Then I'd like the walk.' She tipped her face to Marty's. 'All right?'

'Sounds pretty good right now.'

Roarke came out of the kitchen with a large to-go bag.

'What's that?' Eve demanded.

'Quite a bit of food, I believe. They're boxing up your cannolis, Peabody.'

'Yum. Thanks.'

Roarke turned to Eve, and with discretion, he covered the recorder she wore. 'About that so much sex.'

'It's still on the agenda. Peabody, finish up here. I'm going in to deal with the official transfer. Then go home. You're clear.'

'Sing hallelujah.'

'A question,' Roarke said as Eve switched off her recorder. He took her arm and led her outside. 'You disabled your primary weapon. What about your secondary?'

'Rigged so it wouldn't go above medium stun. You can't kill anybody, even with direct jugular contact, on medium. It seemed safer, in case we got infected.'

'I agree. You know I had a weapon.'

'Yeah, I know.' She sent him a sidelong glance as they reached the car. 'Rigged to medium stun?'

'It seemed safer.' He caught her face in his hands, and despite her quick wince in case any cops watched, kissed her, long, tender, deep. 'I want to keep you, till the end of days.'

'I can live with that. And I'm damn glad this day is about to end.'

She got in the car, flexed her aching toes. And while he drove, adjusted both her weapons to official ranges.

It was safer that way.

A killer wind hurled bitter November air, toothy little knives to gnaw at the bones. She'd forgotten her gloves, but that was just as well as she'd have ruined yet another overpriced pair once she'd sealed up.

For now, Lieutenant Eve Dallas stuck her frozen hands in the warm pockets of her coat and looked down at death.

The woman lay at the bottom of the short stairway leading down to what appeared to be a lower-level apartment. From the angle of the head, Eve didn't need the medical examiner to tell her the neck was broken.

Eve judged her as mid-forties. Not wearing a coat, Eve mused, though the vicious wind wouldn't trouble her now. Dressed for business – suit jacket, turtleneck, pants, good boots with low heels. Probably fashionable, but Eve would leave that call to her partner when Detective Peabody arrived on scene.

No jewelry, at least not visible. Not even a wrist unit.

No handbag, no briefcase or file bag.

No litter, no graffiti in the stairwell. Nothing but the body, slumped against the wall.

At length she turned to the uniformed officer who'd responded to the nine-one-one. 'What's the story?'

'The call came in at two-twelve. My partner and I were only two blocks away, hitting a 24/7. We arrived at two-fourteen. The owner of the unit, Bradley Whitestone and an Alva Moonie were on the sidewalk. Whitestone stated they hadn't entered the unit which is being rehabbed — and is unoccupied. They found the body when he brought Moonie to see the apartment.'

'At two in the morning.'

'Yes, sir. They stated they'd been out this evening, dinner, then a bar. They'd had a few, Lieutenant.'

'Okay.'

'My partner has them in the car.'

'I'll talk to them later.'

'We determined the victim was deceased. No ID on her. No bag, no jewelry, no coat. Pretty clear her neck's broken. Visually, there's some other marks on her — bruised cheek, split lip. Looks like a mugging gone south. But . . . ' The uniform flushed slightly. 'It doesn't feel like it.'

Interested, Eve gave a go-ahead nod. 'Because?'

'It sure wasn't a snatch and run, figuring the coat. That takes a little time. And if she fell or got pushed down the stairs, why is she over against the side there instead of at the bottom of the steps? Out of sight from the sidewalk. It feels more like a dump, sir.'

'Are you angling for a slot in Homicide, Officer Turney?'

'No disrespect intended, Lieutenant.'

'None taken. She could've taken a bad fall down the steps, landed wrong, broke her neck. Mugger goes down after her, hauls her over out of sight, takes the coat, and the rest.'

'Yes, sir.'

'It doesn't feel like it. But we need more than how it feels. Stand by, Officer. Detective Peabody's en route.' As she spoke, Eve opened her field kit, took out her Seal-It.

She coated her hands, her boots as she surveyed the area.

This sector of New York's East Side held quiet – at least at this hour. Most apartments' windows and store fronts were dark, businesses closed, even the bars. There would be some after-hours establishments still rolling, but not close enough for witnesses.

They'd do a canvass, but odds were slim someone would pop out who'd seen what happened here. Add in the bitter cold, as 2060 seemed determined to go out clinging with its icy fingers, most people would be tucked up inside, in the warm.

Just as she'd been, curled up against Roarke, before the call.

That's what you get for being a cop, she thought, or in Roarke's case, for marrying one.

Sealed, she went down the stairs, studied the door to the unit first, then moved in to crouch beside the body.

Yeah, mid-forties, light brown hair clipped back from her face. A little bruising on the right cheekbone, some dried blood on the split lip. Both ears pierced, so if she'd been wearing earrings, the killer had taken the time to remove them rather than rip them off.

Lifting the hand, Eve noted abraded flesh on the heel. Like a rug burn, she mused before she pressed the right thumb to her ID pad.

Dickenson, Marta, she read. Mixed-race female, age forty-six. Married Dickenson, Denzel, two offspring, and an Upper East Side address. Employed Brewer, Kyle and Martini, an accounting firm with an office eight blocks away.

As she took out her gauges, her short brown hair fluttered in the wind. She hadn't thought to yank on a hat. Her eyes, nearly the same gilded brown as her hair, remained cool and flat. She didn't think about the husband, the kids, the friends, the family – not yet. She thought of the body, the position, the area, the time of death: twenty-two-fifty.

What were you doing, Marta, blocks from work, from home on a frigid November night?

She shined her light over the pants, noted traces of blue fiber on the black cloth. Carefully, she tweezed off two, bagged them, marked the pants for the sweepers.

She heard Peabody's voice over her head, and the uniform's answer. Eve straightened. Her leather coat billowed at the hem around her long, lean frame as she turned to watch Peabody – or what she could see of her partner – clomp down the steps.

Peabody had thought of a hat, had remembered her gloves. The pink – Jesus, pink – ski hat with its sassy little pom-poms covered her dark hair and the top of her face right down to the eyes. A multicolored scarf wound around and around just above the plum-colored puffy coat. The hat matched the pink cowboy boots Eve had begun to suspect Peabody wore even in bed.

'How can you walk with all that on?'

'I hiked to the subway, then from the subway – but I stayed warm. Jeez.' One quick gleam of sympathy flicked across Peabody's face. 'She doesn't even have a coat.'

'She's not complaining. Marta Dickenson,' Eve began, and gave Peabody the salients.

'It's a ways from her office and her place. Maybe she was walking from one to the other, but why wouldn't she take the subway, especially on a night like this?'

'That's a question. This unit's being rehabbed. It's empty. That's handy, isn't it? The way she's in the corner there? She shouldn't have been spotted until morning.'

'Why would a mugger care when?'

'That's another question. Following that would be, if he did, how'd he know this unit's unoccupied?'

'Lives in the area? Is part of the rehab crew?'

'Maybe. I want a look inside, but we'll talk to the nine-one-one callers first. Go ahead and notify the ME.'

'The sweepers?'

'Not yet.'

Eve climbed the stairs, walked to the black and white. Even as she signaled to the cop inside, a man pushed out of the back.

'Are you in charge?' Words tumbled over each other in a rush of nerves.

'Lieutenant Dallas. Mr Whitestone?'

449

'Yes, I—'

'You notified the police.'

'Yes. Yes, as soon as we found the—her. She was ... we were—'

'You own this unit?'

'Yes.' A sharply attractive man in his early thirties, he took a long breath, expelling it in a chilly fog. When he spoke again, his voice leveled, his words slowed. 'Actually, my partners and I own the building. There are eight units – third and fourth floors.' His gaze tracked up. No hat for him either, Eve mused, but a wool topcoat in city black and a black and red striped scarf.

'I own the lower unit outright,' he continued. 'We're rehabbing so we can move our business here – first and second floors.'

'Which is what? Your business?'

'We're financial consultants. The WIN Group. Whitestone, Ingersol and Newton. W-I-N.'

'Got it.'

'I'll live in the downstairs unit, or that was the plan. I don't—'

'Why don't you run me through your evening,' Eve suggested.

'Brad?'

'Stay in the car where it's warm, Alva.'

'I can't sit any more.' The woman who slid out was blond and sleek and tucked into some kind of animal fur and thigh-high leather boots with skinny heels. She hooked her arm through Whitestone's.

They looked like a set, Eve thought. Both pretty, well-dressed and showing signs of shock.

'Lieutenant Dallas.' Alva held out a hand. 'You don't remember me?'

'No.'

'We met for five seconds at the Big Apple Gala last spring. I'm one of the committee chairs. Doesn't matter,' she said with a shake of her head as the wind streamed through her yard of hair. 'This is horrible. That poor woman. They even took her coat. I don't know why that bothers me so much, but it seems cruel.'

'Did either of you touch the body?'

'No.' Whitestone took over. 'We had dinner, then we went for drinks. At the Key Club, just a couple blocks down. I was telling Alva what we've been doing here, and she was interested, so we walked over so I could give her a tour. My place is nearly done, so . . . I was getting out my key, about to plug in the code, when Alva screamed. I didn't even see her, Lieutenant, the woman. I didn't even see her, not until Alva screamed.'

'She was back in the corner,' Alva said. 'At first, even when I screamed, I thought she was a sidewalk sleeper. I didn't real-ize . . . then I did. We did.'

She leaned into Whitestone when he put an arm around her waist. 'We didn't touch her,' Whitestone said. 'I stepped over, closer, but I could see . . . I could tell she was dead.'

'Brad wanted me to go inside, where it's warm, but I couldn't. I couldn't wait inside knowing she was out there, in the cold. The police came so fast.'

'Mr Whitestone, I'm going to want a list of your partners, and of the people working on the building.'

'Of course.'

'If you'd give that, and your contact information to my partner, you can go home. We'll be in touch.'

'We can go?' Alva asked her.

'For now. I'd like your permission to go inside the unit, the building.'

'Sure. Anything you need. I have keys and codes,' he began.

'I've got a master. If there's any trouble, I'll let you know.'

'Lieutenant?' Alva called her again as Eve turned to go. 'When I met you, before, I thought what you did was glamorous. In a way. Like the Icove case, and how it's going to be a major vid. It seemed exciting. But it's not.' Alva's gaze swept back toward the stairs. 'It's hard and it's sad.'

'It's the job,' Eve said simply, and walked back toward the steps.

Have you read them all?

Eve and Roarke are back in
CALCULATED IN DEATH
out now